OFFICIALLY NOTED

UNION

D1452922

Copyright © 2022 by TMJ BOOKS

www.tmjbooks.com

All rights reserved.

No part of this book may be reproduced in any form or by any electronic or mechanical means, including information storage and retrieval systems, without written permission from the author, except for the use of brief quotations in a book review.

This is a work of fiction. Names, characters, businesses, places, events, locales, and incidents are either the products of the author's imagination or used in a fictitious manner. Any resemblance to actual persons, living or dead, or actual events is purely coincidental.

THE UNION

LET NO ONE STAND BEFORE WE

TM JEFFERSON

For my Family

1

The tattered, decrepit building on 1st and 3rd street in Mt. Vernon, New York was a dugout for the hustlers and a smoke haven for the addicts. Hundreds of empty crack vials lay scattered along the urine filled steps. Graffiti ridden staircase walls held the names of those past and present and the stench of marijuana lingered through the air, but still, this was home, a sanctuary to more than fifty families.

Three flights up, in an undersized, cluttered apartment, the soothing melody of Mary J Blige's *"My Life"* and the scent of hamburgers and French fries escaped into the hallway.

Sybil snatched open the refrigerator door in search of the last bit of ketchup, but the bottle was empty. "Cleo!"

"Yes?"

"Go over to your aunt's and get some ketchup."

His shoulders sulked and his once playful expression turned grim. "Aww, Ma. I don't wanna go over there." he pouted.

Sybil walked into the living room and stood in front of the television. "I ain't asking you, I'm telling you, now get your ass up and go next door."

Cleo shook his head and poked his lips out. He hated going

across the hall to his aunt Wanda's house, it was overrun with roaches. "But they got roaches, Ma."

Sybil didn't like when Cleo said things like that. Even though she was slightly better off financially than her little sister, she never acted as if she was superior. They were both stuck in the hood. "So do we; this apartment ain't no better than theirs. I told you about talking like that."

Cleo's reason for not wanting to go next door wasn't really the roaches, it was his cousin Mox. The truth is; his fear was being fueled by his own insecurity. He was very aware that Mox is smarter, faster, and stronger than he is, but Mox was naive, hesitant, and unconscious of his own abilities. He put his sneakers on and went to do what his mother asked.

———

"WHO IS IT!" Wanda screamed from the bathroom when she heard someone knocking at the front door.

"I got it, Ma!"

Mox put the controller down, got up from the futon, checked the peephole and then swung the door open, letting his cousin Cleo in. "Cleo, wassup?"

"Wassup." He mumbled, and then nodded at Casey.

The pungent order of sensimilla invaded Cleo's nostrils, and then a cockroach the size of a small *Bic* lighter darted across the 20 - inch television set grabbing his attention, but Mox paid it no mind.

"You scared of a little roach, Cleo?" he joked seeing the fear in his eyes.

"Nah, I'm sayin'... that joint was big."

"Whatever. Yo! Them joints is hot!" he looked down at Cleo's new, white, grey and red Air Max. "Let me rock your old joints since you got those?"

"Nah."

"C'mon, Cleo." he begged. " You said you was gonna look out for me."

"I did look out for you. I gave you those black sneakers."

Mox reached underneath the grubby futon and pulled out a pair of black, soiled *Reeboks*. "I been wearing these every day for more than a year." He shook his head.

Cleo wasn't concerned with how long Mox had been wearing the sneakers; he was still upset at the fact that his mother made him give up a pair of his old ones. If he had it his way, Mox would be walking on his bare feet.

Any opportunity Cleo had to be better than Mox, he took full advantage of. He knew morally it was incorrect, but he wasn't able to shake his envious characteristics. It came from his heart, so it was in his blood.

Switching the subject, Cleo asked, "Y'all got some ketchup?"

Mox went into the kitchen, grabbed the ketchup and squeezed some into a plastic cup.

He held up the cup. "Is this enough?"

The cockroach that was once on the television skirted across Cleo's sneaker. He panicked and his arm brushed against the vase sitting on the mantle, knocking it to the floor.

"Ooooh." Casey crooned.

Mox raised his index finger to his lips. "Shhh... be quiet, Casey."

The crash rattled Wanda's nerves. She reached to pull her pants up and almost knocked the small mirror off the sink. The bathroom door was locked. She was puffing a joint and sniffing a line of coke.

"Mox, what the fuck was that!"

"Damn, Cleo. You just broke her favorite vase." He looked down at the shattered pieces on the floor. "Go head man, take the ketchup and go before she comes out here."

"What you gon' tell her?" He opened the front door.

"It don't matter. I'ma still get my ass whooped."

The bathroom door flew open and the front door closed.

Cleo was gone.

"What was that noise?" Wanda asked. She looked to her youngest, and then down at Mox picking up shattered pieces of her favorite vase. "I know that ain't my vase, Mox?"

He was too afraid to make eye contact. "I knocked it over by accident, Ma." He lied, and that was something he never did.

Wanda's lip curled as it did every time she became angry. She screwed her eyes, balled her fist and shot a sharp, right hook to his ribs. "Get the fuck up and get yo' ass in that room. And take them goddamn pants off!"

Mox absorbed the blow and did as he was told.

At ten years old, he was accustomed to the beatings, so eventually, he learned to block out the pain and visualize more pleasant occasions; but those fantasies never lasted long.

He closed the bedroom door, stripped to his bare skin and waited to endure another lashing. He was cool about it though. His only concern was what her weapon of choice would be.

The iron?

A wire hanger?

Or maybe that bamboo broom Aunt Sybil brought back from Japan?

Either way, he didn't mind taking the ass whooping for his cousin. He thought nothing of it. He felt it was his duty to take the blame because he knew Cleo was scared. His little brother Casey didn't like seeing him get in trouble. He loved his big brother, so he sat back on the dingy futon, crying until he could make no more tears. He rocked himself to sleep.

Wailing screams at 2:30 am woke Mox and Casey from their sleep.

"What was that?" Casey jumped up, wiping the crust from his eyes.

"I don't know. Wait here. I'll be right back."

"No, Mox. Don't leave me." Jumping out the bed, Casey followed his big brother.

The room was pitch black as Mox and Casey tip toed to the bedroom door. Mox turned the doorknob and took a peek into the hallway. It was too dark to see, but he could hear someone's voice. They were saying a prayer.

"If we confess our sins, he is faithful and just—"

As they got closer to the living room, the rumbling vocal sound grew louder.

"—And will forgive us our sins and purify us from all unrighteousness..."

The sour scent of blood perfumed the air and irritated Mox's nose. His stomach muscles tightened and a sudden sweat fell over his body. He fought the urge to vomit and before reaching the entrance to the living room, he stopped short and Casey was on his heels.

"Casey, wait right here," he whispered. "Don't move."

Mox crept through the static dimness; his midnight skin tone merging perfectly with the blackness. Now, only a few steps from the living room, he sensed something wrong and wanted to turn back, but his feet continued to move forward. When he entered the living room, the sight before his eyes churned his insides and the vomit he suppressed only seconds ago erupted through his lips.

His father's butchered, unclothed body was draped over the futon. His hands were tied behind his back in a pipe hitch knot and his throat was slit.

Mox was unable to move. Paralyzed, he watched the tall, wide-body, dark skinned assassin hover over his mother's defenseless, naked figure. The twelve inch blade he gripped was called a Tanto and it was soaked in blood.

Wanda lay stretched across the floor in the middle of the small, filthy apartment, choking on her own blood. She had suffered thirty five stab wounds to the face, chest and neck.

Casey startled his big brother when he brushed up against his arm and attempted to glance over his shoulder. Mox went to shield his eyes from the horrendous scene, but Casey was determined to see. They stood, bare chested and barefoot in their underwear, innocent; focused on the woman who pushed them from her womb, as she gagged, taking her last breaths before their sinless eyes.

The killer slowly turned to the young boys. "Mox," he muttered, wiping the bloody sword onto his sleeve. "Everything comes to an end." He looked at Wanda, bent down, put his hand over her face and closed her eyes. "Sleep, baby..." he whispered, then made his exit.

A milky, drop, CLK 430 crept along the jagged, pothole filled pavement slowing down at the corner of Horton Avenue and Brook Street. The lambent rays from the early morning sun made the polished white paint look like glass.

Wise Earl and two young wolves were holding the block down on this early morning. They watched the glossy, two door convertible pull to the curb and park.

"You young niggas don't know shit about gettin' this money."

Earl hissed. The temperature was almost at a hundred degrees and the air was sticky, condensed and humid. He wiped the sweat from his brow and took a long drag of his cigarette. "Now this nigga here," he pointed to the car, "that nigga gettin' that real paper."

The passenger side door opened and one of the sexiest creatures God created stepped out. Her olive complexion was radiant and her skin was flawless. The tight-fitted, pink shorts she was wearing cupped her dainty, heart shaped ass cheeks perfectly and her well-formed c-cup breast bounced with each step.

Priscilla was a Goddess. She had recently cut her hair short and was rocking the natural look. It completely fit her personality.

She pranced around the front of the vehicle with a bag in her hand. Her cupid shaped, berry colored lips looked juicy enough to bite.

The young wolves gawked at her glowing beauty.

Wise Earl shook his head at their actions. "See... that's the problem wit' you young niggas, you worried 'bout some pussy when you need to focus on the come up."

The beautiful young lady approached Earl.

"Wassup, Uncle Wise?"

"Hey, baby girl." He embraced her. She smelled wonderful. "Tell that nigga to roll the window down."

Earl tossed his hands up and the driver side window slowly came down.

"Uncle Wise, what's good?"

"You tell me, nephew. I know you better step out that goddamn car and come give your uncle some love."

Mox pushed the door open and got out.

He was no longer the short, skinny dark skinned kid he was seven years ago. He was grown up now, 6 feet 2 inches, black as the dead of night and in control of his own operation.

He hugged his uncle and dapped the young wolves.

"What's the word, Unc?"

Earl plucked the remnants of his cigarette and looked at Mox. "The only thing more threatenin' to you besides your enemy, are the people closest to you. Never forget that."

Mox nodded and walked into the corner store. He came out with a bottled water and the newspaper. "Priscilla," He said, getting back in the car. "Get that and let's go."

She unzipped the small *Gucci* carrying bag and handed it to Earl.

"Go fill that up, youngin'."

One of the young wolves took the bag and went around the corner. He returned in seconds handing the bag back to Priscilla.

"You been upstairs, Unc?" Mox asked, ready to pull off.

"Earlier, she up there wit' Casey and Cleo. I'll be through in a minute."

"Aight." Mox pulled from the curb and made the right down Brook Street and then he made another right into the parking lot and pulled in an empty space.

They got out the car, walked to building 80 and took the elevator to the sixth floor. He stood in front of 6A fumbling through his pocket for the keys, finally finding them and opening the door.

As soon as it opened Casey jumped into Mox's arms.

"Whoa, boy; you getting too big to be doing that. Wassup?"

"Nothing." Casey, jumped back down to the floor. He picked his basketball up and continued dribbling.

"Casey!" Cleo yelled from the back room. "Stop bouncing that ball in the house!"

"Shut up!" Mox yelled back.

"Who dat?"

"Who you want it to be?"

"What I tell y'all 'bout all that damn noise in my house." Sybil added. She was in the kitchen washing dishes.

Cleo came from the back room.

"It's this little nigga." He snarled, snatching the basketball from Casey.

"Hey!"

"Hey, nothin'... I told you 'bout this ball. I don't know why you always got it anyway, you ain't no good."

Mox took the ball from Cleo and gave it back to Casey. "Leave my lil' brother alone. Tell him, Casey... you going to the NBA."

Casey's eyes lit up and he got excited. "Yup! And when I get rich, I'ma buy Mox a house and Auntie a house and you ain't gettin' nothing 'cause you always bothering me."

Cleo mushed the 12 year old, making him stumble to the dining table and Casey threw the ball, striking him in his stomach, then he ran through the house.

"You lil' muthafucka!" He growled, ready to chase after him.

"Chill, Cleo." Mox grabbed his arm.

"Get the fuck off me." He yanked away. "Priscilla, why you hang around this guy? I know you can do better than this asshole."

Sybil slammed a dish in the sink. "Cleo, watch your mouth in my house."

"It's this nigga." He pouted.

"It's always somebody else, it's never you." She said, drying off the last dish. "How you doing, Priscilla?"

"Hello, Ms. Daniels. I'm good." She took a seat at the table.

"Why you always sticking up for him? You aint never on my side." Cleo whined.

"Cleo, cut the bullshit and get ready for practice."

He pouted his lips and turned to walk away. He knew better than to talk back.

"Wassup, Auntie?" Mox hugged his aunt. "How's everything?"

"I'm surviving, baby, blessed to see another day."

He glanced around the kitchen. It was always a homely feeling when he stepped through the door. He appreciated his aunt stepping up and taking care of him and his little brother. If it wasn't for her, they would have been dragged into foster care and more than likely, they would have been split up.

After his parents were killed, Sybil took full custody of her sister's two boys. Since then, Mox had moved out on his own, but Casey was still here.

His eyes fell to a picture that was stuck on the refrigerator.

"Do you miss her, Auntie?" He stared at one of the few visual memories of his mother.

"Miss who, Mox?"

"My mother..."

Sybil turned and faced Mox. "Of course I miss her. I think about her every day."

"I do too... you know something," Mox opened the refrigerator and grabbed the pitcher of Kool-Aid. "I wanted to ask you this for the longest, but I was always afraid of the answer."

"Ask me what?"

Mox leaned against the wall. He needed some closure, seven years was long enough.

"Do you remember that night?"

She sighed. "Like it was yesterday."

"Do you know why it happened?"

"I don't have a clue, Mox. I wish I did." She peeled the picture off the refrigerator. "I really miss my sister." Her eyes got watery and a tear rolled down her cheek.

Mox ripped a paper towel from the roll that was on the counter and handed it to her. "Lately it's been on my mind. It just bothers me that nobody knows anything."

Sybil listened to Mox. She knew more than she led him to believe, but she was afraid to expose her dark secrets.

"Sometimes the truth can cause pain, baby."

"No more than it's already caused—"

A knock at the door disturbed their conversation.

"Who is it?"

"Open up lil' nigga."

Mox unlocked the door and Wise Earl strolled into the apartment.

He looked around the peaceful room. Something was going on. It was too quiet for this to be his sister's house.

"What the hell is going on in here? Why y'all lookin' so sad?"

"Uncle Wise, I was just asking auntie if she knew anything about the night my mother and father got killed."

Earl was shocked. His eyes moved from Sybil to Mox, and then back to Sybil. He didn't expect to walk in on a subject so personal. He could tell his older sister had been crying.

"Mox, sometimes things happen and we can't do anything about it. That's life."

"Naw, Unc... I ain't tryna hear that."

"Well, that's what it is."

"That ain't what it is, Uncle Wise. Listen to what you saying, basically, you gave up. Y'all don't even care about what happened."

"It's not that I don't care, because I do. That was my sister, I love her, but—"

Mox cut in. "But what, Unc?"

The room went silent.

"I believe if y'all did know something y'all would tell me..." There was a pause. "Right?" he glanced back and forth. "C'mon, Priscilla." Mox hugged his aunt. "I'm old enough to know now Auntie, and if somebody doesn't tell me, eventually I'll find out on my own."

Earl grabbed his nephew's arm and brought him in close. "I love you boy. Be safe out there, Mox."

"I got you, Unc. Hey, Auntie, tell Casey I'll be through at nine o'clock tomorrow so I can take him to his game."

He walked out the door and Priscilla followed.

Wise Earl shook his head and then looked at his sister. "You gon' have to tell him one day, sis."

2

——————

Priscilla and Mox's unity began only two years prior. It was the summer of 2000 and the upcoming school year, young Mox would become a freshman at New Rochelle high school. At the time he was into sports heavy, baseball and track and field were the ones he favored.

Currently under his Aunt Sybil's care, it was a struggle for her to raise three growing boys. Things were tight, but they managed to get through.

All three of the boys played sports, so the refrigerator was always empty and the laundry was always dirty.

Mox took it upon himself to go out and find a part time job washing cars down at the *Shiny Gleam* car wash in Mamaroneck, which was about ten minutes away. Most the staff was illegal immigrants and young black kids Mox's age, so they didn't mind working with him as long as he did what he was asked to do.

He made a few dollars every week and was able to contribute to the household, contrary to how to his cousin Cleo saw things. Cleo figured he didn't need to work because in a few years he was going pro. But that was in a few years, this was now and Mox was not only pulling the weight of he and his brother, but also Cleo. He never once complained.

It was the top of the morning on a 96 degree summer day when the dark blue Honda Coupe with five star rims and an awful paint job turned into the car wash.

Mox arrived to work fifteen minutes earlier after having an argument with Cleo over the bathroom. Rather than a fist fight, he walked away, figuring he'd be the sensible one.

The blue Honda was the first car to pull up. It was only 8:50 am and they usually didn't start washing cars until 9:15, but when the passenger side window came down Mox approached the pretty creature sitting behind it.

He smiled bright and asked, "Welcome to *Shiny Gleam*. How can I help you today?"

She smiled back, but the driver answered. "Fuck is you smiling for, nigga? Lemme get the full wash, Armor All and all that. How much?"

"Would you like the interior done, sir?"

"Ain't that part of the full wash? I said full wash."

Mox stayed cool. "No it isn't sir, that's why I'm asking."

The driver became annoyed. "I don't want no extra shit, jus' gimme the full wash... and make sure you put Armor All on my shit! Last time them fuckin' Mexicans got me."

Mox continued to ignore his obnoxiousness. He wrote out the receipt and passed it to the pretty female. "Pull up to the yellow line and I'll take it from there."

Once the driver put the car in park, he hopped out and went inside to pay for the wash. His beautiful accomplice stood outside. Mox used this opportunity to strike a conversation.

"Is that your boyfriend?" He inquired.

She didn't even look in his direction. "No."

"Then why you riding with him?"

"Little boy, you need to mind your business. Don't worry about why I'm riding with him."

Mox admired her from head to toe. She was perfect. Her mesmerizing eyes spoke volumes and he was feeling her sense of style. He knew she was older because of the way she dressed. She wore zebra print leggings that showed off her firm thighs, shiny red pumps that accentuated her calf muscles and a tight fitting, short sleeve shirt that emphasized her well-formed breasts.

"What's your name, beautiful?"

She smirked. "Why you wanna know my name?"

"I'm sayin'... I'm just being formal." He extended his hand. "Mox Daniels." He told her.

"Priscilla Davis." She replied, shaking his hand. "Aint you Cleo's cousin?"

"Yeah. Priscilla..." He paused. "I like that name, it fits you."

"Thank you."

"You're welcome. How old are you, Priscilla?"

"Older than you."

"That won't be a problem. I like older women."

They laughed.

"I love your enthusiasm." She said, getting ready to get back into the car. The detailer was wiping the last tire down with Armor All. "Keep it up, you'll find what you're looking for."

"I already did." He responded.

Out the corner of his eye Mox saw the driver coming back out to his car. He recognized the light skinned skinny kid, but he couldn't figure out his name. He was a halftime hustler from the other side of town.

"Yo!" the driver shouted. He had watched Priscilla and Mox talk the entire time. "Why the fuck is you even talkin' to this lame ass nigga?"

"Dee, shut up and get in the car." Priscilla replied.

Dee. That was his name. Deandre Foster.

Mox knew exactly who he was now. Deandre's younger brother is the same age as Mox and Dee is only two years older than both of them.

Once again, he ignored the slick talk and continued to do his work. He would see Priscilla another day and when he did, he would be determined to get her. As for Dee, he wasn't a bit worried about him. Mox already knew who the victor would be if it came down to a one on one.

As they pulled away from the car wash, Priscilla gave Mox a tasteful look and winked her eye. At that point, he knew he had her.

A few days later, a black Lexus GS 300 with stock rims and dark tint slowly pulled into the car wash.

Mox got up from the crate he was sitting on and hurried to the car.

The driver let the window down halfway.

"Welcome to *Shiny Gleam*. How can I help you today?" Mox smiled. The window came all the way down and his smile grew bigger. "What's up, beautiful?"

"Can you take off for lunch?"

Mox turned to see where his supervisor was. "Hold on." He shouted to his co-worker. "Yo, Javier! I'm taking an early lunch, you want a sandwich!"

"Aight! Yeah, bring me one back!"

Mox tossed the drying towel he was holding into the bin and went around to the passenger side of the luxury vehicle. "This joint is nice." He ran his fingers along the custom wood-grain paneling and inhaled the fresh scent of the new leather.

"Thank you," She shifted the gear to reverse and backed out of *Shiny Gleam*.

"Is this your man's car?" Mox watched as she maneuvered the sedan. Her finger nails were manicured and polished light pink and her hair was in its natural curly state.

"No, this is not my man's car. I told you, I don't have a man, and for the record, this is my car."

"This car cost sixty-thousand dollars and you telling me it's yours."

"How do you know the price of this car?"

"I specialize in cars and women." He laughed.

"Is that right?" She was already in love with his humor. "Sixty-thousand dollars ain't a lot of money." She boasted.

"To who?"

"What if I told you that you could make sixty-thousand dollars in one night?"

Mox looked at her in disbelief. "What I gotta do?" He was anxious.

Priscilla chuckled. "Just like that, huh? No questions asked."

"Maybe, one."

"And what would that be?"

"Would I have to kill anybody for it?"

For a moment, Priscilla didn't say a word; she just focused on the road in front of her. Twenty feet ahead, she came to a stop at a red light. "Only if you want to." she answered.

That day Priscilla and Mox ate lunch together at *Subway* and then she dropped him back off at work.

Even though she was three years older than he was, Priscilla liked Mox and the feeling was something new to her. She was rarely interested in guys her age, let alone someone younger than she was, but Mox was different. It was something about his ambiance that caught her attention the first time they met. He was truly eager and confident, not to mention his cockiness was attractive.

After a few dinner dates and two trips to the movies, Priscilla invited Mox over to her apartment.

The cab pulled up to the huge building on Pelham Road.

"Seven-sixty." The driver said. "That'll be six and a quarter."

Mox paid the fare and stepped out into the summery night air. He was rocking a dark blue pair of *Guess* jean shorts, a white short sleeve, three-button polo shirt and his brand new white on white *Air Force Ones.*

He walked into the building and looked for Priscilla's last name on the intercom list. She told him the buzzer number, but it slipped his mind that fast.

Searching through the long list of tenants, he finally spotted her name. *Davis.* He said to himself. He lined his finger up with the name and slid it across to find out the apartment number.

Seeing it was *7C,* he pushed it and waited.

"Who is it?"

"Mox."

The buzzer sounded and he was able to enter the well-lit lobby. The view he took in was surprising. He marveled at how nice the building was. He had become familiar with the debris filled hallways and urine drenched elevators of the projects, but this was a world away from that and it was only ten minutes away from the hood.

Mox checked his outfit in the large, rectangular wall mirror and then rode the elevator to the seventh floor. He followed the sign on the wall and made the right toward *7A-7E.*

When he got to the door, he could hear music, it was cracked open for him to walk right in.

Damn this is nice. The luscious scent of herbs and spices tickled his nose, admiring the paintings on the wall; he noticed each one of them was of African American people.

Mox took a few more steps down the hallway and into the living room where Donell Jones' *Where I Wanna Be* boomed through the surround sound.

"This is that joint!" Mox sang along.

Girl, the love that we share is real
But in time your heart will heal
I'm not saying I'm gone but I
Have to find what life is like
Without you...

Priscilla heard Mox's voice and was moved. She joined in.

But when you love someone
You just don't treat them bad
Oh, how I feel so sad now that I wanna leave...

She grabbed the remote and hit mute. "Let me find out. What you know about Donnel Jones?"

"I like that song right there. My mother was big on R&B so that's pretty much all we listened to. She hated when I put on rap music." Mox laughed at the memory.

"That's cool," She said. "So, that's *two* things we have in common."

"What's the first?"

"Our love for cars."

"Oh, yeah... definitely." Mox looked over the warm, plush apartment. It was nicely furnished and laced with wall to wall carpet, a brown micro fiber sectional couch with matching love seat and a big screen floor unit television. "Damn, you look good."

Priscilla blushed. "Thank you." She was feeling Mox's air. He was unique in a way she couldn't describe, extremely mature and incomparable; a far cry from the ordinary.

Mox spread his arms and went to hug Priscilla.

She had to get on her tip-toes just to wrap her arms around his neck. She was 5'7, but Mox was two inches over six feet.

She looked good rocking a pair of off white linen shorts, a pink tank-top and a pair of white, ankle strap *Louis Vuitton* heels. The perfume she wore was seductive and sweet.

Her soft breasts pressed against Mox's chest and he wrapped his arms around her curvy waist.

After their embrace, Mox went to take a seat on the couch.

"You live here by yourself?"

"Yep."

"Wassup wit' your parents?"

Priscilla didn't mind sharing her personal issues with Mox. It was confusing, but she was comfortable with it. She sat down on the couch beside him and took a deep breath. "Well, my father..." She paused and looked to the ceiling. It was a touchy subject. "I don't even know. As far as I'm concerned, I don't have a father."

"Nah, don't say that. I mean, he's still alive, right?"

"I guess so."

Mox could tell it was difficult for her to explain the situation. He had been going through the same issues with his expression of the traumatic incident in his life, but the more he spoke about it the better he handled it.

"I'm being nosy but, what about your mother?"

The matters of her and her mother's affairs were far more sensitive to discuss than the absence of her father. Priscilla slighted her mother for reasons she withheld from the world, but you could see the affliction in her eyes when it was mentioned.

All she said was, "She's around."

Mox didn't want to force her to talk about it. "Okay. That's good. At least you still have them."

"They're both dead to me."

He wasn't too fond of that statement. "That aint cool, Priscilla. Please don't say things like that around me."

She was rattled by his remark. "Oh, really? Huh..." She turned her lip up. "Well, what's your story, Mr. Daniels? You can't be the only one asking questions. First of all, what color are your eyes? I never seen anybody with eyes that color and what about you mother and father?"

"My eye color is called true amber. I really don't know too much about how and why I have them, but I do know that they're very rare." Mox took a breather and relaxed back on the velvety cushion. He closed his eyes. "As far as my parents... they're dead."

A mini smiled appeared on Priscilla's face and was immediately gone once she understood he wasn't playing.

"You're not joking, are you?"

He opened his eyes and sat up. "I don't joke about shit like that. That's why I asked you not to say what you said." Mox stood up and walked to the window that overlooked Pelham Road. "You should be grateful that both your parents are still here. Never take that for granted because when they do go... it's over. You don't get anymore." He turned and looked at Priscilla. "I wish I could bring my parents *back*."

Before she became too emotional, Priscilla stood and walked over to Mox. "I'm sorry. I didn't mean to—"

He placed his index finger to his lips. "Shh... I'm good, don't worry about it."

"When did this happen?"

"Five years ago."

Priscilla was taken aback. She couldn't comprehend how a person who lost both parents only five years ago was so poised and level headed.

"That shit don't fuck with your head?"

"Hell yeah; every day... I try to block it out, but the fact is, the person who killed them is still on the streets and that bothers me."

"That's crazy." She said, returning to the kitchen. "Excuse my poor hospitality. Would you like something to drink?"

"Sure. A glass of water is cool."

Priscilla poured two glasses of water and sat back on the couch.

"Now, enough with the formalities; wassup wit' this sixty-thousand in one night?"

She laughed. "I knew that was coming sooner or later. Come here, sit down." Mox took his seat next to Priscilla. "I'ma be straight forward with you, I'm usually not this open to people about my personal business, but I like you and I see you've got potential."

"Oh yeah, thank you."

"You're welcome, but for real... you know you can have anything in the world you desire... all you gotta do is believe in it and work hard to achieve it. The boundaries are limitless." Priscilla sipped her water. "This time last year, I was homeless, dead broke and on the verge of a nervous breakdown until I met someone who changed my life. His name is Juan Carlos Ortega and he's a Colombian drug lord. I'm not gonna lie, at first our relationship was physical, but after things didn't work out, we continued to have a business relationship."

Mox was thrown off. "Why you tellin' me this?"

"Because, Mox. This man will give me anything I want. He already gave me another opportunity at life and now it's my turn to give someone else a chance to live out their dreams."

He still didn't fully comprehend where she was going with the conversation.

"Are you serious, or is this some type of joke?"

"No, I'm serious... look." She got up from the couch and went into the back room. When she returned she was holding a brown shopping bag. She placed it on the black and white, marble top coffee table. "Open the bag."

Mox peeled the bag open, reached inside and grabbed the contents out. He placed the two, taped up, rectangular packages on the table.

"What the fuck is this?" He asked.

"What does it look like?"

He grinned. "Look like cocaine to me."

"Exactly."

"You got it all wrong if you think you gon' have me out on some corner slangin' ten and twenty dollar bags of coke. Not gonna happen." He stood up like he was about to leave.

Priscilla grabbed his arm. "That's not what I think. Just sit down and let me explain it to you. It won't take long and if you don't agree, then you can leave, no love lost."

He sat down and finished the rest of his water. "I'm listening."

"One of these," She touched the package. "go for twenty-five thousand dollars in the streets. I get them wholesale from Juan Carlos for only ten thousand; therefore, the profit on each one is fifteen thousand. I'm willing to split the fifteen in half with you if you help me move them."

"Help you?"

"Yes."

"And how am I supposed to do that? Priscilla, I ain't never sold drugs a day in my life. I wouldn't know where to begin."

"This is why I'm here, Mox. I'm gonna show you everything you need to know and I guarantee you in a month's time your whole life will be different. All you have to do is follow my lead."

Priscilla's verbal abilities were immaculate. She could broker a million dollar drug deal and in the same sentence, turn around and slick talk her way out of trouble. It was gift that God had given her and she had Mox hypnotized within minutes, but the crazy part was; her feelings for him were heartfelt and genuine.

"What about your boy, Deandre?"

"Listen, Mox. The only reason I fuck with Deandre is because his sister and I are close. She asked me to put him on so he could help out with their bills and that's what I did, but he ain't you, Mox. He's in that position because I put him there." she rose from her seat and faced Mox. "These niggas out here don't want nothing but a few thousand in their pocket to front with, some new sneakers and a bunch clothes. I know you want more outta life than that, Mox."

They eyed each other steadily. The chemistry was evident and highly explosive. Mox didn't have to say a word; she already knew what he wanted.

"And you ride around in the car with him *because?*"

"Because, he can't be trusted and he doesn't have a business mind. If I give him something I ride around with him until he finishes it. I take my cut and I go, but all that comes to an end the second you tell me yes."

Mox took a minute to process everything Priscilla was speaking on. This type of opportunity didn't present itself on an everyday basis. It was two choices he had; struggle and hope things eventually get better or take action and make an immediate change.

"So, how's this supposed to work?"

They smiled at each other and Priscilla instructed him on everything he needed to do.

November, 2001...

Mox was beginning to establish himself as one of the main suppliers of cocaine in Westchester County, and he managed to stay under the radar because he was smart and he knew how to move.

He hadn't bought a car. He didn't wear jewelry and he was still living in his Aunt's apartment in the projects, but on occasion he would spend the night with Priscilla.

Their mental and physical bond was amplified and Mox's feelings were as strong as he had ever known them to be for a woman other than his mother. Over a year's time, they formed an allegiance on respect, honor and trust. They even came up with a mantra and had it tattooed in the same spot behind their ear. It read; *Let no-one stand before WE* and it was written in script with blood red ink.

Mox was sixteen years old and in love with a woman that was three years older. At least he felt like he was. He had never known the true meaning of love, but when Priscilla was in his presence he experienced completion. It was as if she could almost fill the void of his mother in an odd kind of way.

After the two most important people in his life were taken away so abruptly, Mox pledged to himself that the next person to touch something he loved would die. And his word was bond.

The day Mox accepted Priscilla's offering is the same day she cut all ties to Deandre. Of course he had no idea why she so abruptly stop coming around, but the word would soon hit the wind like a hustler with poor quality work and he would find out that *Mox* was now the one in power.

The unexpected shift in ranking was something Deandre didn't think too highly of. In fact, he was ready to do something extreme; and he did.

The entire day had been tranquil and stagnant. Mox lazed in his boxers on the spongy sofa in Priscilla's living room, punching buttons on the remote control. He was looking for the History channel. It was Tuesday, his day off and he was waiting for her to come back from food shopping.

The house phone rang, Mox leaned up and stared at it lying on the table in front of him. He let it ring until it stopped. He *never* answered Priscilla's phone. If it was her, she would call *his* cell phone.

As soon as he went to lie back, his cell phone rang.

He ruffled through some papers, saw Priscilla's name on the caller ID and fumbled to get it open.

"Hello?"

"Wassup you bitchassnigga!" The caller laughed loudly.

Mox thought it was a joke. "Yo, stop playing on the phone. Where my girl at?"

"Shut the fuck up and listen. I got yo bitch, nigga... and if you wanna see her lil' pretty fuckin' ass again, I'ma need you to go get a bag, put a hunit thousand cash in it and wait for me to call this number back in twelve hours, ya dig?"

Mox took the phone off his ear and looked at the screen a second time. It did say Priscilla. He got up from the couch and went to look out the living room window.

"Who the fuck is this?"

"Oh, you think it's a joke, nigga..." The caller slammed the phone down and Mox pressed the speaker to his ear so he could hear better. He could only make out some rustling and the sound of something being dragged across the floor.

The caller's voice was getting louder. "Hurry up, nigga! Bring that bitch over here!" He picked the phone back up. "You think I'm playing, nigga! I got somebody that wanna holla at you."

A scream came from the other end. "Hellllppp!"

Mox's eyes lit up.

"Shut up bitch!" Mox heard the slap of his hand hitting some-one's flesh. "Say hi to your little boyfriend." He put the phone to her face.

"Mox, help me, please." Priscilla cried.

Deandre snatched the phone back. "A hunit thousand, nigga! Twelve hours!"

Mox dropped the phone and pressed his temples with the palm of his hand. "Arrhhh!" He belted.

When Wise Earl found out his nephew was hustling and then witnessed for himself the magnitude in which he did it, all he could do was offer his prudent knowledge to the young hustler on the come up. He warned Mox,

If you in this game for the sole purpose of getting rich, then you gon'

have to forget about anything you love. Because the second a nigga see you got love in your heart for something, they gon' try to take it away from you.

At that precise moment, Mox could hear his uncle's sharp, raspy voice vibrating in his ear, repeating those exact words.

He was nervous. His hands were shaky and he was pacing back and forth. *Calm down, Mox.* He told himself as he inhaled a breath of the cool central air that flowed through the apartment. He closed his eyes. He tried counting to ten like he had seen someone do in a movie, but every time he got to four his concentration would shift.

Mox hurried to the back room and threw on a hoodie and some sweatpants. He opened the large closet at the back of Priscilla's room, slipped into a pair of sneakers and grabbed the *Northface* book bag that was buried in the corner.

The worriment was swelling and his thoughts were wondering.

I hope they didn't touch her?

What if I give these niggas the money and they still kill her?

"Fuck!" He tossed the bag onto the queen sized bed and stood at the foot with both hands over his face. His breathing was heavy. He silently prayed and asked God;

Why?

Mox bent down, unzipped the bag and started pulling stacks of money out. Once he reached the amount needed, he closed the bag up and went back into the living room.

Paying the $100,000 ransom wasn't a problem or a second thought. If that's what it took to get Priscilla back, it was a small price to pay.

He searched the table and the couch for his phone before spotting it on the floor by the window. When he picked it up he saw a missed call from Javier, his co-worker/Lieutenant.

A thought stumbled into Mox's brain and he quickly cooked up a scheme, but he needed help. He pressed the seven numbers into his phone.

It rang two times and Javier picked up. "Mox, I was callin—"

"Javier, I need your help."

"Yeah, anything, Mox... you alright?"

"I... I can't talk over the phone. I'm on my way to you," he stuttered.

"Aight, I'm here."

Mox went to the kitchen and got the keys to Priscilla's other car. He snatched the book bag and went to meet up with Javier.

Eleven hours and fifty-five minutes later, Mox's cell phone rang. He looked around the room and then he answered it.

"Hello?"

"You got that?"

"Yeah."

Mox envisioned Deandre smiling ear to ear smile.

"Aight, this is what it is... I want you to—"

He broke in. "Hold up, homie..." the phone went silent for a few seconds and then Mox picked it back up. " I got somebody that wanna holla at you."

"Deandre, please... let that girl go!" his mother cried. "They gon' kill us!"

He couldn't believe what he was hearing.

Mrs. Foster and his little sister, Shelly were tied up to two chairs with their wrist and ankles duct taped, confined to a soggy, dark room that reeked of urine. Tears covered their faces, but they kept their eyes on Javier and his two Mexican comrades that were off to the left holding fully automatic weapons.

"Deandre, you there?"

"Yo, I swear to God, Mox... if you touch my mother or my little sister, I'ma fuckin' kill you."

"You *still* makin' threats?" Mox put the phone directly in front of his mouth. "I got your mother and your little sister over here duct taped and tied up. I'm 'bout to flip a coin. Yeah, read between the lines, nigga. Now this is how we gon' do it... give Priscilla that phone and when she calls me and tells me she's safe, I'll let your people go."

Deandre shot back. "I don't trust you."

"You got no choice." He hung up.

Twenty minutes later, Priscilla called Mox and let him know that she made it home safe.

He released the Foster family without harm. Two weeks later police found Deandre dead in his car, parked in the back of the *Stop*

& Shop Supermarket on Palmer Avenue. He suffered two gunshot wounds to the head.

Following the Foster boy's murder, Mox could no longer duck in the shadows and creep below the radar. He was on front-street now. The whole city knew about it, but the police didn't have enough evidence to charge him and he was fully aware of that.

Right after he killed Deandre, Mox went back to Priscilla's to shower and go to sleep.

No nightmares.

No visions.

Not even a thought about it, but his whole world changed after that.

3

A slight glare from the sun's rays squinted through a crack in the window shade as Mox sat at the foot end of his twin sized bed, finishing off a second bowl of cinnamon toast crunch. His attention was on the exclusive news flash that came across the 32 inch screen in front of him.

It had been ten months since the *World Trade Center* bombing and the magnitude of destruction was still inconceivable. He watched as video recordings played back the frightening incident that touched the world. All of his thoughts were on the families that suffered the loss of a loved one and how their lives were abruptly transformed within minutes. He could identify with them. He felt the same pain they did.

The fateful loss of his parents was still fresh on his brain and the only way to cease the reoccurring visions was to find out the truth.

Mox placed the empty cereal bowl on top of the television and looked down at Priscilla while she slept, peacefully.

Reaching down, he tugged lightly on the bed sheets exposing her nudeness. Her skin was flawless; like an airbrushed model in a print magazine, delicate; like an invaluable piece of art; and extremely enticing.

Mox crawled into bed behind Priscilla and inhaled her sweet essence. The pleasurable aroma got him excited and his manhood began to pulsate. It escaped through the slit in his boxer shorts and tickled her ass cheek. He reached around, put his hand between her warm, moist thighs and let his middle finger slip into her kitten.

Priscilla moaned.

Seconds later, her love syrup dribbled down Mox's knuckle.

She reached back, caressed his hardened manhood and whispered. "Get a condom."

Mox rolled onto his back and snatched a condom off the small, wooden nightstand. It was out the wrapper and on his dick in one breath.

He shoved himself halfway inside of her.

Priscilla's walls tightened and she squeezed his muscle.

Mox went deeper.

"Oohh... Mox."

He held her shoulder with his left hand and gripped her waistline with his right. The speed of his stroke increased by the seconds and the slapping sound of her soft ass cheeks against his well sculpted thighs grew louder.

Priscilla buried her face in the pillow and continued moving in rhythmic motion. Grunts of pleasure escaped her lips as she climaxed for the second time.

"Yes, Mox! Fuck me!"

Her assertive sex talk always turned him on.

Mox flipped her onto her stomach and proceeded to thrust himself deep inside of her until he reached his peak.

They rolled over, exhausted, sweaty and out of breath.

Priscilla looked in Mox's eyes. She wiped the sweat from his forehead and kissed his lips. "What's wrong?" She questioned, noticing his mind was someplace else.

The expression on his face was silent and his eyes held a puzzled stare. "Nothing, why you ask?"

Priscilla sat up in the bed. "Because, Mox, we just finishing fuckin' and now you act like you do want me to touch you."

"It's not that, Priscilla."

"Well, what is it?"

Mox rubbed his shiny bald head, pondering. "It's this whole situation with my parents—it ain't adding up to me, things don't feel right."

"Mox, listen." Priscilla got up, walked around the bed and sat on his lap. "I understand how you're feeling, but you can't let this control your life."

The frustration in the pit of his soul was boiling. Priscilla had no idea what it was like to wake up to a bloodbath. To watch your parents, especially your mother, take her last breaths in front of you. Maybe she did go through a few things, who hasn't? But whatever her troubles were, they had no similarities to Mox's experience.

"Stop comparing your situation to mine," Mox moved Priscilla off his lap and got up. "It's different, you still got your mother; she's alive."

"Mox, you know I don't fuck wit' my moms."

"That's because you choose not to. I never had a choice... this shit was cast upon me like a death ridden plague."

"So, what are you gonna do?"

He picked a towel up and tossed it to Priscilla. "I'ma do whatever I need to do to fix it. Take a shower and get dressed... we going for a ride."

An hour later, Mox pulled the polished Mercedes to the curb at the corner of 241st and White Plains Road in the Bronx.

As soon as he turned the corner the area became familiar. His recollection was detailed and vivid, as if a mental picture was embedded in his brain.

His thoughts took him back twelve years and he could see his mother's 1988 burgundy Nissan Stanza with the one hubcap, a blown out passenger side window that was filled in with a garbage bag and malfunctioning brake lights.

That was her baby, as she called it.

Priscilla tapped Mox's shoulder breaking his concentration. "Why did you pull over?"

He took the key out the ignition and let his head fall back onto the headrest. "When I was younger my mother use to move around a lot and I was with her most of the time, whether she was going to get drugs or we were going to church... I was right by her side. I saw plenty of things I probably shouldn't have seen, Priscilla, but at the end of the day those experiences shaped my way of thinking and forced me to become very observant."

Priscilla thought about her own trials as a child and how her mother was the total opposite. She admired Wanda's attempt to be in Mox's life, unlike her mother, who was always quick to chastise and humiliate her every opportunity she got.

"There are things a child's eyes shouldn't see." She said.

Mox looked into the rear-view mirror. "Well, my eyes seen it all."

"Nobody would watch you for her?"

"The only person she trusted to watch over me was my aunt Sybil and she worked a lot, so I *had* to be with her, and then she had Casey and it was all three of us running around in these streets." Mox opened his wallet, pulled out a picture and stared at it. "We would travel all over New York... that's how I learned the highways and all the major streets in the five boroughs." It was a photo of him, Casey and his mother in front of Rockefeller Center.

"Can I see?" Priscilla asked, reaching for the picture.

Mox handed it to her.

"Wow," She smiled. "You and Casey look just like your mother."

The brothers shared a lot of the same features as their mother, from their dark skin tone and structure of their faces to the size and shaping of their lips and ears.

"Everybody says that."

"If you don't mind me asking, where was your father?" She handed the photo back.

"That nigga only came around when he felt it was necessary. If my mother didn't have no money, he didn't wanna be bothered with us."

"That's crazy."

"Not really." He said. "The whole time I knew him, I never felt that father and son bond between us, so his absence didn't really bother me. It might sound a little awkward, but that's what it was."

A silence settled in and for a few seconds they sat staring into the sky, listening to the sound of passing cars.

Priscilla finally spoke. "So, why are we here?"

"Because, I keep gettin' a vision of this store every time I close my eyes," Mox smirked. "My mother loved to smoke weed. I remember her bringing me here all the time. We would go to the store over there," He pointed across the street. "And she would get whatever she needed to get and then we left... I'm hoping one of these dudes can lead me to some information. Maybe somebody in there knows her."

"Mox, that was more than seven years ago. Do you think the same people still work there?"

He pushed the car door open. "I don't know, but I'm 'bout to find out. Come get in the driver's seat and start the car up."

"You don't want me to come with you?"

"Nah, I need you in the car in case something happen and we gotta get outta here."

Priscilla sat behind the wheel and watched Mox walk across the street. He got to the door, pushed it open and entered.

The inside of the store was just the way he remembered it; cluttered, dimly lit and clouded with smoke from the incense that burned all day. The shelves were over packed with early dated vinyl records and up to date reggae CD's.

A tall, brown skinned man with a ragged beard and thick, long, golden dread locks stood behind the cash register.

Mox approached the counter, his ears filled with Peter Tosh's tranquilizing vocals as he sang through the speakers, *Wanted Dred & Alive.*

"Yes, young one... how can mi help you today?" His accent, strong, but clear enough to understand.

Mox focused his eyes on a painting that covered the back wall. It was a picture of a fair skinned man in a suit with a chiseled face, curly hair and a bunch of medals on his lapel. He was sitting at a table.

"Who is that?" He asked.

"Dat's Haile Selassie I... him da emperor of E-t-opia fa four decades!" He lifted his right hand and held up four fingers. "He da reincarnation of Jesus Christ, bredren... him gon' leed us to Zion!"

Mox felt the passion and reverence in his every word. He extended his arm and they shook hands.

"My name is Mox."

"Mox, eh... dat's a very distinctive name, bredren." He turned and called out to someone in the back. "Tyga!"

"Yah?" They yelled back.

"Come to de front!... sorry bredren, mi name Lion." He eyed Mox. "You look familiar, bredren, you from ear?"

"Nah, not really." He reached into his pocket. "I got another question though." Mox placed the picture on top of the counter. "You know her?"

Lion picked the photo up and looked at it closely. He pulled out a pair of rim wire glasses from the front pocket of his shirt and fixed them on his face.

"Bloodclaaat!" He screamed, throwing his hands to the sky. "Tyga, come now!"

"So, you know her?"

Lion sucked his teeth and slowly removed the glasses from his face. Within seconds, his entire demeanor had switched.

A short, dark, broad shouldered Rasta with dreadlocks stumbled out the back room gripping a black 500 Mossberg pump at his waistline.

"Mox, meet Tyga, him a shotta! Now you gwan hafta tell mi a lickle more 'bout why you ear..."

Mox remained calm. "I told you why I was here. That's my mother in that picture."

Lion turned and held the picture up to show Tyga.

"Dat's da dead boy Reginald woman." Tyga growled.

Mox stared at the husky man holding the shotgun. "Yeah, I'm Reginald's son."

Lion whipped his thick, golden locks around and faced Mox. "Reginald your father?"

"Yep."

"Well, mi do a favor for Reginald; a fifteen tousand dolla favor... and him never pay me back."

Mox shook his head. He knew where this was going.

"I'm sorry to hear that, dred, but he's dead now."

"Yes," Lion chuckled. "Mi know him dead, but since him your father... now *you* owe me his det!"

Tyga rushed around the counter and put the barrel of the shotgun to Mox's stomach.

The front door swung open and the nozzle of a double action, black polymer .9 millimeter was the first thing visible.

"Drop that shit slowly or they gon' be sweeping them nasty ass dreds off the floor."

"Tyga!" Lion shouted. "Gun 'eeem!"

"Shit!" Mox cursed. "Priscilla, I told you to stay in the car."

"Seven minutes, Mox. You know the rules." She clenched the baby cannon with two hands while her eyes focused on the shotgun-toting Rasta.

Tyga lowered the weapon, finally dropping it to the floor.

Lion took a step back and raised his hands to the sky. "Mi nah want no problem, bredren."

"I don't want no problems either, Dred. I just want some answers." Mox stated. "I need to know who my mother and father were dealing with... anybody they associated with."

Lion's eyes shifted to the barrel of the pistol. "Mi nah know a ting, bredren." He lied.

Mox bent down to pick the shotgun up. "I think you lying to me, Dred."

"Pussywhole... mi nah lie."

"You like sports, Dred?" Mox grabbed the nozzle of the Moss-berg and handled the 30 inch pump like a baseball bat.

Lion ignored him, sucked his teeth and then shot Tyga a distasteful glare.

"I love me some baseball..." Mox continued. "Last year, I was All American, ranked number six in the country. They called me, M. Daniels." Mox positioned himself like he was at the plate, ready to take a pitch. "It didn't matter if the pitcher could throw ninety five miles per hour..." He raised the shotgun and twirled it like he was about to swing for the fence. "I was tay-king-it-out-the park!" Aiming for his ribs, Mox swung the lightweight weapon with as much strength as he could muster.

The force of the blow shattered Lion's elbow when he tried to block it and he collapsed to the floor.

Again, Mox swung. This time slamming the weapon down on his leg, crushing bones on impact.

Lion writhed in pain, but somehow managed to not scream.

"Hol lon!" Tyga reasoned. He wanted to help. "Mi tell you, mi tell you."

Mox moved toward Tyga. "See, now he's a real friend."

"Tyga, ya nah gwan tell dis faassie boy nuttin'." Lion was furious.

"Yo," Mox nodded at Priscilla. "Shut him up."

Priscilla pressed the cold steel to Lion's lips. "All I need is a reason." She whispered. It wasn't the first time she had held a gun to someone's head and it sure wouldn't be the last.

"Tyga, tell me something before this shit get crazy." Mox cautioned.

Tyga's lip quivered. He was timorous. In all the years he had stood by Lion's side never once had he seen him get treated this way. People feared Lion.

"All mi kno is..." He looked at his helpless friend. "Reginald use to work for de white man, dey call him The Ghost."

"The Ghost? Why they call him that?"

"Because, afta him murder ya whole family—" He paused and looked Mox in his eyes. "Him vanish!"

Mox wasn't at all moved by Tyga's story. "That's it? Where can I find this Ghost?"

Tyga shook his head slowly and a demonic grin appeared on his face. "Ya nah gwan find him... him gwan find you!"

Mox was angry, and when he became angry his inner beast would rear its hideous face. It was like a Dr. Jekyl and Mr. Hyde transformation. One minute he was calm, restrained and well mannered, and then, at the blink of an eye he could become violent, audacious and discourteous.

He could never figure out where this maniacal being derived from, but at times he enjoyed it; it was gratifying. He was able to unshackle those locked up feelings and set them free.

"Go start the car." He hadn't looked at her or said her name, but Priscilla knew it was time to go. She backed away from Lion and stepped out the door.

Mox ordered Tyga to sit on the floor next to Lion.

"I need to get a message to this Ghost guy. Who's gon' deliver it?" Tyga slightly raised his hand and nodded his head. "Good... so we don't need him." He lifted the black 500 and let it explode. The roaring blast was ear-piercing and the slug blew away the top half of Lion's head. Blood, brains and dredlocks were everywhere. "Tell The Ghost we need to speak."

Before Mox left the small store, he checked the back room and came out with a *Puma* duffle bag containing three pounds of high grade marijuana and $65,000 in cash.

He wiped the shotgun of his prints, snatched the photo off the counter and walked away from the scene with no regret.

When he got to the car, he tossed the bag into the backseat and jumped in the passenger. The first thing he said was, "Where you get that gun from, Priscilla?"

"Damn, can I pull off?" She put the car in drive and sped away. "I took it from my brother."

Mox reclined his seat. "You know you could'a got me killed back there."

"I was just tryna help."

"I'm sure you were, but if you listen to me... that would be an even bigger help."

Priscilla cut her eyes at Mox. "I can handle myself."

Mox laughed and they rode in silence the rest of the way back.

4

NOVEMBER 2003

Mox was still working at the car wash, the only difference now was that he controlled a $200,000 a-week cocaine operation and *Shiny Gleam* was his headquarters. As soon as he was put into position, Mox recruited all five of his co-workers and appointed them each a specific job. All he did is answer his phone and count the money. He hadn't touched drugs since the day Priscilla presented the offer to him and that's how he liked it.

The dealings were run so precisely that it never interfered with the daily car wash flow. Nobody saw drugs come in and nobody saw them go out. At the least, Mox would move 7-10 kilo's a week, sometimes 15, but if he really wanted to turn it up, he could easily move 20-30 without breaking a sweat. Priscilla had customers coming in from out of town on a daily basis. It was no longer unusual to see out of state plates pulling into the *Shiny Gleam,* and some days the parking lot resembled a car show, but the supervisors never knew a thing because all the drug flow did was enhance the already profitable business.

Everything Priscilla said to Mox eventually came to fruition. He was young, black, handsome and rich, living a lifestyle most people dream about, but he was never content. Being a drug dealer was never in his plans. In the beginning, all he wanted to do was find the man that murdered his parents. Somewhere down the line he got sidetracked and lost focus.

Not a bit of information on "The Ghost" had surfaced since the record shop murder and Mox didn't have any other leads to go on. A few times he even felt like giving up, but seeing that picture in his wallet always reassured him that he was fighting for something that meant a lot to him. At any cost he was going to find who he was looking for.

When Mox first asked Priscilla if he would have to kill anybody for the money, her response was, *only if you want to.*

After a year in the game he learned that meant; *of course you are.*

The feeling Mox got after he killed Lion was nothing compared to what he felt when he murdered Deandre.

5

Mox came to a stop at the red light at Lincoln Avenue and North Avenue. He looked up in the rear-view mirror and saw a blue and white NRPD patrol car slowing up behind him. He snatched the seat belt and quickly snapped it in. When the light turned green he made the right and went up North Avenue with the patrol car following.

As soon as he passed the bus depot the cop tossed his lights on.

"Fuck!" He cursed aloud seeing the flashing red lights in his mirror. Mox didn't know why he was being flagged. He had his seat belt on and he was doing the speed limit. He pulled the $90,000 Aston Martin to the curb and waited for the officer. When he heard the cop's voice come through the horn, that's when he got nervous.

"Driver! Let me see your hands!"

Mox shut the ignition off and placed both of his hands outside the window.

Two more patrol cars and an unmarked had arrived on the scene.

At 12:10 in the afternoon on a Wednesday, in the middle of North Avenue, in the blistering cold, the New Rochelle police department had Mox Daniels surrounded and he didn't even know what he did.

Pedestrians looked on in astonishment as two officers ran at the car from opposite angles with their guns drawn. One of them snatched the door open and yanked Mox from the driver's seat.

"Yo, what the fuc—"

In two seconds, Mox was faced down on the frosted pavement with a knee in his back and a .40 Caliber to his head.

"New Rochelle police, don't fuckin' move!" He screamed in Mox's ear.

A short, black detective with a terrible receding hairline stepped in.

"Bring 'em up." He told them.

They brought Mox to his feet.

He had tiny pieces of gravel stuck to the left side of his cheek from his face being pressed against the cold concrete, and one of his sneakers had come off.

"Mox Daniels, you're under arrest for the murder of Deandre Foster. At this time anything you say can and will be used against you in a court of law. You—"

Mox went completely deaf for a few seconds. He stared directly at the detective, watching his mouth move, but no sound came out.

One officer shouted. "We got something!" and lifted a black .9 millimeter out the glove compartment.

Mox turned, saw the officer holding the gun up and shook his head.

Priscilla.

He was arraigned on murder and gun charges and then two days later a judge set bail at one million dollars.

COUNTY JAIL - VALHALLA, NEW YORK – (VISITING ROOM)

After a thirty-five minute drive and standing in line for over an hour, Priscilla finally made it to the inside of the visiting area of the county jail. She went through the search, gave the C.O. her slip and was escorted to a table in the far left corner of the room.

It was her first time coming to visit anyone in prison, so she was amazed at how many women came to see their boyfriends, husbands, and family members. What she didn't like was people searching through her shit. Once she got past that, she was good.

As she scanned the room, she counted thirty tables and every one of them was occupied. Every few minutes an inmate and his/her visitors would depart and go their separate ways and two minutes later more visitors and another inmate would be at the table.

Mox came through the door, passed the guard a piece of paper and was directed to his table.

She got up when she saw him walking toward her and they hugged.

Mox embraced her firmly, but not too hard. He rested his face in the nape of her neck and kissed her gently and then moved to her lips. Their tongues twisted, and before they broke away, Priscilla slipped something down Mox's pants.

"Damn..." She said, savoring the taste of his saliva. She pecked his lips once more before she sat down. "That suit is real bright." She tugged at his orange county jumpsuit.

Mox smirked. "Oh, you got jokes, huh?"

Priscilla blushed. She almost couldn't look him in his eyes. She felt guilty.

"I'm sorry, Mox."

He clenched his teeth. "I told you about that fuckin' gun, Priscilla."

"I know, Mox, I'm sorry," tears built up in her eyes. She sniffled and wiped them away. She had been careless and left her gun in his car.

"Listen, baby, don't cry..." He grabbed Priscilla's hands and held them tight. "I'm just a little upset right now and I don't mean to take it out on you. Don't worry about this... all this shit gon' go away."

"What are they saying?"

"They ain't saying nothing. That murder charge is bullshit. I can beat that with the right lawyer." He looked around and lowered his tone. "But this other thing might sit me down for a sec."

"How long is a second, Mox?"

"It all depends. Did you do what I asked you to do?"

Priscilla didn't even hear the question, she was too busy watching the man to the right of them ice grill Mox.

She whispered. "Why he looking at you like that?"

Mox glanced and smirked. "That's Deandre's little cousin, Rudy. I think he wants revenge." he laughed.

"That's not funny, Mox. You better be careful in here."

"I got him taken care of. That's why I told you to bring this." He pointed to his pants. "So, what did he say?"

"Who?"

"Juan Carlos, Priscilla."

She got lost for a minute. "Oh, he said if he does this for you, you're gonna have to owe him a favor."

Mox rubbed his head. "I figured that. Tell him everything is good. Just hurry up." he leaned in to kiss her lips. "Damn, you taste good."

Priscilla couldn't help but smile. It had only been two days and she was missing her man crazily.

The one hour visit had gone by quickly.

"Daniels, time's up." The guard came to the table and handed Mox his pass.

"Okay, a few days and you should be out of here." She kissed him one more time before she turned to leave. "I love you."

It was the first time she said it and it caught Mox off guard. He didn't know what to say back even though he had the same feeling, so he said nothing and let her walk through the doors.

"Daniels, let's go!" The guard shouted again.

Mox was housed in a part of the prison that they called "The Old Jail" specifically because of the old, rusted bars, molded and cracked walls and no hot water. In the summertime, the walls would sweat and in the winter they would be ice blocks, literally. It was just like the jails you see in those old movies; 23 hour lock-down with one hour of rec.

As soon as he got back to his cell, Mox put a sheet up and stripped to his boxers. He reached into the briefs he had on underneath and pulled out two balloons the same length and width as his thumb. He bit the small knots at the top and ripped the latex apart.

The C.O's keys were jingling and Mox knew he was getting closer to his cell. He stashed the ripped balloons and the contents under the thin, county issued mattress and sat on the toilet.

"What the fuck you in there doin', inmate?" The C.O pulled the sheet back and peeked in.

Mox had a magazine in his hand, sitting on the toilet with his draws on his ankles. "Taking a shit, C.O."

He Looked at Mox and turned his nose up. "You gonna fuckin' stink the joint up, inmate. Put some fuckin' water on that shit... and hurry up and get this sheet off my goddamn bars." He let go of the sheet, walked back down the tier and hollered. *"Count in five minutes, ladies!"*

Mox jumped up and pushed the weak mattress to the side. He tossed the ripped balloons in the toilet, flushed them and unrolled the five one-hundred dollar bills Priscilla had given him. The other balloon was full of marijuana.

Getting the contraband into the prison was an easy task for Mox because he knew one of the visiting room C.O.'s. Usually after a visit you had to walk through a metal detector and get stripped searched before going back to your block, but because Mox had a name and he was able to dish out a few dead presidents; he was invisible to the guards.

He peeled off two big faces, folded them up as small as he could and then he threw his orange county pants back on and snatched the sheet off the bars. Before the guard called the count, Mox rolled up a couple of marijuana sticks, scribbled something on a piece of paper and sent the note two cells down on a line.

"On the count!" The C.O hollered.

Mox stood at the entrance of his cell and waited for the guard to make his round.

"Williams!" The guard shouted into the cell next to Mox. *"Williams, get your ass on the gate! It's count time."*

When they called count you had to be on your feet, standing at your gate in full county oranges and there was absolutely no talking.

An hour and a half passed, count cleared and the shift changed.

Mox hopped off his bunk once he heard the C.O call out, *"On the chow!"*

He stood by his gate and waited for the trustee to come by.

"Yo, wassup?" He stopped at Mox's cell. He was a chubby, light skinned kid with corn row braids. "That was you who sent the kite, right?" he slid Mox's food tray through the feed up in the bars.

Mox spoke low. "Yeah... your name Botta Bing, right?"

"Yeah... why?"

"Nah, my boy Javier told me that you and him is good. He said you could get me what I needed. " Mox flashed a few of the marijuana sticks he had in his hand.

"Oh, yeah..." Botta Bing nodded. "Yeah, I got that kite. What's the situation though?"

Mox stuffed three marijuana sticks and the two hundred dollars into his hand. "I need what's on that paper tomorrow morning, and then at lunch I need you to bring four cell's tray over here before you give it to him."

Botta Bing screwed his face up. "That's askin' a lot." he looked down at what Mox had given him. "I'm sayin' that's the nigga Rudy's cell, right? Check it," he looked down the tier. "I don't like that nigga anyway, so whatever problems y'all got, that's between y'all. I'm just sayin'" he shrugged his broad shoulders and made a gesture with his hands. "You don't know me, I don't know you."

Mox smiled. "Exactly."

The next morning Botta Bing tapped on Mox's cell and slid his breakfast tray through the feed up.

Mox got up and went to the gate. "Did you get it?"

Botta Bing passed him a small, plastic tube that looked like perfume. "Yo, what the fuck is that shit?"

"Ebony Dream." Mox grinned. "Make sure you bring that tray over here at lunch."

Later that afternoon Rudy Foster had to be rushed across the street to Westchester Medical Center to get his stomach pumped, but the doctors couldn't figure out what caused it.

The following day Mox made bail and walked out of the county jail a free man. As soon as he stepped into the parking lot, a black guy in a grey suit approached him. "Mr. Daniels," he called out.

Mox kept walking. He sped his pace up. If it was the feds, they were going to have to wrestle him down.

The black guy in the suit called again. "Mr. Daniels, I'm a friend of Juan Carlos."

Mox stopped and turned around. "Who?"

"Juan Carlos." He gave Mox his card. "I just spoke with Priscilla. She told me to meet you here. My name is Charles Woods and I'll be representing you throughout this process."

Mox took the card and looked it over. "Where my girl at?"

"I told her we had a few things to discuss about your case, so she went home to wait for you."

"Ain't nothing to discuss." Mox started to walk off.

Charles pulled a manila folder from his briefcase and tapped Mox on his arm with it. "Somebody was there, Mox."

He spun his neck around quickly. "I don't know what the fuck you talking about. Nobody was no-where."

Charles opened the folder and handed Mox a photo of a young white kid with dirty blonde hair, blue eyes and a few freckles on his nose. "Billy Worsham; works the overnight shift at Stop & Shop on the weekends. Apparently, the night of said murder, Mr. Billy here went to take his break and had his little girlfriend meet him in the back lot. He was giving it to her from the back when he says he heard shots and looked up." Charles and Mox locked eyes. "Billy says he can identify the shooter."

"Fuck!" Mox almost knocked the folder out of Charles' hand.

Charles took a step closer to Mox. "Mr. Daniels, we both know what needs to happen here if you want to continue to operate on these streets. The gun charge is the least of your worries. Ballistics came back and it wasn't the gun that Deandre got killed with." Charles put his hand on Mox's shoulder. "Most you'll do on that is five. I'll see to that, but it's on you to handle this other thing." He grabbed Mox's arm, shook his hand and turned to leave. "Oh, there's a car at the end of the lot waiting to take you to see Priscilla."

Mox stood in the middle of the parking lot, looking into the sky at a school of birds, dancing through the desiccated, wintry air. He wished he could be a bird and fly away from all the trouble that was bringing him down. He wanted to know where those birds came from and where they were headed.

He breathed...

6

The night Mox bailed out of the county jail, he went directly to Priscilla's apartment and it would be one of the last nights they would get to spend together for a long time. When he walked in all the lights were dimmed, but the soft, angelic voice of *Whitney Houston* could be heard from a distance. She was singing about good love.

He entered the bedroom where Priscilla was stretched out across her queen sized bed, wearing a pink, sheer, camisole top with matching crotch-less panties. She was mouthing the words to the song with *Whitney*.

> *NOW YOU'RE HERE LIKE YOU'VE BEEN BEFORE*
> *AND YOU KNOW JUST WHAT I NEED...*
> *IT TOOK SOME TIME FOR ME TO SEE...*

Mox stripped to his boxer shorts and got in the bed beside her. The sweet, inviting, redolent of her *Estee Lauder* White Linen perfume, inflamed his appetite for sex. The few days he spent away felt like a lifetime, and he desired the gentle, sensuous touch of a female.

"Did you know this was my favorite song?" Priscilla spoke softly and caressed his chest. She ran her hand down his chiseled six-pack and into his boxers.

Mox closed his eyes and let *Whitney's* harmonic vocals tranquilize him. He was in a calm paradise, enjoying how Priscilla slowly stroked his rod until it stiffened in her hand.

Mox lifted his head and looked at Priscilla. "My mother told me the music you fall in love with is sometimes a reflection of your inner most feelings."

Priscilla mounted Mox and kissed his lips lightly. "Well, your mother was right." she covered his face with kisses, making her way to sucking his earlobe.

He wrapped his arms around her waist and pulled her warm body closer to his so he could feel her vagina pulsating on his hardened muscle. Priscilla kissed down his neck and onto his stomach, leaving small rivers of saliva running down his abdomen. When she went to slide his boxers off, she said. "I wanna taste you." Mox sat up, moved down to the foot end of the bed and Priscilla got on her knees between his legs. She tugged at his dick with both hands and then she licked around the head. Mox grabbed the back of her neck and shoved himself deep inside her warm mouth.

"Ohhh..." he moaned as he watched her pretty lips slide up and down his tool. She coated his ten inch pole with loads of wetness and made a loud slurping sound while doing so .

Mox plucked at her beautiful, protruding, brown nipples with one hand and kept the other on her neck, guiding her mouth while he passionately fucked her face. They stood and he lifted her 140 pound frame and buried his face in her nectarous, drippy, vagina.

"Oh, my GOD! Baby, I'm cummin!" She tightened her thigh muscles around his neck and choked his face as she convulsed from multiple orgasms.

Mox laid her on her back and positioned himself on top of her. He flicked her nipples with his tongue and slipped his little man inside her steamy wonderland. The fit was perfect. Priscilla reached up, grabbed Mox around his neck and pulled him in close. "I want you to do it slow..." she put her tongue in his mouth so she could taste herself. "Make love to me, Mox." her voice was heavenly and appealing. He carefully nudged his long, dark, third leg deeper and deeper into her swollen kitten while she clawed at his back and tensed up. It felt like he was in her stomach. Mox grabbed her face with both his hands and sucked her soft, sweet lips as he continued his slow, long stroke.

Priscilla felt his cadence increase and he dug further into her canal. "Don't pull it out." she whispered in his ear.

On cue, Mox's body shivered. He sucked her lip harder and gripped the back of her head. "Priscilla... I'm 'bout to cum." He mumbled.

"Cum inside me, baby." She climaxed at the same time he did, and they let out a sigh of ecstasy. They fell asleep engulfed in each others arms as he was still inside of her.

THREE WEEKS LATER, seventeen-year-old Billy Worsham's body was found on the Northbound side of the Sprain Brook Parkway, between Scarsdale and Hastings. He died from multiple gunshots to the chest. He was the only witness in the Deandre Foster case and now he was gone.

The Westchester County D.A knew they could no longer charge Mox with murder, so he plead out to a firearm possession and was promised six years at sentencing, which would be in April.

Mox felt the pressure of being caged as his sentencing day grew closer. He wasn't looking forward to being locked away and he had even thought about running.

Priscilla's hands were shaking as she held the steering wheel and pulled into the county courthouse parking lot. She wanted to stop the car and wail like a two year old, but she had to be strong for Mox. She had to prove to him that she could keep the foundation secure and step up as his woman. It was already embedded in her mind that she would continue to stand by his side during the entire sentence; whether it was six days or six years.

"What are you thinkin' about?" She asked, pulling the key out the ignition.

Mox sat up in his seat and put his hand on Priscilla's thigh. "You."

"What about me?" She placed her hand on top of his.

Mox leaned over and kissed her delicate lips. "I love you." he whispered.

A single droplet fell from the well of her eye and Mox wiped it. He touched her forehead with his lips and told her, "I'll be right back. I gotta take a piss."

"Mox... in the parking lot? What if the police see you?"

"What they gon' do, take me to jail?"

Priscilla couldn't do anything but smile because Mox's sense of humor was one of the main reasons she loved him.

She sat in the car and waited for him to come back.

And waited.

And waited some more.

Priscilla sat in the car for seven hours staring at the corner, hoping Mox would step out the shadows at any given moment, but he never did. That day would be the last time she saw Mox Daniels for a long time.

He managed to evade the law for a whole year without incident. They finally caught up to him in Randolph County West Virginia, living in a trailer, tucked off deep in the woods. He was extradited to New York and sentenced in Westchester County court to six years; all to be served in a state correctional facility.

UPSTATE CORRECTIONAL FACILITY – FRANKLIN, NY (THE SHU)

After serving 3½ years in Clinton Correctional Facility, Mox was moved to Upstate Box because of a tier three disciplinary ticket he received for contraband. His cell had been the target of a shakedown and the C.O.s found a homemade shank taped to the bottom of his toilet. Usually, he would've been charged with a third degree felony, but the hearing judge was lenient. He took away Mox's good time and gave him a year and a half in the box.

The day Mox was transferred from the county jail to the state prison was one he would remember for the rest of his life. He knew from the time he stepped foot off the bus that he was in a different world.

State and county were two variant monsters that could never be compared. Mox knew that in order for him to survive, he would have to play his hand in a different fashion. The rules weren't the same and the players weren't either, so he was compelled to modify his strategy and adjust his game plan.

The SHU (Special Housing Unit) Aka "The Box" is where the state housed it's most vile inmates. If you were sentenced to time in the box, it was because of a fight or some sort of contraband.

Mox had been in "The Box" for over 500 days, confined to a 9 ½ by 12 ft. double-bunk cell for twenty-three hours a day. The beds were two steel ledges bolted into the wall and behind them, a steel door which lead to the recreational yard that was about the same size as the cell. It also had a small writing table, some storage space and a shower on the left side. Everything was controlled by the staff from the outside.

During his time in Upstate, Mox never had a cellmate that he got along with. They were too loud, too dirty or too tough and not one of one of them lasted more than two weeks. It didn't matter how big or how small they were, none of them could fuck with Mox.

With nothing but time, he sharpened his hand skills along with his mind by shadow boxing and practicing meditation. His whole day was scheduled to a tee. He slept for six hours, read for twelve, meditated for five and went to recreation for one.

It wasn't until his last ninety days, that Mox was finally placed in a cell with someone decent.

It was 49 year old Priest from Yonkers, New York. He was serving a thirteen year sentence for a jewel heist he pulled in 1998, and he only had a year left. The papers say he got away with three million in diamonds. The police only recovered diamonds totaling 1.5 million.

Priest was 6'3, 290 pounds, dark skinned and in superior physical shape for a man his age. Mox took a liking to Priest as soon as he stepped through the gate. It was the aura. His cell was clean. Everything was in order, nothing was out of place and it didn't reek of dirty socks and underarms.

They built a connection, and for the first time, Mox could honestly say he found a friend in Priest. They would talk all day. It got to a point where Mox was no longer afraid to share the repressed thoughts of his past. He got a chance to express himself and he wasn't worried about being judged.

One ironic thing they had in common was their fathers were taken from them at an early age. It was something they could talk about for hours at a time.

The days passed with ease, and the time came for Mox to make his return back into the world. It was a bittersweet feeling leaving someone that you had just gotten to know, someone you admired, but Mox had a whole life ahead of him and he still had unfinished business to take care of.

He thought about all that was going on in the world and the blessing of a second chance he had been given. He reminisced on the promise he made Casey in a letter he wrote two years ago.

I promise I'll be there when you get drafted to the NBA. He wrote. And he was going to be able to keep that promise.

"Daniels, on the discharge!" The C.O yelled.

Mox shook Priest's hand and gave him a brotherly hug. "I'ma see you when you touch the streets. Be safe in here."

Priest held his hand firm. "Mox, can I ask you a question before you go?"

"Of course, old man." Mox shot a playful jab at Priest's abs.

"Seriously," He looked directly at him. "If you find him, what you gon' do to him?"

Mox stared and for the first time he noticed the color of Priest's eyes. He was drawn to them because they were almost identical to his, maybe a shade or two lighter. He grinned, knowing what Priest was talking about, but he wasn't expecting a question like that. He thought about it for a second.

"First, I'ma ask him why? And then..." the fire in Mox's eyes flickered. "I'ma kill him."

WHILE MOX WAS LOCKED AWAY, Cleo was playing football. He was considered one of the best defensive linemen in the country his senior year. Colleges across the US were scouting the Daniels boy and success looked like a foreseeable destination. A few months before his senior year came to an end, Cleo was awarded a full ride scholarship to play at Syracuse University. He committed and went on to gain national exposure.

His sophomore year was outstanding. He led the ACC in tackles and sacks, which caught the eye of an NFL scout for the New York Jets. Cleo was destined to become a professional superstar, but his non-compassionate outlook on life hindered his decision making and he chose to indulge within the wrong circle of associates.

Ninety days before the 2006 NFL draft, Cleo was shot in the back of his head, at a birthday party he attended on the lower East Side of Manhattan. He was seconds away from a flat line and the pearly gates. He was knocking on the door, but it wasn't his time to arrive.

Cleo was admitted into the Westchester County Medical Center where he slept in a coma for five and a half months. His lifelong dream of becoming an NFL superstar faded like smoke clouds in a gusty wind.

After a full year of recovery, Cleo's speech, sight and limbs were almost back to normal. Although he had to learn how to talk and walk all over again, his determination fueled his work ethic and he redeemed himself, getting back to his feet as if nothing ever happened.

Cleo came to the realization that his football career was no longer a possibility. It took a minute, but he finally accepted it.

He trained his body daily, going to the gym four days a week. At the time of the shooting, he was an agile 275 pounds, and then after surgery he lost 60 pounds, but gained that back plus more during his rehab. He was naturally a big kid, not to mention, he was light on his feet.

Once he gained his confidence, Cleo started bouncing at nightclubs, mainly in the Bronx and Manhattan area. He built his reputation throughout the club scene as the guy you did not want to bump heads with.

Cleo's knuckle game was as sharp as a thorn's needle. His temperament was reckless and his attitude reluctant. To add, he was disrespectful when it came to women. In his warped mind, he believed they enjoyed it and the foul part was he treated his mother no differently.

Cleo's notoriety grew and he built connections with big names in the drug game, as well as the entertainment industry. He was unsettled about not being able to play professional ball, but the underground lifestyle seemed to satisfy his cravings.

IT WAS May 2010 and Mox had only been home a month, yet he was already living a lucrative lifestyle. He aligned his old crew from the car wash and went back to business. Quickly, he realized things weren't the same as they had been five years ago. He no longer had the connect he once cherished, and a piece of his heart was still missing.

Mox had grown up in prison. He became bold and completely certain of himself. The air he exuded was of a boss and those qualities were the ones Cleo recognized while they were growing up. He was afraid of them.

Mox was back in control of his own situation, in command of his own destiny and governing the fate of others. He was beginning to take full advantage of the distinctive qualities God had given him, and those countless hours he spent alone gave him the time to reflect on how everyone around him had an impact on his life. He was sometimes curious about the motives of his cousin. The resentment was clear-cut in Cleo's actions, speech, and disposition, but as they grew older he learned to disguise it and shadow a lot of his true feelings. Mox hadn't considered Cleo to be at threat, and so he brushed it off as a small thing and remained loyal to his family.

One of the re-connections Cleo made was with his old high school teammate, Mikey T. It was at a night club he was working. After they talked for most of the night, Cleo found out about Mikey's family, the Telesco's. He knew who they were and what they did. He had done some work for Mikey's younger brother, Vito, but at the time he didn't make the connection.

The Telesco's ecstasy ring brought in millions a year. Their only problem was that the labs they had set up were in low income housing areas because they didn't want them in their own communities. It was product placement, but in doing this, it left them open to stick-ups, murders and problems with the local dealers in those areas.

Mikey T asked Cleo if he could align a protection crew for a new lab they were setting up in the Bronx, and that's how the business venture was born.

After seeing that Cleo's crew was official, Mikey brought him to meet his father, Vinny Telesco aka The Old Man.

Vinny took a liking to Cleo. He'd been hearing nothing but great stories of his truth and loyalty, so much that he negotiated a percentage of the gross amount from every lab to Cleo as long as he could assemble a protection crew and put an end to all the robberies and violence around the locations.

That's exactly what Cleo did. But in order for it to be done right, he needed cousin Mox to run the business. He was opposed to once again riding in his shadows, but there was clearly no other choice in the matter if he wanted it to become profitable. He sucked it up and dealt with the circumstances the best way he could.

Together they formed **"The Union"**

Structured identical to the American Labor Union, Mox arranged an organization of four Union rep members, not including himself and Cleo. The common goal was to band together and create better working conditions for employees.

Negotiations such as wages, rules, complaint procedures, hiring, firing, benefits and workplace safety were discussed through labor contracts. If a worker had a problem or a concern, he/she were to inform the elected Union rep of that borough.

From there, a meeting would be set up and the Union rep would present the information to Cleo and Mox, whereas they would come to a mutual agreement.

Each lab employed eight workers. Five in, three out. Two chemists to mix and administer the actual drugs. One engineer controlling the compressor machine, which produced up to 500 pills every three minutes, and two assembly line workers, usually females. They bagged up the bundles which consisted of 1000 pills per bag. The other three employees were armed guards, patrolling the outside areas of the lab.

The rules were strict and enforced in the common area around lab sites. The Union rep's job was to make sure everything ran according to plan. If not, they would have to face Cleo and Mox, and the outcome of that was never a good one.

THE UNION

Javier Ramirez, 24 years old, 5ft 9inches, born in Guatemala. He's the elected Brooklyn Union Rep. He was the one that got Mox the job at Shiny Gleam in 2000. They developed a firm relationship after Havier helped him with the Deandre issue.

Following Mox's incarceration, Javier built his reputation on the streets as a stick-up kid in Yonkers. In 2006, he got pulled over on the New Jersey turnpike with 20 pounds of marijuana and went to the feds for 36 months.

Besides his Union Rep seat, Javier was Mox's most trusted man. He handled the supply of most the lower level Brooklyn dealers and alongside that, he owned car lot where he sold used cars.

Frank Williams, 26 years old, 6ft tall, 205 pounds, from Greenburg. He's the Staten Island Union Rep. Frank earned his nickname, "The Chess Player" because of his strategic moves to elude authorities and out-think his enemies. Back when they worked at the car wash, Frank was on windows and tires, now he's rich, intelligent and handsome with a stronghold on the coke game in Staten Island. Frank was worth millions.

In 2009 he opened up a nightclub in Manhattan called "RED" and hired Cleo as head of security. He also helped Mox get back in position when he came home. He fronted him the buy money on five kilo's.

Mox admired the fashion in which Frank did business. He was always truthful and never afraid to speak his mind. On top of that, he controlled a small army of killers who left no witnesses. Frank was among the few who gained Mox and Cleo's trust.

Nate Barnes, 25 years old, 5ft 6inches, 200 pounds. He's the Union Rep for the borough of Manhattan. Nate is by far the most callous of the bunch and is known for his dark glasses, brash attitude and thirst for blood. A short time after leaving Shiny Gleam, Nate became a hired gun for a Peruvian drug cartel. He has strong ties to some of the world's wealthiest people and is feared globally.

Nate was the person Mox kept in contact with during his incarceration, because he dwelled in the circle of assassins. If anybody could find out information on the man who killed Mox's parents, it was him, so he kept him close.

Papi, 28 years old, 5ft 8inches, 175 pounds. He's in control of the Bronx borough. While working with Mox at the car wash, Papi stashed as much money as he could before leaving and was able to open up two bodegas on the Northside of the Bronx. Mox mainly used the stores as stash spots.

Just like in prison, if it was a weapon you needed, all you had to do was go see the Spanish dudes. On the streets it was no different. Papi had the illest gun connect heard of and anything The Union needed, he supplied. To be the humblest out the crew, Papi had the means to cause the most damage.

The Union would meet with the Italians on the first Sunday of the New Year at the Pallazzo Hotel in Las Vegas to discuss the previous month's earnings and go over the outline for the current quarter. Any disputes Union Reps had toward each other were addressed at the meet and usually taken care of.

The meeting was less than two weeks away and Cleo was hoping that everything would go well. He was aware of the tension between his cousin, Mox and the Italians, but he was pretty sure it could be diffused before things got out of hand. What Cleo didn't know was Mox had his own agenda and he was playing by his own set of rules.

7

A dense fog settled on the quiet night as Cleo stood, gun in hand, red beam dancing on Supreme's forehead. He honestly didn't know how it had gotten to this point, but what he did know was that shit was about to get real.

His heart beat at a high rate and his stomach was in a twist, but he had to get this done. It was his only chance to prove himself to Mox.

His hands, covered in black leather gloves, he held the .40 caliber weapon firmly. His breathing was heavy after running half a block; Cleo wasn't a little dude. He stood 6 ft. 3 inches and weighed in at 302 pounds, so that half a block chase had him wheezing.

"You had to make me run, huh?" Cleo gasped. "It didn't have to come to this." he looked directly into Supreme's his eyes.

Not a speckle of fear was visible. Preme wasn't a sucker; he was a certified gangster. "You ain't built for no bodies, Cleo." He drawled. "You a business man, you ain't no killer."

Cleo thought for a second, maybe he was right. Then again, maybe he wasn't.

"You know what?" He took a step closer. "You absolutely right, Supreme." Cleo placed the cold steel barrel to the middle of his eyebrows. "This is business, never personal."

He squeezed the trigger with his index finger and a round was released through the chamber. It created a deafening sound that could be heard for blocks. The slug blew half Supreme's brain onto the brick wall and his body collapsed to the moist pavement.

Cleo stood still for what felt like minutes, but were actually seconds, staring at Supreme's empty body. Never even realizing how far he had gone. He snapped out of his trance and departed the scene before police arrived.

Mox gripped the steering wheel of the black Denali as it muscled down the highway in route to his destination. He sang along with *Sade's* soft, soulful voice as *Soldier of Love* whispered through the speakers.

I'm a solider of love...

Today, Mox wasn't feeling good and that usually wasn't the case, but because of a sudden tragedy, there was a major shift in the plans.

The music went silent and a beeping sound came through the speakers. It was Mox's blue-tooth connection. He looked at the display on his phone and quickly hit accept. He hoped it was the call he'd been waiting on.

"Wassup?" He answered.

"That little birdie that's been singin' outside your window is no longer a problem." The caller assured.

"Beautiful. That's why I love you." Mox smiled and reached his hand over to caress the leg of the beautiful, young lady sitting in the passenger seat. "Meet me at Vito's spot, tomorrow afternoon. Peace."

Tamika quickly pushed Mox's hand off her leg and sucked her teeth. "Who da fuck was that?"

"What I tell you about minding my business, Tamika. Jus' shut the fuck up and enjoy the ride. Please."

Tamika's neck twisted and she wore a look of astonishment. "Nigga, I don't know who da fuck you think you talkin' to, but I damn sure ain't one of them bird bitches you use to fuckin' wit."

Mox smirked and hit the right blinker indicating that he would be getting off at the next exit. He really didn't like Tamika, personality wise, but she was gorgeous and had a name, and that's all that mattered. Mox wasn't a fool; he knew she was only with him because he was a young, street nigga with a lot of money, but he also had his own personal reasons for befriending her.

"What makes you so different, Tamika?" He questioned. "Sit here and tell me you ridin' in my shit cause you like me. Go head and tell me that lie. You fuckin' me because I got money, Tamika; I'm that nigga!"

Tamika rolled her eyes knowing he was absolutely correct, but she didn't give a fuck. This was her game. She only dealt with dudes that had money and she sure wasn't concerned whether it was legal or illegal. Her mentality was, use what you got, to get what you want.

Once they exited the highway all the roads were pitch black. Mox came to a stop and looked right to left for a street sign to help him figure out where he was. He and Tamika had been on the road six and a half hours in route to Danville, Virginia from New York City.

Once he recognized the area, he relaxed. The light turned green and Mox pulled over to the curb.

"What you pullin' over for, Mox?"

Mox put the truck in park, hit the overhead light, reached to the backseat and grabbed a newspaper article. He glanced at it, shook his head and held it up for Tamika to see.

"You see this?"

The clipping had a picture of a brown skinned kid with wavy hair and a chipped tooth smile. He was standing in the middle of a basketball court holding a ball.

The headline read: **'First round NBA draft pick killed in robbery'**

Tamika looked confused. "I don't understand?"

Mox leaned his seat back and snatched the pearl handled nine from his waistline. He looked at Tamika and calmly placed it on the middle console. "I'ma give you another chance. Please don't lie to me. I'm beggin' you."

Tamika's nerves raged; she was terrified. *I should've listened.* They told her this nigga was crazy. She could barely get the words out. "Ye...yes, I remember."

"Good." Mox smiled. "Now, take a real good look at this kid's face." he said, pointing at the picture.

Tamika took the clipping and put it to her face to see it clearer. She knew who it was, but now he looked even more familiar.

She glanced at Mox.

He smiled. The same smile the kid had minus the chipped tooth. She couldn't believe it.

"You can't believe it right?" Mox was holding the pearl handled weapon in his right hand, pointed directly at Tamika's head. "That was my little brother, Tamika." Mox cried.

She reached for the door handle, but the door was locked. She tried the unlock button, but nothing happened, so she screamed to the top of her lungs. "HELP! PLEASE! SOMEBODY HELP ME!"

Mox switched the gun to his left hand and wiped the tears from his cheek. "Bitch, you can scream for help all you want. Ain't nobody gon' hear you."

He wasn't lying either. The Denali he was driving was a one of one, exclusive, presidential edition. Fit with bombproof exterior, soundproof interior and right now, parked on the side of the road, in the middle of nowhere; the black matte color made it invisible.

Tamika continued screaming, trying to escape the armed fortress. A swift blow to the side of her face with the butt of the gun calmed her down. She curled over, holding her wound, head between her legs.

"I loved my brother, Tamika." Mox sniffled. "He was my heart."

CASEY DANIELS WAS CONSIDERED the best shooting guard to come out of New York in the last five years. He led UCONN to a National Championships and also led the Big East in scoring.

Casey was one of kind. He had just signed a twenty-million dollar endorsement deal with Nike. He earned the top pick in the draft and was headed to Washington to play with the Wizards, but his life was cut short when Tamika and an accomplice robbed and shot him in his hotel room. They took $7,500 in cash, a Hublot wristwatch worth five thousand and his life, which was priceless.

When Mox received the phone call from Cleo about Casey's murder, he wanted to believe it was a joke, but then he realized nobody around him joked about things of that nature. The news was sudden and overwhelming. A horrified feeling of emptiness and discomfort quickly settled in the pit of his stomach. His other half was gone and he *had already been living with the tragic double homicide of both parents. At the time he was given the news, Mox was on his way to celebrate Casey's remarkable accomplishments. Sadly, that intended celebration would be halted forever.*

The only information Mox had on the incident was what Cleo told him about a female named Tamika, who supposedly was the last person seen with Casey in the hotel. That, and a bunch of mixed up stories from the police and media about an accomplice.

A week or so after the tragedy, Mox had Tamika's full name, address, date of birth, phone number, house number, social security number, credit score and anything else he needed to get in contact with her. He followed her and monitored her movements for days until he had her routine figured out, and then he approached her. He knew she wouldn't know who he was because not many people did. He did his best to keep his lifestyle away from his brother's success.

Mox was familiar with the type of female Tamika was. He attracted her kind all the time. It only made it easier for him to turn their social acquaintance into a night of heavy breathing, shit talking and ass slapping. After he fucked her a few times, he led her to believe she was going to assist him in moving some work out of state. Of course her greed, thirst and perilousness went uncontested. There wasn't a doubt in her mind that Mox could possibly be her next victim, but she was clueless as to what was really going on. It didn't take much, and when she went for the bait, she got hooked.

MOX WAS FURIOUS. He gathered himself, cocked the barrel of the handgun and a bullet slid into the chamber. His eyes, filled with fury.

Tears ran down Tamika's pretty face, smudging her make-up. "Please, Mox, don't do this. I'm... I'm sorry."

"My brother had a bright future, Tamika. He was the only one that graduated high school. He was making something of his self and he was my ticket outta this lifestyle. You got him got killed. You fuckin' bitch!"

Tamika looked into Mox's eyes and knew she didn't stand a chance. There was no escaping her fate.

Bizarre and distorted visions of Casey and his parents flashed before Mox's eyes. The gruesome scene in which his mother and father were murdered was right in front of him. He was standing in the exact room. His little brother, hanging over his shoulder, looking down at their parents mutilated bodies.

Mox wiped his face of tears a second time and watched Tamika as she rocked back and forth in the cushy, leather seat; praying. He pressed the gun to her head. "Who set this shit up? Who was you with?"

She never stopped rocking and then mumbled, "I don't know."

"Bitch!" He pressed the weapon against her temple harder. "Stop lying to me."

"I swear, I'm not lying." Through cries she tried to explain. "All they told me was the time they would be there and how much they were going to pay me. When he came in..." her breathing was erratic. "I was in the bathroom." she continued to rock. "Please, God, don't let him kill me. I'm sorry. I swear. I'm sorry..."

"You can get down on your knees and pray to the heavens. Ask God for whatever it is you want, but until you believe those words, the only thing you doing is wasting your breath."

The barrel jumped back and a slug pushed Tamika's head into the passenger seat window. Her brains decorated the glass. Mox reached over, snatched the ten thousand dollar *Tiffany* necklace off her neck, pushed her body from the truck and left her on the side of road, in the middle of Virginia.

8

VITO'S BAR & GRILL - WHITE PLAINS, NEW YORK

T he doorbell jingled when Cleo entered the restaurant. Delicate sounds of *Frank Sinatra* whispered at a low tone and the tasteful aroma of sausage and peppers soaked the air. Cleo always smiled when he stepped into Vito's because he knew he would get a good meal. He waved and greeted the aged white guy standing behind the long, oak wood bar. "Tony, what's goin' on?"

"Nothin' much, Cleo. Good to see ya."

"Same here." Cleo continued to the back, acknowledging the few patrons scattered throughout the restaurant, eating and drinking. He spotted Vito sitting in a booth at the rear with two females. "Excuse me, ladies. Vito, my man. What's good?"

Vito excused himself from the table, shook Cleo's hand and they walked to a different booth. "Mox went too far this time, Cleo." He took a seat. "I might not be able to save you guys on this one." Vito hissed.

"Save us, from what?"

"C'mon, Cleo, yous know how the rules go. Supreme was a made guy. I mean, he ain't family or nuttin' like that, but yous can't just go whackin' off any and everyone yous please. It's structure here."

Cleo laughed and sipped his water. "Structure, huh?" He stared at the man sitting across the table from him. "You wanna know what I think, Vito? I think you're full of shit, but hey," he shrugged his shoulders. "That's just my opinion, right?"

Vito seethed and his body language revealed his distaste. *The nerve of this nigger, walking in here, talking to me like that.* "Cleo, your filthy mouth is gonna get you in a lot of trouble."

Cleo smiled. "We'll cross that bridge when we come to it." He didn't fear the Italians at all. Cleo was willing to go head up with anyone in the way, and the Telesco crime family was not exempt.

Vito Telesco was third in rank, which would make him Capo under the hierarchy. His older brother, Mikey T was the Underboss and their father, Vinny was the Boss.

Vito's Bar & Grill was a front for the underground casino that operated from midnight until 5am. The walls were made of brick, the ceilings, a dark tin and Christmas trimmings hung all year 'round. Rather than booking reservations, Vito designated tables to regular customers once a week. Privileges were allotted depending not on monetary heft or status but, for the most part, on loyalty. Nowhere else in the city could a person own a table like you could own a condominium. Only a select few are admitted in, and those few are well known and respected. Most of them came to Vito's to conduct business that couldn't be handled in an office.

"So, where's your boy?" Vito asked. "It's fuckin' three thirty and he's still not here."

Cleo ignored Vito. He summoned the waiter and ordered a double shot of *Remy Martin*. "Be easy, he's on his way."

Vito mumbled under his breath.

"You said something, Vito?"

As soon as Vito went to speak, Mikey T walked through the door. "My colored brother, Cleo! What the fuck is goin' on guy?".

Unlike Vito, Mikey T and Cleo were the best of friends. They attended high school together and were starting defensive linemen on the varsity football team. Mikey T knew his position in the family; but he didn't have the same views as they did regarding blacks. He possessed a genuine love for Cleo that was real, but he would never go against his blood.

Cleo pushed his seat back and stood to greet Mikey. "My Caucasian twin... Mikey mutha-fuckin T!" he embraced him.

"It's been a minute, eh, Cleo. Good to see you, bro. You still big as a house I see."

They laughed.

"That's good eatin', Mikey. How's The Old Man?"

"Hangin' in there. You know how it is. Lately he's back and forth to the doctor. This freakin' diabetes is killin' him, and you know how The Old Man is. He don't listen to nobody."

While Mikey and Cleo got reacquainted, Vito boiled. Mikey hadn't even acknowledged his brother and here he was, laughing and joking.

"How's my little bro doin'?" He finally asked, tapping Vito's chest.

Vito got up from his chair to hug his older brother. He wanted to tell him how he really felt, but circumstances of that nature could never be discussed in public. Besides, Mikey knew Vito disliked that he showed Cleo so much respect, but there was little he could do about it.

"Could be better, could be worse." Vito answered.

Mikey sat at the table. "Who ya tellin'. So, Cleo... eh, where's Mox?"

On cue, Mox appeared at the front door, black as night, sporting a pearl white, fox bomber with the hat to match. The five-inch Cuban cigar he puffed produced a thick, white cloud of smoke.

"Speak of the devil and in he walks." Cleo laughed.

"Look at this fuckin' clown." Vito barked.

Mikey jumped up. "Hey, cool it, Vito." He approached Mox. "No smokin' in here, bro."

Mox stopped at the table, took another puff of his cigar and blew the smoke into the air.

"Fuck you, Mikey. Tell them white guys over there to stop smokin'. We came to talk business, correct?"

"Correct."

"So, this is my proposal, and rest assured my partner feels the same way. Right, Cleo?"

Cleo didn't speak. He nodded his head. Truth was, he didn't

know what Mox was about to say. They spoke on a few percentages, but Cleo told him it was too early to get those types of numbers. They were just getting in good with the Italians and to demand a higher percentage was something Cleo knew they wouldn't go for.

Mox continued. "We want a piece of Queens."

Vito cut his eyes to Mikey. They held a look of surprise. "Queens?" they said in unison.

"Yeah, Queens." Mox repeated.

"I don't know what you're talkin' about, Mox." Mikey lied.

"You know what I'm talkin' about, Mikey. Astoria. That warehouse. Seven hundred thousand a month. Any of this ring a bell?"

"You're a funny fuckin' guy, you know that, Mox?" Mikey snarled. "You should be here discussing how much compensation you gonna give The Old Man for knocking off one of his major dealers."

"Fuck, Supreme. That nigga was a snitch! Cleo, what's thirty-five percent of seven hundred thousand? Quick."

"Is this true, Cleo?" Mikey asked.

Cleo rubbed his fingers together. "Yeah, it's true." he paused and looked at Mox. "Two hundred and forty-five thousand."

Mox kept smoking his cigar. "It don't matter anyway, Supreme is dead. I came to talk about Queens and our two hundred and forty-five thousand a month."

"The Old Man still needs something," Mikey bargained.

"Well, the Old Man ain't getting shit from me till I get a piece of Queens."

Vito raised up. "Hey, watch your fuckin' mouth, guy."

"Fuck you, Vito."

Cleo stood. "Mox, chill."

"Nah, Cleo. Fuck these EYE-Talians. We don't need these muthafuckas, they need us."

Mikey fixed his tie. "Cleo, talk to your boy. Maybe come back tomorrow. Things might be different, eh?"

"Yeah, tell 'em to shut up, Cleo, before I do it myself." Vito added.

Mox smiled at the two brothers. If he really wanted he could kill them right now, but the chances of him and Cleo surviving were slim to none. The only reason he hadn't started a war was because the money was coming in at rapidly. The Italians controlled the ecstasy market throughout the five boroughs as far as the manufacturing went, but Mox and Cleo provided the muscle and protection for those labs to operate.

They produced thousands of ecstasy pills a day that were sold and distributed to wholesalers who, in turn, re-sell them at market rate which varied from seven to ten dollars a pill. At the time, the four major manufacturing labs were located in Brooklyn, Staten Island, Manhattan and the Bronx. Each factory roughly accumulated five to eight hundred thousand dollars a month in revenue and Mox and Cleo's cut was twenty percent of everything.

The Telesco's thought they were being slick by secretly opening another lab in Queens, thinking Cleo and Mox wouldn't be worried about it. They were wrong. Mox caught wind of the situation and wanted in. Cleo, on the other hand, really didn't care, but what's right is right. They made an agreement and the Italians were trying to renig.

Mox removed the hat from his head and grilled Vito. "Try it, Vito. I dare you."

They eyed each other intensely.

"C'mon, Mox." Cleo tapped his shoulder. "Mikey, we gotta make this thing right. I'll be in contact. And tell the Old Man I said get well."

Mikey frowned, "Sure, Cleo." Then he remembered." Oh, I almost forgot. Sorry for your loss, Casey was a good kid. It's a fucked up situation."

"Yeah, it is."

Cleo and Mox stepped out the door and into the windy, pedestrian filled streets. Four days before Christmas and the holiday shoppers were out in abundance, scurrying to get their last minute gifts.

Cleo pulled his phone out to call a cab.

"You still fuckin' wit' them cabs, huh?" Mox questioned, knowing exactly what Cleo was doing. He couldn't understand why he hadn't bought a car. He had more than enough money.

"I can't find a truck comfortable enough for my big ass," he joked.

He wasn't lying though. Cleo shopped around for a new truck, but the ones he test-drove didn't fit him the way he wanted. He wasn't in a rush to buy a vehicle anyway. He took cabs everywhere he went.

"Man, fuck that cab. I got the truck around the corner."

"Cool, but Mox, you gotta be easy with these Italians. Right now ain't the time to be stirring up a war."

"Fuck them degos, Cleo." He fumed. "Pasta eatin' muthafuckas. I don't trust 'em, and you shouldn't either. Those assholes knew exactly what they were doing when they opened that lab in Queens. They thought we wouldn't find out, but I want mines, and if I gotta get it in blood, so be it."

Cleo knew Mox was hotheaded, but he wasn't about to let stupidity come in the way of millions. He took a deep breath. "We don't need any more problems, Mox. That's all I'm sayin'. We gettin' good money from these dudes and The Old Man's beginning to show some leniency. Let's not fuck up a great a situation."

"It may be great for you, but it ain't great for me. I want more." Mox said, starting the truck.

Gluttony was something Cleo despised. The way he saw it, the only thing greed could get you was a pine box or a hundred years in a cell. He didn't want either. While in the truck, something dawned on Cleo. "Mox, what about the bitch?" he asked.

Mox pulled the truck from the curb. "I left that bitch on the side of the Roanoke River." he laughed loudly.

9

PELLEGRINO'S RESTAURANT, LITTLE ITALY, NYC
DECEMBER 22ND 2010

Pellegrino's Restaurant, located on the infamous Mulberry Street in Little Italy was a fairly new establishment mixed in with hundreds of years of Italian heritage. Tucked away in the cut, Pellegrino's served as one of the Telesco's favorite hangouts. Frequently, you could catch Mikey or Vito sitting at a table, feasting on a plate of penne al la vodka and salad. At times you may have caught Vinny Telesco himself sitting at the bar.

Sunny tossed his cigarette to the ground and stomped on it before he walked through the doors to Pellegrino's. The restaurant was packed. Upon entering, he removed his hat and unbuttoned his wool pea coat. He slid past the two couples waiting to be seated and walked to the bar area.

"Lemme get a straight gin. No rocks." He told the bartender. Sunny looked around for a familiar face. Seeing none, he tossed his drink back and ordered another one. It was like a flame burning in his chest. He was warming up now. His nerves were calming and he was feeling more like himself. He felt normal. The confidence he previously lacked was building up like a snowball racing down the Appalachian Mountains.

His fears evaporated like boiling water in a pot.

He was ready.

He turned to exit the restaurant and stopped short as if he'd forgotten something.

"Hey!" He screamed, turning back, reaching into his pants. The shotgun he lifted from his waist was sawed off. "Mox says, suck his dick!"

The explosion that followed was ear-splitting. Standing patrons fell to the floor and waitresses panicked in fear for their lives.

Sunny put two more slugs into the half of gun, cocked it and pulled the trigger once more.

The smoke clouds were so thick, Sunny could barely see in front of him. The bartender, crouched behind the marble bar, nervously fingered his old .38 snub-nose. He was waiting for a clear shot. Quickly, he stood up and let off four rounds, two striking Sunny in the chest. The impact slammed Sunny's frame to the floor. He tried to crawl to the front door, but he wasn't able to. Just trying to breathe was difficult enough. He gagged on his own blood. His body shook and his heart stopped beating. It was over.

The few customers and employees who didn't get hit scurried to the exit and pushed their way out of the restaurant and into the streets. In the rear of the restaurant, ten feet away from the kitchen, Vito poked his head up slightly above the table that hid him. He was terrified, but he couldn't show it.

He lifted himself up and tried brushing some tomato sauce off his suit. "Shit!" he cursed, checking his body for any wounds. Trembling, Vito pulled his phone from his pocket and dialed a number. Someone picked up on the other end.

"Vito?"

"Mikey, we got a problem."

"LICK THE HEAD. Yeaahh. Ohhhhh. I love that shit." Mox moaned. He bit his bottom lip and let his head fall back on the plush leather.

Kim held his dick with two hands and slid her tongue up and

down his long, heavy shaft. A stream of saliva hung from her chin as she devoured his thick, chocolate Mr. Goodbar. Kim loved sucking Mox's dick. It was huge. Each time she tried to deep throat, she gagged and tears came out of her eyes.

Mox raised his head and palmed Kim's soft ass with both his hands. He slapped her cheek that had a tattoo of black panther on it.

"Ooooohhh! Wait. Open your mouth. Ahhhhhhhh!"

Kim sucked until Mox shot a load of warm, pearl white cum all over her face. She licked her fingers, blew a kiss at the camera and smiled. "Mox, you always taste good."

He picked up his cigar out the ashtray, lit it and then hit stop on his HD camera. "You should be a movie star, Kim." He grabbed his pants off the floor. "I swear to God you put on an Oscar winning performance every-mutha-fuckin-time." He laughed.

"I need a favor, Mox."

"A favor?"

"Yeah. Can I hold some money?" She asked, snapping her bra straps.

"Hold some money?" Mox repeated, sarcastically. But he didn't have a problem giving Kim money. Only because he knew she was an independent female who took care of her responsibilities and this was the first time she had ever asked him for anything other than some dick.

Mox laughed.

"I'm serious, Mox. It's been rough for me raising little man by myself. Shit, every penny I get goes toward bills and the baby. I just wanna treat myself to something nice."

"Where that little nigga's father?"

"Who the fuck knows. I ain't spoke to that nigga since the day I told him I was pregnant." Kim barked. She flicked through the channels on the remote. "And my brother ain't helpin' out either. He runnin' around in the streets somewhere. When was the last time you saw Supreme, Mox?"

Hearing his name made Mox's antennas rise. He was trying to be cool. "Supreme, who?" He asked as if he didn't know.

"My brother, Supreme, nigga. Who else?"

"Oh, Preme," Mox slowly repeated. "Shit, I ain't seen that nigga, Preme in like... two weeks; maybe three." He lied.

Mox had honestly forgotten that Supreme was Kim's older brother, not that it would've changed anything, but maybe he would've thought on it a little longer. He admired Kim and not just because she sucked good dick, but because she was a smart and outgoing person. The few females Mox dealt with were money hungry groupies. Kim was different, but her brother was a snitch, so he had to go.

How could he explain to Kim that her only brother was dead, and on top of that, he was the one who orchestrated the hit. Her poor little heart would be crushed and Mox just couldn't live with that.

With concern in her voice, she said, "Well, I hope he's alright."

Mox's cell phone rang and at the same time someone was knocking on Kim's front door. Seeing the caller ID, he grabbed the phone and answered it.

"Gimmie a second and I'ma call you back." He pressed end before Cleo could speak. "Get the door, Kim."

Mox put his sweatshirt on and glanced down at the Smith & Wesson nine millimeter lying on the end table next to the sofa.

"Who is it?" Kim sang as she pranced down the hallway to the front door. Without looking through the peephole, she undid the locks.

Hulk sneered when the door came open and spoke, "Vito sends his regards." he smiled, lifting twin fifty caliber desert eagles. Two shots pushed Kim's 130 pound body five feet down the hallway. She was dead on contact.

When Mox heard the blast, he snatched his gun from the table, reached in his pocket and slipped the clip in. Quickly, he let off six shots hoping it could buy him some time, and then he got low. "C'mon, muthafuckas!" He whispered under his breath, holding his weapon firmly.

Hulk stepped over Kim's corpse and peeked around the corner. He pushed his back off the wall and let the twin fifties rip. The small missiles tore through the air, crashing into anything in the way. Glass shattered, dust and smoke filled the atmosphere and Mox sat composed, awaiting his chance.

He counted under his breath. "Four, three, two— "Hearing both guns click, Mox knew they were empty. He sprang to his feet gunning like Joe Montana on 4th down with the game on the line.

Every slug that came through the barrel slammed into Hulk's wide chest, dropping him to the plush carpet. He was choking on blood, but he still had a bit of life in him.

Mox waited to see if there were any more shooters and then he made his way to where Hulk was. Seeing him still breathing, he tried to roll the 6'4 240 pound man over on his back, and after two attempts, he finally got it.

"Who sent you?" He growled, shoving the hot gun barrel to Hulk's temple. Surveying the apartment, he could see Kim's petite body lying in a pool of blood, which only intensified his anger. "I'ma ask you again. Who—"

Hulk tried to speak. "Vi... to," his words were low, but Mox heard him. "Said, fuu--ck you."

Mox stood up and emptied the clip into Hulk's stomach.

Vito?

He cut his thinking short and rushed over to Kim. His heart fluttered, and immediately tears washed his face. He dropped to his knees. He couldn't believe it. He picked her up and held her in his hands.

"Kim," He whimpered. "Kim, wake up, baby." Mox wiped the stream of blood seeping from her lips just as he had done with his mother years ago. His heart felt like it was about to explode. Hearing sirens in the distance, he jumped out of his daze and carried Kim's limp body to the sofa.

Mox stood still for a moment, looking around. *Damn.* He thought. *My prints all over this muthafucka.* It wasn't enough time to wipe the entire apartment down, so Mox threw his boots on, snatched his coat and went to make his exit. "Oh, shit." He turned on his heels and went back to get his HD camera. "Definitely can't leave this."

VITO PACED BACK and forth in his shiny, hard bottom shoes, tapping the wood floor with each step. "I can't believe this shit." he cursed.

"Vito, sit down!" The Old Man hollered from his chair. His voice, hoarse from bronchitis.

Vinny Telesco had been watching his youngest son have a nervous breakdown for the past forty-five minutes. He had no clue of the situation, but all the bickering and foul language gave him reason to believe something transpired.

"What happened, Vito?" Mikey questioned.

Nervous, Vito pulled a cigarette from his pack and lit it. Normally The Old man would make a big deal of him smoking in the house, but he let him get away with it today.

"Vito, you hear your brother talkin' to you?"

"It was a fuckin' hit, Mikey. That black bastard Mox put a hit on us."

"Mox?"

"Yeah, Mox."

"When'd this happen, Vito?" The Old Man asked.

Vito took a long drag of his cigarette and blew the smoke out.

"Bout a hour and a half ago." He puffed the cigarette. "I slid down to Pellegrino's to have some lunch, ya know, a lil' penne n whatnot, and this fuckin' junky, umm... what's his name?" Vito thought hard. "Oh yeah, Sunny. Sunny Gallano. He walks in and you know me, I'm duckin' the fuckin' guy 'cause he's always beggin'. So, I'm in the back by the kitchen and all of a sudden I see this fuckin' loser, he's standing in the middle of the joint holding a fuckin' sawed off." Vito took another drag and continued. "So, you know me, Mikey. I go for my rivoltella (Pistol) and we shoot it out." He fibbed.

The Old Man knew Vito was lying about shooting it out. He raised these boys and knew exactly what they were capable of. Vito was a bit on the timid side. He used the family name as a crutch.

Mikey found it hard to believe also. "So, you twos is shootin' it out in the restaurant, huh? Then what?" he inquired.

"I finally got a clear look through all the smoke and I hit the guy." Vito lied again.

"So, you took him down?" Mikey said. "Where does Mox come in this?"

"Fuckin' Sunny screams out his name before he starts shootin' up the place."

The Old Man looked at his eldest son. "Mikey, what you think?"

"I don't know, Pop. Sounds kinda funny to me." Mikey tried to make light of the situation. "I mean, why would Mox get drunk Sunny to do a hit for him? It just doesn't make sense to me."

"It makes perfect fuckin' sense, Mikey. That fuckin' moulie wants to start a war!" Vito argued.

The Old Man heard enough. "Cool it, Vito." he cautioned. "Here's what we do." He turned to Mikey. "Vegas is coming up in a few days; see what Cleo has to say about this. Until then, sit tight."

A dim-witted expression came over Vito's face. "Too late."

"What do you mean too late, Vito?" The Old man questioned.

"It's too late, Pop. I sent Hulk."

"Ahh, nah, Vito. What you go and do that for?" Mikey steamed.

The Old Man struggled to stand up from his chair. He was furious. It wasn't that he was afraid of Mox, it was the fact that he had so much respect for Cleo he didn't want to harm him, let alone go to war with him.

He slung Vito a look that spoke volumes and then faced his eldest. "Mikey. Get Tommy on the phone. Tell him we got a problem."

10

"Chris, make the next right and then a left at the stop sign." Cleo directed, sitting in the back seat of his favorite livery cab. The town car slowed at the stop sign and Chris hit the left blinker.

"One day I might be able to own one of these nice houses back here." He dreamed.

"Nothing's impossible, Chris. If you work hard enough, I'm sure you can get anything you want."

The cab cruised at a moderate fifteen miles per hour down Tall Spruce Circle in Kensington Woods. It was one of the wealthiest areas in New Rochelle, New York.

Cleo sat back staring out the window at the placid scenery. He wished his life could be as simple as some of the families in this community, but it wasn't and now it looked like it was going to get worse.

"One twenty one Kensington Circle, sir."

Cleo pushed the door open and hopped out the Town car. "Aight, Chris, I'm good." He peeled a crisp hundred dollar bill from his stack.

"You sure you don't want me to wait, Cleo?"

"Nah, go 'head. If I need you, I'll call."

Cleo hurried down the driveway to Mox's 3500 square foot

estate. Usually, when Cleo got to the front door it was open because Mox would see him on the surveillance cameras. Today, it wasn't, so he rang the doorbell.

"C'mon, Mox open the door." He whispered. Then he rang it again. After two more rings he stepped back to get a view of the second floor and yelled. "Yo, Mox!"

A shadow moved behind the blinds and then they slid open.

Mox was standing in his robe, holding his AK47 trying to see who was yelling his name. Noticing Cleo, he rushed down to open the door. Cleo barely passed the threshold and Mox was screaming.

"They killed, Kim." He slammed the door shut. He clenched a bottle of Perrier Jouet in his right hand.

"What the fuck are you talkin' about?" Cleo was confused. He followed Mox into the living room.

"Fuck them spaghetti head muthafuckas!"

"Mox, I told you, now ain't the time to be startin' a war. We can't afford that."

Mox looked at Cleo like he was crazy. "I ain't start shit. They kill one of ours, we kill one of theirs. You know how this game is played. Kim didn't deserve that."

Cleo was still lost. "Hold up...hold up. I don't know nothing about Kim. What the fuck happened at Pellegrino's?" he questioned.

"Pelle, who?" Mox laughed, but it wasn't a joke. He took a swig from the bottle then plopped down onto his chaise lounge.

"Pellegrino's, Mox. Don't act like you don't know what I'm talkin' about. You sent that fuckin' drunk in there to shoot up the place."

Mox's brow furred. He stood up and faced Cleo. "I ain't sent nobody to do nothing... and I don't know what the fuck a Pelleninos or Pellepinos or..." He hesitated. "Whatever that is. All I know is, I was getting' my dick sucked and the phone rang. I saw it was you, so I picked up. Right after I said I'ma call you back, somebody start knocking on the door." Mox tipped the bottle again. "Kim went to see who it was and all I heard was a cannon. I had to let a couple go in order to buy some time and then I got low."

Cleo interrupted. "Aight, so what that got to do with the Italians?"

"Are you serious, Cleo?" Mox couldn't understand Cleo's reaction. "That big, pasta eatin" muthafucka spit Vito's name out before I fixed him."

"C'mon, Mox stop lying!"

Mox got offended. "First of all, lower ya muthafuckin' voice in my crib. Second, when have I ever lied about some shit as serious as this?" His eyes were trained on Cleo. "Don't let 'em brainwash you, cousin. You of all people know how I get down."

Cleo didn't know how things would play out. The monthly sit down was days away and here he was stuck in the middle of a potential war with the Telesco Crime Family. "Aight, listen, let me apologize for yelling in your home, but this is what gotta happen." He took a seat. "We got a few days until Vegas, Mox. I know they killed shorty, but I need you to be cool until we sort this out. I spoke to The Old Man and as long as you don't move, they won't move."

Mox shook his head. "I don't trust 'em."

"Trust me, Mox. Please?"

CHRISTMAS DAY CAME and light snow flurries fell from the sky like confetti. Children were out in full swing by 9:30am riding new bikes and racing remote control cars. Hustlers huddled on street corners hustling and the homeless sought refuge from the blistering cold.

Even though Mox had never received a gift on Christmas, it was still one of his favorite holidays. Growing up, he looked forward to waking up early and rushing across the hall to Cleo's house, just to play with *his* toys. Cleo didn't get much either, but it was more than what Mox had.

He put his Moncler bubble coat on and tied a scarf around his neck. He knew to dress appropriately because he would be standing in the wind for most of the day. His phone rang as he was getting into his truck. "Hello?"

"Mox, I think I'ma cool out today. I don't feel like being bothered." Cleo said.

He was anticipating this call. For his first Christmas home, Mox spent a few thousand on gifts for some of the less fortunate kids in the community. He rounded up a few teens from the Boys & Girls Club and they were going to pull up to the projects in a big trailer and hand out gifts to everyone who came out.

"C'mon Cleo, It's my first Christmas back. Don't make me come over there and snatch your big ass out the bed. It's for the kids, man."

"I ain't feeling it, Mox. I got a lotta shit on my mind."

"You ain't the only one. Last night I had to make that call to Kim's people. Imagine how I'm feelin'."

"Word. I might come through. No guarantees though."

"Aight. Peace." Mox tossed the phone into the passenger seat. He knew Cleo wasn't coming. It was the same thing every time with him. If it didn't benefit Cleo in any way, shape or form, he wasn't with it. His selfish ways hadn't changed at all. They just grew worse.

The trailer pulled into the parking lot and the children's faces lit up like Christmas lights. Mox and his handful of helpers stood, smiling. Red and white Santa hats atop their heads and a plethora of toys surrounding them.

Mox lived for days like this because he was once one of the less fortunate. Each time he gave out a gift and was thanked, his smile spread wider. The hood loved Mox, especially this hood.

From his peripheral, Mox spotted a familiar face. He jumped down from the back of the trailer and advanced toward her.

"Priscilla?"

The joyless young lady stared at Mox, trying to recognize his face. Her hair was in shambles and her garments were unkempt. Drug use was obvious, but she still seemed to have a sparkle of flair lingering.

In less than a minute, she recalled his face. *How could she not remember?* She grinned, but then her pleasure immediately turned to sorrow.

"You see what these streets did to me, Mox?"

"You stronger than this, Priscilla." He looked over her haggard frame and wanted to cry.

"You always told me I was strong, Mox, but this shit is stronger." She admitted.

A curly haired little girl tugged at Priscilla's sleeve. "Mommy, I want a present." She pressed.

"Is that your daughter?"

"Yes, and she's gettin' on my last nerve about these damn toys."

Mox kneeled down in front of the little girl. "She's gorgeous, Priscilla. Hi there, beautiful. What's your name?"

The little girl smiled and answered. "Brandi."

"Hi Brandi, my name is Mox and me and your mom are very good friends. Let me ask you something, Brandi. If there was one toy you could have in the whole world, what would it be?"

With no hesitation, Brandi shouted, "Dora!"

Mox couldn't help but to laugh at her glee, but he didn't have a clue what Dora was.

"Okay, what's Dora?" Brandi pointed to a three foot doll sitting on the back of the truck. "Oh, that's Dora. Well, let's go get her." Mox grabbed Brandi's hand and led her through the sea of children while Priscilla followed. He yelled for one of the helpers to get the doll.

"Mox, you don't have to do this."

"Yes I do. Here you go, Brandi." He sat the doll right next to her.

"Thank you."

Mox watched her eyes shine and her lips curl into a smile. This is what life was about; being able to have a hand in someone's happiness. Mox enjoyed these moments.

Priscilla looked at Mox. "Why do you do this?"

"Because if I don't, who will? I sold a lot of drugs out here, you know how it was. I took away from plenty of mouths and destroyed more than enough families pushing work through here." Mox reflected. "I'm in a position now that I'm able to give back to the people that gave to me, so it's only right."

Priscilla eyed Mox. "What about us, Mox?"

In the back of his mind he was thinking the same thing. He and Priscilla had a past that was so strong, the energy could still be felt. They met when Mox was fifteen and she was eighteen. She loved her some Mox, and at the time, she was ready to do any and everything he asked.

Unbeknownst to Mox, Priscilla was a few weeks pregnant when he went on the run. Eight and a half months later, she pushed out a seven pound, five ounce baby girl and named her Brandi.

Priscilla did all she could to contact Mox, but he cut ties to the outside world when he became a fugitive. She even went as far as finding his whereabouts through the internet and writing letters to him while he was incarcerated, but she never received a response. A few years passed and Priscilla became involved with one of her younger brother's friends named Ryan.

Ryan was a local cocaine dealer. He was seeing a few thousand a week and Priscilla preyed on his weakness. She let him let him taste the pink candy and had him wrapped up like a car wreck on the interstate.

Ryan liked to pop pills. One night, he convinced Priscilla to take a double stack ecstasy pill after she'd been complaining about being stressed out. In a time span of less than ninety days, Priscilla became addicted to hard core drugs. There weren't many she hadn't tried, but ultimately, her drug of choice became cocaine.

"I don't know, Priscilla. I guess we went our separate ways."

"No, Mox. You left me. You left me sittin' in a fuckin' parking lot."

"I ran because I was scared, Priscilla."

"Scared of what?"

"Of losing you. I didn't wanna go in there and be stressed out, worrying about what you doing. So, I cut all ties. I felt it was something *I* needed to do in order to get through that situation."

"And how long ago was that? It's been more than five years, Mox."

"You're right, but I don't know what you want me to tell you."

"You don't have to tell me anything." She grabbed the Brandi's arm. "At least say goodbye to your daughter. C'mon, Brandi, we're leaving."

"Don't lie like that, Priscilla." Mox didn't believe her.

"*Lie?* No, Mox. I'm not lying. Look at her eyes. Familiar, huh?"

Mox kneeled down to get a better view and right away his knees got weak. He stared, and Brandi smiled. Her eyes were rare and he knew because his were the same.

Mox stood up and took a moment to think, but Priscilla was persistent.

"Oh, and if that ain't enough... come here, Brandi." She

unwrapped the scarf from around her neck. "What's that right there?" she pointed to Brandi's star shaped birthmark at the top of her back.

Mox felt electricity shoot through his body. It was the same birthmark he had in the exact same location. He started sweating and it was thirty two degrees outside. He couldn't take his eyes off Brandi. He remembered the last night he and Priscilla were together; now, all of a sudden, it seemed like yesterday.

Mox reached to touch Brandi's shoulder and she lunged into his arms. He held her close and tight and then he turned to look at Priscilla, and she was gone.

11

Almost a week passed and Mox still hadn't heard from or found Priscilla. He had no number, no address and not a clue of where she would be. *How could a parent abandon their child?* He thought, but the irony was he had done the exact same thing.

Vegas was hours away, and Mox had a new found duty as a father; to raise his child. If that was the case, he would have no problem stepping up, but his lifestyle was dangerous and the last thing he wanted was to put his baby girl in harm's way.

"How you know she's yours?"

"You saw her, Cleo. She looks just like me."

Cleo grabbed a few chips out the bag that was sitting on the table and stuffed them into his mouth. "I wouldn't trust no fiend."

"Priscilla ain't no fiend. She's just going through somethin' right now. I know her."

"You know her?"

"Yeah, I know her." Mox got defensive.

Cleo could see he was getting under his skin. "So, how you gon' handle this? I mean, a little girl is big responsibility."

"I know, Cleo," Mox rubbed his temples. The stress of the situation was setting in and he didn't know how to deal with it. "The fucked up part is; this whole time she hasn't mentioned her mother."

"That should tell you something. Her mother probably don't give a fuck."

Mox was fed up. "I don't need your negative feedback, Cleo. Keep your opinion to yourself."

Mox glanced at Brandi sound asleep on the couch. Every time he looked at her he saw more of himself. It was surprising and astounding at the same time.

Their flight to Vegas was departing in less than three hours and he was hoping Cleo's girl, Susan would watch after Brandi while they were gone. Mox was a bit skeptical on leaving his child with a stranger, but after reasoning, Cleo convinced him.

Susan had mocha skin, full lips, round hips and big hair. She owned a brownstone on 138th and Amsterdam Avenue in Harlem. She also had an eight year old daughter who looked to be well taken care of, so Mox felt at ease.

"I didn't know you had a daughter, Mox?" Susan took a seat next to Brandi."

"Me either." He laughed. "Susan, you sure it won't be a problem leaving her here?"

"Mox, how many times am I going to tell you, it's okay. Besides, my daughter will be home in the morning so she'll have someone to play with. Trust me, she's good."

Mox looked around at the stylish home, he was impressed. You could tell a lot about a person's character as soon as you stepped through the door to their house, and he knew Cleo wouldn't recommend someone who wasn't trustworthy.

Two and a half hours later Cleo and Mox were on a flight to Vegas.

THE PLANE LANDED at McCarran International on Wayne Newton Blvd.

Mox and Cleo jumped into a limo and headed to the Palazzo hotel. As usual, Cleo wasted no time hitting the casino while Mox went and checked into his room. He had a lot on his mind. A war with the Italians was slowly brewing and making the wrong move could lead to a disastrous ending for them all. He spent the rest of the night thinking about his daughter and drinking his pains away. By the time the sun rose, he was ready to see what the Italians had to say.

One by one, each Union delegate entered the large conference room and took a seat. Mikey and Vito sat at one end of the oak table while Cleo and Mox sat at the other. The remaining four Reps sat in twos on each side, and Tommy, Mikey and Vito's cousin, stood off to the side.

Tommy was ordered by The Old Man to escort Mikey and Vito to the meeting just in case things got out of hand. Tommy stood 6 ft. 5 inches and weighed 290 pounds. His gorilla like features made him hard to look at and his scowl was always minacious.

Mikey stood. "Greetings, gentlemen. Due to a family situation, The Old Man will not be joining us today. So, Vito and I will be speaking on his behalf."

Everyone nodded their head in recognition except for Mox.

Slumped in his chair, sporting a three thousand dollar suit, he blew smoke clouds into the air. "So, you the boss now?" he said, sarcastically.

Mikey smiled and sat back down.

"Mox, let me handle this," Cleo interrupted.

"Good morning, delegates. As you all know, this is the first meeting of the year, so happy New Year to you and your families. Next, nothing has changed as far as Union dues so let's get that out the way first."

At the start of the meeting each Union Rep was responsible for their monthly Union fees. The fee amount varied between boroughs and the total amount was then split between Mox, Cleo and the Italians.

Each Rep opened up a briefcase, said their total amount and emptied the contents into a bag that sat atop the table. It totaled $700,000 cash.

Mikey rose from his seat to address the Union. "Mox, I think I deserve a thank you."

"A thank you? For what?"

"For lettin' you breathe. Only off the strength of Cleo are you still alive."

"Suck a dick, Mikey. If you wanna go to war, fuck it, let's go to war."

Cleo jumped in. "Hold up! Nobody's going to war here. It's too much money involved."

"Well, put a leash on your dog, Cleo." Vito barked. "He's way outta line."

"No, you're outta line, Vito. I didn't start this shit, you did." Mox replied.

"It doesn't matter who started what. We got a problem and we need to get it solved here and now." Cleo told them.

"Cleo, you know I got respect for you as well as every other man sitting at this table," Mikey stated. "But the disrespect will no longer be tolerated; let's not forget who brought you in this."

"So, what are you saying, Mikey?"

"I said it, Cleo. What I say goes. My father started you guys in this business and I'll be damned if I let your hot headed cousin screw it up."

Mox's anger increased. "You gon' let him talk to you like that, Cleo?"

"Cleo's not the problem, Mox. It's you!" Vito shouted.

Mikey walked to the opposite end of the table and immediately Mox stood in defense. Their eyes locked. Tommy stood still in the back with his chest pumped.

"If you gon' make a move, Mikey it better be a good one. Remember, we playing chess here, not checkers." Mox reminded.

Vito sat in his chair, snickering. "Well, it looks to me like you're playing without your Queen." he teased.

Mox thought about pulling his weapon and shooting Vito between the eyes, but that wouldn't be enough for him. He wanted to make them feel the pain and anguish he was feeling.

"You know the body ain't worth shit without the head, right?" Mox hinted.

Vito's face instantly turned red. Nobody threatened a Telesco and got away with it. "You got some fuckin' nerve, Mox. Are you making threats now?"

"Gentlemen," Cleo intervened. "This is going nowhere. All the bickering back and forth ain't solving the problem. We're here to discuss business and all I hear is bitching."

"You're right, Cleo. That Queens issue hasn't been resolved yet either," Mox said.

"You still talkin' about Queens?" Mikey replied. "Nobody's touchin' Queens, that's that."

Cleo sensed the frustration. "Fair is fair, Mikey. We had an agreement and you guys broke it."

"Queens was never part of the deal," Vito chimed.

Mox slowly shook his head and turned his wolf like eyes up to his cousin. "You see how they treat us, Cleo..." he paused and looked each man at the table in their eyes. "You trust these muthafuckas?"

Cleo didn't respond, he just stared. Then he said, "Yeah, I trust 'em."

"Well, I don't!" Mox raised his nine millimeter with the swiftness and precision of a firearm specialist. Simultaneously, each Rep stood with their guns pointed at the Italians.

Tommy reached to draw his weapon, but it was too late.

Mox held his gun firm and approached Vito who was still sitting, scared to death. "Talk that tough guy shit now, Vito."

Mikey kept his cool. "Mox, you're making a big mistake."

"Oh, yeah. Well, we all make mistakes sometimes. What counts is how we deal with the consequences."

"Mox! What the fuck are you doing?"

"Cleo, chill. I got this. Papi! Get the bag, we out."

Mox cocked his gun and put it to Vito's kneecap while Papi grabbed the bag of money. He could smell the Parmesan cheese on his breath from his heavy breathing. He sensed the fear.

Mikey tried to move, but Nate snatched his arm and shoved a pistol to his neck.

On the other side, Javier and Frank held Tommy at bay.

"Don't do this, Mox!" Cleo urged.

Mox looked at Cleo, and then to Mikey. His smile turned poisonous seconds before he choked the trigger and blew Vito's kneecap to shreds. The violent squall could be heard throughout the entire top floor.

Mikey watched in rage as his little brother begged for his life. "You muthafucker!" he shrieked.

Vito fell to the floor, blood spilling from his wound. He had never been shot before, the pain was grueling.

Mox turned to leave, but glanced at Cleo. "You coming?"

Cleo never answered; he just stood up and walked out.

"You think you're gonna get away with this shit, Cleo!" Mikey yelled. "I'm gonna fuckin' bury you!"

"Hey, Mikey. Tell The Old Man I said grazie!" (Thank You) Mox joked.

MOX DIDN'T PLAN to go to Vegas and shoot Vito, but after they killed Kim, he acted on emotion. He had love for Kim, real love. Knowing Cleo wouldn't agree with his original idea, which was to take the Union fees, he promised the Reps a percentage if *they* agreed to hold him down. Before shooting Vito, Mox carefully weighed his options. In his heart, he felt he could handle a war with the Italians, and be victorious in the process. All he needed was Cleo to see things the way he did.

Feathery snow flurries fell from the sky, blanketing the concrete as the 25 mph winds raked the naked trees and ripped its branches. A black Town car came to a complete stop across the street from the projects and Cleo stepped out.

"Meet me back here in one hour, Chris."

Two whole days had passed since the Vegas episode and Cleo hadn't spoken to Mox. He was considerably upset and wanted an explanation. His ties with the Italians were sure to be severed, and even more than that, he now had to keep a close watch of his surroundings and move about cautiously.

Cleo hustled down the wintry strip and into building 60. The overpowering stench of weed, urine and cigarette smoke filled his nostrils upon entry. He stepped onto the pitch black elevator and hit the button to go to the sixth floor. When the door opened, Cleo went right to apartment 6H and knocked.

Inside the apartment, Dana scurried to the back room to warn Mox that someone was at the door.

"Shh..." He put his index finger to his lips and removed his weapon from his waistline. "Go get Brandi and bring her back here." he whispered.

Dana was Mox's best friend growing up. She stood 5'9, mahogany brown skin, sexy heart shaped lips, thick thighs and a firm ass from her dedicated 3-days-a week workout plan. She was well educated, and the only female Mox slept in a bed with and never once pursued sex. They had a mutual respect for each other and Dana only wanted to see Mox prosper. Back when they were younger, he would run to her building and knock on her door after he got a beating. He stood there with dried up tears on his cheek, snot falling from his nostrils and the saddest frown you ever saw. Dana had no choice but to let him in because she knew all he wanted was some of her mother's chocolate chip cookies. She felt bad for Mox. She really liked him as a friend and was one of the few who saw with her own eyes the struggle he was going through.

She tip-toed to the front, grabbed Brandi and walked her to the back while Mox went to see who was knocking. He glimpsed through the peephole and recognized Cleo standing there, frustrated.

The door opened, and Cleo's eyes fell on the gun Mox held in his left hand. "I don't think killers knock on the door," he teased.

"The last one did." Mox clarified. He peered in to the hallway to make sure no one else was there. "What's good, cousin? I knew you'd be coming around sooner or later."

Cleo shook his head with resentment and entered the apartment. "That shit you pulled in Vegas gon' get us killed, for sure. What the fuck is wrong wit' you, Mox?"

"Keep your voice down, Cleo. Brandi and Dana in the back room."

"Mox, you don't get it. You initiated a war with the Italians. This shit is serious."

"It ain't no more serious than going to war with niggas on the block, Cleo. Don't tell me you scared of these dudes?"

"It's not about being scared. It's about being smart and making the best suitable decision," Cleo reasoned.

"The best suitable decision?" He repeated. "Listen, cousin. Our original agreement with the Italians was twenty percent of everything with the possibility of an increase upon us driving the numbers up. Now, tell me if I'm wrong, but from day one until now... those numbers are up, and always have been." Mox sat in the fold up chair next to the sofa and fronted Cleo. "These bastards making millions off us, Cleo, and all we eating is scraps off the fuckin' table."

"You're greedy, Mox."

"I'm not greedy. I'm hungry. You saw that little girl. Ain't no denying that, Cleo. That's my reality and I gotta handle that. This shit ain't even about me." Mox got up from his seat and sat next to Cleo on the sofa. "I got too much love for you to let a nigga hurt you. You know that. We family, nigga, and right now I need you."

"I don't know, Mox."

"Hold up. I'll be right back." Mox went to the bedroom. He came out with the bag from Vegas. "I got three hundred stacks in here and half is yours. I hit Nate, Javier, Frank and Papi off with a hundred a piece, so everybody is good."

Cleo gazed down at the bag full of money. One hundred and fifty thousand was much better than the usual twenty percent they got, but it came at a price that he wasn't willing to pay.

"You had this planned out already, huh?"

Mox smirked. "Not really. I ain't gon' lie. I was gon' take that bread, but then they killed my girl, Cleo. I had to make somebody bleed."

"I don't think you understand what you getting yourself in to."

Mox carefully listened to Cleo's words. "So, you don't want none of this?" He ruffled through the stacks of bills.

Cleo got up from the sofa and gestured to make his exit. "We can't win this one, Mox. Sometimes you gotta know when to bow out."

"I ain't bowing down to nobody. Fuck them Italians!" Mox hissed. "You go over there and try to talk to them muthafuckas and they gon' blow your head off. They don't give a fuck about you, Cleo. You just another nigga. Do you really think Mikey gon' ride with you before he ride with his family?"

"I knew Mikey since we were kids." Cleo reasoned, opening the front door.

"Oh, so what that mean? You think he won't kill you, Cleo? The Union, Cleo; No-one stands before WE!" Mox yelled as Cleo walked out.

12

DOWNTOWN - BROOKLYN, NEW YORK

The stoplight at Hoyt and Atlantic was temporarily out of order and traffic was becoming extremely congested. Horns blared and irritated motorists complained aloud about the chaos on the roads.

Javier clenched the steering wheel and mashed his foot on the brake to avoid smashing into the vehicle two feet in front of him. "Watch where the fuck you going!" He slowly eased up to where the traffic officer stood trying to direct the gridlock.

The officer gestured for him stop and approached the driver's side window. "License and registration." he ordered.

"You just let ten people go pass and now you wanna pull me over? This is crazy." Javier was furious. He couldn't understand why he was the only one getting pulled over. He reached for his wallet and gave the officer his license and then he popped open the glove compartment and searched for the registration. He felt the small .380 underneath some papers.

"You're kinda young to be driving an eighty thousand dollar car. What type of work you do?"

Javier twisted his neck and gave the officer his best screw face. He hated cops, black and white. He was ready to shoot him and pull off, but the traffic was even more backed up now.

"I sell cars." He answered. And he wasn't lying either, but the whole truth was, the cars are stolen.

"Oh, yeah... what kind?"

Javier's hand eased off the pistol. "All types, they're used, here, take a card." he pulled a business card from the middle console and handed it to the cop.

"Javier's Auto" He read out loud. "That's cool. Here you go." the officer gave Javier his license back and let him pass.

The glare from the sunlight was in his eyes so he pulled the sun visor down, made the right onto Atlantic Avenue and ran into some more traffic.

"Shit!" He hit the Bluetooth button and spoke to the system. "Call Rene." he said slowly and clearly so he could be heard. After a few rings a female voice came through the speakers.

"What's up, baby?"

"Rene, I'ma be there in like a half hour."

"A half hour?... My pussy wet right now. You playing games, Javier. I swear I hate fuckin' wit you."

Javier smiled "Oh, word?" He was feeling himself. He knew every time she said that, she meant the exact opposite.

He saw an open in the lane next to him, stepped on the gas and turned the wheel quickly. The Town car behind him was coming too fast and smashed the rear of his new Audi. Javier's body jerked and he was pushed forward into the steering wheel. "Oh, shit!"

"Hello?"

He grabbed the back of his neck and grimaced. "Somebody just crashed in to the back of my shit." He grumbled.

"You alright?"

He turned to look out the back window and caught site of the two, dark suited, gun toting, white men, moving in quick. His survival instincts kicked in and he got as low as he could, opened the glove compartment and snatched the gun. He raised his arm and blindly let off three shots through the back windshield, dropping one of the dark suits.

The traffic officer around the corner heard the shots and radioed for back up. At the same time, a blue and white NYPD patrol car was cruising Atlantic Avenue on the opposite side where traffic was at a minimum. Hearing the shots, he sped up to where the accident was and jumped out the vehicle with his gun drawn.

The other dark suit fired the fully automatic machine gun he held and bullets ripped through windshields, striking innocent bystanders as they sat in the backed up traffic. Javier hit the clutch, shifted gears and smashed his foot on the gas pedal. The cop's gun was blaring and sirens howled in the background. He turned the wheel and tried to maneuver his way out, but only got fifty feet before crashing into a delivery van.

The gunfire was loud and continuous as Javier staggered from the wrecked automobile. He felt his left arm go numb and when he looked down he saw blood leaking from a hole in his shoulder. There was no time to worry about that because dark suit's gun was still spitting out rounds.

After he dropped one officer, the dark suited gunman turned and fired on the traffic cop who was ducking behind cars trying to shield himself. This gave Javier a few seconds to execute his next move.

He hobbled to a grey, Toyota Camry that was twenty five feet in front of him and tugged at the door handle. It was locked. The driver, an elderly white woman, was slumped in her seat with a bullet hole in the back of her head.

Javier smashed the driver's side window with the gun and opened the door. He yanked the dead woman's body from the seat, tossed her to the ground, jumped behind the wheel and escaped the lurid scene with minimal damage.

IT WAS 9:30 pm and the projects were a ghost town. Except for a few stray cats and a junkie here and there, Ryan was the only one out, huddled in the cut on the side of building 80. He let the smoke flow through his nostrils and plucked the clip of marijuana into the grass. When he looked up, he saw a common face approaching. From a distance he nodded and she nodded back. "What's up, what you want?"

"Please, Ryan, jus gimme two for thirty-five this one time. You know I always come straight."

"I don't take short money. Look at these shits." Ryan bragged. "This is the best shit out here." he held two clear, glassine baggies filled with cocaine in his palm.

Priscilla's eyes enlarged at the sight of the irresistible drug. She grew extremely eager and her mouth twitched. "C'mon, Ryan, I'll bring it back. I swear."

He tucked the drugs back into his pants pocket. "I heard that lie a thousand times, Priscilla. You full of shit. Get the fuck outta my face."

Apprehensive and jittery, she crammed her hands back into her pockets, hoping some money would magically materialize. She felt something, dug deeper and pulled out a brand new pair of diamond studded earrings.

"Look. I got these!" She bellowed and shoved the two, half karat stones in his face.

"Let me see those." Ryan grabbed Priscilla's wrist, twisted it and dumped the rocks into his hand. He eyed the beautiful nuggets and then he looked at Priscilla and shook his head. He opted to just turn around and walk off, but his feelings were hurt by her actions. Ryan put the earrings in his pocket.

Priscilla smiled. "Okay. So, what you gon' gimmie for 'em?"

"What I'ma give you for 'em?" He reached into his sweat pants and backed out a chrome .45 ACP with black plastic on the handle.

Priscilla was stumped. She didn't have a clue of what was going on and she had never saw Ryan with so much disgust in his eyes. "What are you doing, Ryan?" she panicked.

The strike was immediate. As soon as the butt of the gun touched her face, blood shot from her nose. She folded, fell to the ground and Ryan stepped back, raised his leg and kicked her in the stomach while she was down.

"You stupid, bitch! I bought these earrings for Brandi's second birthday! You sniffin' that much fuckin' coke, huh!?" He was steamed. He stood over Priscilla as she fought to get back to her feet.

"Ryan, I'm sorry..." She sobbed. Blood was trickling from her nose like a leaky, project faucet. She touched her face and scowled. Her nose was broken. She could feel it.

Ryan cocked his right hand and struck her in the abdomen with a ruthless blow, sending her back to the pavement in agony. "You out here twisted. Get your shit together, Priscilla!" He said, and walked off up the empty project strip.

Priscilla bled on the freezing concrete. Her eyes were closed. She envisioned a life she always dreamt about, a life she once lived. She thought about her daughter and all the people she wronged. Knowing she was better than what the world saw, Priscilla promised herself she would listen to Ryan for the first time and really get her shit together. It was a must.

CLEO LOUNGED in the backseat of the cab, fidgeting with his new phone. "Chris, wassup... you don't seem like yourself today. Is something bothering you?"

Chris kept his hands on the wheel and his eyes on the road. Something was troubling him, but he didn't want to burden Cleo with his problems, so he downplayed it. "You know; regular problems with my girl, nothing crazy."

Cleo knew he wasn't telling it all, but it was his business and if he didn't want to share it, that was fine too. "Okay... yea, I got those problems too."

They both laughed.

Cleo's phone rang and it surprised him. He couldn't figure out how someone had already gotten his new number. He only had the phone for two days. "Hello?"

The caller hung up.

"They starting this shit already." He whispered. Cleo looked up and noticed they had been sitting at the light for longer than usual. "Wassup with this light, Chris?"

He looked up at the light. "I don't know, Cleo. Maybe it's broken."

Suddenly the backside passenger door swung open and Vito

grilled Cleo with a six shot .38 in his hand and one knee wrapped in gauze. "Get in the car."

Cleo spun his head.

The other door came open and a short, fat, slick haired white guy had a twelve-gauge shotgun pointed at his chest.

"I aint going nowhere."

A black Town car pulled up to the open door and the back window came down.

"Hey, Cleo. Get in the fuckin' car!" The Old man hollered.

Seeing how serious he was, Cleo complied. He tapped Chris' headrest. "Go head, I'm good from here." he slowly exited the cab and entered the black Town car with the Mafia Boss. Vinny Telesco.

Chris never looked back. He pressed on the gas, went through the light and continued to the highway.

Another Town car pulled up and Vito limped to the backseat. The slick haired, fat guy jumped in the front seat of Vinny's car and they peeled off.

Cleo looked out the window at the passing scenery. He paid no attention to The Old Man.

"You can't even look me in my face, Cleo."

"It wasn't my fault, Vinny." He tried to explain.

"The fuck if it wasn't your fault. He's been your responsibility from day one." The Old Man wheezed. "You vouched for him, Cleo. If I didn't like you, I'd have Sammy the scar up there put a few in the back of your fuckin' head."

Sammy turned in his seat and smiled. The sight of his discolored, rotten teeth made Cleo's lip curl.

"Turn the fuck around, Sammy... I aint talking to you."

"Just give me some time, Vinny. I'll take care of it." Cleo lied.

"Time's runnin' out. I'm giving you one chance and one chance only. I don't wanna hear any more about Mox."

It took him a minute, but soon enough, Cleo finally caught on to what The Old Man was trying to say. He couldn't believe what he was being asked to do.

Cleo looked at the Mafia Boss for the first time since he'd been forced into the car.

"I can't do that, Vinny." he pleaded.

The Old Man rubbed his hands together, loosened his tie and fixed his beady eyes on Cleo. "It's either blood on your hands or dirt on your grave. Whichever one you choose, Cleo." he hit the button to let the window down and a cool breeze caressed his face. "Jimmy, pull over." he instructed. "Now, get the fuck outta my car."

Cleo wanted to tell The Old Man to fuck off, but he was smarter than that and being ignorant in this situation was only going to lead to one outcome; a casket. One thing was for sure, he wasn't taking orders from nobody. He was going to handle the situation however he saw fit. Fuck the Telesco's.

He stepped out the car and noticed that he was on the side of the highway in between Mt. Vernon and the Bronx, so he reached for his phone and made a call.

"Wassup, Cleo?" A voice on the other end answered.

"It's time to earn your stripes, youngin."

13

Thick, black clouds hung in the air, creating a dull setting to the mornings rise as Mox hesitated to get up from his warm bed and start the day. He stretched and made an attempt to push the heinous visions of reoccurring nightmares from his head. Since witnessing the murder of his parents, a good night's sleep was almost impossible.

He stepped into his slippers, tossed his silk robe onto his back and went to check on Brandi in the guest room down the hall. When he opened the door, she was sitting upright, watching Dora the Explorer on the 40 inch flat screen in front of the bed.

"Good morning, beautiful." He poked his head through the door.

She giggled at his playful antics and replied, "Good morning."

"You know what today is, right?"

Brandi quickly hopped off the bed and jumped into Mox's arms. "Surprise Saturday!" she yelled.

For the past two weekends, Mox would have a gift delivered to the house for Brandi to celebrate Surprise Saturday. It was an idea he came up with after he realized how life was for her growing up with a parent on drugs. He'd gone through the same thing. Suddenly, a sharp flash of light lit the entire room, followed by a rumbling thunder. Torrential rains fell from the dark skies and violent winds ripped branches from the trees.

Brandi threw her arms around Mox's neck and held on with all her strength. Her face was buried in his chest. "Daddy, I'm scared."

Mox held her tight. He brushed her hair back with his hand. "Don't be scared, baby. It's just some thunder and lightning."

"I know, but I don't like it."

Mox smiled, "Me either." he turned and carried Brandi down the steps and into the kitchen. "What do you want to eat this morning?"

"I want pancakes, eggs and umm..." She thought hard. "Oh, bacon!"

"Pancakes, eggs and turkey bacon, coming up."

Another growl roared through the skies and this time the lightning seemed like it was closer. Brandi rushed from the table and attached herself to Mox's leg as he gathered the utensils to cook.

"I got you, baby. Don't worry." Mox kept her by his side while he cooked their breakfast.

As they sat and ate, the severe downpour continued. Mox laughed and watched Brandi drown her pancakes in syrup.

"Daddy, is that God?"

"Is who God?"

"Whoever is making all that noise and rain."

He smiled. "I'm sure he has a lot to do with it."

"How does he make those loud noises?"

Mox sat up in his seat and wiped his mouth with a napkin. He loved that Brandi asked questions. It showed she was curious about the things going on around her. He thought about her latest and tried to explain it the best way he could.

"Alright. You listening?" She said yes. "Now, when warm air rises it mixes with the cool air. Up there." he pointed. "When they get mixed together they form a cloud. The cloud keeps rising into the air and raindrops form inside and they start falling from the cloud. Now, when the cloud reaches a certain height, that's when we have thunderstorms. They're called cumulonimbus clouds."

Brandi dropped her fork on the plate. "Huh?"

Mox laughed. "Alright. I'll teach you that word later. C'mon, let's go put a movie on until the delivery person comes." They got up from the kitchen table and walked into the plush living room. Mox's lair was a bachelor's dream pad. Gorgeous carpets and hand placed tiles covered almost every square inch of the estate. He and Brandi got comfortable on the fine, imported, French-leather chaise lounge and watched *Diary of a Wimpy Kid* on the 200 inch projection screen, until they fell asleep.

Forty-five minutes later, the vibration of Mox's phone on the glass coffee table woke him up him. He glanced at it and then looked at Brandi. She was in a deep sleep.

"Mox, I need to come and talk to you." The caller said.

"You know where I'm at."

"Cool, I'll be through in a minute."

Mox relaxed into a deep nap and when he got up the clock read 4:25 pm. He and Brandi slept the entire day.

He tapped her shoulder to wake her up and realized, Gene; the delivery man, hadn't arrived. It was unusual because he always made his deliveries before 3pm on Saturdays. Mox walked Brandi upstairs to the master bathroom and the doorbell rang. His natural instinct was to look up at one of the 25 camera's he had placed throughout the house, but he remembered the system had been down for the past few weeks.

"Go use the bathroom. This might be the delivery man." He told her and rushed down the hall to his bedroom.

He sneakily pulled the curtain back and saw the dark colored delivery truck parked in front of his driveway. Some of his tension eased at the sight of the well-known vehicle.

Mox snatched the .357 Sig off his dresser on the way downstairs. He definitely wasn't about to get caught slipping.

"Brandi, you alright in there?" He stopped in front of the bathroom, tucked the weapon in the small of his back and let his t-shirt cover it.

Brandi yelled. "Yes! I'm okay!"

"Alright, let me know when you're done."

The bell rang again as Mox hurried down the steps to the front door. "I'm coming, Gene." he turned the knob. "You a little late to—"

The barrel of a shotgun was gawking at Mox's chest and before he got to finish his sentence, the explosive blast sent him flying to the floor. By the grace of God he only caught a few pellets in the abdomen. He rolled over to get from in range of the next discharge and the slug ripped the expensive floor tiles to crumbs. He reached for the Sig tucked in his pants, but he didn't feel it. He panicked and scoured the area. It was lying on the floor, about ten feet away and must have dropped out of his pants when he hit the ground. Mox rolled across the floor like he was on fire and made it to the gun. He palmed it and dashed to the steps where he finally got a few seconds to think while the gunman reloaded.

At first, he didn't recognize the shooter, but then he saw the man sent to take his life was Tommy Telesco.

Mox made it to the bathroom door and called out for his daughter. "Brandi, you still in there?"

"Yes, daddy. I'm scared. The thunder is getting louder."

He touched his side and his hand was covered in blood. The wound was burning. "Stay in there until I tell you to come out, alright?"

"Okay, but I'm done."

"Just lock the door and get in the tub."

Brandi did as she was told.

Meanwhile, Tommy crept up the steps with destruction in his eyes and fresh slugs loaded into his weapon. He was ready to fulfill the order he was given. He raised the shotgun, plucked the trigger and the blast tore away chunks of the hand crafted, wooden banister. Mox ducked and shielded himself from shards of debris in the air. His opportunity came and he let the barrel fly, tossing rounds through the smoke filled atmosphere. A bullet hit Tommy's shoulder. He stumbled and dropped the weapon, but one bullet wasn't enough to immobilize the brawny assassin. After he regained his balance, he picked the shotgun up, but tossed it back down after realizing he had no more slugs. He went for the .38 revolver in the small of his back and capped off two shots, hitting nothing.

Mox inhaled. He paused and thought about his daughter. She was the only reason he had to live. He was not only willing to put his life on the line, but also prepared to take one if that's what it took to make sure nothing happened to her. Light sweat formed in his palm as he gripped the compact cannon. He could hear Tommy's foot-steps getting closer with each passing second. His timing was perfect. As soon as the Mafioso henchman rounded the corner, a .357 projectile smashed into his cheek. The contact from the bullet cracked his jaw and broke his nose on impact.

Tommy went down and Mox rushed over to finish the job. He looked at the helpless tough guy. "At a certain point in our lives we all gotta go, today just happened to be your day." Fire shot from the nozzle of the sig and a bullet landed between Tommy's eyes. Mox didn't have to check to see if he was dead. He never second guessed his work.

The bathroom door opened and Brandi's innocent face appeared in the crack. She glanced down at the bloody giant.

Mox hurried to where she stood. "C'mon, baby we gotta get out of here." He grabbed her arm.

"But, what about Surprise Saturday?" She asked, her voice, sweet and gentle.

"I'll make up for it." Mox scurried through the house with Brandi by his side. He entered his bedroom and emptied the $125,000 that was in his safe into a *Luis Vuitton* duffle bag. He checked the dresser drawer, picked up his HD camera and tossed it in the bag also. His truck was parked at the entrance of the house, but leaving out the front door wouldn't be the smartest decision. His other car was parked in the garage, so he threw the bag over his shoulder and he and Brandi made an exit out the back of the house.

14

Chris turned the wheel and made the right onto Mox's block. A line of unmarked police cars filled the street and homicide detectives were combing the scene.

"I don't think you wanna go down there." Chris warned.

Cleo lifted his head and glanced out the window at the disorder. He couldn't believe what he was seeing.

"Make the U-turn, Chris. Get me outta here."

"Anywhere in particular?"

"The projects."

Six minutes later, Chris pulled the Town car over and Cleo got out and walked into the projects.

After Christmas and New Year's passed, there weren't many people wandering about in the projects. It actually resembled a ghost town. The frosty winds kissed Cleo's cheeks and he tugged at his wool hat, pulling it down over his ears. He slowly approached two young guys as they stood on the strip, engaged in a heated conversation about sports.

"Man, Kobe is better than all them niggas!" Tyrell shouted. The kid he was talking to shook his head and kept his mouth shut. He knew how Tyrell got when he became angry.

"Youngin, wassup?" Cleo interrupted.

Tyrell stepped away from his conversation and greeted Cleo with a handshake. "You tell me, boss. I was out here all night waitin' for you."

"What I tell you about that boss shit."

"My bad. Jus' tryna show respect. That's all."

Tyrell Michaels, the gullible sixteen year old who would do anything to get a name in the hood. He had a few shootings under his belt, but for the most part, he was a low level hustler, looking for a come up. Every now and then, Cleo would come through the hood and drop some work off for Tyrell and his team to move. It was never anything too big. A few ounces of weed, maybe a couple hundred grams of coke. It was more than enough to put Tyrell on, but all he wanted was a rental car for the month, some new gear, and all the weed he could smoke.

Cleo whispered in Tyrell's ear. "Did Mox come through here?"

Tyrell nodded toward the building. "He's upstairs." He told the kid he was talking to that he would see him later and him and Cleo walked into the building.

They exited the elevator on the sixth floor and Cleo knocked on Dana's door.

"Who is it?" She yelled.

Cleo gestured for Tyrell to say his name.

"It's me, Tyrell."

The door swung open and the two men entered the apartment.

Dana was in a tank top and a pair of tight fitting shorts that accentuated her ass cheeks and made her camel toe visible. She had light beads of sweat sitting on her forehead, her hair was pin wrapped and she was breathing fast.

"Fuck you in here doing, workin' out?" Tyrell joked, but his guess was right. A workout DVD was playing on the 30 inch television.

Dana slammed the door shut and locked it after they came in.

"Damn, Tyrell. Do you ever go to school?" She asked.

He brushed past her and took a seat on the sofa. "I can't get money in school."

"Maybe not, but you can get a fuckin' education. Duh." She sassed, rolling her eyes at her little cousin. "Wassup, Cleo? Mox is in the back."

"How you doing, Dana? Can you tell him I'm out here, please."

"Sure."

Dana went to get Mox and Cleo grabbed the fold up chair that was against the wall. He took a seat next to the sofa. "Yo," He whispered. "I hope you don't be tellin' Mox about our business?"

Tyrell straightened up and looked at Cleo. "Nah. Hell no." he shook his head. "Mox be on his bullshit. Him and my cousin always talkin' that school shit. Fuck that. I ain't tryna go to school, I'm tryna get this money."

Cleo smiled and nodded. He knew Tyrell could be manipulated easily and he planned to take advantage. "Aight, cool. Keep this low." He reached into his bubble coat and passed Tyrell a brown bag. "That's two hundred soft and three zones of sour." Cleo lifted his coat and grabbed the gun off his waist. He cocked it and placed it on the small, wooden coffee table. "Have that next week, you heard?"

Tyrell smirked at Cleo and agreed. "I got you."

When Tyrell looked up, Mox was coming down the hall. He was shirtless with gauze wrapped around his mid-section.

Tyrell raised his eyebrows twice to inform Cleo.

"Why you ain't in school?" Mox questioned, as he entered the living room.

Tyrell sighed and glanced at Cleo. "See." he picked the remote up and hit power. "Mox, I don't wanna go to school. Let me hold somethin'?"

Mox told Tyrell to move over so he could sit on the sofa directly across from Cleo. He snatched the remote out of his hand and changed the channel. "You running wit' young niggas now, Cleo?" He picked the gun up off the table and turned to Tyrell. "This you?"

"Nah, that's mine." Cleo reached for the weapon, but Mox pulled away.

"Tyrell, give us a minute."

With no hesitation, Tyrell rose from the sofa, picked up his coat and went to leave.

"Aight, Mox... lata, Cleo."

The door shut and Mox cocked the barrel back on the handgun. He saw a bullet was loaded in the head. He dumped it on the carpet and hit a button and the clip fell out the bottom. "What's good, Cleo?" He placed the empty weapon back on the table.

Cleo smirked. "You tell me. I went by the crib, shit was crazy. You alright?"

Mox got up and went into the kitchen a few feet away. He snatched a bottle of champagne from the fridge and picked up the ashtray with a fresh cigar in it. "Yeah, I'm good. But before I get to that, wassup wit' you and that young nigga? I hope you ain't the one giving him work."

Cleo looked Mox in his eyes and told a blatant lie. "I ain't never gave that little nigga nothin'."

Mox didn't believe him, but he let it ride. "Okay, so we on the same page as far as that goes," he popped the top off the bottle of champagne. "Now, this other thing. This shit just went to the next level."

"I told you to let me take care of it. I knew this shit was gon' get outta hand."

"It's too late for that, Cleo. Don't you understand... they came to house... while my daughter was there. What would you do?"

"I wouldn't have put myself in a situation like that in the first place."

Mox got up and went to where Cleo sat. "You been on some real bullshit these past few weeks. What's good wit' you?"

"You don't listen, Mox. And when you don't listen that's when I get put in a fucked up position."

Mox had no problem reading between the lines. He knew just what Cleo was getting at.

"So, they sent you here to kill me?" He smiled.

Cleo kept a stern face. "Yup..."

Mox walked to the coffee table, picked the gun up and put the clip back in. He cocked it and held it out to Cleo. "Here's your gun... shoot me."

Cleo pushed the gun out his face. "We too strong for that, Mox, cut it out. But you asked so I had to tell you the truth. Yeah, The Old Man ordered you dead and he basically told me that I gotta be the one to do it."

"And what you tell him?"

"I didn't tell him anything, you still breathing, right? I came here to let you know that I'ma ride this out wit' you. I'm loyal to family first. *Let no-one stand before WE*. Remember that?"

Mox smiled. "It took you long enough."

He still didn't fully trust his cousin's actions. There was something about Cleo's body language that made his words unbelievable and Mox detected it the last time they had a conversation, but he never jumped the gun.

Cleo relaxed in his chair. "So, what's the deal wit' Javier?"

Mox took a long swig of the champagne. "He had to get low. Two police got shot. One died; the other one still in the hospital. That shit is crazy."

"So, what's your plan now that we ain't fuckin' with the Italians. Money is gonna slow up, Mox."

"Just be cool. I got a few things I'm working on. You short, you need some paper?"

"Nah, I'm good right now." Cleo responded.

"Listen, trust me, I'ma handle this. Our first order of business is Vinny Telesco."

15

"Pop, hurry up, you're gonna be late!" Mikey screamed as he walked out the front door.

Vinny struggled to his feet from the cozy sofa and then mumbled a few cuss words. He screwed his face at the thought of another doctor visit. It would be the third one this week and he was growing tired of it.

"Goddamn doctors get on my nerves, Mikey."

"I understand, Pop, but ain't nothing I can do about it. Doc says you need to come in today, says it an emergency."

"Everything's a fuckin' emergency according to him."

Mikey held the car door open while the aging, ailing Mob Boss crawled into the backseat of the limousine. And then he slid in beside him.

"Jimmy, Take eighty seven. It'll get us there faster." Vinny's voice was dry and raspy. He coughed.

"Pop, you alright?" Mikey sat up to make sure he was okay.

"Yeah, Mikey. I'm fine." He spit in his handkerchief and put it back in his coat pocket. "Where's your brother?"

"I don't know, Pop. He said he had something to take care of."

"Hmph..." Vinny relaxed on the fine leather and stretched his long legs in the spacious limousine. "The nerve of that guy." He was worried. "You gotta watch over him, Mikey. You know Vito ain't the brightest M&M in the pack."

"Yeah, I know, Pop."

"Just don't let nothing happen to your brother. And what's going on with this Mox situation?"

"Not too much. I haven't heard anything from Cleo."

"He's not gonna do it. Mikey, I want you to handle that. And after Mox," Vinny looked out the window at the passing traffic. "Take care of Cleo."

"But, Pop—"

"But nothing. Just do what I tell you to do."

Vinny sat in his seat, speechless. It was out of his hands. There was nothing no one could do or say.

The partition came down and Jimmy, the driver tried to get Vinny's attention. "Excuse me, boss."

Nobody heard him.

Mikey finally said something. "Why you so caught up on Mox, Pop?"

"I got my reasons."

Jimmy tried again. "Excuse me, boss."

"Yeah, Jimmy."

"I think we're being followed."

Mikey turned to look out the back window but he couldn't see because of the dark tint. He kept his cool. "How far till the next exit?"

"Two miles." Jimmy replied.

The limousine slowed up at the Central Park Avenue exit in Yonkers and the two black Mercedes 500's that were tailing did the same.

"Pull into the gas station." "Vinny ordered.

Jimmy made a right turn into the Mobile gas station and pulled over by two giant gas tanks. The only car there was getting ready to pull off.

Mikey checked his weapon and then reached to open the door. "Let me handle this, Pop."

"Sit down, Mikey. I can take care of myself." Vinny opened his door and stepped into a brisk, light wind that whistled at the few hairs that were left on his head. He buttoned his overcoat and watched the two 500's pull in behind him.

Jimmy removed his revolver from the glove compartment and stepped out with Vinny.

The occupants of the two Mercedes exited the vehicles, but Vinny only recognized Mox and Cleo. He had never seen the other three guys. They all donned dark, tailor fitted suits and shiny shoes.

Vinny kept his hands in his pockets while they approached. "I wasn't expecting any visitors today."

"You should always expect the unexpected, Old man." Mox was standing ten feet in front of him.

"Those are quite knowledgeable words coming from a dead man." He smiled. "Cleo, I thought I asked you to do something?" Vinny studied Cleo's mannerisms. He could tell he didn't want to be there.

"I don't take orders from you anymore, Vinny."

Mikey emerged from the backseat, palming a black pistol. "Is there a problem here guys?"

Upon sight, Mox's men backed out weapons of their own and Jimmy sneakily eased toward the gas tanks.

"However you wanna do it, Mikey. It's your call, but we didn't come here for that."

Vinny fumed. "Put that fuckin' thing down. I told you I'll take care of this. Now, get back in the car."

"You heard your father, Mikey," Mox teased.

Mikey pressed him. "At least I know who my father is."

Mox smiled, and before Vinny could step in, the butt of his gun slammed down on Mikey's face, causing him to drop his pistol. His nasal bone cracked and a stream of blood shot onto Vinny's coat.

Mox cocked the weapon and shoved it under Mikey's chin. "If your gun game was as slick as your tongue you wouldn't be in this position."

"Mox, not here!" Cleo yelled out.

"Hey!" Jimmy screamed. He was standing by one of the giant gas tanks with his .32 revolver pointed directly at it. "Either you guys put the guns down or we all die." He was trembling and the lightweight firearm felt like a 100 pound dumbbell in his hand.

Jimmy was 54 years old and had never fired a gun in his life. The only reason he kept one in the glove compartment was because he chauffeured a mob boss around the city and it made him feel like he was a part of the lifestyle.

"I'm tellin' you, I'll shoot this damn thing and blow half the city up. Put 'em down!"

But nobody budged.

Vinny attempted to calm him. "Easy, Jimmy. I got it. Everything is cool." He grilled the five men in front of him. "What do you want, Mox?"

Without removing the gun from Mikey's throat, Mox dug in his pants pocket and pulled out the photo of him, his mother and Casey. He shoved it in Vinny's face.

"My mother and father were killed in one of your buildings back in ninety five. Did you know 'em?"

"Of course I knew 'em." Vinny stared at the picture. He knew the answers to all Mox's questions. "But I ain't the one you need to talk to."

Jimmy still had his gun aimed at the gas tank and Mikey was bleeding severely.

"I wanna know what you know."

Vinny side eyed Cleo. "Ask your Aunt."

"Leave my mother outta this." Cleo took a step forward.

What did his Aunt have to do with this? Mox was thrown off. He recalled asking if she knew anything about the night of the murder, but she denied it.

Mox eased off Mikey .

"Cleo, you use to be a good kid." Vinny moved forward. "You use to listen to me. Whatever I told you to do, you did." he leaned in close to Cleo's face. "I liked that about you. I ate, you ate. But now... now... you and Nino Brown over here wanna take over the world together, huh? Fuck Vinny and the Telesco's. Well, you know what, Cleo... when you go to sleep with the snakes, don't be surprised when you get bit."

"Fuck you, Vinny!" Cleo snatched his weapon from the inside of his jacket and put it to Vinny's head.

Jimmy screamed again. "You think I'm playing!" He pulled the hammer back with his thumb and had a round ready to go.

"Hey, Cleo. I bet you never told the guys that you were the one who paid drunk Sunny to shoot up the bar and say Mox's name."

"You're a fuckin' liar, Vinny." Cleo went to smash the old man in the head with the gun, but Mox grabbed his wrist.

"We not gon' do this here, Cleo." Mox cut his eyes at Vinny. "This ain't over."

Vinny breathed a sigh of relief once he saw they backed away and re-entered their cars. He hadn't planned on dying, but what he had done was plant a seed of suspicion in Mox's head. He was a wise old man if any. He knew Mox would come for him as soon as he found out the truth. All he did was buy himself some time because if Cleo and Mox were at war with each other it was beneficial to him. He needed them out the way so he could execute his plan.

"I KNEW you couldn't fuck wit' me. You suck!" Tyrell tossed the PS controller at his homeboy Leon. He had just finished beating his ass in Madden for the third time in a row. "You see what I be doin' out there boy." Tyrell fixed his arm like he was a running back holding the ball. He mimicked the replay that was on the screen. "Uh, uh... a lil' spin move, juke to the left. Uh! End zone!"

"Shut up. You better keep your voice down before Dana come back out here and kick us out. I ain't got nowhere to stay tonight."

"True... 'cause she will kick *yo'* ass out." Tyrell laughed.

He and Leon had been crashing at Dana's for the past few weeks. She agreed to let them smoke and play the game in the crib as long as they watched Brandi while she was at school.

Dana didn't have a problem helping Mox with his daughter. She was aware of the circumstances and wanted to be of any help she could. Besides, he was funding her $40,000 a-year college tuition at Mount Sinai School of Medicine. What he didn't know was Tyrell had been watching Brandi every night for the past month, due to the steady babysitter taking a vacation. Dana knew if he found out, he would be overly enraged, but she had no other choice. Tyrell had to watch Brandi until she found someone else.

"Roll up." Tyrell tossed Leon a cigar and a zip lock bag of weed.

Leon wiped his face with his hand and looked at the clock on the wall. "Damn, it's five thirty already, the sun bout to come up." They had been playing the game for hours. "Aight, lemme use the bathroom first."

Two minutes later, Leon came out the bathroom and sat in the fold up chair.

"You ain't flush the toilet or wash your hands?"

"Ain't no water."

"What you mean?" Tyrell hurried to the kitchen and tried the faucet. Nothing.

"What the fuc—"

BOOM! BOOM BOOM! "Open up! New Rochelle police department!" The moment Tyrell's eyes hit the door it was flying off the hinges. "Get on the floor! Now!" The tactical unit officer was dressed in a dark blue fatigue suit, a helmet and full bullet proof body gear, wielding a pump action, 12 gauge shotgun. Three more officers blitzed in and searched the rest of the apartment. An hour later, Tyrell, Leon and Dana were in handcuffs, sitting in holding cells at the police station and Brandi was in the custody of the state.

Dana was livid when the detectives explained the charges and the reason for the raid. She wanted to kill her cousin.

Tyrell had been using the apartment as a trap house and his reckless behavior cost Mox and Dana a huge loss. Police found $290,000 in cash, a half ounce of crack and a quarter pound of weed. The weed and crack was Tyrell's, but the money belonged to Mox. As soon as the word got back to the street, Mox called a "Union" meeting.

MARRIOTT HOTEL – NEW ROC CITY

Mox walked into the 3rd floor meeting room of the Marriott in disarray. He looked defeated and fatigued, like he'd been up for days without a wink of sleep. His eyes held blood and his heart pumped misery while hellish thoughts bounced around his brain like someone pulled the lever on a pinball machine. The burden was coming down on him and the pressure was hastily getting weighted on his shoulders, but Mox was resilient and he vowed to let nothing hinder his committal.

His dress shirt hung out one side of his pants and his shoes were untied as he neared the ash wood table. Frank, Papi and Nate were the only ones physically present because Javier would be attending via iChat and Cleo had gone missing for the last week.

Frank saw the strife on his partner's face. "Mox, don't worry, we gon' take care of this."

"I hope so, Frank. I feel like time might be runnin' out. Anybody heard from Cleo?" They all said no. "Frank, did you get that information I asked for?"

"Yep." He passed Mox a ripped piece of paper with a name and address on it.

> *RITA DAVIS*
> *255 HUGUENOT ST.*
> *NEW ROCHELLE, NY*
> *APT 12K*

Mox tucked the piece of paper into his pocket. "Okay. We gotta make a stop by there when we finish and I gotta go check my Aunt. I also want you to go bail Dana and her little cousin out as soon as possible. I can't have them sittin' up in there. As far as the Telesco's... we fall back for now. We don't move until they force us." Mox sat on the end of the table, tapping his knuckle on the wood. The strain was killing him.

Nate responded. "You sure that's the right thing to do? You know I can make that disappear."

"I know, Nate. I just got so much shit I'm dealing with right now I can barely focus."

Papi stood up. "That's why we here, papi. Ju know we got ju back."

"I think you should let Nate handle that, Mox. Take some pressure off you. That way we can focus on getting Brandi back and handling that other thing." Frank suggested.

Mox agreed. "You're right. Nate, do that; and take Papi with you.

"Hey! You guys forget about me?" Javier broke the tension and made them laugh. He was making his appearance through a video chat from a remote location.

Mox looked amused for the first time in hours. "Wassup, bro. How's the shoulder?"

Javier tapped on his wounded arm to show it was healing. "Muthafucka hit me wit' a forty-five, Mox. I took that shit like a champ, bro. I heard you took one too."

"A few pellets in the side, nothin' crazy." Mox lifted his shirt. The pellets ripped his abdomen to shreds. It looked like a sponge. "You out there takin' care of business, right?"

"Of course. I should be able to set something up soon. I know you'll love it out here. Beautiful women, beautiful weather and easy money. What more could you ask for."

"I bet. Listen, Javier, stay in contact with Papi. Make sure you check in so he can keep you informed. I'ma speak to you later." The computer screen went blank and Papi shut the laptop down.

"Before we step out this door and do what we gotta do," Mox paused and took a good look over his team. "I jus' wanna let each one of you know that I love y'all like brothers. I never had people as close to me as you guys are and I appreciate the love. This shit is genuine. We bosses." He pointed at each man and they rose from the seat they were sitting in. "No one man above the team." Mox placed his right hand over his heart and each man followed suit. "From this day forward we pledge, under oath, to never take the stand against our fellow brothers. To never fuck each others wives and at all times remain loyal..." every face in the room had a cold, focused stare. "Til the heavens turn to dust and hell freezes over; let no-one stand before WE!"

16

S usan leaned against the bathroom sink and let the salty droplets fall from her eye wells to the porcelain tiles. She wiped her face for the hundredth time and tried to catch her breath. "Please, stop." she cried. With each bang on the door, she flinched. She was frightened and exhausted from putting up the fight of her life and barely getting away. The last sixty minutes she'd been living out the most terrifying dream you could imagine, and now she was locked inside her own bathroom, praying that someone would come and save her.

"Bitch, as soon as you open this door, I'ma fuckin' kill you." Cleo had his back against the bathroom door. He clenched a half gallon of *Hennessy* in his right hand and a five inch, wood handle kitchen knife in the other. He was drunk and his disposition was unstable. "Su-san!" he slurred and then turned the cognac bottle to his lips. He lifted his right leg and horse kicked the bathroom door with his size 13 *Timberland* boot.

"Cleo, please, stop! Why are you doing this?" Susan wiped her runny nose and tried to get her hands to stop shaking.

Cleo kicked again, but this time his foot crashed through the flimsy plywood door. He kicked some more to widen the hole and then he got down on the floor and stuck his head through the crack like *Jack Nicholson* in the *Shining*.

"Heeeeere's Johnny!" He laughed so hard he started to cough. "Susan!" he screamed. After several unsuccessful attempts to reach the lock, Cleo finally got smart and used the knife to move the latch.

Susan had nowhere to turn, nowhere to run and nowhere to hide. She had to fight. She thought back on her previous abusive relationships and all the beatings she took from the men who claimed they loved her. *Was this love?* She felt like the only men she attracted were the ones that used physical force. It was a cycle. She watched her father violate her mother time and time again, so much to the point that it became normal, and if it didn't happen, then something was wrong.

She balled her fist so hard, her finger nails cut into her palm and she charged at Cleo as he came through the door. The *Hennessy* bottle slipped from his fingers and hit the floor. Shards of glass and cognac were everywhere.

Susan took a chance and tried to reach for the knife in his hand, but slipped on the wet, glassy tile and banged her head on the enamel steel bathtub. The impact knocked her unconscious and she lay there, on her own bathroom floor, powerless and damn near dead.

Cleo dropped the knife in the toilet and got down on the floor beside her. He was still in a drunken stupor. "Susan." he shook her limp body, but she didn't respond. He lifted her and held her in his arms. "Baby, get up." he used the back of his hand to wipe the blood that leaked down the side of her mouth; the blood that he drew just an hour ago after he slapped her. "Baby," he mumbled. "Get up."

Susan was alive but her breaths were quick, short and faint and if she didn't receive medical attention soon, she would die.

"I'm sorry, baby..." Tears washed Cleo's face. He rocked her in his arms. "I'm sorry..."

His phone vibrated in his pocket and snapped him out his drunkenness. He dug it out and saw it was Mox calling. He quickly hit accept. "Mox, I need your help." He looked down at Susan. She hadn't moved.

Mox could hear the conflict in his voice. It sounded like he was crying. "Cleo, what happened? Where are you?"

Cleo closed his eyes. "Mox, I'm sorry..." his voice got high.

"Cleo!" Where are you?"

"I'm at Susan's." He sniffled. "Mox, hurry up, please."

"Where's she at?"

He whispered into the speaker. "She's sleepin'..."

"Aight, I'll be there, don't move."

25 Minutes Later

"Cleo!" Mox yelled as he pushed the door open to the brown-stone. "Frank, call his phone." he removed the .40 caliber Taurus from the double harness shoulder holster underneath his blazer.

"He's not answering, Mox."

The two men cautiously ascended the steps to the second level and Mox hollered again. "Cleo, you in here?"

They heard some shuffling towards the back of the house.

He could hardly get the words out. "Yeah... I'm...I'm in the bathroom."

When Mox and frank turned the corner, the bathroom door was wide open with a gaping hole in it like someone kicked through it. Cleo was on the floor, holding Susan, who looked to be either sleep or dead.

"What the fuck?" Mox tucked his gun back in the holster and ran over to the bathroom. "Yo, Frank, check the house and make sure nobody else is here." he looked down at Cleo's bloody hands and Susan's beat up face. "What the fuck did you do, Cleo?"

"Mox, I'm sorry..." His face was full of tears and Susan's blood.

Mox snatched a towel off the rack and threw it on the floor, so he wouldn't slip in the glass. He bent down and put two fingers under Susan's chin and felt for a pulse. "She's still breathing. We gotta hurry up and get her to a hospital. Cleo, get up!"

Mox and Frank carried Susan to the car and put her in the back seat with Cleo. Frank got behind the wheel and they rushed through the moderate traffic. They made a right onto Amsterdam and then a left onto 135th street and ran every light until they reached the Harlem Hospital Center.

Mox pulled Susan from the car and waved down the ambulance that pulled up to the emergency entrance. The two EMTs got Susan onto a gurney and into the emergency room without delay. Mox couldn't stay and give any information, so he jumped back into the car and they took off.

After a ten minute ride on the highway going back uptown, Mox told Frank to pull into a *White Castle's* parking lot on Westchester Avenue. He jumped out, pulled the back door open and Frank tried to stop him. "Mox, leave him alone."

"What the fuck is wrong wit' you, Cleo? What you do to that girl?" Mox dragged his three hundred pound frame out the backseat like a bag of laundry.

Cleo didn't even put up a struggle. He just cried. "Mox, I'm sorry..."

"Yo, Mox, it's a lot of police out here tonight. I think we need to keep it moving." Frank was trying to avoid any more problems because they already had enough to deal with.

After Cleo got back into the car, they continued on the highway to New Rochelle.

"Frank, drop me off on Huguenot, so I can go see Ms. Davis."

"Got you."

"And keep this nigga wit' you. Don't let him out your sight."

VITO DOWNED his last shot of *Johnny Walker* and got off the bar stool he was sitting on. He checked his watch, smiled and thought about his late night rendezvous that would take place within the next hour. He hadn't gotten laid in a month.

Tony slid down the bar with a washrag, wiping up spilled drinks and peanut shells. He stopped when he reached Vito. "Boss, you taking it in early tonight?"

"Yeah, I got a hot one, Tony." He fixed his sweater and tapped his pocket to make sure he still had cash on him. "Twin blondes," he cheesed.

"A regular stud ain't you..." Tony laughed. He knew Vito was telling one of his routine lies.

But not tonight, for the first time, he was actually telling the truth.

"Go head and makes jokes, Tony... 'cause in about twenty

minutes, I'll be bangin' two twenty-year olds from the back on a bum knee. You'll be at home... by yourself, of course, drinking stale beer and slammin' lil' Sammy there in your pants. Ha! Now make sure you lock up on time," Vito turned to exit. "And don't rip the skin off your dick tonight, Tony. Take it easy!"

"Fuck you, Vito!" Tony threw the washrag and almost hit him in the back.

Jimmy had been sitting in the limo, parked in front of Vito's for the last twenty minutes, waiting on him to come out.

Vito jumped into the backseat and tapped on the partition. "Jimmy, take me over to the Ritz Carlton, Three Renaissance Square." The limo peeled off and he sat back, stargazing on the adventure he planned on having with the twins. He envisioned all the different positions he would have them in and the thought alone aroused him. He reached into his pocket and pulled out a folded hundred dollar bill. He opened it, dumped the white, powder like crystals onto the back of his hand, and then vacuumed it right up his nostrils. He felt the electricity run through his body and then a sudden numbness washed over him, his eyes rolled and he smiled. He sat, composed and let the high potency drug run its course through his blood stream as he relaxed in paradise. When he finally looked out the window to see where he was, they were just passing the Ritz Carlton.

"Jimmy, where the fuck you goin'? You passed the place."

He kept it steady down Court St. and made a left onto East Post Road and then pulled over and parked behind a black van.

"Jimmy, didn't you fuckin' hear me. I sai—"

The partition came down. "I no think Jimmy hear you, my friend." Papi lifted Jimmy's stiff body from the passenger seat and Vito saw the dime sized bullet hole that sat in the center of his forehead. There was a streak of blood trickling down the bridge of his nose. "I no think Jimmy hear nobody, my friend."

Vito fumbled, trying to grab the pistol off his waistline, but when the door opened he fell into a state of shock. Like a deer caught in bright headlights.

Nate was standing in a black suit, gripping an AM-15 sub machine gun. "Too late, Vito." He let the machine gun blow, and fire shot from the nozzle like a torch. The sub sounded like a jack-hammer going off in the middle of the night. Vito caught every bullet that came out of it. He fell to the limo carpet and half his body was hanging out the door. His blood was splattered throughout the back of the car.

Nate looked down at Vito's bloody corpse and kicked him over to make sure he wasn't breathing. "Papi, vamanos!"

Papi emerged from the driver's seat, tossed Jimmy's hat and jacket back in the car and him and Nate got in the black van that was parked ten feet away and burnt the road up.

MOX STEPPED out the black 500 Benz and walked into the Avalon apartments at 255 Huguenot Street. He gave the desk attendant a fake name and told him he was visiting someone one the ninth floor, but he took the elevator to twelve. He tapped on 12K and waited for someone to answer.

An elderly female voice could be heard from behind the door. "Who is it?"

"Hello, Mrs. Davis... It's Mox. I'm Priscilla's friend."

The lock clicked and the door slowly came open. The older woman standing before him had a familiar face, one that he recognized. Mrs. Davis had a few more wrinkles, but for the most part she and Priscilla looked alike. They were beautiful and even in her old age, she carried a delightful semblance.

"Look at those eyes." She shook her head. "Come in, Mox. I was wondering when you would stop by."

He stepped in and gave Mrs. Davis a kiss on the cheek and then followed her into the living room.

The apartment was a modest one; bare, eggshell colored walls, a micro fiber couch and love-seat, a 32 inch flat screen television sitting on a stand against the far wall and tall plants in each corner of the room.

Mrs. Davis went into the kitchen and poured Mox and herself some water. She sat the two glasses on the table along with a white envelope that had his name on it. She took a seat on the couch. Mox rested in the love-seat next to her.

"Well, it's a pleasure meeting you, Mox. I haven't heard too much about you, but I do know that my daughter loves you." She smiled and sipped her water. "You see that picture over there?" she pointed to a photo on the T.V stand. It was a picture of him and Priscilla the day Mox brought his 430 CLK. They were leaning against the car, parked in front of the dealership. "Whenever Priscilla walks through that door, the first thing she does is pick that picture up and dust the frame. She loves her some Mox."

He got up to look at the picture. He had only seen it one time before. "I love her too, Mrs. Davis. That's why I'm here." Mox picked the picture up and stared at it. A recollection of that day materialized in his brain. It felt like it just happened.

He saw how happy Priscilla was and then he thought on how wearied she looked the last time he'd seen her. He wanted to cry. He wanted to fall out and snivel right there in the middle of Mrs. Davis' living room. His heart was sore and contorted because he believed his self-centeredness was the cause of her stress, and down the line she didn't make rational decisions.

"Have you heard from her?" He asked.

"In the last year, I got two letters from Priscilla. One was mine..." She pushed the envelope on the table closer to Mox. "And this one is yours."

He picked it up and ripped it open:

Mox,

I not writing this letter to apologize for anything I did in the past. If I did it, it was meant to be done. You left me when things got rough and I tried. I tried my hardest to hate every bone in your body, but I couldn't. It's just something that's not allowing me to have any type of animosity towards you, and I can't even explain it.

When I found out I was pregnant with Brandi I was over-joyed. I wanted the chance to speak to you so bad, so I could tell you we were going to have a child, but that never happened.

For six long years I wondered what was going on with you.

I didn't know if you were dead, sick or what. I was lost without you, Mox and it never even crossed your mind that someone on the outside, who truly loved you, was concerned.

Leaving all that in the past; today is a new day and I now have a clear and precise outlook on my life. I've been in this rehabilitation center for the past few months and things are going pretty good. I'm looking forward to coming home and seeing Brandi. How's she doing?

Mox, if it's not too much to ask, my mother's rent is two months past due and I'm not able to take care of her the way I was when I was there. We don't get along, but I did make sure she had a roof over her head and food in her refrigerator. Whatever you can part with will be appreciated.

I should be coming home any day now. The counselors in this program are helping me find an apartment, get a job and enroll back into school. I'm excited. I can't wait to start over and I also can't wait to see my babygirl.

Things are different now, Mox. Maybe there's still room for US.

Love you! And see you soon!!

Priscilla,

P.S. Tell my baby I love her and give her a HUGE kiss for me.

Mox put the letter back into the envelope and sat down. "Mrs. Davis, I got something I need to speak to you about." He wasn't prepared to tell her, but he had to. He was thinking maybe she could help the process go a little smoother. He breathed deep. "I don't know if Priscilla told you, but she left Brandi with me and there's a little problem now."

"What do you mean?"

Mox got straight to the point. "I had someone babysit Brandi while I was working and this particular person's house got raided by the police. They found drugs and money in the apartment and CPS took Brandi."

"Oh, my God... Mox, you have to get her back. Priscilla will go crazy. Oh, poor baby. I know my little angel is scared."

"I know. That's part of the reason for me coming here. I need your help."

Mrs. Davis stood up. "If it has anything to do with Priscilla or Brandi, I'm sorry but I can't get involved."

Mox was stunned. *How could she say something like that? This was her blood.* "I don't understand. This is your granddaughter I'm talking about. I would go get her if I could, but my name isn't on her birth certificate. It has to be immediate family. If you go in there, there's no way they can deny you. We can go get her today."

The distressed expression on her face wasn't the one Mox was looking for. "I'm sorry, Mox, I can't. A long time ago, Priscilla told me to stay out of her and Brandi's life... and that's how it's been since. It hurts, don't get me wrong. I love my daughter and my grandchild, but that's a road that I refuse to travel down again. Priscilla may not have told you how tainted our relationship is and I'm not going to get into it because if she wants you to know, she'll tell you. But, what I will say is, we've never had a good standing between us and that's just what it is. I wish it was different, but it's not."

He tried to understand, but he couldn't. "So, you're not gonna help me?"

"Mox, the only thing I can do for you is pray and have faith in God because he always does the right thing. Sometimes, we may ask why and other times we even doubt him, but trust me, if you have credence and admit Him into your life, He will heal you and guide you down that path of rectitude and spiritual bliss... and then you can begin to understand why things happen the way they do."

Religion was something Mox never delved into, although, during his incarceration, he did thumb through the Bible a couple of times and study a few scriptures out of the Quran, but he wasn't apprehensive on acquiring the knowledge of a single creed. His sharpest memory of God had been the prayer he heard before he saw his mother and father's ravaged bodies.

If we confess our sins, he is faithful and just and will forgive us our sins and purify us from all unrighteousness.

He memorized the prayer from that moment. To him, it meant if he admitted his wrong doings to God, he wouldn't be judged, but forgiven and cleansed of sin.

Mox got up to leave. There was nothing more he could say. He gave Mrs. Davis a hug and a peck on the cheek. "I have no choice but to respect your decision. I wish things were different between you and your daughter, but I see that's something you and she have to handle." He reached into his pocket and pulled out a stack of one hundred dollar bills and a piece of paper with his name and number on it. He counted out two thousand dollars and put the money and his information on the table. "If you ever have a change of heart, I'm only a phone call away. The money is for groceries and anything else you need. I'll make sure the rent is paid until Priscilla comes back so you don't have to worry about that.

"Mox, thank you, but I can't take your money."

He smiled and opened the door. "You got no choice."

17

The teeming rains fell from the dusky clouds that loomed in the air on the pained Friday morning of Vito Telesco's funeral. It was a spectacle. The bosses from all five families were in attendance, including a number of immediate family members and friends who were there to show support to each other in a time of grief.

Vinny's wife, daughter and son stood alongside him under large umbrellas, shedding tears and watching as they lowered the $12,000 gold trimmed casket into the ground. Vito's final resting place would be the St. John's cemetery in Middle Village Queens, NY, where a private mausoleum held the body of one of the most infamous crime figures in history, Salvatore (Charlie) "Lucky" Luciano.

Domenic Conte, the boss of the Gambino family, walked over to Vinny before everyone left the cemetery. He was wearing a long, oyster colored trench coat, shiny black shoes and a matching fedora. He grabbed Vinny's hand and kissed both sides of his face. "Mi dispiace (I'm sorry) Vinny, little Vito was like a son to me. I remember when he was born, God bless him. Hey," he moved in closer to whisper in Vinny's ear. "Hurry up and take care of this fuckin' thing before it gets outta hand. I don't wanna get involved." He patted Vinny on the back and went to get into his car.

Mikey saw the strain on his father's face. "Pop, you okay?"

"I just had to bury your brother, Mikey. What do you think?" Vinny opened the limousine door and got into the back seat.

"Well, if you need me to do anything, just let me know."

The back window came down and Vinny scowled. "I want their fuckin' heads, Mikey, all of 'em... Mox, Cleo, the mother, brothers, sisters, cousins... whoever got the same blood running through their veins is fuckin' dead!" he spat. "You better handle this, Mikey and I'm not joking around."

The window went up and the limousine rolled away.

18

Priscilla spent her last 120 days at the Charles K. Post Treatment & Rehabilitation Center in Brentwood, Long Island. After Ryan humiliated her in the street, she signed into the program. She wanted to make a change for the betterment of herself and Brandi's life. She was aware that at the pace she had been running the streets, it wouldn't have been much longer before she was locked up or killed.

The time away allowed her to reflect on the series of events that led to her decline. Since the day Mox disappeared from her life, everything went downhill. She couldn't digest the fact that one day he was there and they were together, connected like links in a chain, and then, he was gone, and she was abandoned. Things got bad when Priscilla found out she was pregnant. She fell into an unmanageable state of depression, and with Ryan feeding her drugs; it only worsened her state of mind.

It took a few weeks for it to register, but after a while, Priscilla realized Mox wasn't coming back. She was still getting coke from Juan Carlos, but when she got with Ryan he couldn't move the same amount of weight as Mox and the money was coming up short.

After too many losses, Juan Carlos told Priscilla he was no longer doing business with her until Mox returned.

Now, she was pregnant, broke, and had recently developed a new drug habit that she couldn't afford. The only thing left to do was exactly what she vowed to never do, and that was become what her mother had always called her.

Ryan never gave Priscilla a dime, so when she went broke; she had to do for herself. Whatever it took to put food and clean diapers on her baby girl, she did. Plenty of nights, she would starve, because the only money she could hustle up would be enough for some formula for Brandi. She stole everything from bottles of Gerber baby food to an $800 dollar power folding stroller out of *Toys R Us*.

She ran a scam on the department of social services and figured out a way to get more money than she should have been getting. The extra finances helped her secure her own living space. She was able to rent a room for $500 a month.

Every day, Priscilla would tell herself that she was going to kick the habit, but every day, the habit continued to kick her. By the time Brandi was four years old, Priscilla was all the way strung out on cocaine and the effects of the highly addictive drug were more than obvious. Certain areas of her skin darkened and her hair became dry and frizzled. The only thing she thought about was coke. It got so bad that her sinus and nostril tissue were permanently scarred. She no longer loved herself inside or out. She didn't care. She became physically dependent on the drug and needed it to function.

But everything changed the moment she walked through the doors of the treatment center. It felt like a ton of weight lifted from her shoulders as soon as she signed the agreement papers. The first week of her withdrawal was the worst, because her body craved more of the drug than usual and her obsession to use increased. Instead of giving in to her cravings, Priscilla had to occupy her mind with new and unconnected thoughts to distance herself from the norm. She had to become somebody new, and in order to do that she needed to let it all out.

When she started her one-on-one therapy sessions with her counselor, Priscilla was distant and unresponsive. She wasn't comfortable opening up to people she knew, so a stranger was out of the question. It took some time, but eventually, she started to express herself and show some progress.

A couple weeks later, she was ready for the group sessions.

"Hello, my name is Priscilla... and I'm an addict."

On her journey through the twelve step program, Priscilla discovered a new life and gradually shed all the fear and emotions she kept locked inside. It was a new breath and a rejuvenated experience. She listened as other addicts shared their stories of joy and horror and when it was her turn, she was delighted to partake.

"Hello, my name is Priscilla and I'm addicted to cocaine."

"Hello, Priscilla." The group replied.

She continued. "I came here four months ago after my ex-boyfriend beat me up in the streets. I'm thirty years old and I have a six year old daughter who I abandoned, just so I could go off and get high. Excuse me y'all." her eyes got watery and she wiped them.

"It's alright, baby..." A white girl named Jennifer try to calm her. She and Priscilla had met through the program three months ago. They had been cool since. "We all made mistakes that we knew were wrong when we were doing them. It's all good. Jus' let it out." Jennifer was the only friend Priscilla had in the program. Everybody gravitated to at least one person they could trust and confide in and she was just that. She and Priscilla had a lot in common. They were beautiful, young females with daughters, a drug habit and tons of hate in their blood towards their mothers.

Priscilla kept going. "I never told anyone this, but when I was nine years old my mother and father were separated and not too long after she had a new boyfriend. From the day he walked through the door I knew he was the devil. I tried to tell my mother how I felt and she brushed my feelings off. After six months of them dating, she let this stranger move into our house. There were nights I would jump out of my sleep because I felt someone's presence, and sure enough, it would be him, standing over me, drilling me with those satanic like eyes of his." Her tears started to flow again, but this time she let them fall. "It started with the disgusting looks and it escalated to him touching me and eventually he pinned me down in my own bed and raped me." The entire room had an eerie silence and nobody could look Priscilla in the face. "I told my mother about it the next day and you know what she did?" Priscilla paused. "That bitch told me I was lying and she whopped my ass everyday, faithfully, until I told her I made the story up. Till this day she still doesn't believe he raped me."

Her story had the room in tears. Jennifer got up from her seat and went to give Priscilla a hug. They cried and embraced for a minute. Priscilla had just rid herself of dead weight she had been holding onto for twenty years and it felt remarkable. It helped her move on to the next phase of her new life.

All eighteen group members stood up and started clapping. They were proud of the progress Priscilla had made since her arrival, and in a few hours she would be on her way out the door to start her new life.

Jennifer tapped her leg. "Hey, you better not forget about me when you get back in the world."

Priscilla hugged her again. "You know I got you, girl. I told you I got a plan..."

19

T he fairly sized one bedroom apartment smelled of soiled clothes that hadn't been washed in months. The walls were filled with smoke and the carpet was full of dirt. Tyrell sat on the arm of the old ripped up sofa and reached into his left pocket. He pulled out 2 quarters, a dime and 5 nickels.

Eighty five fuckin' cent to my name. He thought.

"Tyrell!"

"What do you want, Ma?"

"Gimme some money."

He looked down at the change in his hand and smiled, but he really wanted to cry. "I ain't got no money."

"So, gimme some drugs." Ms. Michaels staggered out the back and into the living room. She was a tall, slim woman, who once was exceptionally attractive, but after smoking crack for five years, that beauty dwindled away. She had a grubby red scarf tied around her head to hide her bald spots and her T-shirt and sweatpants were unwashed and full of holes.

"I ain't got nothin' ma. No money, no drugs." He pushed some old newspapers to the side and sat on the sofa.

She scratched at a dark spot on her neck. "Well, you gotta get the fuck outta here. I don't need you here if you ain't got nothin'... you might as well go back to where you was."

"I was at cousin Dana's house, but she said I couldn't stay there no more. I ain't got nowhere to go."

"Well, you going outta here... bet that."

"Ma, don't do this to me right now. Please."

"Please my ass, Tyrell. You wanna be grown, take yo' grown ass out there in them streets."

Tyrell cast a hateful sneer at his mother. "Oh, so since I ain't got no money or no drugs I gotta *leave*? You gon' kick your own son out over some foul shit like *that*?"

Ms. Michaels picked up a half smoked cigarette from the ashtray and lit it. "Boy, please..."

"Fuck you then... you crack head bitch!" He slammed the door as he left out.

"No, fuck you, Tye-rell! You no-good-son-of-a-bitch!" She ranted. "You ain't shit and you never gon' be shit! You just like yo' ol' punk ass father!"

It wasn't the first time Tyrell had called her a crack head or a bitch. Their altercations started the day he found out she was using drugs. His heart felt like it had gotten crushed, and on top of that, he got ridiculed for it. That's when the trouble started.

Two years ago, he solidified his hood credibility when he shot and robbed two dudes from out of town at a dice game.

"Yo, that's in the crack!"

"Everything good over here. I told you the rules before we started."

Tyrell stood off to the side watching the local hustlers spar off with the dice like he did every night in the hood. Stacks of money, liquor, weed and women always set the scene for a summer evening, and the gamblers stayed out all night. Some nights, C-low games would go on for hours and then lead into the next day. After five straight hours, the only ones still going at it were Rome and two dudes from out of town.

"I'm not payin' that. It's in the crack. Let me roll over." The short kid from out of town said.

Rome stuffed the dice in his pocket. "You not gon' pay me? Nigga, that's a five hunit dolla ace. You gon' pay that."

The tall kid from out of town said, "My man said let him roll over."

Rome gave Tyrell the head nod and he got off the bench.

"Fuck you and your man. Gimme all that shit!" he pulled out an old snub nose with black electrical tape wrapped around the handle.

"Yo, Rome wassup wit cha—"

"Shut the fuck up!" Tyrell slapped the tall kid from out of town with the old pistol and then went in his pockets and took everything he had. He did the same to the short kid, but when he went to take the chain off his neck, the short kid got bold and tried to grab the gun. He didn't succeed. Tyrell shot them in front of the building and from that day on, the hood would respect him.

After his mother told him he wasn't shit, Tyrell went and rolled his last bag of weed and sat in the park, smoking and thinking of a way to come up. He was out on bail, no money, no work and no place to lay his head. The only thing he owned was that old, rusted .38 snub nose with the tape on the handle. He had to make do with what he had.

Halfway through the blunt, his homie Leo popped up. "Whaddup, Rell?" he took a seat on the wooden bench.

"Coolin, what's good wit' you? Wanna hit this?" he tried to pass the blunt, but Leo said no. "Oh, you quit smoking now, huh?"

"Yeah, I'm chillin'. I gotta get my shit together, Rell. I can't keep doing the same shit. Yo, my moms said she gon' kick me out if I get in any more trouble. Fuck I'ma go?"

"Nigga, my moms already kicked me out. You know how that goes... fuck it." Tyrell inhaled a thick stream of smoke and exhaled through his nostrils. "What you got in the bag?"

"DVD's and socks." Leo opened the bag and took the contents out.

Tyrell laughed and the smoke caused him to cough. His eyes were watery. "Nigga, you sellin' DVD's and socks now, what the fuck is wrong wit' you?"

"I ain't tryna go to jail, that's what's wrong with me. Fuck that crack shit. My uncle fronted me some stock and this shit is good money. Police ain't gon' fuck with me for this shit."

Tyrell shook his head. "Nigga, you trippin'... yo, come wit' me to go see Rome real quick. He 'pose to give me some bread." They got up and walked into building #70. Tyrell was still joking on Leo's hustle. "You a funny nigga, son. What door this nigga live at?"

"I think it's 2C." Leo answered. They walked up the steps and Tyrell knocked on the door.

A male shouted. "Who is it?"

"It's Rell."

The door came open. "What you want, lil' nigga?" Rome said. He kept the door cracked with his foot behind it.

"Yo, lemme holla at you for a sec, my nigga."

Rome opened the door and let Tyrell and Leo in. "Damn, this shit is nice, Rome." Tyrell looked over the situated apartment. Rome had been doing well for himself these past few years. He was one of a handful of hustlers in the projects who were really getting some money. He ran a profitable dope spot on the other side of town that had been in business for the last three years and sometimes he would get Tyrell to do a few things for him. Rome recognized the thirst in his eyes and took advantage of young Tyrell because he was easily swayed. He fed him just enough to keep him hungry and coming back for more, but Tyrell wasn't as stupid as he thought.

Rome knew he came to ask for something. "So, wassup, what you wanna talk about?"

"I need to hold somethin'..."

"You always need to hold something, my nigga. Every time I give you something, you fuck it up."

Tyrell tried to reason. "I'm sayin' my nigga... I know I fucked shit up before, but right now shit is real. I ain't got nowhere to rest my head. I ain't got no bread. I need your help, for real."

Rome wasn't giving in this time. "I ain't fuckin' wit' you like that, Rell. It's too much of a headache." he looked at Leo. "What the fuck you lookin' at? What you got in the bag, Leo?"

"DVD's and socks."

Rome looked in the bag. "Oh, word... lemme get a couple pair of them joints and that new shit that came out Friday... wit' Denzel." Leo gave him the DVD and two pairs of socks. "Okay, I see you Leo. You gettin' money, huh? So, this is what you need that paper for, Tyrell?"

"Man... fuck them DVD's, Rome. I need some real money."

"Nigga, you tryna be Pablo Escobar *tomorrow*. That shit ain't gon' happen. You gotta start at the bottom and put that work in. You know the old saying, *'Rome wasn't built in a day'* " he laughed. "Hold up y'all... I gotta go check on my daughter. She's in the back, sleep." He walked to the backroom.

"Yo," Leo whispered when he saw Tyrell snatch the pistol from his pants. "What the fuck you doing?"

Tyrell palmed the weapon, looked at it and then eyed Leo. "Jus' shut up and do what I say."

"But—"

Rome came from the back and as soon as he entered the living room, he saw Tyrell holding the gun. "What you doing?" his eyes were on the old taped up pistol. "Fuck you got that for?"

Tyrell was nervous. He quickly aimed the gun at Rome's head. "Where the fuckin' money at, Rome?"

Rome grinned. He didn't think Tyrell was serious. He looked at Leo and noticed the panic on his face, so he took a step toward the gun. "Stop playing with me, Rell."

Tyrell took a step forward and gripped the handgun tighter. He wasn't playing at all. "You think it's a joke?" He pulled the trigger and shot Rome in the foot.

Leo jumped at the sound of the gunshot. "Rell, what the fuck are you doing!?"

The impact from the bullet broke Rome's ankle and he fell to the floor in agony. The look he gave Tyrell was a confused one. "You buggin, lil' nigga... chill!" Blood was spilling out the hole in his foot.

Tyrell stood over him and put the gun to his head. "Where that bread, nigga?"

Leo was scared to death. "Rome, I ain't have nothing to do with this," he pleaded.

"Shut the fuck up, Leo, before I shoot your dumb ass too." He bought his eyes back to Rome. "You got five seconds to tell me where that money at. Five..." he started counting down.

"Rell, don't do this, my daughter is in the back. Please."

"Three... Two..."

Rome had to make a swift decision. "Aight... aight." he took a deep breath and looked at the blood coming from his foot. "The money is in the deep freezer, all the way at the bottom." The pain was worsening. "Ta... take it and get the fuck outta here."

"Leo... get that." Tyrell ordered.

His adrenalin was at its peak. Every time he held that gun in his hand he felt powerful. The power was so intense it stimulated his mind and made him believe he was everything he ever wanted to be. It was magician like, and the gun was his magic wand. He could make things happen with just a wave of his hand.

A baby's cry echoed from the back room and right away Rome's neck turned. It was his three year old baby girl, Essence. She had been asleep the whole time.

"C'mon, Rell, let me get my daughter, man." Rome tried to stand up, but his body weight was too much pressure for his wounded limb. He slouched back to the floor. He attempted to crawl to the back room, but Tyrell stopped him with a harsh, soccer kick to the ribs. Rome curled into a fetal position on the cold tile.

Leo came from out the kitchen holding two, giant zip-lock freezer bags filled with money. He was sweating and agitated. "Rome," he whined, shaking his head. "I didn't have nothing to do with this."

Tyrell turned the pistol on Leo. "Shut yo' stupid ass up and wait by the door," he tossed him a shopping bag. "Put the money in that bag."

The baby's cries grew louder by the passing minutes and Rome continued to lose blood. "Yo, Rell, you got everything, man..." he cried. "Jus' go... please, let me get to my daughter."

Tyrell glanced down at the blood and then looked at Rome, begging for his life. There was no way he could leave this apartment without killing him. He knew if he let Rome live, as soon as he was able to walk, he would come gunning for him. He raised the revolver and leveled it to Rome's head. He bit his bottom lip until he split it and tasted his own blood. He was so focused he didn't hear Leo's cries for him to not to shoot.

"Please, don't shoot him," he begged.

Tyrell strangled the pistol's hair trigger and unloaded a slug into Rome's head, and then he pumped the last three in his chest. Besides the gunshots, all you heard was Essence in the back room, screaming her lungs out.

Leo fumbled trying to unlock the door. His nerves were rattled. When he finally got it open, he took off running toward the staircase and Tyrell was behind him.

"Hold up..." Tyrell yanked the back of Leo's shirt preventing him from continuing down the steps. "Let's go up to the roof and go over." When Leo turned around, his face was wet from tears. "What the fuck you cryin' for, nigga?"

"You didn't have to kill 'em, Rell." Leo bawled. The teardrops were flowing freely.

Tyrell took the bag of money from him and snatched him by the back of his shirt. "Get the fuck up the steps, nigga."

They hurried up the stairs to the roof of building #70 and crossed over to building #81. They were the only two connecting buildings in the projects. Before they reached the lobby in #81, Tyrell pushed Leo against the wall in the staircase and pressed the snub nosed barrel to his cheek. "If you say a word about what happened to *anybody*... I'ma kill you. You hear me?" Leo nodded. "Go to the crib, act like nothing happened and I'ma come see you tomorrow wit' some money."

Leo could care less about the money; he was pleased with walking away with his life. He and Tyrell went their separate ways.

20

July 1st 2011

The sun was beating down on the project bricks at a sweltering 98 degrees when Mox hopped out the United taxi cab and rushed to his Aunt's building. Halfway there, he got stopped by his Uncle Wise Earl. "Playboy... you goin' upstairs? I need to holla you at real quick." Uncle Wise was getting old, but he was still as sharp as a scorpion's stinger and his smooth 70's style had yet to be modified. He was an ol' school player who played by the ol' school rules.

Earl had come up in the era of the *"Real Gangsters"* where, if somebody was caught stealing, depending on the value, either your hand would be chopped off at the wrist or a few fingers would go missing. It was the time when guys in the streets had morals and principals. If something got done it was with a reason and not *"just because"* Although this new generation didn't abide by these rules; Uncle Earl did.

"Wassup, Unc... how you been?" Mox could see he had fresh track marks from shooting heroin into his veins. Earl had kicked the habit for a few years, but the monkey was back for revenge.

He followed his nephew into his sister's building. "Maintainin'...

tyrna dodge these goddamn suckers as usual. Hey, you heard about that boy, Rome?"

"Nah, what happened to him?"

"Young boy put somethin' hot in 'em. They found him in his apartment, shot up. Police came and snatched up that young nigga, Leo."

"Get the fuck outta here, are you serious?" Mox had just bailed Dana, Tyrell and Leo out of the county jail. "You fuckin' around again, Unc?"

Earl eyed the marks on his arms. "Listen, nephew. You let me worry about this bitch on my back and let's continue to take care of that business. You hear me?"

They stepped off the elevator and Mox put the key in the door. "You full of shit, Unc. How you expect to conduct business and you noddin' off n' shit?"

Earl frowned. He disliked when people told him the truth about his addiction. "Aight, keep your voice down, Sybil don't know I'm getting' high." he closed the door behind him.

"Oh, word?..." Mox peeked his head in the kitchen looking for his aunt. "Auntie!" he shouted.

"Yes." Sybil came from the back and saw Earl and Mox standing in the living room. "What you want, Mox, I'm watchin' my stories."

"Your brother is back out there getting' high."

Earl's eyes bulged at Mox's words.

Sybil looked at her brother's face and then at his arms, and when he tried to hide the scars, she knew Mox was telling the truth. "I don't know why the fuck you tryna hide 'em for, Earl. Anybody with eyes can see that shit is in you. I was just too naïve. I got blinded and so caught up on believing in you and knowing you could make that change that I forgot who I was dealing with. You know how that saying goes, 'once a junkie always a junkie.'"

Earl got defensive. "I know, I fucked up, but don't act like you this goddamn angel who fell from heaven and you ain't never did wrong. We all done did some shit we regret. Fuck it." Earl threw his hands in the air. "Since my shit is all out on the table, we might as well put *everything* on the muthafuckin table!"

"You right, Unc. We gon' put everything on the table, today. I got some questions and I need 'em answered." Mox looked at his aunt. He saw the discomfiture in the shift of her demeanor. "When's the last time you spoke to Cleo, auntie?"

Sybil walked into the kitchen. "I was just on the phone with him. He's across town."

"Call him back." As soon as the words came out of Mox's mouth the front door was coming open and Cleo was walking in. Mox hadn't seen him since two nights prior, when they had to rush Susan to the emergency room. "Cleo... wassup, you right on time," he smiled.

"On time for what?" he was confused.

Mox wasted no time. "Auntie, I know you been holding secrets from me about the night of my parents murder. I'm not leaving this house until you tell me the truth."

"Mox, I don't have to tell you anything."

Earl cut in. "Yes you do, because if you don't, I will."

"What the fuck are y'all talking about?" Cleo was still lost.

Sybil stayed silent and kept her eyes glued to Earl.

"Cat got your tongue, sis? Let me help you out..." Earl turned to Mox. "That nigga Reginald ain't your real father. We been lying to you your whole life. Your—"

Sybil pulled a picture out the Bible that was sitting on the coffee table and passed it to Mox. "That's your real father."

Mox looked down at the picture and he froze. He couldn't believe he was staring at was his biological father. It had to be true because his eyes told him so.

Sybil explained. "Your mother and I used to go out, a lot. They knew us at every club in the city when we were younger. We were gorgeous, but your mother had that *'talk'*. She could convince a guy to do anything just by having formal conversation. They went crazy for my sister. The day I met *him*," she pointed to the picture. "We were in some club and he approached me. Wanda kept telling me to talk to him and eventually I did. That night, we had been drinking and smoking, so everyone was intoxicated and I did something I probably wouldn't have done, had I not been drinking. That was the first and last time I had a one night stand."

"I never heard from him until three months later, when I saw him leaving your *mother's* apartment. Later, I found out he was a close friend of Reginald, who had been your mother's boyfriend for two years at that time. First, I didn't think anything of it, but when he came around I could see she acted different. When she got pregnant, no one questioned who your father was because we all assumed it was Reginald, but when I saw your eyes, I knew she was lying. Those eyes are rare and only a few people living have them. Your father is one of them."

Mox rubbed his head. He was trying to absorb this new information he was being told. It made perfect sense when he thought about it. His eyes were distinctive and Reginald didn't have eyes like his. He thought back on he and Reginald's relationship and how they never bonded like a true father and son. They had no similar qualities and nothing in common.

"So, what happened the night my mother got murdered?" he asked.

Sybil went on. "Reginald and that man in the picture had done a robbery at the world trade center, a week before your mother was killed. They stole two million dollars in cash and one million in jewels. Reginald convinced your father to stash everything in Wanda's apartment. The night before the murder, your mother and I got into a huge fight about some money and a lot of foul things were said. At that moment she came clean about going behind my back and lying about who your real father was. She told me she was sorry and she said that she would make it up to me by giving me some of the money that was in her apartment. I didn't believe her until she showed me what was really there, and I tell you... I never saw so much money in my life." Sybil's eyes filled up with tears. "Wanda left out to run to the store and I went back into the apartment and stole the money."

"What?" Cleo wanted her to repeat herself. "You stole what?"

Sybil ignored her son and finished her story. "The next day, they came to get the money and it was gone. I heard him torturing Reginald that night, asking him where the money was. I stood by the door and listened to my sister's cries for help while she was being crucified and it was my fault because I could have helped her, but I didn't." Tears washed her face as she confessed her deepest sins.

Mox stared at the picture. He knew this man. "Are you sure *this* is my father?" he questioned.

"Yes, I'm sure, Mox. Why?"

The room was silent.

"Because... I know this man."

Earl was surprised. "What?"

Mox studied the photo. "His name is Priest and I shared a cell with him when I was upstate."

"Oh, my God!" Sybil broke down and tried to cover her face from humiliation.

"So, what you tellin' me is... my father is the one who killed my mother that night?"

Sybil's cries became gut wrenching screams for forgiveness and Earl tried to embrace his nephew to console him.

Mox pushed him back. "Don't fuckin' touch me. Y'all knew this shit all this time." He crumbled the picture in his hand. "I asked you over and over again; both of y'all lied to me. Both of y'all knew the truth from the beginning and you had me runnin' around killin' myself tryna figure this shit out. You don't know half the shit I went through searching for something that was right up under my nose." He crumbled photo harder in his fist.

Suddenly, *'Breaking News'* flashed across the screen and caught their attention.

Casey Daniels was a prominent prospect out of Westchester County that was headed to the NBA before his life was so suddenly cut short. At twenty one years of age, Casey was shot dead and robbed, here at the Marriott hotel at New Roc City last year.

In the winter of that same year, the body of Tamika Hutchins was found on the side of the road by the Roanoke River in Virginia. Police say Hutchins and an accomplice lured Daniels into a room at the hotel and robbed him at gunpoint and then shot him six times, ending his life.

Police have found a missing security tape from the night of Casey Daniels murder at the hotel and they have identified Hutchins' accomplice as this man,

They showed a mug shot of the shooter on Sybil's 37 inch television.

Twenty six year old; Cleo Daniels. Authorities are advising anyone with information on Mr. Daniels' whereabouts to please contact our crime hot-line at 914 -555-5555. Beware, Mr. Daniels is considered armed and very dangerous.

By the time they turned their heads to look at Cleo, his pearl handled, chrome .9 millimeter Ruger was pointed in their direction. He saw Mox reaching for his waist. "You try to pull that shit out and I'ma empty this clip."

"Cleo, why?" Sybil cried.

"Nephew, calm down..."

"Fuck that nephew shit. I know the truth!"

"What truth? What the fuck are you talking about?" Earl tried to get Cleo to settle down.

Through sobs, Sybil uttered, "He's adopted."

Mox and Earl replied in unison. *"Adopted?"*

Cleo waved the gun at Mox. "Yeah, adopted." he pointed his finger at Sybil. "That's not my mother, he ain't my uncle and you damn sure ain't my cousin." he clenched his teeth and gave Mox the coldest ice grill he could muster. "I never did like you, nigga."

"Why you do it, Cleo?" Mox knew there was another person at the shooting, but he would have never imagined it to be someone he thought was family.

Sybil and Earl could do nothing but watch as Cleo put the barrel of the gun to Mox's head. "Because, I never liked that lil' nigga, he stole *my* dream. I was supposed to be the one going to the league, not him."

"That's what this shit is all about? You killed my little brother. He loved you, Cleo. We all love you."

"Fuck your love, Mox! From day one you thought you was better than me. Every girl I liked wanted to be with you..." a tear fell from Cleo's eye. "You knew I liked Priscilla and you still went after her!"

Mox was dumbfounded. "Priscilla? Nigga, since we was babies I been holding your punk ass down. Everything you was scared to do, I did... and I always gave you the credit. I showed you genuine love, Cleo. Fuck if we ain't blood. We grew up together. We struggled together. We ate and fought together, but all this time you had larceny in your heart towards me. People always told me that too.

They used to say, 'watch your back, because your cousin is a snake', but I never believed it. I see for myself now. It's always the ones closest to you that hurt you the most."

"Don't bitch up now. I wouldn't have to do this if those fuckin' Italians would've done what they were supposed to do." Cleo cocked the weapon back. "Yeah... I *was* the one who paid drunk Sunny to shoot up the bar and say your name. I figured they could take care of you and I could take care of them, but things didn't go as planned, so I gotta do this shit myself, just like I did Casey."

Mox tried to grab the gun from Cleo's hand and a tussle ensued. They wrestled until they hit the ground, but Cleo still had a firm grip on the pistol. Mox tried to bend his wrist so he would drop it, but nothing was working. Cleo was using his one hundred pound weight difference to his advantage.

"Cleo, stop!" Sybil begged. Earl tried to help, but Cleo backed him up by aiming the gun at him.

The butt end of the Ruger came down on Mox's jaw and the struggle turned one sided.

Cleo made it to his feet and stood over Mox as he lay on the floor, wounded. "Since you miss your brother so bad, I'm 'bout to send you to meet him." he closed his eyes and squeezed the trigger.

THE LIVERY CAB could barely make it to the parking lot because of all the police cars that were lined up. Priscilla looked out the window as she waited for her change. Paramedics and EMT's were rushing someone to the ambulance on a gurney. She hadn't paid it much mind until she saw Mox's aunt Sybil and his uncle Wise Earl, running alongside the men pushing the small bed on wheels.

She pushed the cab door open and sprang from the seat. All she could see were tubes coming out the mouth of whoever was lying on the gurney. As she got closer, her heart beat faster and faster. She looked at the horror on Sybil's face and knew something was wrong.

When the paramedics whizzed by, it was as if a video frame was playing in slow motion. She saw the only man she ever loved, stretched across a thin mattress, fighting for his life. She reached out to grab his hand, but could only brush his finger-tips because they were moving fast.

Priscilla looked up and then she looked around for her daughter. She didn't see her. The white and red truck with the flashing lights started to pull away and Priscilla jumped back in the cab.

"Hurry up, follow the ambulance!"

21

D r. Callahan rushed into the operating room behind paramedics, who had just rolled in Mox's blood soaked body. "Nurse," she called out. "What's his status?"

"Ahh..." The nurse flipped through some papers on a clip board." Twenty-six year old, black male with a gunshot wound to the head."

The heart monitor beeped and the squiggly lines changed.

"What happened?" the doctor asked.

"I don't know... his BP is decreasing, eighty-nine over sixty." the nurse answered.

Dr. Callahan moved closer to Mox. "Increase the dopamine delivery rate to twelve point five."

"His brain waves are spiking and his blood pressure levels are erratic!" the nurse yelled.

Dr. Callahan stood at the foot of the operating table. He tried to get Mox to speak. "Mox... are you still with us? Mr. Daniels?"

Mox didn't answer, he couldn't respond.

One of the nurses shouted. "We're losing him... get the crash cart!"

THE SURROUNDING chaos agitated Priscilla as she watched the doctors attempt to pump life back into Mox. It was a torturous sight, but she couldn't pull her eyes from it, she hadn't blinked in minutes. Plastic tubes were inserted into his nose and mouth to help with his breathing and nurses did whatever was necessary to keep the bleeding to a minimum.

His clothing was cut and ripped from his body as he lay there, naked, on an operating table, fighting for his life.

As the tears hastily cascaded down Priscilla's cheeks, she silently prayed to a higher power and begged him not to take Mox. *It wasn't his time*, she thought. This couldn't be a part of what *God* had planned for her. She had just gotten her life in order and was willing and ready to start over with the hopes of Mox wanting to be a family. She thought on how long it had been since his easeful touch soothed her tense nerves and made her feel as if there was no one but the two of them on earth. She dreamed of the day everything would be right and the three of them could peacefully grow together and get to know each other.

Her thoughts drifted and an image of Brandi flashed before Priscilla's eyes. Instantly, an overwrought look of concern flushed her face. *"My baby!"* she shouted, slapping the hard plastic window. *"Mox, wake up! Where's Brandi? Oh my God, where's my baby?"*

Doctors quickly pulled the shade over the window so no one could see inside, and two tall, dark skinned security guards made their way to Priscilla. They tried to get her to calm down in an attempt to comfort her, but nothing seemed to work.

Sybil sat in a waiting chair that was pressed against the wall only ten feet away, in a distraught trance. Her nerves were ashake and her palms were clammy. The chatter from the visitors and employees was on mute. Her mind was strained with the events that had suddenly taken place.

A part of her felt free, but yet, she was still saddened at the fact she had held onto a secret so disheartening and so destructive; a secret she knew would taint, sever or even worse, end her once close relationship with her nephew. She tried to cry, but the tears wouldn't fall. Maybe she did have more than a tad bit of animosity towards her sister, more than even *she* believed. Had she been putting on an act, or did she *really* care? Several thoughts alike raced through her brain faster than *Usain Bolt* in the one hundred. She couldn't stop her left leg from shaking. It was a display of fear; an instinct she'd been living with her entire life. Sybil turned her head and saw her brother, Earl. He was propped against the far wall, one leg up, hands in his pockets and his head down. "Earl." She whispered.

He looked in her direction; a brief, indistinct look of confusion. "Ain't no fixing this one, sis." he uttered, shaking his head. Earl was reluctant to speak openly about the situation, and on top of that, he was getting sick. Pellets of sweat started to form on his head. His stomach turned and his nerves twitched. He yawned every few minutes and kept glancing at his watch and then up at the clock that hung on the wall. He was counting the hours it had been since his last fix. *Seventy-two,* He thought to himself. The diarrhea was about to kick in. "Shit!" he imagined he was saying it in his head, but it came out loud. Everyone in the waiting area turned their head to Uncle Wise and he scowled back. "Fuck y'all lookin' at?"

"Earl!" Sybil scolded.

"Fuck that, sis. I gotta use the bathroom." He surveyed the large space. "Excuse me; guard... where's the restroom?"

The guard pointed down the long corridor and Earl took off.

Priscilla relaxed her nerves and tried to bring herself together. She looked at the clock; it read 1:50 pm. Without delay, the panic she had just overcome was slowly settling back in. It slipped her mind that she had to report to the shelter by 2-oclock. If she didn't show up or was late, the case worker was going to push her application to the bottom of the pile. She remembered what her counselor, Mrs. James told before she left.

Priscilla, please don't let me down. These people are expecting you and they're doing me a favor by moving your name to the top of the list. You have to be there by two pm on the day you're released from the treatment center. No if's ands or buts about it. If you don't show up, there's nothing I can do for you. This is your chance to make the change you've been talking about. Don't screw it up...

Don't screw it up. Don't screw it up! She told herself.

Priscilla turned and looked to the operating room where Mox was. The last thing she wanted to do was leave his side, but it was either that or end up on the streets again. The thought of becoming her old self was frightening enough for her to rationalize and make a quick decision. She brushed the tears from her face and took a few steps toward Sybil. "Excuse me, Ms. Daniels, I know that right now you're dealing with a lot... I mean... we all are, but I need to find my daughter. Do you know where she is?" she anxiously waited for an answer, but Sybil didn't even raise her head in acknowledgment, she just looked down at the floor. "Ms. Daniels?" Priscilla tried again to get her attention without being rude.

Sybil finally lifted her head; her face, full of grief. "It's all bad, Priscilla... It's all bad."

"I don't understand?" She glanced at the clock again. *What did she mean it was all bad??* Prsicilla's nerves were about to go haywire, but she remained calm. "When was the last time you saw, Brandi?"

Sybil stared into Priscilla's eyes and the affliction was evident. She could tell by looking at her that she'd been through hell and back. The last time she saw her, Priscilla was strung out on cocaine. She sure didn't look her best. Her hair was ragged, garments were squalid and her spirit was in the mud, but today, today she was a brand new woman, and all she wanted was to see her daughter. Sybil tried to tell her. "She's gone..."

The words hung in the air for a few seconds before they came down and slapped Priscilla in the face. "Who's gone?" she asked, not believing what she thought she heard.

"Brandi... is gone, Priscilla. They took her."

Her face went blank. "Took her?" she sat in the chair next to Sybil. "What do mean, they took her... who took her?" her voice was getting louder.

"Excuse me, miss?" One of the guards stepped over to where she sat. "We asked you to keep your voice down... I'm afraid you're going to have to leave."

Priscilla ignored him. "Who took my baby!" she shouted.

"Miss," The guard went to grab her arm to escort her from the building.

"Get the fuck off me!" she pulled away and faced Sybil. "Who took my baby?" she cried. Tears were pouring from her face and her heart felt like it was about to explode through her chest.

Two more guards came around the corner to help ease the situation, but Priscilla was livid. "Miss, you need to calm down before we call the authorities."

Sybil put her head back down and remained silent. She couldn't imagine the anguish and heartache Priscilla was feeling. The only man she loved was stretched out on a bed, fighting for his dear life, and her young, innocent daughter was in the custody of child protective services.

"Where's my baby!" She repeated, trying to grab at Sybil's shirt, but the guard restrained her and drug her out the waiting area and into the street.

Unlike earlier, the shining sun had taken cover behind a fluffy, grey cloud and the gloom had set in. It was still hot, but now the humidity and dankness was making it sticky and uncomfortable. The frustration and displeasure mixed with the heat only heightened Priscilla's anger. She was confused and didn't have a clue as to where her child was, nobody would tell her anything, and to top it off, she had to be at the shelter in five minutes.

She bent down to fix her shoe and a cab rolled up to the emergency entrance. After the two passengers got out, Priscilla begged the driver to drop her off a few blocks over. When she got settled in she would have to contact her mother to find out if she knew anything about Brand.

The two and a half block ride took only a few minutes, but when Priscilla burst through the Providence house doors at 89 Sickles Avenue, the clock read; 2:05.

She cursed under her breath, *shit!* She was late.

An older, brown skinned, heavy set woman with black shoulder length hair sat behind a desk, rambling into a cordless phone about her baby's father not paying child support. She paused in the middle of her conversation. "You're late."

Priscilla froze, her mouth opened, but nothing came out.

"Yeah, girl... I'll call you back." she rolled her eyes at Priscilla. "Umm hmm... my two-o-clock finally decided to stroll in." she clicked.

"I'm sorry. My name is Priscilla Da—"

"Ms. Davis," She cut in. "Like I said, you're late. You see that clock?" She turned and pointed at the clock on the wall behind her. "It says two-oh-five and your appointment was scheduled for two-o-clock. That means you should've been here fifteen minutes ago. I'm sure they told you about being *on time* in the program."

Priscilla started to say something, but got cut off again.

"You know... you're lucky Mrs. James and I are cool." She reached into a cabinet and grabbed a small stack of papers. "Usually, you would have come through that door late and I would've kindly told you to turn it right around. Are you serious about this?" she asked.

"Yes, very serious... and again, I'm sorry for being late."

The woman sucked her teeth and shook her head. She had seen a thousand Priscillas walk through that door. "Sorry ain't gone get you nowhere in this world, so that's the first thing you need to do..." she placed the papers in a clipboard and pushed it toward Priscilla. "Stop being sorry and be responsible. Chile', don't nobody owe you a damn thing, so don't expect anything, and you won't be disappointed. Now, I don't know your situation or the things you been through in life, but let me tell you this..." she looked directly at Priscilla. "You can't help *nobody* if you don't help *yourself* first... and that's the truth. It took me a long time to figure that one out."

Priscilla listened closely to every word that was said. She watched the woman's body language and it was like this woman knew exactly how she was feeling, like she understood what she had been through, like she walked in these same shoes some time ago. She stepped closer to the desk, grabbed the pen and started to fill out the questionnaire. Her emotions were chaotic and the pressures of life felt like a ton of cement bricks on her shoulders. No longer able to hold it, she broke down and a teardrop slowly descended her cheek. It splashed the paper she was writing on. "God, please help me..." she whispered.

The woman came from behind the desk and grabbed Priscilla's hands to console her. Her palms were warm, moist and shaky from anxiety. "Listen, baby, we're gonna help you. I don't want you to think I was trying to come down on you or belittle you in any type of way. I just have to give it to you the same way someone else who stood behind that desk gave it to me..."

Priscilla lifted her head. "You—?"

"Yup, *me*... I was just like *you*. It was ten years ago when I came strolling through that door." She nodded toward the entrance. "Young, disrespectful with a heart full of hate and a heavy addiction to heroin. I was bad... and now, I'm sitting here looking at you and I know you're a good person. I can see it. You have a good heart; all you need is some guidance. If you're willing to put forth the effort, we will assist you in reaching your goals." She let go of Priscilla's hands and walked back behind the desk. "It's all up to you."

22

The black Town Car barreled down the block and then skidded to a stop on Webster Avenue and Krest. Cleo knew who the driver of the vehicle was, but after what just happened, he was nervous and extremely cautious.

"What the fuck took you so long, Chris?" He jumped into the backseat and pulled the door closed.

"There was traffic, Cleo." Chris put the car in reverse and made an illegal U turn. "I got here as fast as I could."

Cleo stretched across the backseat and tried to regain control of his breathing. The humidity had him drenched in sweat and red splatters of blood looked like ink blots on his t-shirt.

"You alright back there?" Chris asked. He kept glancing in the rear-view mirror.

Cleo grimaced. "Yeah, why?"

"I mean... you are back there breathing hard and sweating profusely... and you do have some blood on your shirt."

"Oh, you mister funny man today, huh?"

"Naw... not like that, Cleo. I'm jus' sayin'."

"What the fuck you sayin'?" He sat up in the seat, but Chris kept silent. "That's what the fuck I thought. No, I'm not alright." Cleo wasn't playing at all today.

"Is there anything I can do for you?"

"Yeah, Chris... shut the fuck up and drive. Take me to Vito's."

Twenty minutes later, the sleek Town Car pulled to the sidewalk in front of the Bar & Grill, but before Cleo exited, he checked his weapon. He gripped the handle firmly and then looked down at the blood on his hands.

It was Mox's blood.

Cleo heard a voice in his head, *why?* But he pushed it from his thoughts and stepped out into the warm, moist, summer air.

He was agitated and confused at first, but when he thought about the situation rationally, he came to the conclusion that there was only one person that could've leaked that missing surveillance tape. For a short minute, he even considered storming into Vito's and opening fire on whoever was within distance, but what good would that do? So, on the ride over, he presumed that Vinny Telesco was the only one that could get him away from the trouble that was shadowing him, and he needed to see him, face to face.

As he stepped closer to the entrance, Cleo's mind was so clouded he wasn't aware of his surroundings and missed the county police car that was parked two spaces up. He pushed the door open to Vito's and walked in. The music played at a low volume and the atmosphere was sedate. Three patrons sat casually on stools along the front of the bar, watching an old war movie while Tony, the bartender, fixed another round. He turned when he heard the bells on the door jingle.

"Aye, Tony, wassup?" Cleo waved, but didn't break his stride. He continued straight to the back.

Tony tried to stop him. "Hey, you can't go back there!" But his words fell on deaf ears.

Cleo walked past the tables, nodding at the few customers who were eating and advanced to the back of the restaurant. He came to a stop when he spotted a small crowd of people sitting at a large table and three dark suited henchmen standing off to the left; two dark haired and one dirty blonde. But his focus solely lied upon Vinny Telesco's pale, wrinkled face. Their eyes locked and Vinny made a gesture to his goons, who quickly stepped to where Cleo stood. "Pat 'em down." he said, rising from his seat.

One of the dark haired henchmen felt Cleo's waist and removed the pistol he had tucked. "Why'd you leak the tape, Vinny?"

"Fuck you and that tape, Cleo." The few guests who sat at the table started to get up and leave. "Everybody, sit down. This won't take long."

After Cleo killed Casey in the hotel, he knew the only way the police could identify him was the surveillance tape, so he reached out to the mob boss because of his strong ties to the city, and magically the tape came up missing. Cleo then swore to an agreement with Vinny that the tape would be destroyed in exchange for a million dollars, but Cleo couldn't come up with the money. A second chance was given when Vinny ordered him to kill Mox, but again, Cleo didn't produce and The Old Man felt like his hand had been forced.

"All the work I put in for you, and this how you treat me? We had an agreement about that tape. You broke your promise, Vinny."

"No, you didn't produce; besides... promises are made to be broken." He raised his eyebrows at his men and they snatched Cleo from both sides.

There was no fighting it, he was outnumbered. The mob boss got within an inch of his face. "You know, Cleo... you got some fuckin' nerve coming here." his voice was dry, and hoarse. "First of all, you're interrupting my fuckin' wine and cheese party." Two of the guest smirked, but this was far from a laughing matter. "I trusted you with my family and what did I get!" his voice went as loud as he could get it. "Huh, what did *I* get, Cleo? You know what *I* got... a dead fuckin' son, that's what." Vinny looked to his left. "Mikey, teach this fuckin' guy a lesson."

Cleo looked to the right and Mikey scowled at him. "What's up, Cleo?" He sounded clogged and stuffy because he had gauze wrapped around his face to protect his nose from when Mox hit him with the gun.

Sensing the situation was about to take a turn for the worse, Cleo tried to reason. "Vinny, wait... I did it... I killed, Mox."

The Old Man smiled, fixed his suit jacket and then returned to his seat. "So, you come here for what; a trophy or somethin'?" a dry giggle escaped his mouth, but the flame in his eyes told another story.

"It's too late, Cleo." He sat back, crossed his right leg over his left and waited.

The sound that the ten inch folding knife made when Mikey flipped it open caused Cleo to twist his neck in an attempt to see what it was. The glare from the track lighting that hung fifteen feet in the air hit the stainless steel blade and made it glimmer. Cleo's eyes grew wide. Mikey gripped the wood handle with revenge being the only thought on his mind. It was weighing on him so heavy, that recently, he became depressed and eagerly violent, which was unlike him. He painfully wanted to avenge his brother's death and the only thing preventing a homicide this evening would be the county police officer who was standing by the entrance, waiting on an order of pasta.

"You scarred my family for life when you killed my little brother." He said, taking a few steps closer to Cleo. "And since I can't kill you right now... I'm gonna leave you wit' a scar to remember me by until I catch you again."

Cleo kept his focus on the knife. "I ain't have nothin' to do wit' your brother's murder."

Mikey ignored his words and placed the razor-sharped blade to the side of Cleo's face. "Every time you take a look in a mirror, you'll be reminded of why you shouldn't fuck wit' the Telesco's."

He slowly dragged the blade south, from his forehead to the bottom of his chin, and as soon as he lifted his hand, Cleo's face opened up like a baked potato split down the middle with butter and sour cream topping.

The high pitched howl he let out was ear wrenching.

He tried to break away, but as big as he was, Cleo couldn't fight his way out the grasps of Vinny's henchmen.

A stream of blood raced down his chest and his tongue could be seen through the side of his cheek.

The police officer heard the shriek, looked up, and started to walk to the back, but Vinny waved his hand assuring him that everything was okay. He had an idea of what was going on, but he and the Telesco's were like family. Even though he was aware of their business, he did his best to turn a blind eye to it.

"You've been nothin' but problems lately, Cleo." Vinny got up.

"Gimme that." he grabbed the knife from Mikey. "I know you heard that old saying, 'never bite the hand that feeds you'... well, you bit me once and I sure won't give you the chance to do it again."

The dirty blonde haired henchman gripped Cleo's wrist and slammed his hand down on the table.

Vinny clutched the knife between his fingers, lifted it and slammed the sharp-edged blade into the back of Cleo's right hand. The pain shot through his arm and he felt the discomfort through his entire body, but he didn't make a sound. He just gazed into Vinny's passionless eyes, searching for a speck of endearment, but nothing was there. The only thing positive about this situation was that Cleo knew Vinny wouldn't have him killed right now. It was too many witnesses.

The Old Man yanked the knife out of his hand and wiped the blood onto Cleo's shirt, "Get this piece-a-shit outta my face."

Two of the henchmen pulled Cleo by his arms and pushed him out the front door. Stumbling to his feet, he barely made it back to the Town Car before he mumbled. "Drive, Chris." He pulled the door shut with his good hand and his wounded hand was wrapped in his t-shirt, but the bleeding was getting heavier.

Chris wasted no time. He started the car, threw it in drive and peeled away from the scene. When he checked the rear-view mirror, he saw the blood on Cleo's shirt. It was definitely more than what had been there before. "Oh shit! What the hell?... we gotta get you to a hospital... Cleo, you alright?"

"No hospitals, Chris... jus' drive." He looked down at the dime sized hole in his hand and could almost see right through it.

"Here, take these." Chris tossed the two hand towels he kept in the glove compartment into the backseat with Cleo. "Use them to slow up the blood flow. Just wrap it around your hand and squeeze it."

Cleo wanted to smile, but just the thought of it made his face hurt. "You a fuckin' doctor now, Chris?"

"Naw, but I saw someone do it on that television show, *Survivor*. It works, trust me."

"Trust will get you killed, Chris."

The Town Car veered to the right and went down the ramp and onto the highway.

"Okay, listen. I know somebody who could help you. You know, fix you up. No hospitals. No police; none of that."

"Get me there... and Chris," Cleo paused and looked at his reflection in the partition as small droplets of blood continued to fall from his chin. "If it ain't what you say it is... I'ma kill you."

23

"**Y**es, daddy! Oooh! Have it baby... this pussy is yours, Franky!" Toya arched her back and rotated her 46 inch, lemon colored hips while Frank plugged her from behind. "Beat this pussy up, daddy... ohhhhh!"

The distinctly, alluring 26 year old Latoya Reid was a 6 foot, 165 pound red-bone with straight, long black hair that hung to the middle of her back. She has, cat-like eyes, a bunch of freckles spread across the top of her rosy cheeks and an ass that belongs in *Straight Stuntin'* Magazine. Her sunny colored complexion makes her look like she's of foreign descent, but the reality is, she's just an old country girl from the deep southern woods of South Carolina who migrated to New York in pursuit of a dream. She and Frank met on the set of a video she had been hired to perform in, and ever since that day, he's been knocking it down.

"Who pussy is this?" Frank thrust his pelvis back and forth, sliding his 9 ½ inches as far into Toya's vagina as possible. "This *my* pussy!"

"Yes! Go deep, daddy... ohhhhh, yeah... take this pussy! Take this puussssyyyy!" Toya's walls were contracting and the sensational pleasures she felt were quite uncommon for her. She came back to back to back, releasing her cream frosting all over Frank's dick.

A sheer coat of sweat covered his body as he physically punished

Toya's love box. His hands were placed at the small of her back, in a diamond position, so he could control all movement. He looked down at her soft, pretty ass, sliding on his glistening dick and smiled. Beads of perspiration slipped from his forehead and onto her ass cheeks as he worked her middle. *All those late nights in the gym were paying off.* His stamina was at its highest level and his performance was at its peak. He stood on his tip-toes and submerged himself in the pussy.

"Ohhhhhh!" Toya moaned. "That shit is deeeeppp, daddy!"

Frank grabbed her waistline and in a sequential cadence he rammed his power rod between her vaginal lips. "Say my name, girl! Tell me who run this muthafucka!"

Toya could barely catch her breath to speak. "Fraaa—"

"Say my name, girl!"

"Fraaann—" She couldn't get it out.

Her shriek of pure joy grew louder and all you could hear was skin slapping, heavy panting, and the headboard of Frank's three thousand dollar queen sized bed banging against the wall.

"Say it, girl!"

"Frrraaannnkyyy, baaaabbbyyyy!"

Frank backed up, rolled the condom off his dick and splashed a load of cum all over Toya's ass. "Ahhhhhh!" he spanked her cheeks until he released the last drop and then he fell onto the bed next to her. His phone rang, but he noticed it was on the opposite side of the bed and out of reach. "Answer that for me." he said.

Toya looked at him, rolled her eyes and picked the phone up from the nightstand. "Hello?"

The caller replied. "Lemme speak to Frank."

"Who dis?"

"Bitch, put Frank on the phone."

Toya sucked her teeth. "Here, nigga." She dropped the phone on Frank's chest and he pressed the speaker button.

"Hello?"

"You lettin' bitches answer your phone now?"

Toya's lip turned up. "Bitches?"

"Yeah, you heard me, video hoe."

"Fuck you, nigga!"

Frank grabbed the phone, took it off speaker and looked at Toya. "Yo, chill."

"Fuck that... you jus' gon' sit there and let that nigga call me all types a' bitches... fuck you too!" She got up and walked out the room.

Frank sat up in the bed. "Nate, what up?"

"I need to see you."

"Why, wassup?"

"Shit got crazy... somebody hit Mox."

"What?"

"Word... said he got hit in the head. It's ugly right now."

Frank's lip dropped and the phone fell from his grasp, hitting the carpet. The only people he could think of that were capable of something like this were the Italians.

His head slumped and he stared down at the phone. He could hear Nate calling for him, but his mind was someplace else. Mox was like a brother to Frank and the rest of the team, and if it meant going to war with the Italians, then bodies were about to drop because regardless of stature, creed or street ranking; nobody touched a Union affiliate and got away with it. Nobody. Frustration, anger and pure ignorance clouded his thoughts as he reached for the phone. "Somebody gotta bleed, Nate. They touch one of ours, we touch two of theirs. You know how this shit go."

Nate felt the exact same way, but the question was, who was getting touched? "Yeah, I feel you, but who?"

"Those fuckin' Italians, who else..." Frank answered.

"Nah, Frank... this shit happened in the hood. I know the Italians got balls, but them shits ain't that big, and them muthafuckas ain't just gunnin' niggas down in the hood like that."

Frank took a minute to think about what Nate was saying. "Okay..." he nodded his head in agreement. "You might be right about that." he tried to think about other instances where they may have had an altercation with someone a while back, but nothing came to mind. "You spoke to Cleo?"

"Not at all, but what you wanna do about *this?* I'm on my way to New Rochelle right now."

Frank wiped his face in confusion, because, for a second he

thought he was dreaming. But when Toya stepped back into the room, he knew shit was real. She was still upset about Nate calling her out her name. "I can't believe you sat there and let that nigga call me a bitch."

If she was paying attention, she would have clearly seen the discomforting look of annoyance plastered on Frank's grill. "Leave it alone, Toya." he warned.

"*Leave it alone?*" Her eyebrows rose. "What the fuck you mean, *leave it alone?* This nigg—"

Frank jumped from the bed and cut her off in mid-sentence. "I said let it go, Toya!" his face was flush with tears.

She was shocked. Her mouth hung open and her eyes were stuck to Frank's face. "I... I..." she didn't know what to say, but Frank let it be known.

"Mox got shot." The words didn't even feel right coming off his tongue.

"What? Oh no... I'm sorry, baby." Toya heard the convulsion in Frank's voice and felt sympathy and deep sorrow for him, Mox and the entire Daniels family. She liked Mox and had actually been given the chance to meet him one night in Frank's club, a couple weeks back. At first impression, she was awed at how someone of his eminence could present himself in such a reposeful and unruffled fashion.

According to the stories she'd been hearing, this guy Mox was being portrayed as some type of brash, gun toting, drug dealer, killing machine, but from her observation she saw he was just a young, street dude with a good head on his shoulders. Combined with the discipline to abide by a set of principles and the determination to get what he wanted, Mox's leadership qualities were easily recognized by strangers.

Frank picked his pants up and started to put them on. "I gotta go."

"Wait..." Toya grabbed his hand. He was shaking. "Baby, where you going?"

Frank pulled away, ignored her question and went to the closet to get his gun.

"Frank, please don't leave." She begged, watching him check the clip.

He placed the gun in his waistband and threw on a three-button, short sleeve Polo shirt. "That's my brother, Toya. What you expect me to do?" he snatched his car keys off the table and stormed out the house. There was nothing more she could say or do; Frank had his mind made up.

Toya watched from the second floor window as he got into his car and drove away. She cried and prayed that everything would be okay, but deep within her gut she knew that was a far distance from the truth.

Tupac's expressive, true-to-life lyrics trumpeted through the *Bose* stereo system as Frank clutched the wheel with one hand and held a blunt in the other. He let the thick ghost like smoke flow through his nostrils while he kept his eyes glued to the road. Pac's vocals were mesmeric. *My Ambitionz Az A Ridah...* The sleek, black 500 Benz hugged the road as Frank pushed the machine to speeds close to one hundred miles an hour. By the time the blunt was done, he was cruising down Horton Avenue, pulling up to the projects.

It was 7:15 pm and the sun was just beginning to set. The dull, red and yellowish rays produced an orange glow that hovered over the projects and the lingering smell of death was afloat throughout the air.

Whether it was a shooting, stabbing, fist fight or just a heated argument, whenever there was an incident in the hood, everybody came outside to be nosy and this night was no different.

The past three days had produced two shootings; one, a murder and the other had yet to be told. Who would have thought that the summer was just beginning to blossom?

Frank stepped from the vehicle and made his way down the strip towards the buildings. When he passed the park area, he was approached by a young kid on a pedal bike.

"Yo, whats good?" The kid said.

Frank slowed his stride to get a good look at the kid. "You know me?" he replied.

He knew something was up with him because it was eighty degrees outside and this kid had on shorts and a black hoodie.

The kid on the bike sped up and cut Frank off before he could get any further down the strip. He jumped off the Mongoose and Frank went to reach for his weapon.

"Yo, chill homie... it aint like that." The kid extended his hand. "Tyrell Michaels. I'm Dana's lil' cousin." he pulled his hand back when he saw Frank wasn't budging. "You Mox peoples, right?"

"Yeah, why?"

"Your man Nate jus' went upstairs. C'mon, I'll show you where it's at."

Frank had met Dana before, but had never been to her house. The kid didn't sound like he was trying to pull a stunt so he followed him into the building.

When they got to the door, Tyrell knocked twice and someone shouted from the inside. "Who is it?"

"It's me, cousin."

When door came open, they walked into the apartment and Frank immediately noticed that Dana had been crying. Her make-up was smeared all over her face from wiping away tears.

The strong stench of cigarette smoke lingered in the atmosphere and clouded the room.

Frank saw Nate sitting on the sofa smoking a Newport and shook his head. "I thought you quit?" He asked?

Nate took a long drag and exhaled the smoke. "I did, but this fuckin' stress is killin' me Frank."

"Jus' be cool. We gon' handle this accordingly. First I need to know what happened... Did anybody speak to Cleo?"

Dana and Tyrell looked at each other and at the same time said, "*Cleo?*"

"You don't watch the news do you?" Tyrell grabbed the remote and hit the power button.

The breaking news story had been playing all day and as soon as they showed Casey's face on the screen, Dana broke down and ran to the back room.

Nate stood up off the sofa and he and Frank stared at the television. The staggering looks on their faces told stories of their own and neither of them wanted to believe that what they were seeing was real, but the harsh realities of life aren't always the most pleasant, especially when you're dealing with these cold and bitter streets.

"Are you fuckin' serious!?" Frank was livid.

Nate pulled another cigarette from his pack and lit it. "I knew that mutha-fucka was a snake." he puffed the stogie and let the toxins enter his lungs.

"Yo, listen." Tyrell turned the television off and took a seat on the folding chair. "It's on fire out here right now, fam. My lil' man jus' got booked for a body yesterday and this shit wit' Mox this morning jus' added more fuel to the flame. Niggas said Cleo hit Mox too."

For a few seconds silence filled the room.

"This shit went all the way to the left, Frank." Nate was pacing now.

"What hospital they got my boy in?" Frank questioned.

His stomach was in knots and tears were building in the well of his eyes, but he knew this wasn't the place or time to show emotion.

"He up the block at *Sound Shore* right now." Tyrell answered. "Yo," He sat on the sofa and whispered. "I know the spot Cleo be at. That nigga go there at least once a week to trick off... I can handle that for you."

"Handle what?" Nate didn't like outsiders intervening in family business.

Tyrell felt the vibe and tried to ease the tension. "Mox was like family to me too... even though we had our differences, I know everything he was telling me was to help me. He wanted me to stay in the books and stay off the block, but I a'int listen. Anyway... this is the shit I'm here for." he reached under the sofa and pulled out his taped up .38 revolver. "Mox looked out and bailed me, my cousin and my homeboy out of jail a few days ago. I got love for that dude, so if some work gotta be put in..." he paused and looked at their faces. "All I'm saying is; I'm that nigga to get the job done."

Frank realized Tyrell was the one who got Dana's house raided and Brandi taken away, he probably felt like he owed Mox.

Nate wasn't feeling it. "All you young niggas want is a name for yourself. We don't need no other niggas handlin' our busi—"

Frank jumped in. "hol' up Nate..." he eyed Tyrell. "lil' nigga say he ready to put in work, let's see what he about."

Nate looked Tyrell up and down. He of all people knew that shooters came in all shapes and sizes and the only way to find out if his word was authentic was to give him a chance. He wasn't one hundred percent sure if giving Tyrell the green light was the right decision, but in his book everybody deserved a shot.

"Fuck it... you only get one chance to make a first impression, kid. I hope you make it a good one."

They went to leave out and Frank stopped at the door. He glanced down at the old, rusted .38 Tyrell had in his hand.

"You gon' need something better than that to put in work." He grabbed the silver Baretta .380 semi-automatic off his waistline and tossed it on the couch.

Tyrell placed the old .38 on the coffee table and picked up the .380. He gripped the wood grain handle tightly. "This is that Canadian joint, right here?"

Frank and Nate wore surprised looks.

"You know your weapons, huh?" Nate reached around his waist, lifted his shirt and grabbed the pistol from the small of his back. He tossed it on the couch next to Tyrell.

He palmed the lightweight, chrome and black handgun. "Ooh, this is that new G2 right here... and it's a forty." Tyrell studied the gun. "It got the good thumb rest, a new trigger safety," he held the weapon with two hands, extended his arm and aimed at an invisible target. "This is that shit the police be using." he pressed a button on the handle and the clip fell from the bottom. "I know my ratchets" he cocked the barrel, put his nose to it and sniffed. "Brand new." he said, placing it on the table.

Nate smiled for the first time. "Impressive, kid. Keep it."

The door slammed and Frank and Nate were gone, leaving Tyrell on his cousin's couch with three guns and the green light to put a hole in Cleo's head.

He sat back, spread his arms across the back of the sofa and the corners of his mouth almost touched his ears.

Less than 72 hours ago, Tyrell was broke, homeless and unaware of where his next meal was coming from, but now he was sitting on a couple thousand stacks, two brand new guns and a chance to earn the trust of Mox's comrades.

Who says crime don't pay?

24

Wise Earl jumped from the seat he was sitting in and approached Doctor Callahan as he exited the operating room. "Doctor, please tell us you got some good news?"

The doctor removed the mask from his face, peeled off his gloves, and took a seat between Earl and Sybil. "I would be lying if I told you everything was going to be okay. Your nephew has suffered a severe gunshot wound to head." he stood up, pulled an x-ray from his clipboard and held it to the light so Sybil and Earl could see. "This, right here, is an x-ray of your nephew's skull. As you can see," he pointed to a small hole. "Right here, is where the bullet entered."

Earl stepped closer to get a better view. "So, where did it come out?" he questioned.

"That's the problem." Doctor Callahan removed his glasses and tried to explain. "See, the bullet traveled along the mid-line of his brain and now it's lodged back here," he pointed. "in the base of his skull."

"So, what that mean?" Earl was getting agitated. "You still a'int tellin' us nothing."

Doctor Callahan put his glasses back on. "Mr. Daniels, if we go in and try to remove that bullet from Mox's skull, there's more than a fifty percent chance he could die under the knife."

"Oh my God!" Tears fell from Sybil's eyes as she slumped to the floor. She didn't want to believe she was the cause of this turmoil, but the truth was an uncomfortable actuality, and in time, all untruth hiding in darkness will be illuminated and unmasked.

Earl picked Sybil up, wrapped his arms around her, and did what he could to tranquilize her discomfort. He was sensitive and sympathetic to her misery because he knew exactly how it felt to be the cause of something tragic; there were demons in his closet too. "Is there *any* good news, Doc?" Earl asked.

"The good news is, Mox's heart is still beating. The bad news... his brain is severely damaged."

"A *coma?*"

"Yes," Doctor Callahan lifted the x-ray again to show Earl. "When the bullet entered the skull, it damaged these areas right here." He pointed. "Damage to these parts of the brain can sometimes result in amnesia or dementia."

"So, you tellin' me when he wake up he a'int gon' remember what happened?"

"If and when he wakes up... memory loss is a possibility. I'm sorry Mr. and Ms. Daniels, but that's all the information I can give you at the moment. We'll continue to do everything we can to keep Mox alive. You got my word on that." he turned to leave.

"Doc, hol' up." Earl caught up to him before he got too far down the hall. "How long you think he gon' be in this, *coma?*"

Doctor Callahan shook his head. "I don't know, Mr. Daniels... could be one day, could be one year. It's all up to Mox. If he fights, I'm sure he can make it."

Earl watched as the doctor turned on his heels and continued down the corridor. He made his way back to Sybil sat in the waiting area. "Excuse me, nurse," he called to a young lady who had just left out of the room they moved Mox into. "Is it possible we can see my nephew now?"

The young nurse looked down at her watch. "Sure, you've got twenty minutes until visiting hours are up, but before you go in, let me tell you; he's not responsive and it looks a lot worse than it is."

Earl ignored her warning and went to get Sybil to come with him into Mox's room. "Sis, c'mon, they said we got twenty minutes."

She sat still for a second and then got up and they walked toward the room, holding hands, but before they could get inside, Sybil panicked. "I can't do this!" she snatched away from Earl, ran back to her seat, buried her face in her lap, and cried.

Earl was fifteen feet away from the room, but it felt like he was taking a thousand steps to get there. His heartbeat sped up and he kept swallowing saliva. The closer he got to the door, the more real it seemed.

He turned the knob and slowly pushed the door open. The medium sized room was painted sky blue and there were two beds, but one was empty. A quick glance around and Earl's his eyes fell on the heart monitor next to the occupied bed.

Beep... Beep... Beep...

The frigid temperature and the eerie sounds coming from the machines gave Earl the chills. Next to the heart monitor was an oxygen machine, an IV and a breathing module.

"Damn, baby boy..." Earl could barely look at Mox. He was lying on his back, his head was wrapped in gauze and his arms were straight at his side. Earl took a few steps closer and the repulsive sight of Mox's swelled face numbed his nerves and churned his insides. He gagged and a warm sensation rose in his chest, causing him to grab at his stomach and reach for the trash can. He wanted to vomit, but nothing came up. He wiped the saliva that hung from his lip and tried to bear the emotional scene. The beeping of the heart monitor sounded like it was getting louder by the seconds.

Beep... Beep... Beep...

"Damn, nephew..." Earl managed to get to the chair that was beside Mox's bed. He sat down and stared at the tubes that were in his nose and mouth and a tear slid down the side of his face. "C'mon, baby boy, you gotta wake up." he whispered. "We need you out here, Mox. Your family needs you. You gotta fight, nephew." the tears started to fall with ease. "Mox, I'm sorry..." Earl cried his heart out and begged God to help Mox recover. He felt another presence in the room and thought it was his sister. When he turned to look, it was Frank and Nate, standing in the doorway.

Frank was waiting for Mox to jump up from the bed, smiling,

and tell everyone this whole thing was a joke, but that didn't happen. He tried to move, but his legs were frozen.

"You gotta take care of this, Frank." Earl sobbed.

Frank's eyes were watery from seeing Mox lying in that hospital bed, but when he saw Earl crying like a child, it only intensified his aggravation. He brushed the dampness from his eyes and looked at Earl. "Let no one stand before we." He mumbled and then he and Nate exited.

PRISCILLA'S first overnight stay in the shelter felt like the longest day of her life. For weeks, she sat in the inpatient program, dreaming of the day she would be able to hold her daughter again, only to come home and hear she's gone. Sitting on her cot, with her arms wrapped around her knees, pressed against her chest, she closed her eyes and thought back on the day's events. A whirlwind of emotions spun inside of her and the attempt to suppress the pain was useless. She could no longer hide how she was feeling. The tears came down like a waterfall. Priscilla opened her eyes and looked around the large room. The nasty colored green walls made her insides quiver and the fetid stench of old, dirty clothes clogged the air.

Damn, I gotta pee

She stepped off the cot and walked down the dark isle of the dorm to the restroom, and in passing, she counted the cots aligned alongside the walls. It was twelve on each side, but two were empty. When she pushed the door open, a cloud of smoke smacked her in the face and made her lip turn. She heard movement, and one of the stall doors flew open. A tall, slim, brown skinned female with bulging eyes and ashy lips came stumbling out.

"Oh," She sucked her teeth. "it's jus' the new girl. We cool... right?" she inquired.

Priscilla stared at the scraggily woman. She was high, disheveled and very edgy. "I don't care what y'all do in here. I jus' came to use the bathroom."

Another woman stepped out the stall. "She bedda mind her

muthafuckin' business." She stopped in front of Priscilla. "Bitch, you fuckin' up my nut."

Priscilla acted like she didn't know what was going on. "Huh? I jus' came to pee." She tried to get around the woman and go into the stall, but she was much bigger than Priscilla. "Excuse me."

"You a pretty bitch, a'int you." She went to touch the side of her face, but Priscilla moved. "You sure you don't want me to come in there wit' you?"

Priscilla wasn't surprised at the advance. She thought it would've come a little later than sooner, but she was anticipating it. Her girl-friend, Jennifer, had already schooled her to the occurrences that would take place in these shelters. She mentally prepared Priscilla for what she was about to encounter, because living in these shelters was similar to living in prison. The major difference was; staying at the shelter was a personal choice. You didn't have to be there if you didn't want to.

She ignored the heavy set woman's words and nudged her way past the two females and into the stall.

The crummy bathroom was typical of a government facility. It reeked of sour urine and feces, and the toilet seat was stained with dry blood.

Nasty bitches.

When she exited the stall, the slim, brown skinned chick was leaning against the sink, puffing on a cigarette. "What's yo' name?" She blew smoke out and tapped the ash in the sink.

"Priscilla."

"Umm hmm... well, my name is Kim, and that bitch there," she said pointing to the door. "That was Mother Nature... she run this shit. If I was you, I wouldn't get on her bad side; she known to have a not so very good temper." Kim offered the remains of her cigarette to Priscilla.

"No thank you. I don't smoke." She finished washing her hands and went to grab a paper towel from the dispenser, but Kim blocked her.

"Bitch, you actin' like you too good to smoke wit' me?"

Priscilla snapped, snatched a handful of Kim's hair and pressed the side of her face against the cold, filthy tile on the wall. She leaned in close enough to smell her stale breath. "If you even think of fixing your lips to call me a bitch again... I swear to God that will be the last thing you ever say."

Kim wasn't aggressive at all, so she never attempted to fight back, but as soon as Priscilla loosened her grip, a straight edge razor grazed the bottom of her chin.

She jumped back, grabbed at her face and Kim swung the flat, rectangular blade again leaving a two inch gash across Priscilla's arm. She stood there, smiling, holding the razor. "Bitch!"

Priscilla caught a glimpse of her face in the mirror and then looked at the blood dripping down her hand and thought twice about her next move. "This shit a'int over, bitch." She whispered, snatched some paper towels, wrapped her bloody arm up and went back to her cot. Her first day of re-entry into the world had proved to be by far one of the worst days of her life, and yet, she still had so much to go through in order to fulfill her plan. She tried not sleeping, but the weight of her lids felt like a bag of bricks and the next time she opened her eyes it was fourteen hours later.

Priscilla looked up and noticed she was no longer in a dorm, this was somebody's room. The walls were painted a yellowish/orange color, which made the sun's rays more glaring, and despite the warm temperatures, a cool breeze flowed through the huge bay window that overlooked the yard. Priscilla lay, staring at the old ceiling fan, watching the wooden blades go round and round.

"You finally woke up, huh?" The woman's voice sounded familiar, but Priscilla couldn't see clearly. She lifted her head, squinted and tried to make out who this person was coming through the door. "You done got yourself mixed up in something already." She said, shaking her head.

When she finally came closer, Priscilla recognized the woman from the front desk of the shelter. "Where am I?"

"You're still here at the shelter, but you're in my room." The woman placed two aspirins and a glass of water on the table next to the bed. "I found you passed out this morning when I made my round through the dormitory... must'a lost too much blood. Poor baby, you were almost dead. Good thing the nurse got here on time this morning. I don't know what I would've done without her help."

Priscilla coughed and her head felt like it was about to explode. "Owww... my head is pounding." She looked at her hand and instead of the paper towels she used; it was now wrapped in a real bandage made of gauze. "How bad is it?"

"Not too bad... here, take these and lay back down." She handed Priscilla the aspirins and the water. "That scar on your face there, may be a lifetime memory."

Priscilla forgot about getting cut on her face. She couldn't feel a thing. "My face?" she panicked and reached for her cheek.

"No, don't touch it." The woman grabbed her arm. "You'll just make it bleed again. Nurse Betty had to stitch you up real good. You got seven on your face and five more on that arm. You wanna talk about it?"

Priscilla shook her head no, and lay back in the warm bed. She shut her eyes and a vision of Brandi made her spring right back up. "My baby!" she pushed the covers off and attempted make an exit, but the loss of blood debilitated her completely. She was too weak to hold her body weight and collapsed to the floor.

"Girl, you gon' kill yourself. Now stop being so hardheaded and let me help you." The woman assisted in getting Priscilla back into the bed. "Now, ain't nobody said you got to stay here, if you wanna leave, you know exactly where that door is, but think about it first."

"I need to get my daughter back, please..." Priscilla complained.

"Okay, listen... there are rules that everyone abides by in here. First off, let me start by saying, everyone here calls me Ms. Kathy. Like I told you before, I was once in the same exact spot you're in now." Kathy took a seat on the bed next to Priscilla. "Anyway... the rules as stated are; curfew begins today. That means you're in this house by seven-thirty pm every night for the next thirty days. No exceptions. Next, no outside company at all; third, for the first ten days you are on a probation period, which means you do not leave the house unless you are told to; fourth, you will participate in household chores. Every morning you will be assigned a task for the day. Failure to complete that task will result in disciplinary actions, and last but not least, absolutely *no* drug use whatsoever. Are we clear, Ms. Davis?"

"Ten days?" Priscilla couldn't get past not leaving the house.

"Yes, ten days. Do you have a problem with that?"

"Yes, I do because I need to find my daughter." She felt the puddle about to overflow from her eyelids.

"Where is she?"

A river of tears rushed down Priscilla's face. "I... I don't know..." she sobbed, uncontrollably.

Kathy rubbed Priscilla's shoulder. "Well, I wanna help you, so tell me everything that happened..."

25

The array of dazzling colors and explosions lit the warm ebony sky on the evening of July 4th, while the smell of gun powder lurked loosely in the air for a few miles. School kids raced up and down the strip, lighting fireworks; each time, almost blowing their little fingers to oblivion. It was the day of independence; our independence, and it was a day when families put aside differences and came together to share laughs, food and fond memories. Generations of cousins, uncles, aunts, nieces and nephews, all who share the same bloodline, united on this day in celebration.

In the park, directly across from building #60, Tyrell sat atop a bench in a tank top, blue, Nautica beach shorts and a pair of white, Air Force Ones. He was fresh and he was in power. He split the cigar down the middle, dumped the guts into the grass, sprinkled in the green buds and rolled it. When he reached for his lighter, it wasn't in his pocket, so he went to ask one of the kids who were lighting fireworks, but from the corner of his eye he could see someone coming up the walkway.

"What's good, O.G? Lemme get some fire from you?" When the dark figure stepped closer to the light, Tyrell immediately recognized who it was. "Oh shit, Uncle Wise, wassup wit' you?"

"Ain't nothin' good, yougin'" Earl went into his pocket and

handed Tyrell a lighter. "Jus' left that damn hospital..." He said, shaking his head.

Tyrell lit the blunt and took a long drag. "Oh, word... how that go?"

"It's sad, man... shit is real sad." Earl took a seat on the bench next to Tyrell. "Just the fact that I got to sit there and see my nephew suffer so much and ain't shit I could do about it." He pulled a cigarette from his pack and lit it. "I mean... I ain't never saw Mox in a position where he was down... never. Ever since he came up, he stayed at the top. He's a winner, man, and to see him all bandaged up like that and his face all fucked up... that's some crazy shit. Feel me? He ain't responsive, he ain't giving nobody no signs... I don't know, man... I'm praying for the best, but prepared for the worse. Ya dig?"

In between smoking and listening to Earl, Tyrell was serving his customers. "Hol' up, Unc." He turned to the female that waited by the gate. "How many you want?"

The shoddy female with a scarf tied around her head flashed ten fingers and approached the bench. "I'ma dollar short... I got forty-nine." She passed him two crumpled twenty dollar bills and nine singles.

Tyrell looked to see if it was clear, reached into his pocket and pulled out a zip-lock baggie full of crack. He counted out ten pieces and handed them to the female. "I want my dollar when you come back."

"You know I spends money, nephew... I got you." She said, skipping away.

Tyrell faced Earl. "Mox is a strong dude. I know he gon' pull through." He stuffed the money in his pocket.

"Yeah, I hope so." Earl replied. "You getting' money out here, huh?"

Tyrell blew the smoke through his nostrils. "Yeah, you see me. I got this shit in the chokehold." He pulled the baggie from his pocket. "Look at these shits... these is nickels, them niggas over there selling dimes and they shit ain't half the size of these." He dumped a few in Earl's hand.

After he took a drag of his Newport, Earl smiled, because he knew quality work just by looking at it, and what Tyrell had was top of the line cook-up. "How you able to do this?"

"I got a sweet connect."

Earl studied the small, white rocks. "You cookin' it yourself?"

"Yup... they call me 'Chef Boy R'..." he laughed. "Why you wanna know anyway, Unc... you don't fuck with this shit."

"Sure don't." Earl gave the rocks back. "But I'll tell you this... you sittin' out here on this bench wit' a pocket full a' stones and a stack a' cash, smoking weed and slangin' like it's legal... fuck is wrong wit' you?"

Tyrell lit his blunt after it went out. "I'm hungry, Unc... gotta get this bread, but shit aint pumpin' like I thought it would."

"You *hungry?*" Earl stood up. "When hungry niggas see food they eat. You can't tell me you don't see this goddamn plate in front of yo' face... you hungry ain't you, nigga?" Tyrell nodded his head. "Well... eat."

"I'm out here. You see me eatin' it." He inhaled the smoke.

Earl shook his head. "Nah, yougin'... you jus' nibbling off the plate right now. It's *real* money out here and you playin' games."

"Shiitt..." Tyrell stood up. "You mus' got me confused, old man," he raised his tank top and exposed his two guns. "We don't play games over here."

Earl smiled and then laughed. "Nigga, you got guns too? You must'a bumped yo' goddanm head, boy."

"Shit real out here, Earl." Tyrell pulled one of the guns off his waist and cocked it. "If a nigga think he comin' up in here to take mines," he aimed the weapon at a glass bottle that sat on the stone wall about forty feet away. "He got it fucked up." The gun ruptured, blew the glass bottle to shreds and nobody even turned their head. The sound of the shot was hidden in the fireworks.

Earl could do nothing but shake his head. "You need guidance, youngin'... let me tell you something." He plucked his cigarette. "I made Mox a whole lotta money out here. Ironically, from these same benches we standin' in front of right now. When that car wash shit popped off, that nigga was gettin' so much work he didn't know what to do wit' it... mind you, prior to this, Mox had never sold a drug a day in his life, but it was in his blood; he jus' didn't know it.

He use' to call me and be like, meet me in the back, Unc. So, I go back there and he hands hand me a shopping bag wit' a sneaker box in it." He pulled another cigarette from his pack and lit it. "I take the bag upstairs, crack the box open and it's two fuckin' keys in that bitch."

Tyrell knew Mox was getting money, but he had no idea he was doing it like that. "For real?"

"No bullshit. I had my young wolves out here... you remember Damion and Daren, right?"

"Hell yeah... the Wolf brothers, what happened to them dudes?" Tyrell asked.

"They was down for a second on a attempted murder rap, but new evidence jus' came forth and they got released today. My boys be up here tomorrow night." Earl sucked in the smoke and let it filter through his nostrils. "What I'm saying is... you need a team out here. If you organize this shit right, you can make millions... I'm tellin' you. Fuck wit' me... I'll make you rich."

Tyrell was skeptical on accepting Earl's advance because he was mindful of his track record, but he did know for a fact that Uncle Wise was a certified hustler. His eyes went to Earl's arms. "You still fuckin' around?" he could see the track marks coming down from his biceps.

Earl was embarrassed. "Look at me, youngin'..." he held his trembling hands out in front of him. "I'm sick. I ain't did nothing since the night before Mox got hit."

"I don't know, Unc... I don't think I could trust you."

"That's cool... shit, I wouldn't trust me either, but it ain't about trust, yougin. It's about respect and being real wit' each other. If I can't do something, I'ma let you know I can't do it and I expect the same from you, but at the same time, I put my all into whatever it is I get involved with. I can guarantee you one hundred and fifty percent on my end... We can debate about this all day, but there's only one way to find out..." Earl shook the youngster's hand and walked out of the park. "I'ma see you tomorrow."

Tyrell thought about what Earl spoke on and came to the conclusion that he was right. Without a team there was no way he could expand and take his hustle to the next level. He needed manpower and Wise Earl was going to provide that. Since his home-boy, Leo, went down for the murder, the only person he dealt with on that level was his other childhood friend, Six.

Corey Bellows aka Six was a seventeen-year-old, six foot two inch high school dropout with a golden bronze skin, short, coarse hair and a missing front tooth that gives him a distinctive, menacing appeal. He and Tyrell lived on separate sides of town and went to different schools, but became good friends as kids when they played pop-warner football.

Corey was into his books, so a lot of his peers would shy away from him, and most times, view him as a nerd, but Tyrell took a liking to him. He was conscious of Corey's knowledge and truly appreciative of his friendship. The two had been comrades for more than eight years.

Born on the west side of New Rochelle, Corey lived with his mother, father and baby sister in a one family, three bedroom house, on Third Street. His mother worked in Pelham as a home health aide five days a week and his father drove city buses for the Westechester Bee-line Bus Company. Up until last year, Corey lived the life of the typical teenager, raised by strict, middle class parents, but everything changed on the night of his sixteenth birthday.

It was 2:30 am when Corey strolled into the silent, dark house, hungry and a bit tipsy. He had just come in from a get together that one of his friends arranged for him and he could no longer take the pain and growling of his stomach, so he opted to fix himself a grilled cheese sandwich before he went to sleep. While he waited for his food to finish, the water he had been drinking to sober up was ready to come out, so he went to use the bathroom. He figured by the time he came out, the sandwich would be done, but the only problem was, after he relaxed on the cushioned toilet seat, his eyelids started to put on weight and drifted into a deep, soundless sleep, sitting on the porcelain chair. When Corey woke up his arms and legs were wrapped in bandages, he was lying in a hospital bed and a doctor was standing directly over him.

He looked up at the pale, Caucasian male and asked. "Where am I?"

"In the hospital." The doctor replied.

"*Hospital...* why?" He had no recollection or idea of the previous events.

"There was an accident."

Corey tried to sit upright. "*Accident?*" he looked around. "Where are my parents?"

The doctor shook his head. He disfavored being the person who had to break the bad news to people, especially young kids. "I'm sorry, son... they didn't make it..."

The news headline read: TEEN SETS HOUSE ABLAZE WHILE PARENTS SLEEP

Corey got charged with two counts of first degree murder and was forced to fight his case from inside prison. He sat in the county jail, unable to make bail for more than a year, awaiting a trial that only lasted two weeks, but the end result was not guilty. He had just been released two days ago.

"Whaddup, homey?" Six approached the benches, extended his hand and shook Tyrell's hand.

He was shirtless, showing off his new chiseled frame and all the tattoos that covered his body. His off white, beach shorts sagged slightly off his 36inch waist and he let the strings hang on his crispy, pearl white Nike's.

"Six, what's good?" Tyrell responded.

"Aint shit," he took a seat on the bench. "Yo, you know what's crazy?"

"What's that?"

"Most people in the hood don't even know what the fourth of July represents. They just be happy to see some fireworks and eat a few burgers n' shit." Six laughed and then pulled a cigar from his pocket, split it and let the guts fall to the concrete.

"I guess I'm most people then..." Tryell smirked. "I mean... I know it got something to do with Great Britain and the declaration of independence n' shit, but that's about it."

"Honestly, as black people we shouldn't even be celebrating this shit because the reality of it is... we weren't free then and we're still not free now."

Tyrell nodded in agreement. "You right about that."

"Fuck the fourth of July... lemme get a light." Six lit the blunt and took a deep pull. "So, wassup... it's slow out here today?"

"Nah, it's moving. I ran through half a pack already."

"Okay... yo, I jus' seen that funny lookin' nigga, Gahbe, on the block... he stuntin' hard too."

"Fuck, Gahbe!" Tyrell got tight and screwed his face up. "Old ass nigga... I'm tellin' you son, if I catch one of them in here makin' a sale; I'm poppin' on 'em... I ain't got no words for niggas."

"Damn, son... it's like that?"

"Yo," Tyrell hopped of the bench and stood directly in front of Six. "Look at me, my nigga..." he flashed the two weapons on his waist. "I don't fuck wit' that nigga, Gahbe at all. That bitchassnigga is the reason my moms is fucked up on this crack shit now... I'm tellin' you, Six," he clenched his jaws. "If any one of them niggas step foot in here, my shit going off."

Six stared at him. "Yo, you wild, my nigga."

"Nah, I aint wild... we bout to get rich, nigga." Tyrell eyed Six. "I don't know, Six... you was talking alotta G' shit when you was locked up... it's time."

"Time for what?"

Tyrell smiled, pulled a gun from his waistline and tossed it to Six. "Time to put that work in."

26

An entire month had gone by and Priscilla was beginning to settle into the shelter. Being it was the only place she had to go, she put her pride aside and focused on getting her life together. At all cost, she avoided any type of drama that would deter her from completing her goals. A few times she even had to hold her tongue.

After three weeks of job searching, Priscilla was ready to give up on the hunt and figure out a second alternative to appease her financial woes. It was stressful and the irksome interviewing process was starting to wear on her conscience and deplete her self-esteem. But just when she was ready to throw the towel, a call came from an employer.

"PRISCILLA, HURRY UP." Ms. Kathy was holding the phone. She whispered. "I think it's a job."

Priscilla rushed out of the dorm and grabbed the cordless. "Hello?"

"Hello, Ms. Davis... this is Catherine Welch, hiring manager at Stop & Shop supermarket. How are you doing today?"

"Fine, thank you."

"Well, I'm calling because we've looked over your application and I've also spoken with Jim, who you did the interview with... and we would like to know if you're still interested in working here and if so, when can you start?"

Priscilla's eyes lit up and a smile widened her face for the first time in a while. "Ughh..." she was so excited she couldn't speak. "Ummm.. yeah, I'm very much interested. I can start tomorrow if you need me to."

Ms. Welch loved Priscilla's enthusiasm. "Great, but since tomorrow is Sunday; how about you come in at nine am on Monday and we can take care of the paperwork?"

"Monday sounds great... see you at nine... and thank you."

Ms. Welch said bye and hung the phone up on her end. Priscilla was caught in a befuddled shock. She didn't realize she was still holding the phone to her ear, but no one was on the other end.

"Well," Ms. Kathy held out her hands, waiting for a response. "What happened?"

Priscilla stayed silent for a few seconds, blinked her eyes and then placed the phone on the front desk. "I got the job..." she still couldn't believe it. "I got the job, Ms. Kathy!"

"Yay!" Ms. Kathy hugged her because she was proud of her accomplishment. She witnessed the strain and struggle Priscilla had been going through, and coming from a similar place, she could sympathize with why she would sometimes act the way she did.

So, for the past week, Priscilla had been getting out of bed at 6:30 am, taking a shower, eating breakfast and heading out to Mount Vernon so she could punch the clock by 7:30. For the first time in her life, she had a job. It may not have been the job she wanted, but she was grateful and accepting of the blessing. Even on the mornings she didn't want to get up, God gave her the strength to spring from the bed, put a smile on her face and make the best of the day.

She was determined.

She was eager.

For eight hours a day, Priscilla watched as the cashiers scanned bar-codes, requested price checks and handled money. In a way, it reminded her of the days when she was hustling drugs, but she washed those thoughts from her mental and maintained focus. Once she learned the ins and outs of the checkout area, she quickly devised a plan to make things run faster. The results of a faster moving line would be more tips.

For two days straight, she watched the cashiers at each checkout line to see who was processing the customer's items the fastest. When she figured out who it was, she approached him. "Hey Randy," Priscilla closed her line and made her way toward the frail white kid working at the register next to her. "Did you take your break?"

Randy thought about it. "Nope, this line been crazy today... I'm ready to."

"Well, c'mon... I need to talk to you about something." Priscilla threw the charm on thick. "I got this sandwich too..." she held up a bag. "I know I'm not gonna eat the whole thing so you can save your money and take the other half of this."

"What kind is it?"

"Ham and cheese."

Randy licked his lips and smiled. "Oh yeah, that's my favorite."

He may have believed it was just a coincidence, but Priscilla knew otherwise. She had been doing her scouting work and overheard him mention his love for ham sandwiches while they stood out front on break.

Randy took care of the last two customers on his line, flicked the 'closed' switch and hurried out to the front. "So, what is it that you wanna talk about?" he said, holding the half sandwich in his hand. He took a bite and mayonnaise got stuck on the side of his mouth.

"I know I only been here a few days, but I been watching you on that register and you be moving." Priscilla tapped him on the side of his arm.

He tried to reply but he had a mouth full of food. "Excuse me... I don't mean to toot my own horn..." he took another bite. "But, I am the fastest cashier on the day shift." Particles of bread, meat and cheese flew from his mouth.

"I know; that's what I'm saying..." She was stroking his ego, but at the same time, he *was* the fastest cashier. "So, how does that work, do you get to choose your baggers?"

Randy stopped eating for a minute. "Well, since I am top dog, I do get to choose who I want on my line."

"Is that right?"

He grinned. "Yup."

"So, why is it that you have the slowest bagger in the store at your register?"

"Oh, Tara?" He cheesed. "I know she's slow, but she's pretty and I like her."

"But, if you had a faster bagger you could make more in tips; how much are y'all gettin' now?"

Randy scratched his head. "On a good weekday, maybe twenty dollars; on the weekend, twenty-five or thirty."

"That's it? Man, we over here pulling in at least fifty dollars a night... and that's a regular night. Let's not even discuss the weekend."

"Fifty dollars? Stop lying."

Priscilla made a cross on her chest with her fingers, kissed her palm and raised her right hand to the sky. "All truth."

"Okay... cool, but let me ask you something?" he said.

"I'm listening."

Randy finished the half sandwich and tossed the bag into the garbage. "You shared your delicious lunch with me and brought me out here to tell me that I'm the fastest cashier, or is there something else?"

"Actually, there is..." Her voice got low. "If you and I were a team in there, we could make a lot of extra money. Think about it, a whole twenty-five extra dollars a day in your pocket, sometimes even more."

Randy contemplated. "I don't know, Priscilla... what about, Tara?"

"What about her?" Priscilla moved in closer. "Randy; you and Tara been working here together for how long?"

"Almost six months."

"In that time has she ever greeted you, smiled at you, or even looked your way?"

He thought about it. "Ummm... not really."

"See, that's what I mean... Tara's not worthy of you, Randy. You're handsome, smart and independent. I'm sure there's plenty of girls out here waiting for a guy like you to come scoop them off their feet."

He blushed. "You think I'm handsome?"

"Of course I do... now, I want you to go in there and tell Tara that she's no longer bagging at register eleven... show her you're the man, Randy." Priscilla was trying her best not to laugh.

"On one condition." He pointed to the bag in her hand.

"This?" she held up the bag. "But what will I eat for lunch?"

Randy shrugged his shoulders. "Hey, you wanna bag at my register... hand over the sandwich."

Priscilla threw on a fake expression of sadness and passed the bag to Randy. The truth was, she had never eaten pork in her life. When they went back inside, Randy walked right up to Tara and made it clear that she would no longer be bagging at his register. She got upset and threw a slight tantrum until Priscilla checked her.

"Listen, bitch... take yo' lil' skinny ass down there somewhere and bag groceries. I got this now."

Her first move had been made.

Priscilla worked strenuously every day and raked in hundreds of dollars in tips throughout the week that she tucked away in her stash. The only way she could make anything happen was to have some money. On the job, she never bothered to make any new friends; she kept quiet and extracted herself from the daily doings of her fellow employees.

She was in her own world.

At 4:30 every afternoon, she would punch out, grab something to eat and hop on the number 42 bus back to New Rochelle. And every day on her stroll back to the shelter, Priscilla would wince at the grim site of the hospital that housed her love. But on this day, that little voice in her head would get the best of her. When the bus doors came open, the splatter of the torrential rains sprinkled Priscilla's cheeks before she could lift her umbrella.

"Be safe, Ms. Davis... have a good night." Tom, the bus driver said.

She stepped into the wet streets and looked up at the overclouded, dark skies, and that's when she heard it. *Priscilla...* She looked around, but the only things moving were the cars traveling up and down the roads. *Priscilla...* She heard it again, this time, she thought she recognized the voice. It sounded like Mox. Priscilla turned her head and her eyes fell on the hospital. She hadn't seen Mox since the day she returned home and her last visual recollection of him was not a pleasant one. It had been a frightening situation that replayed in her brain every time she thought about him. It was time for her to make a decision. It was time for her to face the fear.

Without a second thought, she made her move. In the blink of an eye, Priscilla was walking through the automatic doors to the entrance of the hospital. The cool air sent a chill through her body as soon as she stepped into the lobby. She shook the excess rain from her umbrella, wrapped it up and brushed her wet shoes onto the carpet. When she got to the information desk, a young, short haired, brown eyed blonde girl with a pair of specs sat behind the glass.

She smiled and said. "Welcome to Sound Shore. How can I help you today?"

Priscilla looked around. She never cared for hospitals. They made her sick. "Yes, I'm trying to visit my friend... his name is, Mox Daniels."

The blonde nodded her head and proceeded to tap the keys on the keyboard in front of her. "Yes... Mr. Daniels has been moved from the third floor to the second floor, which is a good thing." She said, as she continued typing. "Oh, I see it right here... he's in room two oh seven. That's the second floor. When you get off the elevator, you make a right." She slid Priscilla a name-tag and a pen. "Write your name on that and keep it with you."

When the elevator opened, Priscilla slowly stepped out and made the first right as directed. After brief thought about what she was doing; she felt a shift in the pit of her stomach and perspiration began to build on her brow and under her armpits. She used the back of her hand to wipe her forehead and when she looked up, room 207 was directly in front of her. If she hesitated, there was a chance for her to turn on her heels and walk away, so she grabbed the knob and gently pushed the door open.

"Oh, excuse me... I'm just finishing up here. I should be done in a sec."

The first thing Priscilla noticed was that the woman standing next to Mox's bed, wearing nurse scrubs, was pretty as hell.

She was short, maybe five feet four inches with brown shoulder length hair, a golden, bronzed complexion and a nice shaped body.

"Is he awake?" Priscilla took a step closer.

The nurse removed her gloves. "I'm sorry... Ms.?"

"Ms. Davis." Priscilla extended her hand.

"How are you? I'm Jasmine. I've been Mr. Daniels' nurse for the past few weeks... ummm... Miss Davis... Mr. Daniels hasn't been awake since he's been admitted."

Priscilla stared at Mox, lying on the hospital bed. It was an unpleasant sight. In all her days of knowing him, he had never looked so overthrown, so worn out and so powerless. She struggled to repress the tears, but the weight of her emotions was too much to bear and her eyes could no longer contain the waterfall. Jasmine could see the grief plastered all over Priscilla's face; she could sense the love in the room.

"I'll leave you two alone for a minute." she fixed the sheet that was covering Mox and left.

Besides the beeping of the machines and the slight sound of his breathing, the room held an awkward quietness that sent a chill through Priscilla's spine. She eyed the motionless figure lying before her. "Mox..." she whispered. His skin looked dry and discolored from lack of vitamins and moisturizer and it was obvious he had lost a few pounds over the weeks. "Baby, I'm here..." droplets spewed from her eyes.

She placed her hand on top of his.

His skin was dry and rough.

He made no indication of response.

He just lay there, eyes closed, taking short breaths.

Priscilla squeezed his hand. "Baby, wake up..." she sobbed. "Mox, don't do this... I need you. Brandi needs you." Vivid images of past memories flashed before Priscilla's eyes. *The first time they met. Their first kiss. The first time they made love.* And then, Brandi's bright smile appeared and Priscilla felt her spirit being whisked away. The pouring rains tapped against the second floor widows and Priscilla's cries grew louder, causing her tears to fall faster. "Pleeeeeaaase don't leave me, Mox..." She bent down, pulled her shoes off and got into the hospital bed beside him. "Mox..." she brushed his face with her hand. "Baby, you gotta be strong, you gotta fight, Mox." she laid her head on his chest and for a second it reminded her of the past times they shared. Priscilla closed her eyes, got in as close as she could and wrapped her arm around his torso. "You gotta fight, baby..." Lying in that bed, next to the only man who had ever cared for her, enabled Priscilla to realize how beloved a life really is and how much she had taken for granted.

She thought about her mother. Her daughter. Mox, and herself.

For Priscilla, this was a test; a test of her strength, will and courage; a test to see if she could move beyond the disturbing past experiences and devote every minute to building a solid, communicable relationship; a test to see if she could open her heart and truly love another human being; a test of her diligence; a test of her faith.

Staring at the ceiling, she made a promise; a troth, to herself and to Mox, that from this day on she would stand by his side until he was able to fully recover and return to his normal state. Meanwhile, she would do anything in her power to find Brandi's whereabouts and get her back. It was time for Priscilla to throw her game face on and turn the heat up in the kitchen... It was time for her to make a return.

27

The music played at a moderate level as the drinks flowed and cries of laughter filled the atmosphere in Vito's Bar & Grill. The Party-goers mingled among themselves in celebration of Billy Telesco's return home from a four and a half year prison bid for an assault charge. Mikey stood at the center of the dining area, raised his glass of champagne and yelled. "Felicitazioni!" (Congrats!) and the entire room followed suit. Billy Telesco aka 'The Butcher' was Vinny's oldest nephew and had been labeled a certified knuckle-head by his longtime peers. He earned his nickname, 'The Butcher' as a hard boiled teen who never took kindly to the word 'no' and honestly loved the sight of blood.

As a youth, Billy was into stick-ups and friendly extortion as he rose to power on his way to becoming a made man. His lanky figure and brash demeanor could never go unnoticed when he entered a room, and those that knew him well, kept their distance.

—————

FIVE YEARS AGO, on a foggy September evening, in Queens Village NY, twenty-four year old Billy 'The Butcher' and twenty-one year old Mikey T strutted into the Silver Moon Diner at 23520 Hillside Avenue. They were hungry, tired and fed up with how the day's events played out. All they wanted was a hot meal and a few stiff drinks.

"I'm tellin' ya', Mikey, I should'a wacked his fuckin' ass when I had the chance." Billy was heated. He was dressed in his usual designer, slim fit, Valentino suit, shiny black shoes and dark shades.

They pulled chairs from under the table and sat down.

Mikey replied. "Naw, if you would've done that, then you really wouldn't have gotten paid. I think he got the message."

A waiter approached the duo. "Welcome to the Silver Moon, my name is Dick and I'll be your waiter this evening." He placed two menus on the table. "Can I get you guys something to drink?"

Billy chuckled. "Yeah, Dick." He laughed again. "Bring us a bottle of that expensive French shit you all got back there."

Dick pulled a small drink menu from his pocket. "Will it be the Chateau Lafite, Marguax or the Haut Brion?"

Billy's smile turned to a serious scowl. "Do I look like I know what the fuck that is? Pick one... now, beat it... Dick!" he pounded his fist on the table in amusement.

The waiter turned his lip, sucked his teeth and pranced off in a fit.

"Be nice, Billy..." Mikey giggled.

After forty minutes at the table, Mikey was stuffed and Billy was tipsy, due to finishing half the bottle of wine by himself.

"Hey, I gotta take a whizz." Billy got up, walked through the dining area, down a short corridor and into the men's restroom. On his way out, he thought he saw a familiar face, but he didn't stop until he got back to the table. "Mikey, doesn't that look like that fuckin' scumbag, Jimmy Rovelli over there?"

Mikey tried not to be obvious and glanced over. "Yep, that's him."

"I knew it." Billy downed the rest of his wine and wiped his mouth with a handkerchief. "Lemme see your gun, Mikey."

"I leff it in the car."

"You leff it in the *car?* What the fuck, Mikey... fuck it." He stormed off toward the kitchen, and when he returned, Mikey caught a glimpse of the ten inch carbon steel blade he was gripping. He tried to stop him, but it was too late.

"Hey, Jimmy... lemme talk to you for a second." Billy forced a fake smile and held the steak knife at his side.

Hey, Billy... what's going on? I know you didn't just come from the kitchen, you working here now?" he smirked. He acted nonchalant, but Jimmy knew exactly what Billy wanted to talk about.

Billy matched his smirk. "Yeah... somethin' like that. Hey... where's that ten large you owe me?"

Jimmy's chipper expression turned to a glower. "C'mon, Billy... this is not the place or the time to discuss this; we both know that."

Billy looked at Mikey and then clenched the knife tighter. "Jimmy... you must think 'cause you wake up every mornin' and slip into your little blue suit that you garner some type of authority or somethin'."

Jimmy looked down and saw the knife in his hand. "Billy, don't do it. You know you can't get away with this."

"Who said I gave a fuck about gettin' away." He reached out, snatched Jimmy by his collar and put the blade to his throat.

Jimmy's wife scurried to his side. "Please, don't hurt him."

"Bitch, shut up!" he pressed the stainless steel harder into Jimmy's neck. "Mikey, c'mere."

A nervous Mikey T wanted to hesitate, but he knew better, so he hurried to where Billy was.

The other three couples that were sitting at their respective tables, dining, pushed their food to the side and rushed for the door.

Mikey got in close on Billy's ear. "You know this guy's a fuckin' cop, right?"

Billy displayed his thirty-two's. "I know..." he whispered. "That makes it all the better."

"Billy, please... gimme a week." Saliva slid down the side of Jimmy's mouth.

"You been dippin' n dodgin' me for two months, Jimmy. It's the principles." He laughed.

Jimmy begged. "Pleeeaaasee."

"Mikey... grab his hand."

Jimmy's wife was screaming at the top of her lungs.

Mikey snatched Jimmy's arm and slammed his hand on the table.

"The pinky, Mikey... I want the pinky."

"Please... no!" Jimmy wailed.

Billy sneered at Mrs. Rovelli. "Next time, it'll be his dick!"

He raised the knife and smashed it down on Jimmy's pinky finger.

"Ahhhhhhhhh!"

You could hear the splitting of the bone on contact. Blood shot from the wound and sprinkled Billy's expensive suit. "Shit!" he jumped back and attempted to wipe the stain, but only smeared it. "You muthafucka!" he lifted the blade and went to strike Jimmy a second time, but Mikey grabbed his arm.

"That's enough, Billy!"

Mrs. Rovelli snatched a handkerchief, wrapped it around her husband's bleeding hand and pulled out her phone. "I'm calling the cops, Jimmy!"

"Gimme that goddamn phone." Billy snatched it from her hand and flung it into the wall, shattering it to pieces. He looked down at Jimmy's severed finger and smiled. "You'll get this back when I get my money." and he tucked the bloody extremity into his pocket and walked out.

ON THE GROUNDS of Billy being a made guy, the department made a deal with the Telesco's that would exonerate Mikey of all charges and induce the minimum sentence of four years on Billy; and those four years flew by.

"Great to see you back home, kid," Vinny hugged his nephew and kissed the sides of his cheeks.

"Good to see you too, Unc... but I'm still pissed about missing Vito's funeral."

Vinny grabbed the young Mafioso by the shoulder and led him through the crowd and to the bar. "Don't get your nuts in a bunch over it... some things we have no control over... excuse me..." Vinny put his hand to his mouth and coughed. "Tonight, we celebrate your freedom. Hey, Tony... get me that envelope I gave to you earlier."

Tony reached under the bar and slid a manila envelope down to Vinny.

"What's this?" Billy shook the envelope when Vinny handed it to him.

"That's what it's about now, Billy, get as much of it as you could."

Billy stuck his hand in the envelope and pulled the stack of fifty's from it. "Thanks, Uncle Vinny."

"No problem, make sure you get laid tonight and call me in the morning. I got a job for you."

Billy smiled and began counting the bills when Mikey walked over. "You ready to get ya' balls out the sand?" he gestured to a tall brunette with huge tits and a slim waist that was standing about thirty feet away.

Billy licked his lips. "It's been long enough, Mikey!"

The bells on the front door jingled and when Billy looked up the face staring back at him was one he sure didn't expect to see.

"Billy Telesco... You still look the same." Jimmy said, walking in with his partner.

Over the years, he had put on a few pounds, so Billy didn't recognize him at first glance. He removed the shades from his face and walked to the bar.

"You got some fuckin' nerve showin' up here, Jimmy." Billy got off the stool and shot him an ice grill.

"Now, now, Billy... don't you think it's been long enough? I mean... I've forgiven you." Jimmy smirked. "I see you're still wearing those cheap ass suits."

"Fuck you."

"Did he just say fuck *me*?" Jimmy pointed at himself and then looked to his partner. "Naw, I think *you're* the one that's been gettin' fucked, little Billy. Hey, I heard you got butter fingers... how many times you drop the soap!" he and his partner broke out in a boisterous laughter.

Billy reached out, snatched Jimmy by his throat and whipped a steel handled blade out the inside pocket of his suit jacket.

Jimmy's partner unlatched the weapon on his waistline and drew it on Billy.

"Grab his hand, Mikey!"

Mikey froze.

"Put the weapon down!" The officer warned.

"Mikey! Grab his fuckin' hand!"

Jimmy tried to speak, but Billy tightened his grip.

"Drop the fucking knife!" His hand was shaking. This was the first time he ever drew his gun on a civilian.

Billy shifted his attention to the officer. "If you was gon' shoot, you would'a done it already... fuckin' rookie." his focus went back to Jimmy. "This time, I'ma cut ya' fuckin' dick off!"

"Hey! Hey!" Vinny pushed his way through the crowd. "Jimmy! Put the goddamn knife down and let 'em go."

"But, Unc..."

Vinny's eyes got beady and his temper flared, his old age was beginning to get the best of him. "Don't fuckin' but me, Billy... jus' do what I say." He covered his mouth and coughed hard.

Billy put the blade away slowly and loosened his grip on Jimmy's neck. "You're lucky... fuckin' prick." He looked down at the badge on his chest and spit on it. "Fuck the boys in blue..."

Jimmy's partner went to grab Billy's arm, but a straight left hand landed on the tip of his nose and his top lip. The rookie stumbled back, touched his nose and blood dripped down his hand. "You bastard!" he grumbled and went to charge Billy.

"C'mon, muthafucka!" Billy flashed the knife again, but this time he was going to use it.

Mikey stepped between the two. "Not here, Billy." he put his arm around him and they walked to the back.

Jimmy was wiping the saliva off his badge. "You going back to jail, Billy!" he shouted.

"Nobody's going anywhere." Vinny tossed a clean handkerchief to the bleeding rookie. "Clean yourself up." he turned to Jimmy. "You had no fuckin' right comin' here in the first place, you work in the city... what the hell you doin' in Westchester County?"

"No disrespect, Vinny, but..."

Vinny cut him off. "Get the fuck outta my restaurant..."

Jimmy knew better than to challenge Vinny, so he tapped his partner on the shoulder and the two blue suits walked out.

28

C hris pressed the brakes and then hit the lights on the Town Car as he cruised across the empty street. The dark vehicle merged with the black night atmosphere, came to a full stop and he parallel parked between a blue work van and a Cadillac truck. "Is this close enough?" He asked.

Cleo blew the smoke from his cigarette at the roof and then looked down at the chrome lined, Romanian AK-47 that sat in his lap. "Yeah, this is good."

He pulled out a pair of black *Nike* baseball gloves from the back of the front passenger seat, slipped one on his left hand, and then picked up the thirty round magazine that was next to him. He pressed the cartridge into the weapon and glanced at his reflection in the tinted window. "I'ma make these muthafuckas pay for what they did to me..." he had fifty-six stitches on the side of his face and his right hand was fully wrapped in a bandage.

Chris looked in the rear-view at Cleo. "How long we gotta wait?"

Cleo made a pained expression when he lifted the AK with his injured hand, but he managed to pull the hammer back and a bullet slid into the chamber. "Until I say move." He pressed a button on the door panel and the window came down. "It's nice out here tonight." a relaxed summer breeze entered the vehicle and kissed his face. "Chris, you ever read *The Art of War* by Sun Tzu?"

"Nah, why you ask?"

Cleo settled back in the seat, grasping the military issued firearm. "When I was back there on that kitchen table at your homeboy's house, gettin' stitched up, I thought about a quote I remembered from that book... Sun Tzu said, *in conflict, direct confrontation will lead to engagement and surprise will lead to victory*" Cleo pressed the button and the widow went back up. "If I would'a been thinkin' like that from the start, I wouldn't have been on that table..." he brushed the side of the weapon. "This time I got a surprise for that ass."

An hour and twenty minutes passed, but Cleo was just as alert as he had been when they pulled up. Besides a passing car every ten minutes, the streets were abandoned and the only establishment open was the Bar & Grill, directly across the street from where the Town Car was parked. Cleo heard what he thought was laughter, so he looked up and saw the door to the Bar & Grill was open and patrons were funneling out.

He tapped Chris on the shoulder, awakening him from his doze. "Chris, wake up... it's time."

"HEY POP, could you grab my keys for me... I'm gonna drop Billy off to the hotel." Mikey said while he waited by the exit.

Billy pushed the front door open to leave. "Ahh, don't worry about me, Mikey... I'm alright."

"Oh yeah..." Mikey looked down at Billy's feet. "So, why you ain't got no shoes on, tough guy?"

Billy dropped his eyes to the cement and burst out in laughter. "Way to go, Mikey!" he stumbled out the exit and into the desolate night air.

"Pop, you alright... you need a ride?" Mikey asked.

Vinny swirled the shot of whiskey in his glass, downed it and then ordered another one. "Yeah, I'm okay, Mikey... go ahead and get your cousin home safe. I'll see yous tomorrow."

"Cool..." Mikey scratched his head, trying to think about where he parked his vehicle. "Shit!... hey, Billy, where the hell did I park the car?"

Billy was bent down, trying to get his shoe onto his foot. "Do I look I know where the fuck you parked, Mikey."

"Alright, calm down... we'll find it."

Partygoers were filing out of the restaurant when a dark colored car with no headlights came barreling down the block.

The roar of the engine made Billy lift his head. "What the fu—"

"I DON'T THINK that's him, Cleo..." Chris hugged the steering wheel and eased off the gas.

"Slow up... slow up." Cleo let the window down halfway and then fastened his hand around the weapon. "That's that mutha-fucka, Billy... I heard he was home, pull up on 'em."

Chris hit the gas, sped up and made the tires screech as he came to a full stop right in front of Vito's Bar & Grill.

"Welcome home, Billy!" Cleo yelled and then aimed the high caliber weapon out the window.

He squeezed the trigger and fire shot from the nozzle. The ear popping sounds echoed throughout the vacant streets and the 7.62 caliber bullets pierced flesh and tore away portions of the concrete structures. Spent shell casings jumped from the flame spitting war gun as Cleo emptied the thirty round magazine at his adversaries.

A bullet struck Billy in the neck before he could attempt to get to the ground and blood shot into the air.

"Billy!" Mikey watched as his body crumbled to the cement. He reached for his shoulder holster, backed out his chrome, 9 millimeter Beretta and returned blind fire, shattering the windows of parked cars alongside the street, but aimlessly missing his intended target. An older; married couple, exiting the restaurant walked directly into a shower of stray bullets and were cut down on contact.

"Pull off, Chris!" Cleo tapped the back of the headrest, ducking back into the vehicle.

The nose twitching redolence of burnt rubber and gunpowder mixed with the nauseating, stench of death lingered throughout the air.

"Nooooo! Billy..." Tears flooded Mikey's eyes as he kneeled

beside his first cousin and tried to lift his limp body from the warm ground, but the dead weight was too much for him to manage. When he looked down, his jacket and hands were covered in Billy's blood.

Screaming sirens could be heard in the distance and the sound was moving in closer with each passing second.

Vinny heard the shots from inside and made his way out to the street in a panic. He could barely catch his breath. "Mi... Mikey, you hit?" he coughed and caught a glimpse of the blood spilling from underneath Billy's body. "Goddamnit, Billy..." he reached down and shut his eyes.

Mikey tried to stand up, but his shattered ankle wouldn't allow him to. "I think I took one in the foot, Pop." He lifted his pants leg and saw the red juice covering his shoe; instantly he felt the burn.

"Shit!" Vinny spat. He could see the flashing lights closing in. "Gimme that..." he grabbed the hot pistol from Mikey's hand, stuffed it in his jacket and called to his longtime comrade. "Hey, Sal! Get him outta here."

The lurid display of death was a picturesque scene that mimicked a classic mob flick. Parked cars riddled with bullets.

Billy Telesco's stiff corpse lolled across the filthy pavement, soaking in a pool of blood. He was in his best suit, most expensive pair of shoes and his *Hermes* tie was flipped over his shoulder. The two innocent bystanders, lying on top of each other, blanketed in blood; were dead at the front entrance of the restaurant.

"Yo, lemme get a pack of Newport and three of those Dutchies." Tyrell slapped a twenty dollar bill onto the counter.

"Ty, you see this shit?" Six was staring at the fifteen inch television affixed to the back wall of the bodega. "Somebody hit the Italians last night... shit crazy."

Tyrell turned and looked up at the local news report on the screen.

I'm standing only fifteen feet away from where the notorious

Italian mob gangster, Billy 'The Butcher' Telesco and two others were gunned down late last night in a hail of bullets.

Reports say the victims were leaving a 'welcome home' celebration for the mob affiliate, when a dark colored vehicle rolled up to the front of the restaurant and one of its occupants opened fire.

This restaurant, Vito's Bar & Grill, is owned by reputed mob boss, Vinny Telesco, whose youngest son, Vito, was murdered less than a month ago. Vinny Telesco was said to be inside at the time of the shooting and police have yet to identify the other two victims. For more on this story, tune in at seven pm.

This is Kathy Lee, reporting live from White Plains, New York, for channel Twelve News.

"Damn... son jus' got home." Six shook his head.

Tyrell got his change, took his bag off the counter and moved to the exit. "Word... nigga probably ain't even get no ass yet. That's fucked up." he giggled.

In a little over a month's time, Tyrell, with the help of Uncle Earl, assembled a team, flooded the streets with product, and proceeded to make his mark in the drug trade. His crew consisted of Uncle Earl, the Wolf brothers; (Damion and Daren) and his longtime friend, Six. On average, Tyrell's weekly profits would total 25 to 30 thousand dollars. He controlled the flow of crack cocaine within the gates of the projects and his clientele was growing by the hour. He felt the need to expand further into the surrounding area, but he was knowledgeable of the repercussions that would occur with that move, so he prepared himself.

The clouded sky gave off a murky tint and a cool September breeze whizzed by, blowing pieces of loose garbage into the street as Tyrell and Six exited the corner store. A group of seven or eight hustlers were gathered about fifty feet up the block in a detached circle, badgering a short dark skinned kid who was about to roll the dice.

"Watch his face when he ace!" one of the men shouted.

The short dark skinned kid shook the dice in his closed fist and blew on them three times. *"Scared money don't make no money, if I ever go broke—"* he unleashed the square ivory cubes from the palm of his hand and they bounced off the wall and rolled across the cement. *"I'ma take yo' money!"* they landed on four, five and six.

"That's some bullshit!!" One of the dicers complained.

"Fuck all that... pay me, nigga." He collected his winnings around the circle. *"Twelve hunit comin'... all downs a bet, everything good in my bank, call em' out!"* he bent down and schooled the dice.

Tyrell and his partner were approaching the circle when Six thought he saw Dana crossing the street on the opposite side.

"Ain't that your cousin?" He pointed out.

"Yeah, that's her... she ain't fuckin' wit' me right now." he chuckled. "Fuck that tho... I want some of this money." he stepped closer to the circle, pulled out a stack of cash and started flipping through the bills. "What's in the bank?"

Without turning around, the dark skinned kid answered, "It's five hunit left, what you want?"

"I want the whole thing...stop it up."

The words caught dark skin's attention and he turned to see who was speaking. When he acknowledged it was Tyrell, he smiled. "You sure you can cover that, lil' nigga?" he grinned.

Tyrell returned the smile. "I can cover anything you put in there... lil' nigga." he dropped the stack of hundred dollar bills on the ground in front of him.

Dark skinned picked the dice back up and went into his routine. "This Gahbe's block, nigga!" he raised the dice over his head, gave them a good shaking and then tossed them against the wall. "Show me six, bitches!"

The dice hit the wall and one bounced off someone's shoe. When they stopped, two of them were face up showing the number three, and the last one lay in a crack showing the number one.

Tyrell reached down and picked up his stack of money and the dice. "Three, three, one... nigga, pay me, that's a ace." he said.

But Gahbe was opposed to losing. "Nah, that was in the crack... I ain't payin' that."

The hostility in his voice made Six step up and say something. "You ain't bout that life, Gahbe, you know better than that."

"Who the fuck is you?"

Six answered by pressing the cold steel of his .45 against Gahbe's cheek. "How bad you wanna know?"

Two of the dicers took off running and the few that stayed, were in too much of a shock to move; they just watched.

Tyrell got excited. "That's what the fuck I'm talkin' 'bout, Six! Handle that shit! Boy... I was startin' to wonder about you." he laughed.

"Empty ya' pockets, nigga..." Six looked at the other dicers and then waved the gun at them. "All y'all niggas... hurry the fuck up!"

Gahbe was mumbling something under his breath.

"You said somethin', homie?" Tyrell was close enough to kiss him.

His teeth were clenched, but his words were clear. "Y'all gon' pay for this... word."

Six shoved the gun back in his face. "Shut up, nigga... gimmie that watch, gimme that chain... oh," he looked at Gahbe's hand and saw the diamonds shimmer in his pinky ring. "And gimme that fuckin' ring too." he pulled it off his finger and stared at it. "This shit nice right here, kid. Look at this shit, Ty."

Tyrell grab the ring and examined it. "This shit icy, Six... lemme get this?"

"It's yours, kid."

"Good lookin'..." Tyrell put the ring on *his* pinky. "Perfect fit too... yo, hurry up, cars comin' down."

Six stuffed all the money into a plastic bag and then cocked his weapon back.

"Easy, my nigga, don't do that shit right here." Tyrell grabbed his arm.

Six moved in close on Gahbe and whispered in his ear. "You lucky." he went to put the gun back on his waistline and had a second thought. "Fuck that." he gripped the barrel and slammed the butt end of the firearm into Gahbe's nose and a shot went off. Gahbe stumbled on the uneven cement; fell against a parked car palming his bloody face and Six ran off into the projects with Tyrell in tow.

29

P riscilla was resting on a single bunk, staring at a fly, trapped in the light fixture that was mounted to the ceiling. In the back of her mind, she was rooting for the fly to escape its confinement by finding the hole it had once came in through. In a sense, it reminded her of her own struggles and how she was once a prisoner of a certain lifestyle. She thought about what it took to overcome her pain, suffering, and lack of self-confidence. She realized how difficult it was to make that transition and break free from her self-slavery. In spite of her misfortunes, it felt good to stand on her own feet and accept responsibility for her doings.

As she gazed, her eyes fell to the bare walls, and she reflected on the last couple months of her life. She was fortunate that there was still breath in her lungs, but her heart had been shattered into three pieces, and two of those pieces were missing. After Ms. Kathy located Brandi's whereabouts, she revealed the news to Priscilla, and ever since, she's been able to breathe a little bit easier. Knowing that her daughter was in a safe environment settled Priscilla's nerves, but the fact that she had been in the custody of CPS enraged her. The first thought to enter her mind was to become rash and extremely violent, but instead, she came to understand that her old ways of handling things would only make the situation more detrimental and further devastate her chances of getting her daughter back. The process in which she had to endure was a monotonous and tiresome struggle, but it would be the only route to travel at the present time. In order for Priscilla to regain full custody of Brandi, she needed to show the department of CPS that she was able to keep a paying job, secure adequate living arrangements, and stay alcohol and drug free.

Today, Priscilla had the day off and wanted to use it to relax and reflect on what she needed to do. Her open custody case with CPS had been going on for two weeks and everything seemed to be in good standing as far as she was concerned. The only dispute she may have had was about having to enter into another drug program after she had recently completed one.

"Priscilla!" Ms. Kathy shouted from the front desk.

She looked at the clock on the wall and then jumped out of the bed. "Yes, Ms. Kathy?"

"Somebody's on the telephone for you... I think it's your job."

My job? It was an hour before she had to be at her drug program. "I hope they ain't asking me to come in today..." she reached for the cordless. "Hello?"

"Hello, Ms. Davis... this is Mr. Porter from Stop & Shop, how are you doing today?"

Priscilla rolled her eyes. "I'm doing pretty good."

She couldn't stand Mr. Porter. He was a black guy trying to be white with no indication of his own heritage, and just as ignorant as could be. His horrible breath and the sound of his high pitched voice annoyed most people he came in contact with, so he was definitely a loner.

"Well, that's good, Ms. Davis. I'm calling you today because it is very urgent that I speak with you. Is it possible for you to stop by today?"

Speak with me? She was stumped. "Umm... I guess that's not a problem. Can I come in now?"

"Sure; the sooner the better."

"Okay, see you in about twenty minutes." She hung up.

Twenty-two minutes later, Priscilla was knocking on Mr. Porter's office door.

"Yes, come in, Ms. Davis." He was wearing his usual, black slacks, black shoes, white collar shirt and a burgundy tie. He pushed some papers aside and sat on the front of his small, steel desk. "Thank you for coming in on such short notice." he reached back and grabbed a folder with some papers in it. "Unfortunately, it has been brought to my attention that we may have ourselves a slight problem." he passed Priscilla the folder. "Do you know anything about that?"

When she opened it, the first word she saw was: Grievance

And then she thumbed through the rest of the papers and they were all grievance slips that had her name on them.

"What is this?" she asked, handing the folder back.

"You tell me... I've gotten one of these every week since you've been working here. The reason I took so long to address it is because things have been really busy around here, but it seems like you and Ms. Holland have an issue. Is this correct?" His eyebrows raised and he waited for an answer.

Holland? Priscilla couldn't pin-point the name, but it was definitely familiar. "I'm sorry; I don't know anybody by that name."

Mr. Porter had a hard time believing her. "C'mon, Ms. Davis... *Tara Holland?* The girl who worked at the register you're currently working at."

"Tara!" She snatched the folder out of Mr. Porter's hand and looked through the papers a second time. "No this bitch didn't..." she mumbled.

"Excuse me?"

"Nothing..." She checked every slip and at the bottom of each one was Tara Holland's John Hancock. "This bitch is lying." Priscilla tossed the folder onto the desk.

Mr. Porter stood up. "Ms. Davis, please... watch your language."

Priscilla was fuming. "Fuck that... that bitch is telling a bold face lie. I hope you don't believe any of this, Mr. Porter?"

"Well, Ms. Davis you're making it very hard for me not to. What I need to know is... how did you get on that line that you've been working on?"

Priscilla shook her head, she couldn't tell him the truth because that would get Randy in trouble. "Regardless of how I ended up at that register, she's lying on me. I never once threatened that girl's life."

"You know something," He walked to the coffee maker that sat on a table in the left corner of the office and poured a fresh cup. "In matters such as this, we usually call the police and let them handle it, but seeing that I've never had a personal problem with you, I opted to just handle it myself—"

Priscilla cut him off before he could finish. "Okay... so, what does this mean? What are you gonna do, cut my hours, make me do extra work, what?"

Mr. Porter took a slow sip of his coffee and then peered up at Priscilla. "I'm sorry, Ms. Davis, but I'm afraid we're going to have to let you go."

The humming of the air conditioner was the only sound heard for a moment and then Priscilla spoke. "Are you serious?" she smiled and tried to laugh it off. "Let me *go?* I know you're not gonna fire *me* over some lies this little white bitch is makin' up."

"Ms. Davis, you know the final decision is not mines to make. I'm just doing my job."

Priscilla was getting nervous. "Wait..." she sat back down in the chair facing Mr. Porter's desk. "I don't think you understand... I really need this job, Mr. Porter. I'm in a difficult situation right now and in order for me to get my daughter back I need to be working. Can you please reconsider?"

Mr. Porter slurped at his coffee. "That's not my concern, Ms. Davis, that's your problem. Please, slam the door on the way out."

Priscilla lost her temper. "What?" she jumped in his face. "Fuck you, you inconsiderate muthafucka!" and she turned to exit.

"Fucking junkie..." He said it low and didn't think Priscilla heard him, but as soon as he went to put the cup of coffee to his lips, a closed, right hand collided with the side of his face and the hot, steamy liquid was everywhere. Mr. Porter didn't know whether to grab his pounding jaw or his burning chest. "Shit!" he stumbled back into the desk.

Priscilla hesitated and then scurried to the door and down the steps. She could see the exit, but there was so much distance in between, she almost felt like giving up. The only security guard in the store spotted her out the corner of his eye and figured she was a customer trying to steal something and run out, so he gave chase. Priscilla dashed through the 'dry foods' aisle and nearly slipped on the fresh, waxed floors. When she rounded the corner, one of her arms brushed against some boxes of oatmeal and knocked them to the floor.

"Hey! What the—" A middle aged, caucasian employee was straightening the shelves and got pushed into them when Priscilla bumped him. He got to his feet and joined the security guard in the foot race.

Everyone's eyes, customers and employees included, were fixed on Priscilla as she frantically raced through the store. She continued down the long stretch to the exit, turned her head to see how far of a lead she had on her captors and practically ran over an old lady pushing a cart out of the sliding doors. "Excuse me! Sorry!" she yelled back, making it out to the front of the supermarket.

Not knowing which way to go, she had to make a swift decision, but her focus got thrown off when she heard the guard calling out. "Hey, you, stop!"

She stepped off the curb and bolted into the street, unaware of the black Porsche truck going 20 miles per hour, coming right at her. In order to avoid a deadly collision, the driver had to mash the brake to the floor, and even in doing that, he still hit her.

As soon as he heard the thud on the paneling of the car, he threw the vehicle into park and hopped out. "Oh shit!" He rushed to Priscilla's aid and tried to help her up.

"Ow!" She pulled back when he reached for her arm. "Don't touch me." When she lifted her head, her eyes locked with his and she was frozen for a second; hypnotized by his beautiful, passionate, caring stare.

His skin was the color of almond, his eyes, a slight Hennessy tint and the fragrance he exuded smelled like success. "I'm so sorry. I swear to God, I didn't even see you." He apologized, but noticed Priscilla kept looking back while she was trying to get up. "Is something wrong, you alright?"

"Hey!" The guard screamed out again.

The driver turned and saw the two people running towards them.

Priscilla finally made it to her feet. "Please... can you get me outta here?"

He opened the back driver's side door. "Hurry up, get in."

She dove into the back seat, stretched across the fine leather and her rescuer peeled out of the parking lot. He stomped on the gas and floored it down Sanford Blvd, continuously checking his rear-view for anybody trailing. "Where am I going?" he asked, eyes focused on the road. He checked the mirror again and could see Priscilla was in pain.

"Jus' drop me off in New Rochelle, please..." The injury was getting the best of her, but she couldn't let it be known.

"Okay, cool..." When he crossed the Pelham borderline, he slowed down in case a patrol car was somewhere in the cut, lurking. "What's your name?"

"Priscilla."

He came to a stop at a red light at the intersection of Lincoln and Webster Avenue. "Priscilla, my name is Quiane."

"Qui... what?" She wanted to smile, but the pain was too much.

He giggled and pulled off when the light changed. "Quiane," he repeated. "But, people call me, Q."

"Okay... Owww..." The pain was searing.

"I think you need to get to a hospital. Your arm might be broke."

Priscilla hated being told what to do. "Please, Quiane... Q, whatever... just drive."

"No problem." He came to another stop light and asked. "Left or right?"

"Make the right... and you can let me out down the block."

As soon as Quiane pulled to the curb, Priscilla hit the unlock button and rushed out of the truck.

"Hol' up! Wait... where you going?" He clicked his seat-belt and hopped out after her. "Priscilla... shit..." she was walking too fast for him.

Without turning around, she yelled. "Thank you, Quiane!" and continued down the block.

He knew he wouldn't be able to catch up to her, so he went back to his truck and cruised down the block when she turned the corner. From where he parked, he could see her entering a building, so he waited a few minutes and drove by slow. *Women's Shelter?* He was shocked when he saw the sign on the building. He made the right, went back around the block, and parked a few car lengths away from the front entrance of the shelter. For thirty-five minutes, Quiane was in his truck, parked, thinking, anticipating, and hoping to get a second chance at seeing Priscilla. She was beautiful and he was uneasy about what occurred; all he wanted to do was make sure she was alright.

A blue and white patrol car cruised down the block past Quiane's truck and slowed to a stop in front of the shelter. Not even a minute later, an unmarked detective vehicle came up the street from the opposite end and pulled next to the patrol car. Quiane sat up in his seat and put the key into the ignition when he saw three officers exit the two vehicles. Ten minutes later, two of the officers walked out of the building, followed by Priscilla, who was in hand-cuffs, being escorted by the third officer.

"Shit!" Quiane put the truck in drive and drove off.

30

J asmine fluffed the pillow and placed it back under Mox's head. "Good morning, Mr. Daniels. How are you today?" she went to the window and let the shade up, causing the lambent sunlight to fill the room. "Did you get some rest last night? I heard you were up pretty late."

Mox opened his only good eye and stared at the same picture on the wall that he'd been looking at for the past few days. It had been a week since he snapped out of his coma, but he had yet to utter a word. The only thing he did was put on a half a smile and nod his head; and that only happened once while Jasmine was talking to him. No one had been by to visit since Priscilla, so the only people to know of his recovery were the doctors and nurses. Every day, for eight, sometimes ten hours, Jasmine would come in to work and tend to Mox's every need. When she first started the job, she had mixed feelings on taking care of someone in a coma. She didn't think she could handle the responsibility of supervising another person's life, but with time came knowledge, and after a few weeks it became second nature.

Jasmine took to Mox even more after she read about his story in the papers. Her heart held regret for all the misfortune he had to withstand and the abrupt transitions he had to encounter. He hadn't said a word to her, but she felt connected to him, almost a part of him, as if they had known each other for most of their lives.

She would arrive at 8:30 am to feed, bathe and massage Mox. Over the past couple of days, his skin had begun to regain its color and texture, almost back to its original state. Every day, Jasmine would read books to Mox, sing for him, play games with him or just sit there and talk to him without him ever expressing the slightest inclination of feeling or speaking a word. He was the perfect listener. He didn't complain, he didn't shout and one of the best parts was, he didn't ask for anything. What Jasmine did notice was that he also never gave up on himself. He fought, every second of every day. It was a struggle, but the work was paying off.

"Look what I brought in for you today." Jasmine pulled out an iPod from her purse and placed it on the desk beside Mox's bed. "I programmed a few songs in it already, so, whenever you wanna listen to some music, all you have to do is hit this little, white button right here." she pressed the button and *Amerie's song Why Don't We Fall In Love* came on. "Ohhh... I love this song!" Jasmine sang the words to Mox.

WHY DON'T WE,
WHY DON'T WE,
WHY DON'T WE FAAAALL IN LOOOOVVEEEE...

She turned the volume down. "You know how you hear a particular song and it brings you back to the first time you heard it... or it makes you recall that special memory of something or someone... that song right there brings back a lot of memories for me; some of them bad ones, some of them were good." she grabbed the fingernail clipper off the table and began clipping Mox's nails. "It just amazes me how the human brain works."

Mox relaxed and let his head rest on the pillow while the music eased his nerves and rejuvenated his soul. Everything Jasmine did for him, he was appreciative of and as soon as it was possible, he was going to thank her for everything. If it wasn't for her, Mox wouldn't have made it as far as he had. Her caring heart and loving soul was keeping him alive, and there was no way he couldn't acknowledge it.

A knock at the door broke Jasmine's concentration. "You can come in, Mr. Daniels." She pulled her gloves off and tossed them into the trash. "Oh, I forgot to tell you that you were getting a visitor today, Mox."

"Is he awake?" Uncle Earl stepped in, removed his *Kangol* hat, and closed the door. He was wearing oatmeal colored, linen pants, chocolate suede penny loafers and a V-neck fitted t-shirt to match.

"Yes, he is. He still hasn't spoken a word, but he is slightly responsive and very coherent. He can see you out of his good eye." She grabbed her clipboard and went to exit. "I'll leave you two to talk."

"Hey..." Earl tapped Jasmine's shoulder before she walked out. "What happened to his left eye?"

"When the bullet entered, it permanently damaged his iris and optic nerve, causing it to remain inoperative. For a while it'll be sensitive to light, so its best that he keep it covered with a patch."

"So, you mean to tell me, he's not gonna see out that eye ever again?"

"Not likely."

Earl shook his head in disgust. "Damn... does he know?"

"Yes, we've explained everything to him."

"Fuck." Earl clenched his *Kangol*. "Excuse me."

"It's okay." Jasmine opened the door to leave. "If you guys need anything, just press the blue button on the remote that's attached to the bed."and she exited the room.

"Damn, baby boy..." Earl took a deep breath and stared at Mox as he lay in the bed. He wanted to cry, but he had to muzzle his emotions and remain strong for his nephew. He pulled up a chair and sat next to him. "You lookin' much better, nephew. I see you getting' some of your color back. I know I ain't been around lately, but I got my hands tied up in a few things. Aye, Mox... look at me, baby." he stood up so Mox could see how good he was looking. "I done put on about twenty-five pounds. I got money in my pocket, I'm laced up." he grabbed the gold and diamond pendant hanging from the Figaro link around his neck and kissed it. "And best of all... I ain't got high since the day you got shot... and that's the truth,

Mox. I ain't gon' sit here and lie... shit, it was rough as hell kickin' that shit, but I'm maintaining. The worst part is over."

Mox focused on the poster hanging on the wall.

"Nephew," Earl scooted his chair in closer to the bed. "I got somethin' big lined up..." his voice was low. "I need you wit' me, baby boy. I need you to get healthy so we can really get this money. It's out here, Mox."

"I'm fucked up, Unc..." For the first time, Mox spoke. It was a hoarse mutter, but Earl heard it, smiled and patted Mox on his hand.

"You gon' be alright, champ."

"I don't know..." he paused to catch his breath. "If I can fight this shit... Unc..."

Earl sucked his teeth. "Shiiit... aye, Mox... remember when you were little, like five or six years old? You use to beg me every day to teach you how to ride a bike and I kept on tellin' you to wait. Well, I guess you got fed up wit' me sayin' that and you took it upon yourself learn how to ride. First of all, I tried to tell you that the bike you were trying to learn on was too big, but you weren't tryna hear at me, so I watched you. I watched you every day for one whole week while you learned to ride that bike. You musta fell about a thousand times, but each time, you got right back up, bruised knees and all, and got back on that bike to try again." He giggled, paused and then looked in Mox's face.

"That was determination, Mox. That was focus. That was you making a vow to self, sayin' that no matter how difficult the task is, you were gonna conquer it. Man... no bullshit... I think you started on a Tuesday and by that weekend you were speedin' all through those projects on that bike. I was proud of you, Mox. I couldn't do nothin' but smile when you cam flyin' by me, cheesin'. You remember what you said to me?"

Mox didn't speak, he just nodded his head yes.

"You told me you could do anything in the world, Mox... you remember that?"

A tear dribbled down Mox's cheek.

"This shit ain't no different..." Earl could no longer hold his emotions captive as the water spilled from his eyes. "You gotta fight, Mox... and goddamnit, you better not give up on me, champ." he wiped the tears from his face with the back of his hand and then checked his *Rolex* for the time. "Listen, man..." he sniffled. "I gotta go take care of a few things, but I'ma come back tomorrow to see you. You want me to bring you somethin'?"

Mox shook his head, no.

"Aight, cool... oh..." Earl reached into his pants pocket, pulled out a picture and tossed it into Mox's lap. "Your aunt is about to move down south and she thought you might like to keep that wit' you. Love you, nephew... see you later."

The door shut and Mox's head dropped to the photo in his lap. It was the photo his aunt Sybil had kept on her refrigerator for the past ten years; the photo of his mother. Mox took a deep breath, exhaled and let the tears spill from his eye.

TORRENTIAL RAIN POURED from the heavens, followed by a deep, growling thunder, and then a glaring strike of white lightning lit up the sky. The projects had been empty all day, devoid of any doings whatsoever; a desert. To make matters worse, two different unmarked detective cars had been rolling through every ten to fifteen minutes. Tyrell and Six kept dry under their large umbrellas as they stood in front of building #70. "Yo, Ty... who dat?" Six asked, watching a dark Town Car pull up to the gate.

Tyrell took a few steps to the middle of the walkway and tried to make out the vehicle. "I don't know, Six. It look like them boys though. You got that on you?"

"Nah, I stashed it in the bushes."

Tyrell heard the doors come open and walked back to the front of the building. He and Six held their ground and watched the two, six foot white men in dark suits stroll up the strip in their direction.

"Hey, Mikey... what's the number of that building?" Sammy looked around at the numbers on the two buildings. One had #70 on it and the other had #60.

"Uhh..." Mikey looked at the buildings. "I think it was sixty... yeah, pretty sure it was. We gotta go up to the sixth floor."

Mikey Telesco and one of his gunmen, Sammy Mallano, trudged through the soaking rain waters and into building #60.

"Who the fuck was that?" Six skipped up the slanted red wall, dipped into the bushes and came back holding a chrome handgun. "Yo, Ty, that wasn't no police."

"Chill... keep that low." Tyrell warned. "Hol' up... lemme call my cousin." He whipped his phone from his pocket and found Dana's number in his contact list, but after three tries he stuffed it back in his pants. "She ain't answering..."

"What door is it, Mikey?" Sammy's Brooklyn accent was deep and rich.

"Six H..." Mikey replied as they stepped off the elevator.

Sammy grabbed the black leather gloves out of his pocket and slipped them on his large, rough hands. "So, who is this broad?" He lifted a Walther P22 from his waistline and then screwed on the sound suppressor.

"Her name is, Dana... supposed to be one of Mox's broads."

Sammy cocked the weapon. "Dana, huh?" He put his ear to the door and then backed up. "You know... I been hearing a lot about this Mox character.... heard he took a bullet in the face... who the fuck he think he is... the Terminator?" Sammy chuckled. "Aye... knock on the door."

Mikey tapped on the door three times.

Sammy cut his eyes and shook his head. "You gotta be kiddin' me... Are you serious? Mikey... you got a pair a balls in your pants or a goddamn pussy cat? Knock on the fuckin' door already."

Mikey balled his fist and banged on the door three more times.

"Who is it?" Dana yelled from behind the door.

"It's maintenance!" Sammy smiled and peeked at Mikey.

They could hear her footsteps getting closer and then the sound of a lock being unlatched and then another.

Sammy gripped the weapon with his index finger placed on the hair-trigger, ready to fire.

When the door came open, Dana was standing there with the biggest smile on her face, until her eyes dropped to Sammy's hands. "I thoug—h..."

The shots sounded like three small balloons being popped and then Dana's body collapsed to the floor.

Sammy tucked the pistol into his inside jacket pocket. "A message from Vinny... don't fuck wit' the Telesco's!" And then he spit on Dana's corpse.

"Them niggas been up there for a minute, right, what you think we should do?" Six was anxious.

"Be easy... we jus' gon' play it cool for now, see how this shit play out." The rain started to slow up, so Tyrell let his umbrella down. "Matter fact... I'ma run up the back staircase to see if Dana's upstairs. Stay here, I'll be right back."

When Tyrell made it to the fifth floor, he could hear chatter coming from atop of him on the sixth. He took the steps two at a time and then pulled the stairway door open.

The hallway was packed.

Someone yelled out. "The police said they're on their way!"

Police? Tyrell nudged his way through the speculating tenants.

He saw a trail of blood leaking out of one of the apartments. "Excuse me." his heart sped up and a cold sweat came over him. "I know that ain't..."

He felt a hand on his shoulder trying to turn him around. "Tyrell, c'mere baby... don't go over there." the soft voice warned, but it was too late. The crowd split and Tyrell saw Dana, his first cousin, slumped in a river of her own blood, at the entrance to her apartment. He forced his way through the crowd and ran to the hallway window. In the midst of the teeming rains, Tyrell could see the two gunmen hurrying out of the building. He balled his fist and pommeled the thick, glass, window, trying to get Six's attention. "Yo! Yo! Six! Yoooooo!"

Six stood in the rain, oblivious to Tyrell's cries of vengeance from six flights up, as he watched the two suited men get into their car and drive away. By the time he did look up, the hallway was full of people. The backdoor slammed, Six turned his head and Tyrell came flying down the steps.

"Fuck!' He screamed loud enough to be heard for miles as he watched the Town Car speed away. He turned to Six with fire flaring in his eyes. "You ain't hear me fuckin' bangin' on the window!"

Six was stumped. "Nah... I ain't hear nothin'... what happened?"

He didn't need an answer once he took a good look at Tyrell's face. The tears explained it all.

31

Among the ramblings, laughter, shifting of chairs, arguments and orange suits, Priscilla could barely remain seated in her chair. Nervous, anxious and afraid of the truth, she focused on the Caucasian woman's eyes across from her as the words began to spew from her mouth. "It's gonna be hard, Priscilla. I suggest you take the plea." she said.

"A *plea?* And where does that leave me?"

"Well, first off... they'll lower the charge from a D felony to a B misdemeanor. That alone keeps you from seeing any state time. What happens then is, once you accept the offer, the judge will more than likely sentence you to ninety days jail time."

Priscilla crunched her brows and turned her lip up. "Ninety days?" she shook her head. "I can't do ninety days. I can't do another hour and you're sitting here telling me to take ninety days... I have to get my daughter."

The veteran lawyer took a deep breath and tried to be cordial. "Ms. Davis... I don't know how to tell you this, but you getting your daughter back anytime soon is far from a reality. You screwed your chances when you fractured that guys jaw. You're lucky he's not pressing charges."

Priscilla got angry, made a fist and pounded the small table. "Ain't nobody gon' stop me from getting my daughter back! Not

234 | TM JEFFERSON

you, not them... nobody!" she shouted. "She's mines!" the tears came down rapidly. "That's my daugh—ter..." she almost couldn't get the words out through her cries.

"Everything alright over here?" A tall, fair skinned C.O. asked.

The lawyer responded. "Yes, everything is good. Sorry, sir."

Priscilla buried her face in her arms and sobbed.

"Ms. Davis, there's something else..." The lawyer pulled out a stack of papers that were stapled together and placed them on the table. She tried to explain the situation to Priscilla. "Since you faulted on your attempt to regain custody of Brandi, someone else has stepped in."

Priscilla raised her head. "What? What are you talkin' about, someone else?"

The lawyer ran her finger down the piece of paper, looking for the name. "Oh, a Ms. Anna Mae Davis is now an approved applicant for custody of Brandi. It says here that she's your mother, is this correct?"

Priscilla's heart skipped a beat, dropped to the floor and then broke into tiny pieces and withered away. "My mother?" She was visibly on the brink of destruction. "I swear to God on every bone in my body if that woman touches a hair on my daughters head... I'ma kill her wit' my bare hands."

"Ms. Davis, you need to calm down."

Priscilla stood up. "Calm down my ass... bitch, you must think I'm stupid. You think I'ma let them take my baby away from me, you're fuckin' wrong!"

Two C.O.s rushed the table and surrounded her. "Have a seat, Davis!" one of them advised.

When she ignored the direct order, the taller C.O pulled his cuffs off his waist and his partner grabbed Priscilla by her arms. They forcefully escorted her back to her cell block. A feeling of discomfort suffused her entire body as she was being dragged off like an animal. "Nooooo! Please don't let them take my baby!" she dissolved in tears. "Please, don't let them take her from me!"

THREE DAYS LATER

"Davis! You got a visit!" The C.O screamed from the bubble.

Priscilla got up from her bunk and walked into the bathroom. She brushed her teeth, washed her face, combed her hair, and changed into some fresh oranges. The past three and a half weeks she spent at the Valhalla county jail had been a living hell for the first time offender. Despite all the wrong she had done throughout her travels, this had been the only instance where she had been in real trouble. The county jail wasn't too much a far cry from the shelter, but the structure was totally different. There was no option to come and go as you please, and the thought of being told what to do and when to do it didn't sit well with Priscilla. Her cell was freezing, the food was disgusting and the inmates were filthy, but there was nothing she could do about it. Priscilla had to bear the brunt, suck it up and make the best of a bad situation. She walked to the C.O.'s bubble.

"Don't go down there starting no shit today, Davis... they were easy on you last time; next one won't be so nice." He handed her a pass and she waited for an escort to walk her down to the visiting room. When they got there, Priscilla was the only inmate awaiting a search to enter the visiting area, so she got through in a hurry.

"You're at table nine, Davis." The C.O directed.

While she walked towards her table, she could see that her visitor was a female by the way her hair hung past her shoulders. *I hope it ain't this lawyer bitch again.* She thought as she got closer. When she came around the table and saw who it was, she didn't know whether to smile or to cry, so she did both. "Oh my God, Jennifer!" Priscilla spread her arms and the two friends embraced for the first time in months.

"Girl, you lookin' good..." Jennifer complimented.

They took their seats at the table.

"How did you know I was in here?"

"I was here the other day, visiting my punk ass baby father and I saw you wild out on that lawyer chick." Jennifer laughed. "What happened, how did you end up in here?"

Priscilla sighed. "Jen... I done been through so much bullshit since I left the program, it's crazy. I was staying at the shelter for a minute and I even had a job working at Stop & Shop in Mt. Vernon."

"So, what the hell you do to get in *here?*"

"This lil' bitch at the job was droppin' slips on me, saying I was threatening her. So, on my day off, I get a call from one of the managers and he tells me he needs to talk. I go in there and this self-centered muthafucka fires me, not giving a fuck about my situation and the fact that I needed the job in order to get my daughter back... so, I punched him right in his goddamn nose."

"Wow... so what happened wit' Brandi?"

Priscilla dropped her head. "They got her in the system, Jennifer. I need your help."

Jennifer was stunned. "The system? How— never mind..." she reached over, lifted Priscilla's head and held her hands. "Listen, girl... I told you when we were in that program that if you needed *anything,* all you have to do was say it. I meant that, Priscilla." she let go of her hands and sat back in the chair. "I don't have many friends, but I do consider you one of the few... and a good one at that. Whatever you need me to do, I got you."

Priscilla smiled and got up to give Jennifer a hug.

"Davis, sit down!" The C.O. yelled.

"Thank you so much, Jennifer." She said, taking her seat.

"No problem, girl. How much longer you gotta be in here?"

"I go to court on Monday. That'll make a full month I been here. If I accept the plea and get the ninety days, I'll have a month left, because you only have to do sixty days of the ninety."

Jennifer nodded her head. "Okay... so that's not too bad. Well, tell me what you need me to do, so I can get on it."

Priscilla went into detail about what she needed from Jennifer and stressed the importance of how much she appreciated her help. An hour later, she left the visit feeling assured that Jennifer would do the right thing and stay loyal to her word. Her friend's helping hand assisted Priscilla in easing her mind and focusing on the time she needed to do. Being stressed out in prison would only lead to more problems.

SWEAT FELL from Cleo's face as he kept a steady pace, jogging on the treadmill. He looked at the timer and it read, 7 minutes. "This shit ain't no joke, Chris. I don't think I can last for three more minutes."

"If you want it, you gotta work hard for it, Cleo. Keep pushing." Chris encouraged.

After Cleo murdered Billy Telesco, he needed a safe haven, so, being the good friend; Chris let him crash in his basement until he figured out his next move. Chris owned a country style, two bedroom, townhouse that was stashed away in the woods, in Rye, New York, a few minutes off the Cross County Parkway. It was hidden in a secluded area, so being spotted was the least of his worries. Besides that, Cleo had begun to shed some weight, due to his excessive cardio training. His overall appearance had taken on a change in the last few weeks. His facial hair had grown, giving him a rough, edgy look and the 30 pounds he dropped had him feeling and looking like a new man.

The treadmill slowed to a stop and Cleo jumped off. "I feel like Mike Tyson in his prime." he bounced on his toes and threw a few jabs at the air. "These niggas can't fuck wit' me!" He looked into the 6 foot wall mirror that leaned against a heavy bag and marveled at himself. He was feeling like a leader; doing what he wanted to do, whenever he wanted to do it, living life on his terms and his terms only, calling the shots, making decisions; being a boss. But deep within, he feared the truth, the truth of the real him and those unforgotten memories that would forever stay embedded in his brain.

As he stood, gazing into the mirror, his mind brought him back to a place he was reluctant to visit. He thought about the neglect, abandonment and malice of his birth mother and still till this day, Cleo couldn't understand how a person who held a child inside of them for nine whole months could do such a horrible thing. He closed his eyes and remembered the day Sybil told him the truth about his mother.

"CLEO!... Mox! Stop that goddamn fighting in my house!" Sybil yelled at the two rumbling youngsters.

"He started it!" Cleo squealed as they got up from the floor.

"Stop lying, Cleo... you jus' mad because I beat you at your own game."

Cleo was embarrassed. "Shut up!" he sucker punched Mox in the stomach and ran off to the back room.

Sybil saw what happened and darted out kitchen to catch him, but the door slammed before she could get there. "Cleo, open this damn door!" she yelled, turning the knob.

"No!"

She ran back into the kitchen and found a butter knife in the drawer. "You must think I'm playin' wit' you, boy." She fidgeted at the lock with the knife, trying to get the door open. Seconds later, she got it. "What I tell you about puttin' your hands on your cousin?" Sybil scolded.

Cleo sat at the edge of the bottom bunk, crying and holding onto an envelope.

"What the hell you cryin' for, what is that?" She snatched the envelope from his hands and when she saw what it was, her bottom lip dropped. "Oh, God. Cleo, did you read this?"

He didn't answer; he just wiped the tears and looked up at her with a face full of anguish.

"I'm sorry, Cleo..." Sybil sat next to him on the bed. "Listen, your mother's not a bad person, she just happened to make some not so good choices in life."

Cleo's voice was low. "So, it is true?"

Sybil took a deep breath and tried to figure out how to tell him the truth. "Listen, Cleo... your mother and I were best of friends back when we were in high school. Your mother was gorgeous. She had that look; tall, petite and extremely beautiful. All she ever wanted to do was be a runway model. That's what she talked about. Day in and day out, every conversation had something to do with modeling. She dreamed of making it big and moving to Paris somewhere. We joked a lot, but that was one thing she was truly passionate about." Sybil gathered herself when she felt her emotions starting to build. She pulled a tissue from her pocket and patted the tear on her cheek.

"When we were in high school, there was this guy named Michael Brown who was the star of the varsity basketball team at the time. Well, all the girls in the school were dying to get a piece of Mr. Brown, but Michael had the biggest crush on your mother. He would've gone to the end of the earth for her if need be. Whatever she asked for, she got. The only problem was; your grandfather was not having it. He could never accept the fact that the Brown family was from the projects. He hated the Brown family... for what reasons, I don't know, but, what I do know is your mother and Michael secretly got together and a few months later, she ended up pregnant. Boy was your grandfather pissed."

Cleo quietly listened to Sybil. He was trying to absorb every word she was saying.

"At first, he tried to make her get an abortion, but she wouldn't do it and he couldn't force her to, so he acted as if everything was okay. Then, he played on your mother's dream of becoming a model and made her believe having a child would destroy her body and she would never get the chance to walk the runway. She believed him, and two days after she gave birth to you, I got a knock on my door.

"GIRL, WHAT THE HELL YOU DOIN' out the hospital?" Sybil brushed the crust from her eyes and stepped aside to let her best friend enter the apartment.

Vivian's hands shook as she rushed through the door, holding her newborn, wrapped in a blanket. "Sybil, I need the biggest favor in the world." she put the baby down on the couch and sat on the wooden coffee table.

"And what's that?" Sybil reached down and picked the newborn up.

"I need you look after my son."

She rocked the baby in her arms. "Look after him... where you goin?"

Vivian got up and paced the living room floor. "Sybil, I got a dream." She said, reaching into her purse for a cigarette. "Right now, I don't have time for no cryin' baby."

"Cryin' baby?" Sybil was shocked. "Vivian, this is your child. You carried this child for nine months and now you just gon' give 'em away?"

"No... I'll be back, I promise." She lied. "I jus' need some time, Sybil. A little bit of time to sort this out and do what I need to do. I can't be a world famous model if every ten minutes, I have to worry about this baby."

Sybil looked down at the baby in her arms. He was sound asleep, unknowing of the world in which he had been brought into. "I can't take care of no baby, Vivian. I got my own responsibilities."

Vivian put the cigarette out in the ashtray. "Please, Sybil... jus' for a few months, and as soon as I get myself in order, I swear to God I'll be back for him." she quickly walked to the door and opened it. "You got my word on that."

Sybil tried to put the baby down and catch her before she walked out. "Wait... Vivian... I can't..." The front door slammed and Sybil was left standing, holding a three day old baby boy. She shook her head, sighed and looked at the precious human life in her arms. "I don't know the first thing about takin' care of no baby." she voiced aloud. "At least she could've told me your name..."

SYBIL HELD the envelope in her hand and looked over to Cleo. "And that's how you ended up here. Nobody asked questions or anything. You were jus' a new addition to the family, and it's always been that way. When the people close to me asked where the baby came from, I always told them you were adopted. "

"Who gave me my name?" He asked.

"My brother, Earl came up with that name for you. He helped me out a lot in the beginning and that's why we're so close." Sybil ripped a piece of paper out of a notebook and wrote something on it. "Here, this is your mother's real name, last address and phone number. Maybe, one day you could write to her." she passed Cleo the paper.

He stared at it and asked. "What does she look like?"

"Hold on..." she went into the other room and came back holding a picture.

When Cleo saw the picture he couldn't believe his eyes. His mother was beautiful. She was tall, brown skinned with big lovely brown eyes and a physique that you only saw in magazines.

"She's pretty ain't she?"

Cleo nodded yes.

"Cleo," Sybil sat back on the bed next to him. "We need to keep this between us. Can this be our little secret?"

He nodded yes again, but in his heart, he didn't agree and he knew one day the truth would come out.

CLEO SNAPPED out of his daze and went to the corner of the basement, to his bag, and pulled out his wallet. He thumbed through some papers and found what he was looking for.

"Wanna take a road trip, Chris?" He asked, looking down at the small piece of paper with a name, number and address on it.

"Where we going?"

Cleo just smiled and said. "South..."

32

Frank's establishment, Club RED, was located between West 16th St. and 10th Avenue in lower Manhattan. Prior to it becoming a night club, the space housed a wholesale market, that, after a few years, eventually went out of business. After obtaining a bachelor's degree in business management, Frank decided to put his education to use and legitimize a significant portion of his illegal drug money. He renovated the space and had a night club built. Club RED had two floors, two large half circle bars, six 40 inch flat screen televisions and the color red everywhere.

The spot was filled to capacity as Frank and Nate, fitted in three thousand dollar designer suits, relaxed on the ritzy suede V.I.P couches in a cordoned off area at the rear of the club. A champagne bucket filled with ice, two bottles of Ace of Spade, and a few drinking glasses were on the table in front of them, not to mention, they were surrounded by a bevy of beautiful women. Frank tapped Nate on his shoulder and leaned in close to his ear. "Did you tell him to be here on time?" he glanced at the Rolex on his wrist.

Nate nodded yes and then sipped his bubbly.

"Well, where the fuck is he?"

A few minutes later, a six foot, 300 pound, black, gorilla looking security guard made his way to where Frank and Nate sat. "There's a gentleman out here accompanied by two others, saying they're here to see you, boss."

"Let him in." Frank replied.

When the bouncer came back, Tyrell, Six and Uncle Wise were following him.

"Gentlemen, have a seat." Frank greeted the men and offered them drinks.

"So, wassup?" he looked at Tyrell.

"Man... I done looked all over for that nigga, Cleo, and one thing I do know is... he ain't in New York."

Frank didn't believe that. "What the fuck you mean he ain't in *New York?* Where can he go?"

"I don't know, but he ain't out here. I had my people check every borough, every nook and every muthafuckin' cranny... he ain't out here, Frank, I'm tellin' you."

The disappointment was obvious. "You told me you was gon' handle this." Frank stood and faced Tyrell.

"I am."

"When?"

Tyrell caught the eye of a seductive, red-bone goddess with short blonde hair, walking by, and winked at her. Then he said, "Don't worry, Frank... I got this. In the meantime, let's toast."

"To what?"

Tyrell raised his glass. "To the power of the muthafuckin' dollar!" he shouted and they all did the same. He stepped in a little closer to Frank. "I'm pretty sure you know Uncle Wise, but this is my partner, Six." he said.

"Hey, Frank," Uncle Wise downed another cup of bubbles. "I went by to see Mox the other day... y'all been by there?"

Lately Frank had been feeling guilty about not going to visit Mox, but he attributed it to working long hours, running the club, and maintaining his drug business. He knew it was a worthless excuse, but that was the only way he could bring himself to justify his actions. Mox was like a brother to him and now he felt like he should've made a better effort to be there for him.

"I can't do, it Unc. I'm not even gonna lie. I know I been fuckin' up by not being by his side, but I can't see my boy like that; that shit hurts too much."

"How is he?" Nate jumped in.

Uncle Wise poured another drink. "He's doing much better. I spoke to him on the phone today and he said they were gonna move him to a rehabilitation center, in Greenwich Connecticut."

Frank and Nate replied at the same time. "*Connecticut?*"

"That's what *I* said... I guess that's what it is though. I think they moving him on Monday."

"Hey, Frank. I think we should take a ride up to CT and check on him." Nate suggested, but was ignored.

Frank refilled everyone's glass with champagne and then summoned the waitress and ordered her to bring two more bottles.

Tyrell sat down next to Frank on the couch. "I need a favor, Frank... actually, two."

"I'm listening."

"What you know about this dude?" He slid Frank a piece of a napkin with a name written on it.

Frank leaned over and showed Nate the name. "What he got to do with anything?" he asked.

"He had my cousin Dana killed."

"*Dana?* Get the fuck outta here... when did this happen?"

"'Bout a week ago... they're having her funeral tomorrow."

Frank thought about the situation and realized the Italians weren't going to let up, *but Dana?* That was something he would've never expected. "Damn... I'm sorry to hear that, but you think you ready for that?"

"*Ready?* Shit..." Tyrell glanced at Six. "I came into this world ready."

"You know it's sharks in that water, kid. Don't jump in if you can't swim, you might drown."

Tyrell let the words sink in and thought about what Frank was trying to tell him. He was just a child, a teenager, trapped in a world of sin that was ruled by grown men, where every choice he made had to be decisive, quick witted and vigorous. He knew he was short the manpower to wage a war against the Telesco's, but his emotions were blinding his perception of reality. "They killed my cousin, Frank..."

he took a sip of his champagne and then wiped his mouth with the back of his hand. "I'ma murder every one of them muthafuckas..."

Blonde hair walked by again, but this time she stopped, bent down and whispered something in Tyrell's ear. He smiled and said, "Yeah, jus gimme a minute." When she stepped off he turned to Frank. "Who the fuck is *that* bitch?"

Frank shrugged his shoulders. "I seen her around a few times, don't know her though. What's this other favor you talking about?"

"I been gettin' my feet wet in the game a lil' somethin'... and uhh, I got my team." He looked back at Earl and Six. "Uncle Earl is guiding me in the right direction, but I need some more help. I figured that's where you could come in."

Frank was confused. "I don't get it."

"Listen," Tyrell lowered his voice just enough so that Frank could hear him. "Word is, you the king of coke."

Frank smiled and then he shook his head. "Do you realize what you just sat here and told me? You want me to supply you, and you being guided in the right direction by a fuckin' *dope fiend?*"

Uncle Earl heard every word. "Aye, Frank you better watch your mouth."

"No disrespect, Unc, don't take it the wrong way."

Earl was fuming. He hadn't felt this way in years. It was like he was living his second childhood and he was ready to take it back to the old school one more time just to show these so called gangsters how shit was done. He was itching for Frank to say something else slick. Mox's homeboy or not, he was about get it. He was about to bring the old Wise Earl out of retirement. "Take it the wrong way my ass, *you* said it, muthafucka. You better curb that tongue before I remove it."

"Fellas, easy... easy..." Nate squeezed between the two men. "Let's not even go there wit' it tonight. It's a bunch of beautiful women in here, we got champagne, good music... lets just relax and enjoy ourselves... please."

The men separated and continued to enjoy their night.

Tyrell bumped Frank on the shoulder. "So, I guess that means no?"

GREENWICH WOODS REHABILITATION CENTER
ONE WEEK LATER

After progress while in the hospital, Mox was moved to a rehab center in Greenwich, Connecticut to further his development. The 217 bed facility was set on elegantly landscaped private and secured grounds, and had a wide variety of staff to cover all aspects of the rehabilitation process. Mox was in room 403, which was located on the far west end of the building. His window overlooked a giant lake and hundreds of miles of nature's greenery. He sat quiet in his wheelchair, facing the window, rubbing his beard, staring out at the sunshine of the midday, and trying to figure out a way to get back home. He took a deep breath and inhaled the aroma of the fresh fall season. A tap on the door caused him to turn around and see who was entering his room.

It was one of his doctors. "Mr. Daniels, how are you doing today?" he inquired, closing the door after entering.

"Not too good, doc." Mox was talking regular again, but he was still physically weakened. He barely had enough strength to cross his legs. "How come I can't remember certain things, doc?"

"Things like what?"

"You know, small shit like... my favorite color or favorite food. Shit... sometimes I can't even remember what happened."

The doctor pulled a pen from the front pocket on his shirt and jotted down a few words on his clipboard. "I see... What about your name, birthday... things like that?"

"I remember those."

"Umm hmm..." The doctor flipped the pages on the clipboard and sat in the chair alongside the wall. "Well, Mr. Daniels... I believe you may be suffering from a slight case of either amnesia or dementia."

"Amnesia?"

"Yes, nothing severe, but it will take some re-learning of some of your basic motor skills. Do you have any family members that can bring in old pictures or something?"

Mox looked out at the marvelous landscape. "Nah... no family, it's jus' me."

"Okay, that's not a problem, sir. Tomorrow morning we can get started on your therapy. It's all up to you, Mr. Daniels. If you make the effort, the work will eventually pay off." The doctor closed the clipboard and left the room.

Mox rolled himself to the front of the dresser and gazed at his reflection in the mirror. He placed his left hand over the patch on his eye, took a deep breath and a tear came rolling down the right side of his cheek. The battles had taken a toll on his physical abilities and he felt beneath himself. He felt useless and forgotten, worn out and battered. He didn't understand how he'd been able to take another breath and more than often, he thought about why God chose to keep him here and remove everyone else from his life. The telephone rang and it startled Mox for a second. He wondered who could be calling if no one knew where he was, but then he thought about Uncle Wise and went to pick it up. "Hello?"

The voice on the other end was deep and groggy. "You know this ain't over until every one of you monkeys is in a grave." And the caller hung up.

Mox knew who it was. He squeezed the cordless phone in his hands and then tossed it into the mirror, causing shattered glass to cover the top of the dresser. If the Italians knew where he was, it was only a matter of time before they showed up for a visit; that is, if they weren't already in the building.

33

P riscilla stepped out of the county jail, looked up to the cloudless azure sky and thanked God for giving her another opportunity to do the right thing. The positive attitude she adapted from being in the program and staying at the shelter had been lost the second that police officer put those cuffs on her wrist. The passive, cordial and respective Priscilla was not getting the job done. It was time to make a change.

"You better smile, girl. You outta there now." Jennifer greeted her friend with a big hug and handed her a brown paper bag.

Priscilla ripped the bag open and started counting the bills.

"It's all there, don't even trip... but that sweat suit..." Jennifer frowned.

"I know, I know. Don't even start."

"Girl... hurry up and get in this car so we can go shoppin'."

Priscilla opened the passenger door to the 2009 Nissan 350 z. "This is a nice car, Jennifer. Let me find out you gettin' some paper out here..."

"I damn sure ain't gon' be out here starving."

The two women got into the vehicle and took off for the highway.

"Did you get the info I asked for?" Priscilla questioned, snapping her seat-belt in.

"Yep," Jennifer dipped through the traffic, hit the blinker and turned onto the Sprain Brook parkway. "Now listen... I went through hell gettin' this info, but it was for a good cause, so I'm not complaining. Okay, first... Mox is doing much better, they say he's talkin' and movin' around." Priscilla's face beamed with pleasure when she heard Jennifer mention Mox's recovery. "The only thing is... they moved him to some rehabilitation center, in Greenwich Connecticut."

"*Greenwich?* Why would they send him there?"

"I have no idea, but the address is in the glove compartment."

"What about Brandi?" Priscilla was anxious.

"Okay... the good news is, your mother wasn't able to get custody of her, but she has been placed with a family."

"Dammit!" Priscilla's voice went high. "Oh my God... I can't imagine what my baby is goin' through." Her eyes started to water up. "How am I gonna get her back now? Lord... please... help me."

Jennifer touched Priscilla's shoulder. "Don't worry about it, girl, everything gon' be alright. I got a plan. I know exactly where she is, and we can get her back, but we have to move fast."

"Jennifer, please... I'll do anything to get my baby back in my arms..." A tear rolled down the side of her face. "Anything..."

After a few hours of shopping in the Westchester Mall, Priscilla and Jennifer made their way downstairs to the Cheesecake Factory to eat and discuss the details of the plan.

"Dang, girl, slow down... that food ain't goin' nowhere."

Priscilla looked up with a mouth full of food. "You ever ate a Valhalla food tray?"

"Hell no..."

"Well, me either." She wiped her mouth with the napkin in her lap. "The whole time I was there, I didn't touch those nasty ass trays... all I ate was honey buns, soups and pre-cooked rice."

"I see..." Jennifer laughed. "You put on a few pounds too."

Priscilla rolled her eyes. "Please, don't remind me." She took a sip of the virgin daiquiri in front of her. "So; what's this plan you talking about?"

A waiter came by to collect their empty plates and refill their drinks.

"Okay... look. I found the family that Brandi is staying with. It's some white lady and her husband down in Harrison, she-"

"Is she alright?" Priscilla was apprehensive.

"Yes, she's fine. They got money, so she's well taken care of... trust me."

Priscilla was still worried. "Are you sure? How do you know?"

Jennifer reached into her handbag and grabbed her phone. "Here... look."

It was a picture of Brandi, in a park, playing on the swings.

Priscilla stared at the phone. "This is all my fault." she said, feeling guilty. "If I would'a done better, she wouldn't be in this situation. I can't blame anyone but myself." she sniffled and the agony of separation got the best of her, causing her to break down and cry, like a child who couldn't get what they desired.

Jennifer rubbed her shoulder. "Stop beating yourself up, Priscilla. I told you, I got a plan... we can get her back."

She looked up. "How?"

Jennifer dabbed at the corners of her mouth with a napkin and sipped her water. "Every Saturday afternoon they bring Brandi to the park for an hour, to let her run around. The same park, the same hour... every weekend, and each time it's the same routine. I got it mapped out... look, all we gotta do is be there when they are, and as soon as she takes her eyes off her... we snatch her! What you think?"

As bad as Priscilla wanted to buss out laughing, she didn't. The situation was too serious, but she couldn't help but to find a bit of humor in the matter. "That's it? That's your plan?"

Jennifer attempted to keep a straight face, but Priscilla's smirk made it impossible.

"I'm sayin'... it's a start."

They laughed together.

"A *start?*" Priscilla said. "You had a whole month to think about what the plan was and this is what you came up *with?*"

Jennifer tried to convince her. "I'm telling you... I know it can work."

"I guess it's gonna have to work." she replied, finishing her drink. "It's the only thing I got right now... so, what about the other thing?"

"Oh, he said he wants to meet with you, tomorrow afternoon, in the city."

The next morning, Priscilla rose out of bed as the fulgent sun ascended into the crisp luminous sky. A cool breeze brushed her face and the flute like chirping of a House Sparrow sitting on the sill reminded her of how fortunate she was. Her feet touched the lush two thousand dollar carpet and she got down on her knees, clasped her hands together and bowed her head in prayer. *God, grant me the serenity to accept the things I cannot change; courage to change the things I can; and wisdom to know the difference. Amen.*

The door opened shortly after she finished and Jennifer sashayed into the room, wearing just panties and a bra, holding a tray with a plate of food and a glass of orange juice. Her body was amazing. She had a permanent tanned complexion that gave her a glow, long, dirty blonde hair, a nice handful of breasts and an ass like a Brazilian porn star.

"Good morning, sleeping beauty." she giggled. "I wanted you to wake up to a surprise, but you're already up, so... here you go." she passed the tray to Priscilla and then pulled the curtain on the window open to let more light in.

Priscilla sat at the edge of the Queen sized bed with the tray on her lap, staring down at the food, trying to figure out how Jennifer knew everything she liked. Turkey bacon. French toast. One fried egg, a bowl of diced fruit and fresh squeezed orange juice. "Are you a physic or something?" she joked, picking the fork up.

"Why you say that?"

"Because, everything on this plate is my favorite."

"Really? This is my breakfast every morning." Jennifer picked the remote up, pushed power and the 50 inch screen television mounted to the wall lit up.

Priscilla finished off the bowl of fruit. "Not to be in your business or anything, but how the hell can you afford a place like this?"

Jennifer owned a one bedroom, townhouse style condo on North Main St. in East Hampton, Connecticut. The seven hundred square foot home had cathedral ceilings, a loft bedroom, jetted tub and a separate shower enclosure. At the time she bought it, Jennifer paid $110,000 cash, but with the renovations, it's now worth well over $150,000.

She smiled at herself in the giant mirror attached to the sandal-wood dresser. "Do it the right way..." she seductively licked her lips and then winked her eye when she saw Priscilla was watching. "And you can get anything you desire from a man."

"Eww, nasty."

"Shut up." Jennifer tossed a scarf at Priscilla. "Don't act like you ain't never did something strange for some change."

"Huh... haven't we all."

For Priscilla, it felt good to be able to laugh and enjoy the moment, because for the past few months she had been seeing more gloomy days than bright ones. The effects of her burdens were weighing heavy on her mentally. It was impossible to push aside her problems and act as if nothing was wrong, so she took responsibility for her actions and decided the only way things would change, is if she had a hand in changing them. She got up to bring the dishes back into the kitchen, but didn't get out the door.

"Oh shit, Priscilla...look!" Jennifer turned the volume up on the television.

Haitian authorities say they seized six hundred and sixty pounds of cocaine from a hidden compartment on a private boat, about fifty miles west of the capital city this morning. The three hundred kilograms have a wholesale value of three million dollars and a street value of over ten million. The seizure comes amid increasing pressure to bring an end to the drug smuggling in Haiti, which United States government believes is a main shipping point for Columbian cocaine bound to the states.

"Wow." Jennifer's eyes were glued to the television. "I wouldn't even know what to do with all them drugs."

Priscilla thought different; she knew exactly what she would do with them and she also understood the ins and outs of the coke game. "Somebody's gonna be *really* pissed today."

"I bet they are." Jennifer hit power and went to her closet to find some clothes to throw on. "Forget that, we got a nine o clock appointment at the hair dresser and your meeting is at two."

"Hair dresser?"

"Yep, I'ma have my girl, Vee, at the shop, hook you up. Watch... you gon' love it."

Two hours later, Priscilla stood in front of the full body mirror at the back of the beauty salon in a stupefied gaze, trying to figure out who the person was staring back at her. "Oh-my-God... look at my hair." she reached back and felt the long, silky weave that was sewn into her roots.

Jennifer was probably the most excited. "I told you she was the best! Oohh, she hooked you up!" she examined Priscilla's new hair. "This is really nice. I might have to get mine done like this." She laughed. "How much do I owe you, Vee?"

"Eight hundred."

Jennifer peeled off ten one hundred dollar bills and handed them to Vee. "Enjoy the rest of your week, Vee. I'll be in next week so you can trim my edges."

When they got back into the car, Priscilla was still in shock. "Eight hundred dollars, Jennifer? Damn..."

"It's a lil' pricey, but it's worth it. That Indian hair is the best you can get. Don't worry about it... that was my gift to you; now we gotta hurry up. You only got an hour before your meeting."

Priscilla was so wrapped up in the way her hair looked, that the meeting slipped her mind. "Oh shoot, the meeting... what am I gonna wear?"

"THAT LOOKS HOT ON YOU!" Jennifer complimented as Priscilla fixed the straps on her rose petal colored, convertible Jersey gown.

"One strap or two?" she asked.

"I think you should go with the two." Jennifer answered. "I'll meet you downstairs in the car."

Priscilla gazed at her reflection in the mirror and thought about how far she had come. All the drudgery she had put herself through prepared her for what she was about to encounter. It was like the turning of a page to a new chapter in her life; a clean slate; a fresh start; a brand new beginning. She fixed the straps on her shoulder and went downstairs to meet Jennifer in the car. On the drive to

Manhattan, Priscilla was antsy and impatient, but truly excited about attending her meet up. If everything went as expected, she could end up in a prominent position; a space that she hadn't been accustomed to in a long time.

Jennifer slowed up and pulled to the curb at 190 Sullivan Street. "This is the place." she said, reaching into her purse. She handed Priscilla a phone. "If you need anything, just call me. My number is already programmed."

Priscilla got out the car and walked past the four tables outside and entered the restaurant.

A short, overweight Spanish guy behind the bar greeted her. "Hola, senora. Welcome to Salon de Tapas." A small, candle lit diner located in a well-trodden section of Manhattan, Salon de Tapas was beloved for its prompt service, wide variety of tapas and reasonable pricing. The six small tables with burning candles, along the brick wall were all vacant.

Priscilla took a seat at the last table, about fifteen feet away from the kitchen, and she waited. After thirty-five minutes, she made up her mind to leave. She got up and started to call Jennifer.

"You leaving already?"

Before she took her eyes off the phone, she recognized the voice. It was one she could never forget. That familiar scent she knew too well, tickled her nose and made her smile inside. "It's been a long time, Juan Carlos." She took a step forward and reached out to shake his hand. His appearance hadn't changed. He was still the tall, pretty boy with the curly black hair, gold Cuban link chain, and chipped tooth.

"You look beautiful." He said, removing his $4,000 Brioni dinner jacket.

When he took his seat, he picked up the menu, and the glare from the light above hit one of the flawless diamonds in his pinky ring.

"I see you're still living a lucrative lifestyle."

"Everything you see is not always what it appears to be."

"Here you go with your philosophies."

Juan Carlos looked over the menu while he continued to talk. "You know how this business is, Priscilla. You get respect when you attain a certain level of success, and even then, that respect is short lived. Those who once respected you, now become jealous and envious of you, and depending on the situation... they may even have bad blood towards you. There's always someone that wants your spot. Don't ever forget that." he looked into Priscilla's eyes. "There's no time to get complacent in this business... it's all about your next move."

The waiter approached their table. "Are you ready to order, sir?"

"I'll just have a seltzer water with some fresh lime, please, and the television remote control. Priscilla, are you hungry?"

"No, I'm fine. I do need your help though."

He smiled. "That's funny. I need your help too."

Not long after, the waiter returned and placed the glass of seltzer water and a plate with fresh, sliced lime next to Juan Carlos. "Here's the remote, sir."

"I already know what you need," he said to Priscilla. "I've been in this game long enough. I can see it in your eyes, but in order for you to get what you want, I'm going to need you to take care of something for me." he dug into his pocket and pulled out a picture.

"Who is she?" Priscilla looked at the salt and pepper haired woman.

"La Capitana... she's in charge of the second biggest cocaine distribution ring in the U.S., and by far, the most ruthless bitch on the face of this earth. She was once a business partner of mine, but the stipulations of our venture weren't to her liking, so she decided to play for the other team." Juan Carlos hit a button on the remote, and the television that was mounted to the wall on the other side of the diner came on. He flicked through the channels until he found what he was looking for. "Have you seen this?"

It was the same breaking news story she watched at Jennifer's house.

"I saw it this morning."

"Three hundred birds, Priscilla." He shook his head and then rubbed his face with his hand. "There's no way I can let this go uncontested."

"And where do I come in?"

"I need someone outside of my people for this."

"And so you choose me?"

"I wouldn't ask if I didn't think you were capable of getting it done... besides, Mox owes me." Juan Carlos grinned and winked his eye at Priscilla. "You want something. I want something... if we work together, I'm pretty sure we can come to an agreement that would benefit all parties involved."

Priscilla was in awe of his proposition. "You're asking me to take someone's life, Juan Carlos. I don't know if I'm ready for that..."

"When a general sends his troops into battle, do you think for one second he's not aware of the capabilities of his soldiers?" He picked up a lime and squeezed the juice into his water. "He's absolutely cognizant of their abilities, Priscilla. This is why he is the general... It's all about catching your enemy off guard. No matter how well thought out the plan is, you can never account for the element of surprise."

"Yeah, but what if it doesn't go right... then what?"

I would never lead you into something I thought you were unqualified for, Priscilla. It's only as difficult as you make it. I got everything set up. All you have to do is show up and execute the plan."

"Show up and execute the plan, huh?" Priscilla sat back and a look of hostility came over her face. There was no other option. She had gone every route she could possibly go and time was something that was not on her side. A decision had to be made, and it had to be made quick.

Juan Carlos looked at Priscilla and raised his eyebrow. He didn't even wait for her answer. He just got up, wrote a phone number on a napkin and walked out of the diner.

34

S prinkles of rain descended the dark sky as the churchgoers filed out of the chapel. All the smiling faces were an indication of the good word from Rev. Miguel Diaz, who was the congregation's senior pastor for the last ten years at the Bronx Spanish Evangelical Church.

"Would you like me to sit and wait, La Capitana?"

"No, I'll be just fine. Wait for me in the car."

The brawny, slick haired bodyguard did as he was told and went to wait in the car.

Priscilla, unseen, wearing a black suit skirt, black shoes, and matching gloves, stood across the street, watching the church empty out. If a move was going to be made, the time couldn't have been any better. Her eyes were focused on the target as she remembered the details Juan Carlos explained to her. *La Capitana never leaves the house without armed guards, so the only way to get close to her would be on a Sunday afternoon, at church, while she's making her confession.*

The thought of taking someone's life while they confessed their sins didn't sit right with Priscilla, but it was too late. The call had been made, and the clock was about to expire. In the back of her mind, she knew if she didn't go through with this, Juan Carlos would have *her* killed. It would have nothing to do with their personal relationship; everything thrived off business.

She crept across the dampened street when she saw the target going back into the church. Pellets of rain splashed her face as she moved closer and closer to the entrance; her thoughts racing through her brain like the 450 Motocross.

La Capitana turned the knob on the confession room door, sat down on the small wooden stool, and faced the grated window to confess her sins. She made the sign of a cross with her hand and bowed her head. "In the name of the Father, and of the Son, and of the Holy spirit; my last confession was one month ago. I sit before you to confess my sins of murder, adultery and dishonor. I am sorry for these and all the sins of my past life. Lord Jesus, son of God; have mercy on me, a poor sinner."

The priest spoke. "Give thanks to the Lord, for he is good."

They made the sign of a cross together and then she said. "For his mercy endures forever... Amen."

The Priest got up and left, but when La Capitana reached for the door knob, it was already opening.

Priscilla slithered through the small, cracked door like a cheetah in the jungle after nightfall when hunting its prey. Knife in hand; their eyes locked and she whispered. "You scared?"

The lump in La Capitana's throat stalled her words, but they eventually came out. Her voice was soft, but firm, and her focus was directly on Priscilla. "You should be asking yourself that question. Hurry up and do your job."

Fear was an emotion that had been left out of La Capitana's life as a child. The only thing she had ever been afraid of was dying poor and being buried in a cardboard box.

Priscilla hesitated, and then she lunged at her target. The 5 ½ inch parkerized blade sunk into La Capitana's soft flesh. As Priscilla shoved the knife inside of her, she felt the blade hit a bone. She grabbed the back of her neck and pushed harder, causing the stainless steel dagger to go deeper into her abdomen. A spill of blood crawled out the side of La Capitana's mouth and her body relaxed. Minus the faint beating of Priscilla's heart and the sporadic short breaths La Capitana held onto, the room was silent. Priscilla let her body crumple to the hard wood floor, stepped over her and exited the church unnoticed.

"YOU HAVE TO EAT SOMETHING, Mox, c'mon... it's been two and a half days." Jasmine tried to convince Mox to touch the plate of food in front of him.

"I'm not hungry."

"At least try one of my cookies. I stayed up all night baking these for you."

"I didn't ask you to do that, so don't sit here and try to make me feel guilty about it."

Jasmine was open-mouthed. She had never heard Mox speak in such a fashion. "Sorry for caring... sheesh."

It was the second day in a row Jasmine had come to visit Mox at the rehabilitation center and it was the second day in a row she had been thrown shade.

"Jus' leave me alone right now, Jasmine. I don't feel like being bothered."

"Is *that* what I'm doing, Mox?" Jasmine was outraged. "Bothering you? I've done nothing but help you from the day I walked into that hospital room, and now that you're getting a little better you're feeling yourself. Fuck you, Mox!" Jasmine snatched her purse and jacket off a hanger in the closet and stormed out the room.

"Jasmine... wai—"

The door slammed, and once again, Mox was left alone; solo, just him, and his curious thoughts. The exact thoughts that continued to strain his mental and demolish his self-confidence. Mox's recovery hadn't been advancing as rapidly as he'd expected, and he still hadn't gained the strength to stand on his feet. The determination was still present, yet, his faith was becoming slighter and more displaced.

He rolled himself to the dresser, stuffed his earphones into his ear, and pressed play on his iPodTouch.

The elevator was closing and Jasmine nearly ran into Priscilla and Jennifer trying to catch it before it went back down. "Excuse me, sorry." She apologized, brushing by the two women.

Priscilla recalled the face, but couldn't figure out where she had seen her before. "I know her from somewhere..." she mumbled.

They continued down the long corridor stretch and stopped in front of room 209 and Jennifer said, "I think this is the room."

But Priscilla's mind was someplace else. "I knew I recognized that girl's face. That's the chick from the hospital..."

"Huh, who?" Jennifer had no clue as to what Priscilla was rambling about.

"The bitch that jus' got on the elevator. She was at the hospital when Mox was there."

"At the hospital, so what is she doing here?"

"I don't know, but I'm damn sure gonna find out." She turned the knob and pushed the door open.

Mox had his back turned when Priscilla and Jennifer walked in and didn't realize they were present until he heard the door close.

"Who is that?" He said, turning in his wheelchair.

Priscilla stiffened at the sight of his uncovered eye, a chill shot through her body and the hairs on her arm stood up. For a moment, she was scared, but there was no denying the fact that her love for the man sitting less than ten feet away from her was continuously burning like a wild brush fire. Before a word was said, an avalanche of tears slid down her face, smudging what little bit of make-up she had on.

"I miss you, Mox..." she bent down to give him a hug and he wrapped his arms around her.

"Please... get me outta here." he begged.

Jennifer watched as the two embraced and shared a long awaited moment. She finally got to see the man she had heard so much about, and even with one eye, he was still as handsome as ever.

Priscilla wiped her face and began searching the room for Mox's belongings. "Where's the rest of your stuff, Mox?"

He rolled back to the dresser and picked up his iPod Touch . "Right here."

"That's it?"

"This is all I need. Who is she?"

"That's Jennifer."

Jennifer waved.

"I don't know her."

"She's my friend, Mox... she's helping me get Brandi back."

The minute he heard Brandi's name, it was like everything

paused and life went silent. He looked at Priscilla, blinked and a single teardrop rolled down the side of his face. "I fucked up, Priscilla..."

"Mox, not now, we gotta get you outta here." A river of tears were building in her eye wells, but she managed to hold them back. "Jennifer, help me get him out that chair."

"I can't walk, Priscilla..." he dropped his head in shame.

"Well, you're gonna start today." She draped one of his arms around her neck and Jennifer did the same. "Now, stand up Mox."

He didn't even try. "I can't."

"Mox, don't tell me you can't. Stand up."

He conjured all the strength he could, and tried to stand on his feet, but it wasn't enough.

"I can't fuckin' do it, Priscilla!" Spit flew from his mouth and he let his body fall back into the wheelchair.

Priscilla snatched him by the collar of his t-shirt and got in his face. "Don't fuckin' embarrass me in front of my friend." Tears fell into Mox's lap. "Now, stand up before I push you out this chair and leave you right here on this goddamn floor."

Mox was startled; he heard Priscilla use that tone before, but never with him. His breathing got heavy, he tightened his jaw and he lifted himself out the chair just enough for Priscilla and Jennifer to hold him up.

"I told you. I knew you could do it, Mox."

Priscilla was happy that he hadn't given up, but she was also conscious of the effort, sacrifice and devotion it would take to reconstruct him. They managed to get Mox onto the elevator, downstairs, through the lobby and into Jennifer's car. The forty minute drive was a silent one. Priscilla, with her seat back, gazed lazily out the window at passing traffic, and Mox, leaned over in the backseat, slept most the way back, due to being under the influence of pain medication he was prescribed.

When they made it back to Jennifer's house, she helped Priscilla get Mox inside and then she got back into her car.

"You sure you don't need anything? I probably won't come back until the mornin'... I got some running around to do."

"We're good." Priscilla replied. "Go 'head, take care of your business. We'll be fine."

"Alright... later. Bye, Mox."

Mox was propped up on the brown, leather sofa with agony etched on his face and chagrin in his heart.

Priscilla locked the door and then sat next to him. "Mox," she put her hand underneath his chin and raised his head. "We're gonna get through this, baby. I want you to know that I'm here for you every step of the way, but you gotta help me out. You gotta focus every bit of energy you got into this recovery, and let go of the anger and resentment... that's the only way it's gonna happen."

Mox was aware of the exertion he needed to put forth in order to restore his mind and body; he was just praying that the devil hadn't captured his soul. He reached over, grabbed Priscilla's hand and looked in her eyes. "Only God can bring me through this... it's his call."

The doorbell rang and it broke their concentration.

"Who is it?" Priscilla walked to the door, peeked through the peep hole and then unlocked it when she saw who it was.

"Good afternoon." A short, Spanish guy in a brown suit was holding a box. "I have a package for a Ms. Priscilla Davis."

She checked him out from head to toe. It looked like a UPS suit, but she knew it wasn't. "That's me." she said, reaching for the box.

"Here you go, m'am... have a nice day." He strolled off and got into a big brown truck.

Priscilla ripped a card off the top of the box and read it:

We're even now...

let Mox know I said, get strong.

Enjoy...

Juan Carlos.

She carried the box to the living room and placed it on the coffee table in front of Mox.

"Who was that?"

Priscilla tossed the card into his lap.

"*Even?* What is he talking about? What did you do, Priscilla?"

She cracked the box open and dumped the contents onto the table. It was ten, individually wrapped kilograms of fishscale cocaine. Priscilla smiled and nodded her head. "We back in business, baby..."

35

A chill November breeze snuck through the cracked window of Tyrell's brand new black on black, Camaro SS. He looked around to see where it was coming from, and noticed the passenger side window was slightly open. He tapped Six's chest with the back of his hand. "Yo, Six... Six... wake up, nigga."

"Huh?..." Six wiped some slob from his bottom lip.

"Close my fuckin' window, you letting my heat out."

A tap on the driver's side window made Tyrell jump and reach for the gun under his seat. The person on the outside of the car was saying something, but couldn't be heard because the window was up. He pressed the button and let it roll down. "Goddamn it, old man... you 'bout to get ya' stupid ass shot."

The scraggly old timer had an ashy, ripped up, leather jacket on, old Levi jeans that looked like he'd been painting in them, and a pair of Timberland boots that were two sizes too big. His beard was haggard like he hadn't seen a barbershop in years, and what few teeth he had left in his mouth were rotted and discolored.

"You know I come bearin' information, lil' nigga." He said.

Tyrell tossed the mean ice grill at the old jack. "What the fuck I tell you 'bout that lil' nigga shit, Trash Can..." he pulled the gun up and placed it on his lap.

"Call me by my name and I'll call you by yours."

"Mann... we call you, Trash Can... 'cause you look like you jus' hopped out a muthafuckin' trash can, nigga!" Tyrell and Six keeled over with obnoxious laughter.

"Whenever you ready to cut the muthafuckin' jokes, I got some real shit to spit at cha..." Trash Can went to turn and walk off.

"Aye! Bring yo' ass over hear, nigga." Tyrell couldn't stop laughing. "Nah, for real... c'mere, wassup?" he was nearly wiping tears from his eyes.

Trash Can snatched the half of cigarette that was nestled in the bridge of his ear and lit it. "Fuck the word on the street... I seen it wit' my own eyes." He took a long drag and let the smoke funnel through his nostrils. "Your boy Leon back on the streets."

They sat up in their seats at the same time.

"Fuck you talking about?" Tyrell's smile went flat and everything became serious.

"I ain't talkin' 'bout shit. I jus' told you, I saw the lil' nigga."

Tyrell opened the door and stepped out the car. "When?"

"Five minutes ago, in the Chinese restaurant; over there on Lincoln n' North."

"Lincoln n' North... yo, Six... get in the driver's seat." Tyrell ran to the passenger side, cocked his weapon and threw his hoodie on. "Aye, Trash Can!" he grabbed a knot of one hundred dollar bills out of his pocket and peeled one off. "Here." he handed the bill to the old man. "Go get yo' ass in the shower or something, ya heard. You fuckin' stink."

Trash Can snatched the money out of Tyrell's hand. "Fuck you, lil' nigga. Go handle your business."

Six and Tyrell rode around the block, parked in front of the laundromat across the street, and walked into the Chinese restaurant. Leon was sitting at a table so immersed in his plate of food, that he hadn't even acknowledged Tyrell and Six were there.

"Whaddup, nigga?"

The sound of Tyrell's voice startled Leon and he almost choked on a spoonful of rice. "Oh shit, wassup, Tyrell?" he stood to give him a pound, but was ignored.

Tyrell squeezed into the seat right next to Leon and Six stood there with a mean mug stuck on his face.

"You... when you get out?" he questioned, sensing the fear in Leon's movements.

"Umm... this morning. I was gonna come see you in a second, but I was starving. I had to get something to eat."

Tyrell picked up a piece of Leon's chicken from his tray and bit it. "Is that right? Lemme ask you a question... and before you answer." He pulled the skin off with his teeth and tossed the bone back into the tray. "Please don't lie to me. How did you make bail?"

"Oh," Leon's nerves were jumping through his skin. He was listening to every word Tyrell was saying, but his attention was on Six. "Umm... my grandmother put up her crib for me."

Tyrell looked at Six and then back to Leon. "Your grandmother? Leon, you fucking lyin' I known you all my life and I know your whole family. Your grandmother died five years ago."

Leon tensed up. "I'm not lyin', Rell. Not my mother's mom, my father's mother. She lives in North Carolina."

"I don't believe you, Leon." Tyrell stood up. "I hope you ain't go out like a sucka."

"Huh? Man, Tyrell... I ain't got no reason to lie to you." Leon felt the tension.

Six butted in. "Everybody else doing it."

"I'm not everybody else..." he responded. "Look, Tyrell, we been friends since kindergarten... I know you don't think I told on you?"

"Did you?"

"Hell no!" Leon started breathing harder. "I would never do no shit like that."

Tyrell smirked. "Come take a ride wit' me."

"C'mon, Rell... It ain't even gotta be like this." Leon knew what 'Take a ride' meant.

"Leon," Tyrell shook his head. "Either you come willingly or by force... it don't matter to me."

Leon's expression was cheerless, he sensed the danger lurking. "Where we going?"

"Don't worry about it... I wanna show you something." The three men walked to the car. "Get in the front, Leon." Six jumped in the backseat, Tyrell hit play on the radio and 2Pac's *Last Muthafucka Breathin* came through the speakers. They rode on the highway for twenty minutes until Tyrell got off the exit and pulled over at an abandoned building on East 147th street, in the Bronx. Leon swallowed the lump in his throat and surveyed the area as they pulled into a vacant lot that housed a ramshackle building. The volume on the radio went low and the only thing you could hear is the sound of the gravel under the slow rolling tires. Tyrell came to a complete stop and looked at Leon. He was scared to death sitting in the passenger seat.

"Get out."

Leon took a deep breath and his right hand started twitching. "C'mon, Tyrell... please man..."

Six slapped him on the back of his head. "Shut yo' punk ass up and get the fuck out the car."

The three of them walked one hundred yards to the entrance of the abandoned building. It was torn down, ragged, and in need of some serious renovations.

"This shit crazy, right." Tyrell tapped Leon's arm. "C'mon, let's go inside." The inside of the building was worse off than the outside; cracked and shattered walls, a battered staircase, and a stench that could make your stomach turn and your eyes water. Tyrell fished a rolled blunt from his pocket and put fire to it. "Remember when we was kids, Leon... and you use to be rappin' all the time n' shit." he blew smoke into the air. "You still be rappin'?"

"Yeah."

"That's good. Check this out. In a few months, I'ma be investin' some money into this place. I'm thinking 'bout buildin' a studio and startin' a label."

Leon smiled. "For real?"

"Word, and I want you to be my first artist."

"Whew..." Leon sighed and looked up to God to thank him. "I thought you was bringing me out here for something else."

"Something else?" Tyrell chuckled. "This nigga's buggin', Six. What... you thought I was bringin' you down here to kill you or something, nigga'?

Leon tried to laugh it off, but his heart was beating so fast he was about to have an attack and kill his self. "Nah," he lied. "I'm jus' sayin'... we all the way down here; I didn't know what the fuck was goin' on." He laughed, but when he realized he was the only one, he stopped.

Tyrell shook his head. "You a scary ass nigga, Leon. Man, I would never do no shit like that to you, here." he passed him the blunt. "You my nigga, right?"

Leon nodded his as he inhaled the potent weed smoke.

"Cool... yo," Tyrell started tapping his foot. "I gotta take a piss... I'll be right back." he trotted over to a dark corner.

"You rap too?" He asked Six and turned around to the barrel of a gun pointed at his head.

Tyrell yelled from a distance. "Six, hurry up!"

Leon was frozen stiff, his eyes halfway out the sockets. "Please, don—" The blast blew a piece of Leon's face off and he fell to the gravel.

Tyrell jogged back over. "Fuck is you waitin' for, shoot that nigga again."

Six complied.

"Took you long enough, nigga." Tyrell grabbed the gun from Six. "Gimmie my shit.

They got back into the car and drove away.

"LOOK," Jennifer pointed to a white and grey house at the corner of Cliff Avenue and 2nd Street. That's the house right there." she said as they cruised by.

"Go around again. I didn't see it." Priscilla lied.

"Girl, we can't be ridin' around in Pelham like this. These cops don't play."

"Alright, just one more time... please."

Jennifer circled the block a second time and Priscilla couldn't believe her eyes.

The front door of the house came open and Brandi stepped out, followed by a middle aged white woman. *"Button your jacket Brandi, it's cold out."*

Priscilla heard the woman's voice and stared at Brandi's angelic face. Jennifer was going 18 miles per hour, but it seemed like she was doing 5. Priscilla wanted so bad to jump out of the car and wrap her precious child in her arms, but she couldn't; because she would delete any chances she had of getting her back.

"Look at my baby..." is all she could say as they floated by. She sniffled and did her best not to cry. "We gotta do something, Jennifer. I can't go another day without my baby."

"What are we gonna do? It's too cold for them to be in the park." Jennifer replied.

Priscilla's mind was working in overdrive. "I got a plan..." she said. "I'm gonna get my baby back, whether they like it or not... she's mine."

TWO HOURS LATER

"Where the hell you get these from?" Jennifer questioned, looking at herself in the mirror.

Priscilla was standing right next to her. "A friend lemme borrow them, crazy right?"

"Crazy ain't the word... these look just like UPS uniforms."

When Priscilla realized snatching Brandi from a public park would be too risky, she thought about the day Juan Carlos sent her the package and the disguise one of his men used. Once she got in contact with him, he wasted no time sending over two uniforms and a decoy truck to set the plan in motion.

"Hol' up... lemme practice." She pretended to knock on a door. "*Knock! Knock!*.. that's me knocking on the door, right? Okay, so when they answer, I'ma be like... how you doin', m'am. I have a delivery for you today." Jennifer broke down laughing at herself.

"Wait. Wait..." Priscilla was laughing along with her. "If you do that, we definitely going to jail. But for real, c'mon, let's get this over with because I been separated from my baby for too long."

Jennifer slowed up and pulled the big brown truck to the curb at 207 Cliff Avenue. "You sure this gon' work?" the nervousness was settling in.

"Just do exactly what I told you and everything is gonna be fine."

The two women exited the truck and Jennifer went to the front door as planned, while Priscilla tip toed around to the back of the house, undetected.

After three knocks, she could hear someone coming to answer the door. "Who is it?" the woman asked.

"Umm... Umm... Delivery, m'am! UPS!" she shouted.

The door started to come open.

Priscilla pulled a lock-pick out of her pocket, slid it into the key hole and jiggled it until the door popped open. She moved cautiously through the dark kitchen, past the dining room and into the living quarters, very careful of knocking something over. The television was on, but nobody was downstairs to watch it. Priscilla heard Jennifer holding a conversation with the middle aged white woman.

"So, you sure you didn't order this, because this is your address, right?" Jennifer backed up and glimpsed at the number on the front of the house. "Yep, two oh seven."

"Yes, that's my address, but I didn't order that."

Jennifer was stalling the best she could, wishing Priscilla would hurry up. "Well, m'am... I don't know what to tell ya'. If I was you, I would just take it. Hey, they're the ones who sent it to the wrong address."

Priscilla eased up the staircase and went to check the first room to the right of her. She turned the knob and pushed the door open just enough to see if anyone was in it. When she saw it was empty, she moved to the next few rooms that were about ten feet down the hallway. The next two produced nothing, but it looked like somebody was in the bed of the fourth room, so Priscilla sneakily entered. She tugged on the cover and the occupant of the bed rolled over. It was Brandi. Priscilla snatched the cover off when she saw it was her and tapped her leg. "Brandi... Brandi, wake up, it's mommy."

Brandi adjusted her eyes to the faint light, looked into her mother eyes and smiled. "Mommy, I miss you."

Priscilla picked her up from the bed and gave her the warmest, fondest hug she could give. She breathed deep and thanked God for putting her child back into her arms.

"Mommy missed you too, baby..." Her tears fell like drops of rain in a severe thunderstorm.

Brandi's excitement turned to fear. "I don't like it here, mommy..."

"Okay, baby... mommy's taking you home." Holding Brandi in her clutches as if her life depended on it, Priscilla quietly dipped back through the hallway and headed for the stairs. A toilet flushed and a door opening caused Priscilla to stop in her tracks.

"*Rose, is that you?*" A male shouted.

Priscilla heard footsteps and took off down the staircase, darted through the living room and escaped out the back door.

Jennifer kept peeking past the woman's shoulder trying to see if everything was alright and she caught a glimpse of Priscilla rushing through the back of the house. She wrapped her conversation up instantly. "Well, if you don't want it, fuck it... I'll take it. Have a great night. Bye!"

36

Christmas of 2011 came quicker than a virgin in his first piece of pussy. It was the same day, one year ago that Mox was reunited with Priscilla and discovered he had a daughter named Brandi, only to have Priscilla disappear like a crack head in debt to a dope boy. Since then, everything had taken a turn for the worse and Mox was on the bad end of a long stick, but the complications he endured within the last 365 days had brought him to where he was today; still breathing, a man with dignity, morals and a heart of stone. Determined, dedicated and disciplined, Mox was again ready to take to the streets, only this time, he didn't plan on losing.

Once Priscilla rescued him from the rehab center, Mox's recovery became much smoother. Of course, there were times when he really wanted to quit, but then that sweet, heavenly smile that Brandi wore pushed all thoughts of giving up out the window. Reconditioning himself was far from an easy task and without the help of Priscilla and Jennifer, Mox may not have made it. The days when his body completely shut down and he couldn't move, Priscilla was there; bathing him, feeding him and making sure he took his prescribed medicines.

At times, it got so bad that Mox would unconsciously go to the bathroom on himself and Priscilla wouldn't question cleaning him up. She was there, step for step while he strengthened his body and began to walk and exercise. She read books to him every night; books like, *The 48 Laws of Power*, *The Art of War*, *The Prince* and many more. Not only did she assist in his physical reconstruction, but also his mental reformation. She was building Mox up; building him up to be the man that God had destined him to be; a leader; a doer and not just another nigga with power. A wise man, a strong man; a family man.

With the return of Brandi, Mox and Priscilla's bond grew daily because they were able to interact with each other frequently. It was the first time in Brandi's life that her mother and father were in the same household and it was beginning to feel like a real family.

Mox turned the water off and stepped out the shower. He eyed himself in the foggy mirror and smiled. His weight was up and his daily workouts were showing major results. He snatched a towel off the rack, wrapped it around his lower body and went to leave out the bathroom when a knock on the door startled him; and then it came open.

"Oh shoot. Excuse me..." Jennifer burst in the door. Her eyes were stuck on Mox's glistening chiseled pecks. "Umm, nice chest." She grinned and slammed the door shut.

Even though Jennifer was kind enough to let the trio crash at her house, Mox wasn't too keen on making a new friend. It was something about Jennifer that he couldn't put his finger on, but in due time, he would find out. He walked out the bathroom and into the room that he and Priscilla were occupying. "I don't like your friend, Jennifer." He said.

Priscilla got up from the bed and put her arms around his neck. "Mox, you don't like anybody". She kissed him on his cheek. "How could you not like her, she's helped us out so much."

"At what cost, Priscilla?"

"Mox, don't be like that. Brandi enjoys her company."

"Keep that bitch away from my daughter. You hear me?" When she didn't respond, he said it louder. "Do you hear me?"

"Yes, Mox... damn, bite my head off."

"I'm not playin', Priscilla. I don't want her around my daughter."

"That's gonna be kinda hard being that were staying in *her* house, Mox."

A bang at the door startled them and Jennifer walked in the room like she had seen a ghost. "Oh my fuckin' God! Look at this shit." she picked the remote up, hit power and turned to the local news. They almost missed it.

Once again, Priscilla Davis is wanted for questioning regarding the kidnapping of her seven year old daughter, Brandi Davis, who was in the custody of her foster parents at the time of the abduction. Any information or tips on the whereabouts of Ms. Davis, please call 555-CRIME-STOPPERS.

Mox just shook his head. "*Kidnapping?* We gotta get outta here."

"Where are we gonna go, Mox?" Priscilla was still in awe of seeing her mug shot plastered on the television screen.

"I don't know, but we gotta make a move. Where's Brandi?"

"She's downstairs." Jennifer replied. "Hey guys, my friend has this place upstate. It's vacant, it's paid for and there ain't no neighbors in site for two miles. Y'all can crash there if you want."

Priscilla looked at Mox. "What you think?"

He side eyed her.

"Where is it, Jennifer?"

"About three hours north, in the Catskills."

Mox turned his lip. "In the mountains? Oh, hell no... I ain't going back up in them mountains. You must be crazy."

"Mox," Prsicilla tried to convince him. "We don't have many options."

"There's always another option." He said. "I want y'all to stay in the house. I gotta go see somebody. Priscilla, let me get your keys."

"Mox, you shouldn't be driving."

"I'm fine, trust me..."

She tossed her car keys and he walked out the door.

For the first time in four and a half months, Mox was about to step foot onto the same streets that almost ended his life. The same streets that he showed so much love to, but in the end, there was never any reciprocation; the same streets that claimed the lives of his most cherished loved ones, leaving him to feel vanquished and uncertain of his own future; these same streets he called home; that he'd been absent from for days on end, but now, he was ready; he was prepared, willing, determined and overly eager to make his reappearance a grandiose one, and that's exactly what he was going to do.

Priscilla didn't want him to go, but she knew he wouldn't listen. "Be careful, Mox." was all she could tell him.

Mox got behind the wheel of Priscilla's black Audi A8 and adjusted his seating. It felt like forever since he had driven a car, but as soon as he hit the ignition, it was like he hadn't lost a day. He admired the cars exquisite detailing and the plushness of the fine, autumn colored, leather seats; it was like sitting in the cock pit of a G5 Jet. As he navigated the streets in route to his destination, Mox repeatedly glanced in the rear-view mirror, catching sight of the patch that covered his eye. He was trying to get used to it, but with each brief look, his heart grew heavy and cold.

When he reached his destination, he valet parked the car and then walked into the apartment building on a surprise visit.

"Who is it, goddamn it!" Earl shouted when he heard someone knocking on the door.

"It's me, Unc... open up."

Earl caught wind of the voice and smiled big. "I know that ain't who I think it is..." he unlocked the door and could have sworn he was dreaming. "Nephew!" he grabbed Mox's shoulders and brought him in close to hug him. "Man... you don't know how much I missed yo' ass, boy."

"I missed you too, Unc."

"Yeah, man... c'mon in here."

Mox looked around at the stylish, yet modern set up Wise Earl had. "This is nice, Unc. I'm proud of you."

"Thanks, man... glad you like it. Sheeiit... goddamn rent two thousand dollars a month. If you ask me, they need to have a few more amenities in this muthafucka." he chuckled.

"I see you on your Don Juan Chino shit, huh?"

Earl smirked, rubbed his beard and then fixed the belt on his silk robe. "A lil' sumptin' sumptin'... Have a seat. I wanna introduce you to somebody." He swaggered off to the back room.

Mox took a seat on the leather sectional that was in the middle of the living room. He surveyed the wall hangings and one picture in particular caught his attention. He quickly hopped up and went to give it a closer look.

Earl appeared from the back room. "Nephew, meet Baby G... my fiancé."

When he turned around, he was shocked.

Baby G wasn't a baby in any way, shape, form or fashion. She was 5 feet 2 inches, dark chocolate skin, long black hair and cake that could feed a party of a hundred.

"Hi, Mox." She said. Her voice was soft and prissy.

"Wassup." He couldn't help but to stare. "I see you got you a young one, huh Unc?"

Earl poured himself a shot of Cognac from his mini bar. He sniffed the yak and swirled it in his glass. "Yeah, she may be young, but goddamnit she ain't dumb... ain't that right, baby."

Mox took his seat back on the couch. "So, wassup Unc. What the streets lookin' like?"

"You know how these streets is, Mox." Earl sat in his leather recliner chair directly across from his nephew and lit a cigarette. "These young niggas fuckin' up the game. They out here shootin' everything movin'."

"Word... it's like that, huh? I got a plan though, Unc... the perfect plan."

"You know as well as I know, ain't no such thing as the perfect plan. You gotta get what yours and get the hell out. It's that simple." Earl reached under the recliner and pulled out a Gucci messenger bag. He tossed it to Mox.

"What's this?"

"A lil' token of my appreciation for all the love you showed me through the years." He blew smoke into the air.

Mox unzipped the bag and pulled out a black jewelry box. He opened it.

"Ohhh... this is nice." He eyed the white gold and diamond pinky ring. "This for me, Unc?"

"Yeah. There's something else in there too."

He put his hand back into the bag and came out with a stack of one hundred dollar bills. "This what I'm talking about." he held the stack of bills in front of him. "This shit right here rules the world.

They say it ain't everything, but I've come to learn that you can't do anything without it."

"You right about that, nephew. So, what you gonna do? I see they got Priscilla's face all over the news. How's the baby girl?"

"I gotta get a spot so she can lay low. I need to make some moves, Unc. I don't trust these niggas no more... I need your help."

"You gon' find, Priest?"

Mox stuffed the cash back into the bag. "You know I am... but first, I wanna find that nigga, Cleo."

37

SUMTER, SOUTH CAROLINA

"It's dark as fuck out here, Chris." Cleo looked to the passenger seat and Chris' head was tilted against the window. He was snoring like a bear. "Yo, Chris." he tapped his leg. "Chris, wake up. We here." Cleo made a right into the driveway of 1648 Radical Road and put the car into park. The house was a single story flat, built on three acres of land and it was right next to the woods. He sat in the pitch blackness, debating whether he should go in or not. The pit of his stomach was rumbling and his palms were building up with sweat by the seconds.

What if she doesn't even live here anymore? he thought.

"You goin' in?"

He jumped when he heard Chris' voice. "Don't scare me like that." Cleo turned the car off. "Yeah, wait here while I go see wassup. And get in the driver's seat. It's your turn."

Cleo got out the car, fixed the gun on his waist and walked down the driveway to the front of the house. He could barely see in front of him, and he nearly tripped, climbing the four steps leading to the front door. The sounds at night in the country were much different than sounds after dark in the city. Cleo wasn't excited about being in town for too long. He knocked on the door loud enough for someone to hear it, but there was no answer, so he knocked a second time, and again, there was no answer. He went to leave and a latch opened on the door.

It was a woman's voice. "Who you come here to see?"

Cleo spun on his heels and looked at the woman wearing a night gown, standing in her doorway. She looked exactly like the pictures, beautiful. For a second, Cleo got lost in her loveliness. He couldn't believe how much he resembled her. A thought ran across his mind and he wanted to become a kid again, so he could leap into her arms, give her a great big hug and tell her he loved her, but in actuality; his heart held a massive amount of hate towards her.

"It's me, ma... your son." Cleo said.

The woman pushed the screen door open and stepped onto the porch to get a better look at this man claiming to be her son.

"I ain't got no son. You at the wrong house, now get off my porch."

Cleo knew she was lying. She looked exactly like the woman in the picture he had in his hand. "So, your name isn't, Vivian?"

"No, my name ain't, Vivian... now, I ain't gon' tell you again."

Cleo held up the picture. "This ain't you?"

She squinted her eyes to get a better look at the picture and the way she reacted told the truth. "Where'd you get that?"

"Sybil gave it me."

Silence settled in.

"I'm sorry, Cleo..." she finally admitted.

He screwed his face. "Yeah, you are sorry, a sorry excuse for woman."

"Cleo don—"

"Don't, Cleo me... How the hell you know my name anyway?"

Vivian fixed her gown and sat in the wicker chair that was on the porch. "Sybil and I kept in contact until you were three years old. She would send me pictures every Christmas. Listen, Cleo... I know you're upset and you have every right to be, but we're here now and we can start over."

"Start over?" Cleo laughed. "Lady, you musta bumped yo' goddamn head. You abandoned me... left me wit' one of your friends and never came back to check on me... not even once." his eyes started to get glossy and his lip quivered. "You wanna start over? We never started anything to begin with." The tears slid down his face. "The day I found that letter was the worst day of my life, and from that day on, I capsuled so much anger, that after a while, I exploded." He mimicked an explosion with his hands. "People say I'm losing my mind..." Cleo's grin turned sinister. "More and more, I'm starting to agree with them..."

"Well, if you don't want to start over, why are you here?"

"I'm here for closure..." Cleo turned his back on her and walked away.

"Cleo, come back..." She called out, but he kept walking.

When he got back into the car he laid his head on the headrest and let his eyes close.

"You alright?" Chris started the car.

Cleo opened his eyes, sat up and looked at Chris. "Nah... hol' up." he pushed the door open, walked back to the house and knocked on the door.

"Cleo, is that you?"

"Yeah."

When the door opened, Cleo lifted his gun and pointed it at her face. She opened her mouth, but nothing came out.

He gripped the weapon, keeping a steady aim. "You're the reason I'm not able to love. You fucked my life up." He closed his eyes and squeezed the trigger. Three shots.

38

Mox sat on the couch and waited for Frank to give him a reasonable answer. "I'm waiting, Frank."

"Mox, I told you, I was busy."

"Busy? You was too busy to come see me in the hospital, that's what you telling me?"

"I got a business to run."

"Fuck your business, Frank!" Mox was furious. "I was dying in that muthafucka and you niggas was sitting back countin' money!"

Nate tried to reason. "It wasn't like that, Mox."

"Well, what was it then, tell me... because from what I see ain't too much work been getting done. Where the fuck is Cleo?"

"Mox, we been looking for him..." Frank explained. "Even put the young kid, Tyrell on him... nothing."

Mox paced the rug in Frank's living room. "I expected more from y'all. We supposed to be a union, a team. What happened to that?"

"Nothing happened, Mox. We still are a union." Frank replied.

Mox picked his leather jacket up, put it on, and opened the door. "Are we?"

The feelings Mox had toward his brothers were bittersweet. He was unsettled and disturbed at the fact the he'd been hospitalized for months and they hadn't taken the time to see if he was okay. He felt like when things took a turn for the worse, the only people by his side were Priscilla and Uncle Earl, and those were the people he least expected. There was plenty of unfinished business to be handled, but Mox was no longer relying on anyone other than himself to take care of it. He would handle things on his own from here on out. He jumped in the Audi, hit the ignition and stepped on the gas.

———

LIGHT SNOW FLURRIES fell from sky and the brisk February winds tugged at Tyrell and Six's face, as they stood in front of the building. "You fucked shorty last night?" Tyrell was being nosy.

"You know I did." Six laughed. "Her and her friend."

"Yeah right. You lying."

"Scouts honor."

Tyrell didn't believe him. "Man, fuck a scouts honor... put that shit on yo' momma, so I know it's real." He didn't realize what he said until seconds later. "Ohh shit... my bad. I ain't mean nothin' behind that."

"It is what it is, Rell... she gone now, ain't shit I can do about it." Six passed Tyrell half of a cigarette.

"You a strong ass nigga, B. Even though me and my moms don't get along, I think I might fuckin' bugg out if I was to lose her."

"I feel you... Yo, who this nigga?"

A man in a black flight jacket approached them. "Excuse me, Tyrell?"

"Yeah, wassup?" Tyrell had his hand on his gun.

"I'm Leon's father, Mr. Smalls..."

He eased his hand off the weapon. "Oh yeah, Mr. Smalls, I remember you."

"I've been looking for you to ask you if you've seen Leon since he came home?"

"He's home?" Tyrell played the dummy role.

"Yeah, my mother put up her house for him to get out. He has court in the morning and no one has seen him."

Tyrell and Six looked at each other.

"Nah, I ain't seen him around here. If I do, I'll let him know you're looking for him."

"Thank you. I appreciate it." Mr. Smalls stepped off.

Six turned his head to Tyrell. "You fucked up…"

39

Mox let the hot water run on his back while he pondered his next move. Uncle Wise found out Priest had been released from prison and was back to his old ways, so it wouldn't be too hard to catch up to him. He also discovered Cleo was hiding in the south, trying to blend in with the country folk.

Mox envisioned the day he would finally get the chance to see his father eye to eye and he could feel his hands wrapping around his throat, choking the life out of him. The memories hadn't gone anywhere and Mox's hate towards his father only grew stronger. He pulled the shower curtain back when he heard the bathroom door open. "Who is that?"

Priscilla walked in, dropped her towel and stepped into the shower with him. She wrapped her arms around his neck and stuffed her tongue in his mouth. Her saliva was warm, savory and sweet like honey.

Mox reached down and slid his middle finger into her saturated kitten and tickled her clitoris with his thumb.

"Ohh, Mox, I'm 'bout to cum..." She rotated her hips on his finger until her cream dripped down the side of his hand.

Mox pulled his finger out and licked the juices. Priscilla reached down and brushed his manhood until it was solid and then guided him into her wetness. The hot water beating on their bodies was soothing and sensual. Mox pinned her back against the tile and submerged himself deep within in her love. He stroked her kitty slow, long, and hard.

"Yes, Mox... ohhh..." She felt his body stiffen and his muscles jumped.

"I'm cumin, baby..."

Priscilla compressed her vaginal walls and pulled the cum out of Mox. "Oh sheeiiit!" He grabbed her by the waist and let it all go inside of her. When they finished, they washed each other and went to get in the bed.

Priscilla's head was on Mox's chest. "Do you love me, Mox?"

He smiled. "Of course I do. Why would you ask that?"

"Because..." She was afraid to say it.

"Because what?"

Priscilla didn't want to start an argument, and if she said something, that's exactly what would happen. But this particular issue had been on her mind for a few days and she wanted answers. "Who is, Jasmine?"

Mox was surprised to hear her name. "That's the nurse that was looking after me when I was in the hospital."

"Why do you have her number?"

Why you going through my shit?"

Priscilla was getting upset. "Mox, I asked you a question."

Mox knew the question she really wanted to ask, and if so, he was prepared to lie.

"So, you're not gonna answer me?"

"What you want me to tell you, Priscilla?"

She sat up against the headboard. "I want you to tell me the truth, Mox. Are you fucking her?"

Mox shook his head. "Nah." he lied. Since his return home, he had been to see Jasmine twice.

"You're lying, Mox."

"You asked me a question, I told you the answer and now I'm lying?" He pushed the covers off and got out the bed. "You know... it's hurts me to think that you don't believe me."

"Well, you know what hurts even more, Mox?... watching the person you love, fall in love with someone else and there's nothing you can do about it. That shit hurts." Priscilla's eyes started to water. "I spoke to her Mox, she told me everything."

"I don't know what you talking about."

"She told me how she took care of you and how y'all got together when you came home. All this shit about you wanting to be with her and you wanna get away from all this bullshit in your life... is that what I am to you, Mox... bullshit?"

"Priscilla..."

"I've done everything for you, Mox. I showed you how to play this game. I was there for you when you were locked up, when you got shot and through the recovery, and in return you give me your ass to kiss."

"Priscilla..."

"No, fuck you, Mox." She pulled the covers over her head and went to sleep.

PRIEST CHECKED HIS WATCH. "It's almost that time boys. Y'all ready?" he reached into the bag he was carrying and pulled out four masks.

"What the hell are those, Priest?"

"We going with something different this time, fellas. No more movie stars... we mobsters today."

Two weeks ago, Priest had been released from state prison and he was already about to pull his third bank heist. He and his three cronies were stashed in a basement, about half a block away from the HSBC bank on Tarrytown Road in White Plains. If everything went as planned, Priest would come off with at least two million in cash.

"Here, take this, Slick." He passed him the John Gotti mask.

Slick said, "Okay... I get to be Gotti for the day."

"Here, Mel." Priest tossed Mel the Vinny the Chin mask.

"This is that, Vinny the Chin muhfucka, right?"

Priest answered. "Yeah, that's him."

"Yo, Que... this you." He handed Que the Sammy the Bull mask.

Que couldn't figure out who it was. "Who the fuck is this?"

Mel took it out of his hand, looked at it and started laughing.

"That's the rat... Sammy the Bull!" he laughed louder. "You gotta be the rat!"

"Nah, fuck that, Priest... why I gotta wear the rat joint?"

Mel couldn't stop laughing.

"Cool out, Mel. Que, it don't matter what mask you get, just put the shit on."

Que was upset. "Man... I'm not wearing that, fuck that."

Priest got in Que's face. "Put the fucking mask on."

Que saw how serious he was, and complied. Plus, Priest was a hundred pounds heavier, so a fight was out of the question.

"Lemme see your gun, Que."

Que passed Priest his nine millimeter.

"Now, see... you look good as Sammy the rat." Priest cocked the gun and emptied the clip into his chest. "Anybody else feel like talking to the police? Alright then... proceed."

40

Since their argument, Mox had been holding the couch down for the last few days, in Jennifer's living room. She didn't mind; her home was their home until they figured out where they wanted to live. During the day, Jennifer did a lot of running around so she was rarely there, but recently she claimed to be on vacation from work and decided to lounge out at the crib.

"Wassup, Mox?" she tried to strike up a conversation.

Mox sat back on the couch, flicking through cable channels. "I'm chillin', wassup wit' you?"

"Nothing much." Jennifer sat down next to him on the couch. "Can I see your eye?"

Mox ignored her.

"Look, I know you don't like me, but I think if you get to know me, you'll think different." She tried to rub his leg, but he pushed her hand away.

"You buggin'."

"Am I? I know you and Priscilla are goin' through y'all shit. I'm sayin'... we can keep this between us."

"Keep what between us?"

"Whatever we do. If you don't tell, I won't tell."

"You ain't shit. I knew you was a snake the day I met you."

Jennifer stuck out her tongue and wiggled it like a snake.

"I know you wanna fuck me, Mox. I see the way you undress me with your eyes." She stood up, pulled her sweatshirt off, and straddled Mox.

"Jennifer, get off me before Brandi wakes up and comes down here." He tried to push her off, but she wouldn't budge. His phone rang. He looked at it; It was Uncle Earl. The front door opened and Priscilla walked in.

The first things she saw were Jennifer's C-cups bouncing and the back of Mox's head.

"What the fuck!" She dropped the bag of groceries in her hand.

Mox turned his head, saw it was Priscilla, and pushed Jennifer off his lap. His phone kept ringing.

Jennifer didn't bother covering up. "Wassup, Priscilla?"

Mox picked his phone up. "Hello?"

Uncle Earl was on the other end. "The white bitch is poison! She's a Telesco!"

"What?" he dropped the phone and looked at Jennifer.

Priscilla's tears were falling like Alicia Key's hit single. She snatched the gun from the small of her back. "I'm not gonna let you hurt me no more." she aimed it at Mox.

Mox grabbed the pistol from his waistline and pointed it at Jennifer. "This bitch is setting us up, Priscilla!"

Priscilla's hands were trembling as she steadied the barrel to Mox head. "No more lies, Mox."

"Priscilla, put the gun down. Do you even know who this bitch is?"

Mox knew he recognized Jennifer from somewhere, she was Mikey T's little sister. He recalled seeing her in a home portrait years back, when they played ball together.

"I don't care, Mox... it doesn't matter anymore. Nothing matters. I did all I can do." She moved in closer.

Mox had his gun at Jennifer's head and Priscilla had her gun to Mox's head.

Jennifer joked. "Look at this, the perfect love triangle."

"Shut the fuck up!" Mox screamed. "Where's your ID?" he picked her bag up and dumped it on the carpet. Her ID card landed by Priscilla's foot.

"Pick it up, Priscilla... tell me what it says."

Jennifer was trying to figure out a way to make a move. "He's lying, Priscilla. He's just tryin' to cover up the fact that we've been fuckin' since he came here."

"Don't believe her, Priscilla. What does the card say?" Mox's grip on the gun was getting tighter.

Prisiclla picked the ID card up and read it, slow. "Jenn-i-fer Tel-es-co..." She dropped the card.

"Daddy!"

"Mox!"

A shot went off...

41

When the shot rang out, Mox's instinct was to lunge for Brandi. Again, she screamed, "Daddy!" and raced down the steps.

"Brandi, get down!"

The bullet struck Jennifer in the middle of her forehead—she was stretched across the living room floor—blood, seeping from the small dimple in her skull. Priscilla's face was flushed with gloom as she clasped the handle of the murder weapon. Her soaking eyes dropped to the corpse; one deep breath, then another.

"Priscilla, let's go!" Mox yelled. He held Brandi in his arms at the front door.

Priscilla looked up. The fear she saw in Brandi's eyes was heart wrenching. Her only seed—a child, subject to the jagged realities of a world she never asked to be birthed into. A beautiful baby girl, who was unconscious to life's rights and wrongs, oblivious to decision making, but included in every decision made. This wasn't the life for a child. This wasn't life for anyone. She gripped the pistol tighter and the tears came down faster. A sour, dreaded feeling bubbled at the base of her stomach. Priscilla murmured. "Do you really love me, Mox?" Silence lingered in the gunpowder-filled air, and her eyes were locked on Mox's face. "Do you love your daughter?" Her arm was moving upward, and the gun was still in her hand.

"Priscilla, put the gun down and let's go."

The small droplets continued to cascade down her cheeks. "I gave you everything, Mox." She inched her pointer finger around the trigger. "What's left to give?" Her voice was low and barely audible.

Mox stood in silence. His focus was keyed on Priscilla's trigger finger. Quickly, he moved to her eyes. They were riddled with agony and defeat, stress and despair. He saw in them the beautiful young lady he met years back. She was still there—just fighting to be released; struggling for a chance to be loved.

"Don't do this, Priscilla. You know I love you. I've never in my life loved a woman the way I love you. Look..." He took a step towards her, Brandi clutched in the fold of his arms. "Look at our daughter."

"Stop lying to me, Mox!" Her voice gained volume. She was less than ten feet away with the gun pointed at his head.

Mox glanced down at Jennifer spread across the floor. The look on her face was sickening. He raised his head, and with his good eye, he peered down the barrel of the loaded handgun. "In about five minutes," he whispered. "This whole spot gon' be surrounded with police, and ain't no way I'm letting them muthafuckas take me back to that hell... so, either you shoot me right now, or put that fuckin' gun down and bring yo' ass on."

Minutes later...

"Brandi, make sure you have your seat-belt on." Priscilla rushed to start the car. She jammed the key into the ignition. "Where we going?" she turned to Mox.

For the first time in his life, Mox didn't have a plan. He hadn't had time to think this one through. "I don't know, but we gotta get the fuck outta here. Now."

Priscilla adjusted the rear-view and put the car in gear. She took one more glance at Mox, smiled, and then mashed on the gas pedal.

"DAMNIT, SIX, WE FUCKED UP!" Tyrell slammed his fist on the table.

"Nah, nigga... *you* fucked up. *You* gave the order."

Tyrell snatched a chair from underneath the table, sat down, and placed both hands on his head. "I don't believe this shit, fuck!" The decision he made to have Leon killed turned out to be the wrong one, and now the burden of his death weighed solely upon his shoulders. Trying to include Six was a physiological move, but truthfully, he knew it was his doing and his doing alone.

"These are the muthafuckas you looking for, champ?" Boom Bam, an ex-football player turned hood legend, came from the back room and dropped a piece of paper on the table in front of Tyrell. They were in his apartment. He was Tyrell's best worker. "They definitely ain't from around here," he said.

Tyrell picked the paper up and stared at the two faces. "Is it them, Six?"

"Yep," six nodded. "That's them muhfuckas. I remember those faces anywhere."

"What the fuck these two white boys doin' in the hood, and who the fuck are they?" Tyrell was baffled. "Boom Bam, you can't find out who these dudes are?"

In college, Boom Bam was a computer expert, so, in the hood, he used his talents to support his lifestyle. He had the ability to hack into anything that could be hacked, and Tyrell summoned his expertise to get the video footage from the cameras set up in the lobby of the building. The task had been completed in a matter of minutes.

"Already done, champ." He dropped another piece of paper on the table. "This is serious business right here, y'all ready for this type of shit?"

Tyrell read the printout and then angrily crumbled the paper in his hands. "I don't give a fuck if that nigga name is John Gotti... they took somebody close to me. I'ma make 'em pay for that shit. I put that on everything." His thoughts drifted back to the last time he saw his cousin, Dana. It was equivalent to traveling down an empty passageway—one that had been avoided for specific reasons. His grip tightened and he crushed the paper. He bit down on his back teeth and clenched his jaws. Measure for measure—eye for an eye, it was the only way. Losing a loved one—an extremely close loved one, birthed an animal not even Tyrell could contain. His initial introduction to the streets was money oriented, but now—now murder was becoming habitual, and his sensibility to love and human life had lessened.

Boom Bam and Six stood in the kitchen, watching Tyrell as he went through his motions.

"I knew this lil' nigga was a bug-out." Boom Bam looked at Six. "He gon' get you killed."

Six was fearless, but he wasn't stupid. He acknowledged that the odds were beyond evenly matched. In fact, there were no odds according to him. *How could two young dudes from the projects wage war against a mafia crime family?*

"I think you need to take some time with this one... think it over a lil' bit." he said.

Tyrell looked up. "You think *I* need to take some time? *I* huh, what the fuck happened to *we*? It was just *we* this, *we* that... what happened to that shit, Six?"

Six didn't think he would catch it, but Tyrell was sharper than what most people assumed.

"I'm sayin', I—"

"You what?" When Tyrell stood up, Six got tongue-tied.

"I—"

"That's what I thought. Don't bitch up on me now, Six. It's crunch time, baby."

"I ain't bitchin' up, Rell. I'm jus' sayin'... we need to come up with a plan if we going at these dudes. We gotta use our brains on this one."

Tyrell reached into his pants and pulled his gun out. He held it in his palm while looking at Six. "You don't need brains when you got bullets, Six." He cocked the weapon and passed the barrel under his nose. Inhaling, he stared at Six and said, "Either you with me or you against me, and if you against me... you a dead man walkin'."

A shiver flowed through Six's body. He knew if it came to it, Tyrell wouldn't hesitate to kill him. He'd seen it done—he'd been a part of it. A choice had to be made, and time was more precious than a newborn baby.

Boom Bam's doorbell rang and they all looked at each other.

"Go see who it is, Boom..."

He walked to the door, put his eye to the peephole, and then looked back at Tyrell and Six. "It's the lil' nigga, O who used to stay in the hood. He probably wanna spend some money."

Tyrell tucked his gun and then fixed his shirt over it. "Let 'em in."

When the door opened, a five foot tall, young kid with a protruding belly, blue jeans, and a hoodie entered the apartment. "Whaddup, Boom? I need five hunit, soft." The kid reached into his jeans and came out with a wad of bills. He looked up at Tyrell and Six, and then took a seat on Boom Bam's sofa.

Tyrell caught a glimpse of the kid's face when he pulled his hoody back. "Yo, Omar, what the fuck you doin?"

"Oh shit... Rell... wassup?" Omar got up from the couch and walked to Tyrell. "I ain't even know that was you. Boom keep it mad dark in here, you can't see shit."

Tyrell hadn't seen Omar in years—since his mother had been sober and held the responsibility of caring for a few neighborhood kids. Back then, they played together, ate together and shared the same couch when it was nap time in the Michaels' house. And now, it looked like they were in the same line of business—the coke game.

"You hustlin' now, huh?" Tyrell smirked and his attention went to the pile of money Omar had laid out on the coffee table. If he was coming to buy five hundred grams at thirty dollars each, then it had to be at least $15,000 on the table.

Boom Bam appeared from the shadows, holding a beat up Nike shoe-box. He took a seat in his old, ragged, wooden rocking chair that was opposite of where Omar sat. He put the box on the table. "Y'all know each other?" he asked.

"Yeah, we know each other." Tyrell replied. "My mother use to watch this nigga. We practically grew up together... Yo, Omar how your moms doin'?"

"She's dead." he said, without a flinch.

"Damn, son. My condolences to you and the family. Where you at now?"

Omar cut his eye at Tyrell. "Homey, you asking alotta questions, wassup wit' that?"

"Fuck you mean, wassup wit that?"

"You heard me, nigga." Omar stepped back and went to reach in his hoody, but Boom Bam jumped to his feet and got between the two young men.

"Y'all niggas chill the fuck out. This is my shit!" he growled.

Omar kept his hand in the front pocket of his hoody, "Who this nigga think he is, Boom?"

"Omar, sit yo' ass down." Boom Bam lightly shoved him towards the sofa. "Cool off, nigga." He turned to Tyrell. "Why you always starting shit?"

Tyrell smiled and let out a slight chuckle. "You right, Boom. My bad."

Being the mediator, Boom Bam diffused the situation before it became hostile. He couldn't understand the mentality of today's youth because he'd grown up in a different era—an era where you fought your problems out if it came to it. But this was the norm. He'd been watching kids kill kids for the past ten years, and it was becoming an epidemic.

"Y'all fucking retarded. I truly believe it's an entire generation of crack babies, and all y'all doing is knocking each other off." Boom Bam shook his head and then sat back in his chair. "That money right, O?"

"My money always right, Boom. You know that..." Omar paused and turned to Tyrell. "Wassup wit' your man, he good?"

Tyrell kept a straight face and held his composure, but what he really wanted to do was shove his gun down this bitchassnigga's throat and make him apologize for his rude behavior. But he was easy. He sat back and played the fool as expected.

Boom Bam picked up a half-smoked cigarette from the ashtray and lit it. "He cool." he answered, letting the smoke filter through his nostrils. He pulled a digital scale out the box along with a zip-lock bag filled with cocaine rocks. While they conducted their business, Tyrell and Six acted as if they were invisible, but they heard everything that was being said.

"Yooo," Omar was putting $1,000 stacks together and placing them to the side. "I ran into that nigga... umm..." He couldn't remember the name. "That big nigga that use to play football from out here, I think his last name is Davis or some shit like that."

"Who, Cleo?" Boom Bam questioned.

"Yeeaahh, that nigga. I bumped into son down in SC. He was doin' his numbers. I think that nigga on the run for something though... he be mad nervous n' shit."

"Word?" Boom Bam brushed it off and never thought twice about it. He knew what Cleo was on the run for—shit, the whole hood knew why Cleo was on the run, but what Boom Bam didn't know was that Tyrell was involved.

After he weighed out the product and they made the exchange, Omar went on his way, but before he left, he said something slick. "Yo, Rell..." He was halfway out the door. "You was never a tough guy. Don't try to be one now. Boom, I'll see you on the next trip."

Tyrell got up and reached for his gun, but Boom Bam stopped him.

"Chill, Rell... he'll be back."

42

A delicate mist entwined with light flurries descended from the darkened sky as headlights from passing vehicles on the expressway served as extra light on the vacant streets. Tricia pranced up and down the strip in her wig, fake fur, tight skirt and four-inch heels, awaiting the arrival of a potential trick. A burning cigarette sat between her index and middle finger, while her eyes followed the dark grey Mercedes Benz that slowly passed. "Get yo' skinny ass off the strip!" the passenger yelled.

"Fuck you, bitchassnigga!" The Benz pulled away from the curb and Tricia plucked the cigarette into the street. "Ol' broke ass nigga," she mumbled, checking the watch on her wrist. Headlights from a black Audi pulling into the parking lot forced her to shield her eyes, but she was adamant on seeing who the driver was. When she noticed it was a female, she sucked her teeth, rolled her eyes, and sashayed back into the lobby of the motel.

"Why did you tell me to get off at this exit, Mox?" Priscilla questioned as she tried to find a space to park.

"Because, we hot, Priscilla. Since you and your little friend back there wanna do secret missions n' shit... this is what we gotta do."

Priscilla badly wanted to snap and curse Mox out, but she remembered Brandi was in the back seat. "Whatever you say, Mox."

She mumbled, put the car in park and they exited the vehicle and entered the motel lobby.

The poignant aroma of badly cooked food filled the cramped lobby space, causing Mox and Priscilla to turn up their nose. "Damn, it stinks in here." Mox complained.

Tricia stared at the couple as she sat in a chair off in the corner. "Hey, Daddy." she said, smiling hard.

Mox heard her, but he ignored her.

Priscilla heard her and replied. "Bitch, you blind?"

"What?" Tricia stood up. She and Priscilla were almost the same size and height.

Priscilla let go of Brandi's hand and took a step forward. "You heard me, bitch. Are you blind?"

A sharp clicking sound caught Priscilla's attention. "Naw, but I bet you bleed." Tricia clutched an old school box-cutter in her right hand. She kept it low, but Mox saw it and stepped between them.

"Fuck is wrong wit' you?" he snatched the skinny prostitute by her weave and shoved her into the corner.

"Hey!" The attendant behind the glass yelled. "No fighting! I will call cops!" he shouted in his heavy foreign accent.

Tricia bounced against the hard plastic window and the razor fell from her grasp and hit the floor. She fixed her wig and skirt and bent down to pick up her weapon.

"You bedda get that bitch before I cut her."

"Try it, bitch. I dare you." Priscilla replied. She had her finger wrapped around the trigger of the gun in her pocket. After she was cut the first time, she vowed to never let it happen again.

"Priscilla!" Mox yelled. He felt Tricia take a step towards him, so he turned around. "Get your stupid ass outta here before you fuck around and get hurt."

Tricia mumbled a few words and then slithered out the front entrance, but kept an eye on Priscilla the whole time.

"Can we get a room, please?" Mox asked the attendant.

He stared at the couple with his dark eyes and then looked down at Brandi.

"How long?"

"One night."

"Forty dollars for the short stay, seventy-five for the night."

Mox turned to Priscilla. "You got money?"

"No."

He turned back to the attendant. "Hold on, I'll be right back." Mox breezed by Brandi and Priscilla and walked out to the parking lot. "Fuck!" He cursed himself as he headed back to the car. The burden of being financially unstable was eating away at his conscience, and he had no clue how he could make things right. He hit the unlock button on the car keys and searched through the vehicle for any loose bills that may have been lying around. "It gotta be something in here." he said aloud.

After rummaging through the entire interior of the car and finding nothing, Mox popped the trunk and prayed for a miracle. He dug through a black bag that was full of Priscilla's clothes. As he continued to come up empty handed, he tossed garment after garment back into the trunk and his frustration grew more intense. He glanced over his shoulder and saw Priscilla and Brandi watching him from inside the motel lobby.

He started to say prayer as he pulled out the last pair of Priscilla's jeans, but he felt something in her left pocket. He reached in and came out holding two $100 bills. Mox shoved the remaining clothes back into the bag, slammed the trunk and kissed the money up to the sky as he walked towards the lobby. "Here," He said, pushing a hundred dollar bill through the hole in the glass. "One night, please."

"Where'd you get that money from?" Priscilla asked.

"Mommy..." Brandi was crisscrossing her legs and she looked agitated. "I gotta use the bathroom."

"Yo, can you speed that process up a lil' bit? My daughter gotta use the bathroom." Mox said.

The attendant stared at Mox from behind the glass. He picked his fork up, dug in his plate and ate a mouthful of food. After wiping the side of his mouth with a napkin, he said. "ID"

"Gimme your ID, Priscilla."

"I don't have my ID, Mox... I don't have anything. We left everything back there... and I asked you where'd you get that money."

"Shit!" Mox was heated. "Does it matter where I got the money from, Priscilla, huh? This is it... this is all the fuckin' money we got right here. This one, one hundred dollar bill." He shook his head and paced the tight area. "I can't believe this shit."

"ID please. No ID, no room." The attendant said.

Mox approached the glass again. "Look, man..." he said. "I'm in a fucked up situation as you can see. I really need this room. How 'bout I throw a extra $25 on it and you just pass me those keys?"

The attendant didn't say a word he looked at Mox with a grin on his face. Seconds later, a set of keys fell through the hole in the glass.

"Thank you." Mox grabbed the keys. "C'mon, Priscilla."

"No traffic! And no smoking!" the attendant yelled as they walked out.

Mox went to get their belongings from the car, while Priscilla took Brandi to the room. As soon as they made it to the room, Brandi rushed into the bathroom to handle her business. Mox returned to the room a minute later and took a seat in the chair next to the window, while Priscilla sat on the bed. "Please tell me you didn't leave those keys in that house."

Priscilla sighed and shook her head. "What do you think, Mox? You rushed me. I left everything. What part of that don't you understand?"

Mox stood up and paced the floor. "How the fuck you leave ten kilos in that house, Priscilla?"

"First of all... lower your voice and stop fucking cursing at me!"

Mox sat back in the chair and squeezed his temples. It couldn't get any worse. They were on the run, broke, and the work they thought they had was gone. Out of nowhere, a sharp pain stung the entire right side of Mox's body. He grabbed the back of his head and bent down between his legs in excruciating pain. Priscilla didn't realize what was going in until he collapsed to the floor, holding his head.

"Mox... what's wrong? Mox! Mox!" She rushed to his side, trying to lift him off the floor.

"I'm good... I'm good..." He held onto the bed to stand up. "What the fuck just happened?"

The toilet flushed and they looked towards the bathroom as Brandi walked out.

"Brandi, you alright?" Priscilla asked.

"Yes," she answered.

Mox fixed himself and went into the bathroom to splash some water on his face. As he gazed into the cloudy mirror, his thoughts went back to the shooting. Cleo had the pistol in his hand. It was pointed directly at Mox's head. He cringed when the shot went off, and it seemed as if it were happening all over again. The sharp pain resurfaced and Mox almost fell into the tub. Luckily, he caught hold of the shower curtain and somehow got back to his feet.

What the fuck is wrong with me? He kept asking himself. And then he remembered. Before he was released from the hospital, the doctor told him he would suffer sporadic pains throughout his body, but he never thought they would feel the way they did. He ran the cold water from the faucet, splashed a handful on his face, and dried off with a towel that was on the rack. By the time he stepped out from the bathroom, Brandi was knocked out, laid across the bed.

"Damn... she was tired," he said. "How you feeling?" Priscilla didn't answer, she just rolled her eyes. "You still mad, Priscilla?" Mox walked to the end of the bed where Priscilla sat. "I know you hear me talking to you." He bent down and gazed into her eyes. "Gimme a kiss."

"Move, Mox. Don't touch me." Priscilla pushed him out of her face.

"I can't have a kiss?"

"No. Go kiss your other bitch."

Mox looked at Brandi to make sure she was asleep. "My other bitch, what are you talking about, Priscilla?"

"Mox, don't fuckin' play stupid with me... you know the bitch I'm talking about."

"Priscilla..." Mox went to grab her arm, and she stood up and slapped the left side of his face.

"I said don't fucking touch me!"

A silent stillness settled in. Mox grabbed his cheek and shook his head. It took everything in him not to react, but one slight glance at his sleeping beauty on the bed and his mind was made up. "I'm goin' out." He said, snatching the car keys off the table.

Priscilla didn't ask where he was going, she just listened as he walked out and slammed the door. Her hands began to shake, and tears welled up in her eyes as she sat at the edge of the bed, jumbled and lost in her thoughts. *Was this a test of their loyalty? How strong was their love?* She asked herself a thousand questions, and finally concluded that Mox was the only man she loved and the only man she wanted to be with—the man she wanted to spend the rest of her life with.

43

Mox slowed to a stop when the traffic light turned red at Watson & Leland Avenue. He glanced at the gas gauge and noticed it was almost on empty. He thought about how much money he had in his pocket. "Fuck!" he banged the steering wheel with a closed fist. When he looked up, the light was changing to green. He pressed the gas pedal and cruised by two bystanders that were on the corner. As he passed, he recognized one of the men and pulled to the curb. "Yo, Bing!" he called out.

"Who the fuck is that?" one of the men mumbled. He was wearing a hooded sweatshirt, jeans and ACG boots. He tapped his partner, took a step back, and reached into the front pocket of his sweatshirt.

"Who you?" the other man asked.

Mox cut the car off and started to get out.

"That's Mox?"

"Yeah, nigga... wassup?"

The chubby Spanish kid with braids looked back at his partner and gestured for him to put his weapon away. "Everything good," he said, approaching Mox. "How you, what the fuck happened?" He was staring at the patch on Mox's eye.

"Shit got real. Nigga shot me in my face... tried to dead me."

"Yeah, I see... goddamn." They shook hands and Botta Bing

introduced his homeboy. "Yo, Mox, this my nigga, Luck. Luck, this is Mox. We was in the joint together for a minute... so, what's good, fuck you doin' over here?"

Mox looked around. The streets were barely alive and the only movement was a passing taxicab every few minutes. "You busy? Come take a ride wit' me."

Botta Bing peered up the block. "Shit kinda slow out here anyway." He walked around to the passenger side and opened the door. "Yo, Luck, hold this shit down. I'll be right back." Mox pulled away from the curb and kept straight on Watson Avenue. The quiet Audi engine purred and the music played at a moderate level.

"So, what's good?" Bing asked. He saw the annoyance on Mox's face as he handled the steering wheel. "I see you got something on your mind, huh?"

Mox shook his head and kept one hand on the steering wheel. "Honestly, I got a bunch a' shit on my mind. Kinda fucked up, Bing... I need a come up."

Botta Bing watched as the traffic passed. "A come up, like what?"

"A few hunit thousand... something light."

"Shiiid... the only way you getting that is if you take it."

"Show me where it's at."

"You serious, huh?"

Mox looked to Botta Bing and then pulled the car to the curb and parked. "Look at me, my nigga," he said. "This is it. This all I got. If I gotta go upside a nigga head to get mines... then so be it. But one thing for sure... ain't no way I can live like this."

Bing sensed the urgency in Mox's voice and paid close attention to his body language. He could tell if a person was being honest or not, just by the way they maneuvered. He knew Mox's words were truthful and he was willing to help him out. "So, what you working wit'?"

Mox turned and stared. "I told you..." he ran his hand over the steering wheel. "This is it. This everything I got right here."

Botta Bing pulled his phone from his pocket and dialed a number. After a brief conversation, he told Mox to pull off and directed him to their next destination. Fifteen minutes later, he pointed to a garage they were coming up on and told Mox to pull into it.

Mox eased off the gas and made the right turn into the cluttered garage. He turned the lights off and snatched the key out of the ignition. "Fuck is this shit?" he asked, looking around the dark, dampened space.

"Chop shop, nigga... gon' see what my man can give you for this joint." Bing said.

Mox looked around Priscilla's car. He knew she would have a fit once she found out he got rid of it. It was only thing she had—it was the only thing *they* had. "How much you think I can get for it?"

"I don't know," Botta Bing knocked on the hidden steel door at the rear of the garage. It was covered with a *Wu Tang Clan* poster. "We about to see." he said, as they waited.

Less than a minute passed and someone on the other side of the door answered. "Who dat?" his voice was deep and he had a heavy Jamaican accent.

"Bing!" Seconds later the door came open and Mox followed behind Botta Bing as they entered the hidden area. It was a dimly lit space that had a cool breeze flowing through. Mox noticed the several parked cars to the far left and the faint aroma of marijuana.

"Wha gwaan bredren?" A tall, slinky Jamaican with a shiny bald head, crooked teeth, and a matching suit greeted.

"Every ting cool," Bing answered. He switched his accent to mimic the Jamaican. "Mi have a nice toy fa ya', Ras."

The Jamaican scratched his chin and sucked his teeth. "Um hmm..." he pointed to the door and the three of them walked out. "Two tousand eleven Audi..." He said, opening the front door. He sat down in the passenger seat. "She ot?"

"Huh?" Mox didn't understand him.

"I said, is she ot?"

Mox looked to Botta Bing.

"Nah... she good, Ras," Bing replied. "It's paid for right, Mox?"

"Oh... yeah, yeah... paid in full. Everything's legit." Mox assured.

The Jamaican continued to inspect the car. He popped the trunk and walked around to the back of the vehicle where Mox and Bing were standing. "Mi give ya' twelve tousand cash."

"*Twelve stacks?* Nigga, we look like crackheads to you?" Bing was insulted.

Ras sucked his teeth even harder. "Mi nah call ya' crackhead, bredren."

"We need twenty-five." Bing said.

"Blooood claaaatt... mi nah give ya' twenty-five, bredren. Twenty-five too high."

"Twenty-five or nothing." Bing's negotiating skills were superb. *Always go with the high number* was his motto. He looked Ras dead in his eyes without blinking.

"Eighteen, bredren..."

"Fuck outta here." Bing tapped Mox on his shoulder and turned to leave. "C'mon, son, we blowin' this joint. I'ma take you to my man in Queens... he gon' treat you right." He said. His voice was low, but loud enough for Ras to hear him.

"Hol' on, hol' on..." Ras sucked his teeth once more and cut his eye at Mox. "Twenty-two?" he said.

Bing looked at Mox and Mox nodded.

"Twenty-two might do." Botta Bing said. He really wanted to crack a cheese smile from ear to ear, because he knew Mox was going to look out for him after this deal. "How long before you gon' have it?" he asked.

"Mi have it now, bredren, gimme tree minute." Ras said. He walked back into the garage and returned in less time than he predicted. When he came back, he was holding a black bag that he tossed to Mox. "Count it."

After Mox counted the money, they left and Botta Bing flagged down a taxi cab. "Take us to Harlem." He announced to the driver, who had tan skin, short black hair and a pointy nose. "And roll the windows down. I can smell ya' hot ass breath all the way back here."

"What's in Harlem at one o clock in the morning?" Mox inquired as he slid into the backseat of the Town Car.

"We gon' see my man, Snap. He got some shit. This the city that never sleeps, kid, get used to it." Bing tapped the back of the driver's seat. "Yo, I asked you to roll the windows down, man. It fucking stinks back here." the driver ignored him and kept his eyes on the road, so Bing tapped the back of his seat a little harder the second time. "Yo, Habibi roll-the-fucking-windows-down, please?"

The driver finally looked into the rear-view mirror. "My name is not Habibi."

"I don't care what the fuck your name is... just roll the windows down."

For the first time, the driver turned in his seat to see the face of the man who was cursing at him. His eyes met Botta Bing's and then he looked at Mox—the windows slowly came down. He was aware of the recent area shootings and figured he keep his mouth shut, even though he hadn't had the best day himself.

"Fuckin' Arabs..." Bing mumbled. He relaxed in his seat and stared out the window. It took them twenty two minutes to reach 131st street and Adam Clayton Powell Jr. Blvd. in Harlem.

Mox passed Bing a twenty-dollar bill. He paid the driver and they stepped out of the vehicle. He surveyed his surroundings as soon as the door shut, and the cab pulled off. Harlem was unfamiliar territory. He barely knew Botta Bing, but here he was, standing in the middle of the street with over twenty thousand cash in his pocket and not a weapon within arm's reach to defend himself. But he moved on instinct and went with his gut feeling. As far as he was concerned, Botta Bing was a stand up dude. He looked out for Mox when he really didn't have to. So, on the strength of that alone, Mox had respect. Although the streets were a different playground, he knew how to play his cards and Mox knew not to overstep his boundaries.

They crossed the street and headed into the Saint Nicholas Housing Projects, but Mox stopped short. "You got me in a nigga projects at one in the morning? I ain't feeling this, my nigga," he said, watching a car cruise down the block.

Botta Bing let out a sigh and shook his head. "My nigga..." he reached in the waistline of his pants, pulled out a black handgun and cocked it, placing a round in the chamber. "Ain't nothin' gon' happen to you. I got you, my nigga... that's my word." He cautiously looked around and then stuffed the gun back into his pants.

Seeing the gun eased Mox's nerves. He felt better about the situation, so they continued their walk into the building. Upon entering, a few muffled voices were heard in the staircase around the corner and the sour, potent smell of marijuana lingered in the air. Bing and Mox kept their eyes and ears open, but didn't pay too much attention to the chatter a few hundred feet away. They took the elevator up four flights and approached apartment 4D.

Botta Bing knocked on the door. "When we get in here, just let me do all the talking." he said.

They heard footsteps coming towards the door and then the lock clicked. "Come in, Bing." Someone behind the door said. "Lock it behind you."

Bing and Mox entered the apartment. It was hot and it smelled like someone was cooking. The short hallway leading to the living room was pitch-black and Mox could barely see in front of himself; he almost bumped into Botta Bing. As they walked further into the living room, a shaded lamp sat atop an end table in the left corner, providing minimal light—just enough to see the person's face you were talking to.

Snap pulled a cigarette from his pack, lit it and took a seat in his favorite lounge chair. "So, what's good, Bing. What can I do for you today?" he asked, taking a hard drag of the cigarette. He was short, dark skinned, overweight, and trying to hold on to what little bit of hair he had left on his head. But deep in his heart, he knew he needed to cut it.

"I need a few pieces." Bing said, pushing some clothes on the couch aside so he could sit down.

Snap turned to Mox and exhaled the smoke through his nostrils. "You ain't gonna introduce your friend?"

Bing stood back up. "Oh, yeah... my fault. But the last time I bought somebody through you told me you didn't wanna meet 'em."

"This ain't last time," Snap replied. "And this guy looks interesting."

"That's my boy, Mox." Bing said.

"*Mox?*" Snap took another long pull of the cigarette and blew the smoke in Mox's direction. "What happened to your eye?"

"I got shot."

"Damn... you gotta be a strong muthafucka to get shot in head and live to tell about it. I guess God was on your side, huh?" Snap plucked the ashes into a plastic cup that was sitting on the coffee table in front of him. "You a cop?"

"C'mon, Snap, you kno—"

"Shut up, Bing." Snap sat up in his seat. "I'm talking to Mox right now. I asked you if you was a cop?" he questioned again.

"Nah, I ain't no cop." Mox could see he was easing his right hand down into the cushion of his chair, more than likely reaching for a gun. He must have blinked his eye, because before he could even think about what to do, a pistol was pointed at his head.

"Oh. Alright..." Snap clutched the black and chrome weapon with the confidence of a sharp shooter. "Because, I don't mind shooting a couple of them muthafuckas." he let the clip drop from the bottom of the gun, caught it, pulled the barrel back and then dumped the bullet that was in the chamber onto the carpet. He smiled at Mox and tossed the gun to Botta Bing.

"How much?" Bing asked, looking over the shiny, new weapon.

"A stack."

"How many you got?"

"How many you need?" Snap asked.

Botta Bing looked at Mox and saw him flash two fingers. "Two." He said. "And lemme get like ten boxes of bullets."

"That's it?"

Bing looked to Mox again for an answer. "Nah... I need something big too... street sweeper type shit." Snap thought on it for a moment, and then told Bing and Mox he'd be right back. When he returned, he was holding a large duffle bag and wearing his signature sinister grin.

"Something like this?" he pulled a black machine gun from the bag and aimed it at the far wall. "What you think?"

"Yeah..." Bing smiled at the sight of the weapon; violence excited him. "I think that'll do for now." He glanced to his right, and Mox was giving him the head nod. "Yeah, we good wit' that."

After they got the money situated, Snap found his cleaning kit and touched the artillery up before they left. Due to his time spent in the military, he became a divine weapons specialist and could tell someone any and everything they needed to know about a gun. He was highly skilled in that area. His ability to dismantle and reassemble a weapon in less than 60 seconds was phenomenal and always a surprise.

Mox watched as Snap's hands moved quick and quiet. He hadn't smiled or said a word—it was total concentration. He had all three guns cleaned and ready for use in less than fifteen minutes. Once he finished, he pulled another cigarette from his pack and lit it. "All ready to go." he said, blowing smoke through his nostrils. "Make sure that money right, and slam the door on the way out. I gotta take a shit. I'ma see you later."

Snap disappeared into the back while Mox and Botta Bing gathered the weapons and left the apartment. They opted for the steps instead of the elevator. Dodging the urine puddles and piles of trash that littered the staircase, they finally made it to the lobby and out the building. Botta Bing waved a cab down in no time. "Yo, come see me in the AM. I'ma take you to my other peoples and get you some wheels." He said, seeing the cab pull up.

Mox gave him a pound, reached in his pocket and handed Bing a stack of twenty-dollar bills. "Good looking, Bing..." He got into the backseat of the cab. "A nigga ain't got too many people he can rely on. I appreciate that shit."

"No doubt, my nigga, be safe." Bing closed the door and the cab pulled off. As soon as it was out of sight, he pulled his phone out, dialed a number and walked down the block.

44

When she heard the key jiggling in the door, Priscilla sat up, pressed power on the remote, and fixed her hair as if she wasn't just in dreamland. She glanced to her left, to make sure Brandi was sleeping, and indeed, she was—curled up, with her feet hanging off the bed.

Mox entered the room, thinking Priscilla and Brandi would be sleep. He didn't want to disturb their rest, knowing their situation, but as the door opened wider, he could hear the television. "You still up?" he saw Priscilla sitting up in the bed.

"Why are you coming in here at four o clock in the morning, Mox?"

"I had to take care of something."

"You had to—" she stopped herself in mid-sentence and got up from the bed. "You know what... gimme my keys. We been in here all night, Mox. Your daughter and I are hungry. That didn't cross your mind?" she reached for her pants that were folded on the chair.

"I had to get rid of the car."

Priscilla let her pants fall to the floor and she plopped down on the bed. "What are you talking about, Mox?"

"I had to sell the car so we could get some money." He pulled the wad of cash from his pocket.

"I know you didn't sell my fucking car, Mox." Priscilla was in disbelief.

Their voices caused Brandi to squirm in the bed and roll onto her stomach, so Mox pointed to the bathroom and Priscilla followed. As soon as the door closed, she went off. "You sold my fucking car! What the fuck is wrong with you, Mox? Did that fucking bullet fuck you up that bad?"

Mox grabbed her shoulders, pinned her against the wall and got right in her face. "Keep ya' voice down before you wake my daughter up." He stared in her eyes. They were getting watery "What we got, Priscilla, huh?" Before she could say anything, he answered. "Nothing! Not a fucking thing! And you worried about that car... you can't be serious. I don't think you get it... we're on the run. this shit ain't no game. We needed money, so yeah, I sold the car."

Priscilla took a deep breath and shook her head. "I can't live like this, Mox. I can't do it."

"You don't have a choice, Priscilla. What you gonna do, turn yourself in? 'Cause I know you don't think I am, and Brandi is staying with me."

"*With you?* And what are you gonna do, Mox, live on the street... going from hotel to hotel? That ain't the life for a little girl, and you know it."

"That ain't the life for nobody, Priscilla, but right now it's our life." Mox leaned against the wall. He couldn't look in her eyes; it hurt too much. "I don't wanna lose y'all, I swear I don't, but I ain't never going back to that hell."

Priscilla's cries grew heavier and the tears dripped faster. "I don't know what to do, Mox. I don't..."

"Let me take care of us, Priscilla, on everything I love... ain't nothing gonna happen to either one of you." He snatched the bankroll from his pocket again. "Look, I got twenty thousand. In a few hours, I'ma get us another car and we'll be good. We should have enough for a half a brick after that. We can take that and start over. Fuck everything else."

Priscilla fell into his arms and let her tears flow. She let all of her worries out on his chest. Hoping and praying that every word he spoke would be true. Although she knew that going back to the life-style would jeopardize everything—*what else was there to do, where else was there to turn?*

Mox held her soft, warm body in his arms. She felt good in his clutches. It was the best feeling in the world—a feeling of fulfillment, pleasure and solace. He squeezed tighter; inhaling her sweet, lustful scent—it made him smile inside. He held on for dear life, never wanting to depart. He stepped back and looked at her puffy, red eyes. Mox wanted to cry. It pained his heart to witness the love of his life go through so much sorrow. The discomfort she felt—he also felt it, and whatever he could do to change it, he would do. He lifted her chin, moved in closer, and their lips met.

"Mox, I—"

"Shhh..." Mox put his finger to her lips. "I got you.," he whispered, stepping over to the shower. He turned the water on and made sure it wasn't too hot and then he started to undress her.

Priscilla wiped her tears and got into the hot shower. The warm beads of water alleviated some of her built up strain as she stood under the shower-head. She looked at Mox and a half a smirk appeared on her face as she reached her hand out to him. "Come on..." she whispered.

Mox stripped off his clothes and stepped into the shower behind her. He grabbed a washcloth from the rack, and some soap, and began washing Priscilla's back. He washed her entire body from head to toe, and then she did the same to him. He whispered in her ear. "Do you trust me, Priscilla?"

She didn't verbally respond. She wrapped her arms around his waist and pulled him close. "Fuck me." She said, shoving her hot tongue in his mouth.

He reached down, palmed the cuff of her ass cheeks and squeezed until his dick hardened, and then he slid his middle finger into her steaming vagina from the back. Halfway in, he felt the wetness building, and Priscilla let out a short sigh of pleasure. Mox spun her around, put her back against the wall—while the soothing hot water rained on their bodies—and Priscilla slightly raised her leg to let him slide into the middle.

She reached down, squeezed his ass cheeks and forced Mox to thrust himself into her. The temporary pain was her pleasure. It was something she desired—something she longed for. Her eyes rolled to the back of her head and she tightened the walls of her vagina around Mox's stiff erection. "Fuck me, Mox. This is your pussy, baby..." She brushed the tip of her tongue across his bottom lip, and Mox dug deeper. He pushed himself so far into her kitty, it felt like he was touching her back.

"I love you, Priscilla," he whispered.

Their fuck session lasted twenty minutes before they climaxed and drifted to heaven. The entire time, they thought Brandi had been sleeping, but in fact, she was up. She had her ear pressed against the bathroom door, trying to figure out what her parents were doing. All she could hear was running water and faint moans. She had an idea of what was going on, and cracked a smile before jumping back into the bed.

After a few hours rest, Mox was back up and ready to tackle the day's agenda. He knew for sure they couldn't stay in one place too long, so while they slept; he plotted their next move. "Priscilla, wake up." He tugged at the covers. "I'ma make this run, and I'll be right back. I left some money for you and Brandi to eat." He pecked her forehead and headed for the door.

"Mox," Priscilla called. He turned around before stepping out. She smiled and whispered. "I love you..."

"I love you too, babe, see you in a minute."

MOX JUMPED out the taxi at the same spot he met Botta Bing the previous night, but the block was empty. He walked a couple hundred yards down the strip and took a peek into the corner store, but no one was there either, so he waited. He waited almost two hours before he saw Bing come bopping up the block.

"Damn, nigga, I been out here all morning waiting for you. It's cold as fuck, too."

"I know my, nigga, my bad." Bing apologized, passing him a brown bag.

"What's this?"

"I got the call you was out here... so I know you ain't eat. I stopped by the breakfast spot before I came, had to fill up the tank." Bing rubbed his belly and giggled. "You ready?"

"Yep."

"Aight, let's do it." He flagged a cab down and told the driver to take them to Brooklyn.

Mox purchased a Black Buick Regal with leather interior for five grand. He slapped a dealer's plate in the rear windshield and he and Bing did 90 mph all the way back uptown, to the Bronx.

"Yo, Bing good looking." Mox sat in the driver's seat.

"No problem, Mox," Bing gave him a pound, pushed the passenger side door open and got out. "Be safe out here... don't let them suckas get one up on you. If you need me, you know where to find me."

Mox nodded and pulled off, merging with the already flowing traffic on the busy Bronx Borough Street. Before he returned to the room, he did some shopping. Besides the underclothes and toiletries he bought, he also snatched two Boost Mobile phones and a few extra sim cards. He was conscious of the consequences and aware that life on the run wasn't sweet, and one slip up could cost them their freedom, so Mox followed his plan to the tee; never leaving anything out.

He needed to replenish old relationships and make them new again. It was imperative that he get back on his feet, and he knew just the person to contact. As soon as he found another spot for Priscilla and Brandi to stay, he would go through the necessary channels to get the phone number he needed.

BRANDI RUSHED to the door when she heard a key enter the lock. "Daddy!" she shouted, attaching herself to Mox's leg as he stepped through the door. "Mommy brought McDonalds."

"Oh yeah, where is it?"

Brandi threw on her sad puppy face. "We ate it all."

"You *ate* it all? And you didn't save Daddy any? That ain't right."

Brandi laughed when Mox put his sad face on and acted like he was crying. "Don't cry, Daddy, McDonalds is right across the street." She giggled. "You can go get some more."

Mox dropped the bags he was carrying, reached down and scooped Brandi into his arms. He kissed her forehead and her cheek. "You know Daddy loves you, right?"

"Yes."

"You love, Daddy?"

"Yes."

"Does Mommy love Daddy?"

Brandi looked at Priscilla and then back to Mox. "Yeeesssss!" she sang, in the most innocent, child-like voice.

Mox put on a smirk and looked at Priscilla. "Let's get outta here."

45

"Yo, that don't look like a zone, mane."

"It's all there. I wouldn't short you, homey." Cleo assured. "I don't do business like that."

The kid standing in front of Cleo was tall and skinny. He had cornrow braids, a white t-shirt, blue jeans, and a pair of dusty Jordan's. He held up the plastic baggie with the large rock of cocaine in it. He examined it a few more seconds and then tossed it back on the table in front of Cleo.

"Nah... I don't want that shit, mane. Lemme get my bread back."

"Get your *bread* back?" Cleo stood up from behind the table. "Nah, I don't work like that. Get the fuck out my gate."

"C'mon, mane... it's like that?

"Yeah, it's like that." The kid reached down to grab the plastic baggie off the table and Cleo pulled his gun out. "I said, get the fuck outta here... now."

The only thing he could do was put his head down and walk out the trailer. He knew Cleo would kill him if he made another move, and that little bit of work wasn't worth getting killed over. He realized he should've taken it when it was given to him. Now he was leaving with nothing, and on top of that, he felt humiliated.

Cleo tossed the gun onto the table next to the bag of cocaine and lit his blunt. "Yo, Whoadie, lock that door." he said.

Whoadie was Cleo's right hand man since his relocation to the south. They met through a female who was a mutual friend to both of their respective women. Immediately, they took a liking to each other and formed a bond. Whoadie was just the type of person Cleo was looking for; somebody of his caliber—someone just as grimy, self-centered and disloyal as himself. Someone he could expunge easily, with no regrets.

"If you see that nigga come back down that road, you know what to do." Cleo said.

"Umm hmm..." Whoadie nodded. He was 5 ft. tall, 150 pounds, brown skinned with nappy box braids. His pants were always sagging, and it was like his white t-shirts came with stains on them, but his gun worked like new, and he was itching to put it to use.

Cleo hit the blunt and passed it. "I went through a whole thing last night." He said, counting a stack of money. Since his departure from New York, Cleo settled in the small country town of Oak Grove, South Carolina. He fit in perfectly. It wasn't much going on, and that's just the way he wanted it. He was renting a trailer home, tucked away on Wren Road, and after a robbery he and Whoadie pulled, Cleo was supplying the town with cocaine. He was making $20,000-$30,000 a day, and he didn't have a worry in the world. The last thing he was thinking about was Mox and all the bullshit back home. "Yo, Whoadie... roll up another joint and come help me count this money."

April 2012 - New York, New York

Gloomy, clouds hovered over the city's skyline, causing a cool breeze to drift off the Hudson River. It had been raining only twenty minutes ago, and it looked like the sun wanted to break through the clouds; only it couldn't. Mulberry Street wasn't crowded, but it also wasn't empty. A handful of pedestrians milled about the restaurants and retail shops as they did daily.

Inside Pelligrino's restaurant, Vinny Telesco relaxed in his seat at his usual table in the rear of the establishment. An empty plate and half a drink was in front of him, and a handkerchief was tucked in the front of his shirt. "Aye, Mikey... what time is it?" he asked his son.

"Two o'clock, Pop, you got somewhere to go?"

"No, Mikey, I jus' wanna know the damn time. Is it too much?"

"Not at all, Pop... not at all..." Mikey went back to reading the day's paper when the sound of the jingling bells on the door made him turn around.

A teenage kid with the same name as Vinny's oldest son came rushing through the door. "Vinny! Vinny! Mikey!" he shouted, running to the back.

Mikey jumped from his seat and stopped the kid once he passed the bar. "Hey, hey, hey... hold up, kiddo. What's the rush?"

Young Mikey was out of breath. "There... there... there's a dead... dog out front."

"A dead dog?"

"Yeah, c'mon." young Mikey snatched older Mikey's hand and led him outside.

"What the fuck! Scooter!" Mikey yelled, rushing to the sidewalk. He kneeled beside the bloody German Shepard that was sprawled across the pavement. "Please... no... Scooter, wake up!" he picked the dog's head up and put his ear to his mouth to see if he was still breathing. "Scooter, wake up..."

Scooter was Mikey's pet dog that he had for more than 10 years. It was his best friend. When everyone else got on his nerves, Scooter always made him feel at ease. He was the true definition of *'Man's Best Friend'* and now he was lying on the cold pavement with a steak knife in his ribs, and a note attached to it. Mikey pulled the knife from his dog's chest and read the note:

You're about to meet Scooter in heaven muthafucka!

Mikey smirked and shook his head at the piece of paper. As he was lifting his head, he heard the sounds of a motorcycle speeding up the block. By the time he looked up to see who it was, it was too late.

"Say hello to Scooter, muthafucka!" Tyrell was on the back of the motorcycle, dressed in black, aiming an assault rifle at Mikey. He squeezed the trigger, disbursing rounds through the air like miniature missiles, and anything in the way of those bullets met its fate. The few people that were on the street, scattered for their lives as they watched those beside them get gunned down.

"Be out! Be out!" Tyrell nudged Six, who was on the front of the motorcycle and they peeled off down Mulberry Street.

"TURN THE CHANNEL, baby, I ain't tryna watch this bullshit all night." Uncle Earl took a puff of the *La Cubana* cigar he had between his fingers and blew the smoke to the ceiling.

"But, I was watching this, Earl." Baby G replied.

"Bitch, turn the muthafuckin' channel fo' I slap the shit outta yo' stupid ass. That's your problem... you don't fucking listen. When I tell you to do something... goddamn it, do it."

"Alright, alright," She picked up the remote. "What channel you wanna watch, baby?"

"I don't know... put something informative on, the news or something." Earl puffed his cigar again, this time letting the sweet smoke filter through his nostrils as he relaxed in his Jacuzzi sized tub, watching the 40-inch television on the wall. "Right there, right there..." he said, telling Baby G to stop at the channel 12 News. "Turn it up. I can't hear shit."

"...The incident happened this afternoon, right here in broad daylight, on busy Mulberry Street." The reporter explained. "The gunmen were said to be riding on a motorcycle prior to pulling up in front of this restaurant and opening blind fire. In the midst of this horrifying incident, three people were killed, and two more were injured. Mikey Telesco, son of alleged reputed mob boss, along with thirteen year old Michael Penella, and an unidentified middle aged woman were all gunned down not far from where I stand."

"Shit!" Earl jumped out the tub and snatched his towel off the rack. "I know this muthafucka didn't just do this shit." He had a strong feeling on who the gunmen were, and he knew retaliation would come sooner than later.

"What's wrong, baby?"

"Nothing. Go get me some pants... and hurry up." Earl dried himself and rushed into the master bedroom behind Baby G. He threw his pants on and tossed a shirt over his head. "Bitch, what the fuck is you sitting there lookin' stupid for? Get the fuck up and go start the car."

"You're not telling me anything, Earl... what's going on?"

Uncle Earl ignored Baby G and went to the closet. He snatched a small box from the top, opened it and pulled out an envelope. The contents of the envelope contained the combination to his safe on the other side of town. He checked to make sure it was there, and then he stuffed the envelope into his pocket.

Before Baby G opened the door to go downstairs, someone knocked. She turned in shock and ran back towards the bedroom. "Baby," she whispered. "Baby... somebody's at the door," she pointed.

Earl dropped the book bag he was holding, unzipped it, and pulled out his chrome.38 Special. "Move," he pushed Baby G to the side. "Go wait in the room."

"But, Earl..."

"Bitch..." through clenched teeth, he scolded her. "Go sit yo' ass in the goddamn room." He tucked the pistol in his waistline and covered it with his shirt as he approached the front door. "Who is it?" he asked.

"Priest."

"Who?" Earl wasn't sure he heard right.

"Priest!" the man shouted.

Earl shook his head. "Fuck..." he mumbled, and then checked his waist to make sure the pistol was secure. He undid the lock and opened the door. "Priest, what a surprise." he said, inviting him into his home.

"It shouldn't be a surprise," Priest replied, walking into the apartment. "You should be expecting this visit. It's long overdue."

"*Overdue?*" Earl shut the door and locked it.

"Yeah, overdue;" Priest looked around at the well decorated apartment. "I been locked up for a long time, Earl. I know you been eatin'... I see it."

"Wait, wait, wait... hold up. Let's keep our voices down, I got company." Earl led Priest into the living room and offered him a seat.

"Nah, I'll stand." He insisted.

"Well, at least have a drink with me." Earl offered. He walked to the mini bar and held up two glasses. "Yak, or champagne?"

"Neither," Priest was serious. "Listen, Earl, I didn't come here to have a toast, sit on your couch and relax. You know why I'm here. Now stop bullshittin' before I get upset."

Earl sensed the tone in Priest's voice. He also saw the shift in his demeanor. "Okay, cool..." he said. "But I thought we discussed everything that needed to be talked about; and besides... I don't think this is the right time or the right place."

"Oh, it's the right time... and the right place." Priest was through playing games. "Where the fuck is my money, Earl?"

"Your money?"

"Yeah, *my* money," Priest reached for the gun in the small of his back. But Earl was quicker. He had his weapon drawn a few seconds before and when the shot went off, Baby G almost jumped out of her skin. The hot bullet hit Priest in the stomach and sent his 200 pound body crashing to the carpeted floor. His gun fell from his hands and Earl kicked it from his reach.

Priest tried to sit up, but the pain was too much to bear. "You better kill me... muthafucka..." splatters of blood shot from his mouth.

"Looks like you gonna need to say that prayer for yourself this time." Earl held the gun with both hands as he steadied his aim on Priest's head. "Don't worry, you ain't gonna be needing that money where you going..." He clenched his jaw and got ready to squeeze the trigger. "Tell my sister I said hi..."

Priest looked up and saw Baby G walking out of the room. "Your whole life is a lie, Earl..." He smiled, and a stream of blood and saliva hung from his lip. "You should'a killed me when you had the chance... now, you can tell her yourself, muthafucka." He rolled on his side and the blast from Baby G's gun echoed throughout the moderate sized apartment.

Earl collapsed and fell through the glass coffee table, shattering it to pieces. Baby G somehow helped Priest get to his feet and they stumbled out of the apartment, without being seen.

46

ONE HOUR LATER

"Uncle Earl!" Mox called out, seeing the front door was cracked open. "Hold on, Priscilla. Wait here." He pushed the door wide open and tip toed down the short hallway. "Uncle Earl!" he called again, but no one answered. The sounds of a television could be heard, but no voices. When Mox stepped into the living room, his eyes dropped to the floor where he saw his uncle stretched out, face down, in a pile of shattered glass. A stream of blood was coming from the hole in his back where Baby G shot him, but he was still breathing. "Priscilla, take Brandi downstairs!" Mox yelled, pulling his phone out. He dialed 911 and told the dispatcher an old white woman was being robbed. Before they could ask Mox a question, he hung up.

Priscilla didn't need to see what was going on. She knew by the sound of Mox's voice there was a serious problem, and for him to tell her to go back downstairs meant he obviously didn't want them to see it. She snatched Brandi's hand and they took the stairs down to the lobby and out to the parking garage.

"Unc... wake up." Mox was taking a high risk staying back. He went even further by trying to turn his uncle onto his stomach so he could breathe. He understood if he touched anything, he would be a potential suspect, but he couldn't turn his back on family; he hadn't been bred that way. "C'mon, Unc..." he struggled to lift the dead weight. "Gotta get you up."

Mox managed to get uncle Earl into an upright position, which helped him take in more oxygen, but if the paramedics didn't arrive soon, he was going to die. The bullet struck his right shoulder blade and was lodged between his chest and back. He was wheezing and his lips started to change color.

"Mox... go..." he could barely get the words out, but Mox heard him.

"You know I don't wanna leave you here like this, Unc, but I ain't got no choice." Mox peeked out the living room window to make sure police hadn't shown up. "Tell me who did this to you," he said. Earl stared at the wall in a daze. His eyelids were getting heavier by the seconds and his breathing was becoming erratic. He didn't answer. "Unc..." Mox bent down, put one hand on his uncle's shoulder and got right in his face. "Tell me who did this to you so I take care of it... c'mon, Unc."

Earl was slipping into an unconscious state. His eyelids were fluttering and his mouth was twitching, but no words were coming from his lips. Mox heard the faint police sirens in the distance and got up to leave, but Earl grabbed his leg. He looked at his uncle—helpless, and on the verge of death, and when Earl looked into his nephew's eyes, a wave of guilt consumed his entire soul. The tears spilled down his cheeks as he tried to get the words out of his mouth.

"C'mon, Unc... hold on, baby... you gon' be aight. Breathe, Unc... breathe..."

Earl finally caught enough breath to mumble what he expected to be his last words. "Your... fa...ther..." his voice was just above a whisper, but Mox heard it clearly.

"My father?"

Earl nodded. "Priest." He whispered again.

The room became silent for less than a few seconds. Mox listened. A dog was barking, birds chirped and a train was passing through the station. He listened for the sirens and they were getting closer. His vision was getting blurry. He looked down at his hands and it looked like he had one hundred fingers. Mox felt woozy and suddenly, a sharp pain shot through the right side of his body and weakened his knees. He reached for the arm of the couch, but his body weight was too much to hold up and he fell to the floor. The last thing he saw before closing his eyes was a silhouette of someone coming through the door.

THE ONLY LIGHT in the black sky was the full moon that looked close enough to touch. As the weed smoke funneled through his nostrils, Tyrell leaned against the trunk of his car. He thought about all he'd been thorough. The road he traveled had been a long, rough one, but he managed to weather the storm and come out on top. The only thing left to do was to buy his mother that nice house he always promised her. And at the rate he was going, that house would be purchased sooner than later.

Furthest from his mind, was what had taken place only hours ago. A war with the Italians was in full swing. It was a battle he knew he couldn't win, but his pride wouldn't let him back down; especially after they murdered his cousin. What did bother him was the fact he had also murdered a child—an innocent child—a child who had no knowledge of what was going on.

Tyrell puffed the weed again and watched as a black Cadillac cruised down the block past him. It was unusually warm for a mid-April night, and everyone was taking advantage of the beautiful weather. Three nicely dressed young ladies crossed the street on their way to the corner store and walked pass Tyrell, giggling like they were talking about him. He knew all three of them.

"You just gon' walk by me like that, Chrissy. I thought we was cool." he said.

"You're full a' shit, Rell." Chrissy replied, turning around. "You were supposed to call me yesterday. What happened?"

"I got caught up. I didn't forget, though. I had some business I had to take care of."

"You didn't forget, but you also didn't call."

"I'm here now though... wassup?"

Chrissy's two friends were telling her to hurry up. "I gotta go. Maybe I'll see you later."

"Hold up, Chrissy..." Tyrell tried to get her to stop. "lemme me holla at you for a sec'."

"Chrissy, c'mon!" one of her friends shouted.

"They're waiting for me, Rell. I'll talk to you later."

Tyrell watched Chrissy's ass bounce as she walked away. "Fuck them bitches," he laughed. "They just mad ain't nobody tryna holla at them."

"Them bitches is broke anyway." Six added. He was sitting in the passenger seat of Tyrell's car with the door open.

"Yo, hold me down. I'm about to check mama love out real quick. I ain't seen her in a few weeks."

"Aight... I'll be right here."

Tyrell crossed the street and walked into the projects. The lights along the path to the building were shot out, so he could barely make out the few people standing on the strip. A small radio played and the overwhelming stench of potent marijuana was prevalent in the air. He heard a few *'wassup's'* and continued into his mother's building. He knocked on the door once and realized he still had his house key, so he checked his pockets, found it, and then opened the door.

The apartment was the usual mess. Dirty clothes and miscellaneous garbage was strewn throughout the entire living room. It was nowhere to sit. He had to move a pile of laundry just to see a seat on the couch. Tyrell looked around in disgust. He was ashamed and fed up with his mother's living conditions.

"Ma!" he called out as he maneuvered through the rummage.

"What, Tyrell?"

"Where you at?"

"I'm in the bathroom, goddamn it. What you want?"

"Pack your shit... I'm gettin' you outta here."

"Boy, please..."she replied. The toilet flushed and she came out the bathroom. "And where am I goin', Tyrell?"

"Anywhere," he said. "I can get you an apartment uptown in that new building if you want."

"*Uptown?* Tyrell you gotta have money to live up there. I ain't got no goddamn money."

"Don't worry about the money, Ma. I'll take care of that... just pack up your stuff."

"I don't wanna go, Tyrell."

"Why not?" He couldn't understand why his mother wanted to stay in the projects.

"Because, I said I don't want to." She picked up a half-smoked cigarette from the ashtray and lit it. "I don't know anybody over there, Tyrell. All those damn white people. I don't wanna be bothered with that."

"So, you rather live like this?" he looked around at the mess she was living in. "In the projects your whole life. I thought the main goal was to get out."

"Get out and go where, Tyrell? Ain't nowhere for us to go. You wanna go up there and live with all them damn white people, you go right ahead. I ain't goin' nowhere... now gimme some money."

Tyrell knew once his mother's mind was made up, there was no persuading her to change it. Nothing he could do or say would make her feel any different. Her words were stone—the final say. He stared at her for a moment, trying to figure out why she felt the way she did, but he couldn't understand it—he didn't understand how you could struggle all your life, and then turn your cheek to an opportunity. It was something he would never understand.

He pulled a wad of cash from his pocket, peeled off $1,000 and gave it to her. "Let me know if you change your mind." he said, as he left out. "Make sure you pay some bills with that money too, and don't smoke it up."

Ms. Michaels's took a long drag of her cigarette and plucked the ashes on the floor. "Tyrell, please... as far as I know, I'm the mother." she told him. "You don't tell me what to do, I tell *you* what to do."

Tyrell shook his head and closed the door. He went down the back staircase instead of the front because it was faster, but had no idea someone was there waiting for him. As soon as he pushed the door open to go down the steps, Gahbe was waiting with his gun drawn.

"Surprise, nigga," he whispered, pushing the barrel of the revolver in Tyrell's face. "Told you I was gonna get that ass." Tyrell was caught off guard—slipping, but he kept his calm. If he could reach the gun at the small of his back, Gahbe would have a problem on his hands. "Run yo' shit, nigga..." he demanded. With his free hand, he searched Tyrell's pockets. But when he went to touch his waistline, Tyrell moved. "Move again, nigga, and I'ma leave you right here." He promised.

Tyrell stayed silent. He knew Gahbe was scared; and he knew a scared victim would shoot him in a heartbeat. He watched his hand shake while he held the gun. "You scared, nigga..." He mumbled and tried to reach for the weapon, but Gahbe had a tight grip. Tyrell pushed him into the hallway door and tried to take off down the steps, but Gahbe was on him. He leveled the pistol, aimed, and pulled the trigger. The echo from the blast was ear piercing. The slug tore a chunk of flesh from Tyrell's left leg, but he managed to make it out the building, alive. He stumbled down the entrance steps and hobbled down the strip towards the block. Gahbe realized he fucked up when Tyrell wasn't lying at the bottom of the steps, dead. He had to prepare himself for the repercussions, because they would come, and they would come sooner than later.

47

W hen Mox opened his eye, he was greeted by the most beautiful smile. The same smile he had fallen in love with years ago.

"Hey, baby. How you feeling?" Priscilla asked. She rubbed his head and then caressed the side of his face. He tried to sit up, but she made him stay in the bed. "Where you going?"

"Where are we?" he looked around and saw Brandi lying on the small leather love-seat at the other end of the room.

"The Harlem Flophouse," she answered. "Don't worry, we're good here."

Mox scanned the room. There was a large walnut dresser opposite the bed. The floors and door entrances were all made from real wood and the lighting was dim.

"How we get here?" he asked. "I don't remember anything."

"You passed out, Mox."

"Passed out?"

"Yes..." she said. "Uncle Earl's house... you don't remember?"

"*Uncle Earl's house?*" Mox's memory was blank. He couldn't recall anything that happened. He let his head rest on the pillow, closed his eye, and took a deep breath. "Why was I was at my uncles house, and how the hell did I pass out?"

Priscilla hesitated. She didn't want to tell him what happened, but she had to. She couldn't look him in the face when she said it. "Uncle Earl got shot, Mox."

"What you mean he got shot?" Mox sat up in the bed. "When did this happen?"

"It must've happened right before we got there. You told me to go back downstairs and wait for you, but you took too long, so I had to come and see what was going on. When I got back to the apartment, I saw you and uncle Earl lying on the floor."

Mox rubbed his head. He was trying his hardest to remember something—anything. After a few minutes, pieces of what took place were slowly popping into his memory. Eventually, he had enough pieces to put together at least what he thought had happened.

"I know who shot my uncle." He said.

"Who?"

"The same person who killed my mother..."

Priscilla dropped her head. She couldn't begin to understand the distress Mox had to deal with, knowing that the man who killed his mother and shot his uncle was still walking the streets. She knew his ego wouldn't allow him to let it go, and no matter what she said, there was no deterring him from finding this man and taking his life.

Mox got up from the bed and tried to get himself together.

"Where you going?" Priscilla questioned.

"We need more money. I need you to make that call."

"But, Mox—"

"Let's not argue about this, Priscilla. Just make the call."

Ten minutes later, a meeting was set up for Mox to meet with the connect; Juan Carlos. But before that happened, he needed to make a visit to the Men's Warehouse to purchase a suit. In order for Juan to take him seriously, he needed to look the part. Mox learned early that money attracted money, and first impression was everything. Although he and Juan had known each other already, they hadn't personally done business, so this was something new. Mox bought a navy colored slim fitting suit for $700, and a pair of black imperial wing tipped shoes for $200. He was ready to go.

Two hours later, Mox was pulling up to the front entrance of the Malaga Restaurant located on 73rd street in Manhattan's Upper East

Side. The valet parked his car and he was greeted by a short Spanish guy with a bald head, thin mustache, and a clean suit.

"Mox?" he asked.

Mox nodded.

"Mr. Carlos is waiting for you.

The two men entered the restaurant. It was small, but well lit. Mox looked around at the pictures on the wall. The atmosphere reminded him of someone's home. It was comfortable. They walked past the granite-top seating areas and neared the rear of the restaurant where Juan Carlos sat at a table in the corner, by himself. He stood and smiled when they approached. "Mox." He extended his hand.

Mox shook his hand and replied. "Juan Carlos, pleasure to finally meet you."

"Yes, yes, it is. Wow..." He looked Mox up and down. "I remember the last time I saw you. You were sitting in the car when Priscilla came by to see me. You were a kid then, Mox. You're all grown now." Juan Carlos embraced Mox. He hugged him tightly, patted him on his back and offered him a seat. "C'mon... sit down, let's talk."

Two red handkerchiefs, two plates and two champagne glasses adorned the table top, and a slim, average height Spanish woman with an apron on and her hair in a bun came from the back to take their order.

"How are you today, sir, would you like to start off with a drink?" she asked.

"Veronica, this is my good friend, Mox. Mox, this is my niece, Veronica."

"Nice to meet you," Mox shook the young woman's hand. "Yeah, I'll have some water, please."

"Veronica, bring us two orders of patatas bravas please." Juan Carlos said. "So, what's up, Mox? Talk to me."

Mox relaxed in his chair. "It's like this, Juan..." he explained. "I'm fucked up in the game right now. I got a lil' bit of paper to play with, but I need more."

"And you come here because?"

"Because, I need your help."

"Haven't we been down this road before, Mox, what happened? What's gonna make this time different from the last?"

Mox took his time answering the question. He knew Juan Carlos wouldn't give him anything without proving himself first. "I grew up," he said. "I'm not the same young dude without any direction. I know exactly what I want now."

"And what's that?"

He looked directly into Juan Carlos' eyes. "More money than I can think about counting." he replied. Mox knew how the game was played, because he played it; and he played it well.

Juan Carlos kept a straight face. He wasn't easily excited by anything. "I don't know about this, Mox. Every time I turn on my television, I see you and Priscilla. I'm taking a big risk dealing with you two." The waitress came back with two plates of food and placed them on the table. "Thank you, Veronica..." he waited until she left and continued. "Last time I spoke to Priscilla, she said it was over. What brought about this sudden change?"

"What else am I gonna do? I got a baby girl to take care of and can't stand to see her not being able to get what she wants. I gotta provide that."

"Mox, you're a smart kid, always have been. I think you can do anything you put your mind to. It's up to you to want more. More for yourself—for your family."

"Exactly," he agreed. "And that's why I'm here, today... because I want more, but I'm not a greedy person."

Juan Carlos giggled. "I see," he said. "You barely touched your food."

"This shit is spicy. What the hell is it?"

"Patatas bravas, it's cut up white potatoes in a spicy tomato sauce. Good, right?"

Mox nodded, as he stuffed his mouth with the fiery potatoes. The two sat, ate and finished their plates of food and then Juan Carlos ordered a bottle of wine. Veronica brought it out and poured the men drinks.

"So, tell me, Mox... what exactly is it that you want me to do?"

Mox wiped his mouth with the handkerchief and sipped his wine. "I need two," he said. "I got fourteen."

"Fourteen, huh," Juan Carlos rubbed his mustache and smirked. "Fourteen is only enough for a half of one, and you want *two?*"

"I know I'm a lil' short, but this is all I got, Juan. You know if I didn't need it I wouldn't be asking."

Juan Carlos stared into Mox's eye and carefully studied his body language. He knew every word he spoke was sincere. "This is it, Mox," he replied, finishing the last bit of food on his plate. "This is the last time I do you or Priscilla a favor. I'm done."

"Thank you, Juan. I really appreciate this." Mox smiled.

"One question," Juan said. "How do plan on moving this work with all this other shit going on?"

"I got some people I used to deal with that moved south. I'm going to see them."

Juan Carlos snapped his fingers and the short Spanish guy with the bald head appeared out of nowhere. He spoke to him in Spanish and sent him off. "Everything is good. Your product will be in the car when you're ready to leave. Now, where's my money?"

Mox reached into his pocket, pulled out the wad of cash and slid it to Juan Carlos.

"This is fourteen?"

"Everything I got."

Juan Carlos fingered the stack of money and then slid a few bills back to Mox. "Don't ever say I didn't look out for you." They shook hands and Mox got up to leave.

48

M ox made a right turn into the parking lot and pulled into an empty space between a Jetta and a Astro work van. He put the car in park and he, Priscilla and Brandi got out. The air was still. Not a breeze within miles, and the illuminated sun was shining bright. They walked through the front entrance of the hospital, and immediately, Mox felt a chill throughout his body. He despised hospitals and everything they stood for.

"You alright?" Priscilla asked. She could see the discomfort in his actions.

"Yeah, I'm good. How 'bout you?"

"I'm fine."

They continued down the corridor and approached the information desk. Two young black security guards sat in chairs behind a small wooden table. One of them—the younger looking of the two —was reading a magazine while the other guy watched sports on his iPhone. Neither one of them were paying attention, so the three of them slid right past. Mox pressed for the elevator and they took it to the second floor.

"What's the room number, Priscilla?"

"Two ten," she answered, holding onto Brandi's hand. "I think this is it right here."

Mox turned the doorknob and slowly pushed the door open. He could see someone lying in the bed. He knew it was his uncle, Earl. "Wait here with Brandi for a second while I see what's going on."

Uncle Earl sat upright in his bed. His shoulder was wrapped in bandages, and he also had three Band-Aids on his face. His eyes were glued to the television and he held the remote in his hand, flicking through the channels. He hadn't acknowledged Mox enter the room.

"Hey, Unc, is that you?"

Earl turned around with a half a smile on his face. "Hey, wassup, nephew. Y'all come to get me, huh? Good, cause I wasn't about to spend another day in this muthafucka."

"Yeah, Unc, we here for you." he lied. "Don't worry, I'ma get you up outta here." Mox had no clue they were letting his uncle go. It just so happened they showed up on the exact day of his release. "How you feeling?"

Earl got up from the bed and started to gather his belongings. "I feel like shit, nephew. The food sucks, and every nurse that came through that door was horrible looking. They need to employ some pretty women up in here."

Mox laughed. "Yeah, I feel you, Unc."

Just as the two of them finished giggling, Jasmine walked in, followed by a not so happy looking Priscilla. She looked at Earl and then Mox, and she smiled. "Mr. Daniels, how are you today?"

"I'm fine, nurse," Earl answered. "Damn you—"

"What the fuck is this bitch doing here, Mox?" Priscilla cut in. She wasn't about to hold her tongue this time.

Mox was lost. He had no idea what was going on, and was just as shocked as Priscilla. He hadn't thought about the possibility of bumping into Jasmine while visiting his uncle, but he did know she worked there. "C'mon, Unc... let's get you outta here." He ignored Priscilla, but still felt the darts she was shooting at him from across the room. He knew her eyes were glued to him, so he didn't even turn around.

"Aww shit..." Earl sensed the tension and saw the fire in Priscilla's eyes. "Is that my baby girl right there?" he asked, diverting everyone's attention to Brandi.

"Mox, I asked you a question."

"Excuse me," Jasmine said. "I didn't mean to cause any problems. I'm just here to do my job."

Priscilla kissed her teeth and rolled her eyes as hard as she could. "Bitch, nobody was talking to you. Mind your business."

"Let's go, Priscila." Mox ordered.

"Oh... so now you don't wanna speak to your lil' friend, huh?"

"Stop it, alright."

"No, Mox, you stop it. Ain't this the bitch you was fuckin' behind my back?"

Jasmine tried to avoid Priscilla's rant, but she wasn't about to be disrespected. "I'd appreciate it if you stop calling me out my name. I'm pretty sure you know what it is."

"Bitch, I'll—" Priscilla lunged at Jasmine, but Mox was right there to intervene. He grabbed her arm and pushed her into the hallway. He had her back pinned against the wall.

"Don't do this shit in front of my daughter. What the fuck is wrong with you?"

"What's wrong with *me?* You're the one who fucked that bitch!"

"Lower your fucking voice."

"Fuck you, Mox. You better let that bitch know."

Jasmine had heard enough. "Alright, that's it." she dropped the clipboard she was holding and stepped towards the door where Priscilla and Mox stood.

"Ut oh... cat fight!" Earl shouted and grabbed Brandi's hand. "We better get outta here, Brandi. They trippin'."

Jasmine swung and almost hit Priscilla in her face, but Mox caught the blow because he was in the middle of them. Priscilla went to swing back.

"Priscilla, chill!" he warned, but she wasn't listening. She tried to escape Mox's hold and swing again, but she couldn't.

"Get off me, Mox!" She screamed. Tears of anger rolled down her cheeks. "Bitch, I'ma fuck you up!"

During the commotion, Uncle Earl gathered his things, and he was ready to leave the hospital. "Y'all need to cut it out. Got this baby seeing all that nonsense. Control your women, nephew." He laughed.

"This shit ain't funny, Unc." Mox said. He was still holding

Priscilla. He didn't want to let her go, because he knew she wouldn't stop once she got started. When he turned around, he saw the two security guards coming their way. "See, now this. Priscilla, you know we can't afford to get caught up in this dumb shit. Let's go." He pulled her by the arm, but she jerked away and broke his hold. Before Mox knew what happened, Priscilla was on top of Jasmine like a lion pouncing its prey.

One hand was full of Jasmine's hair, while she pounded her face with the other. The momentum caused them to fall to the floor and Priscilla landed on top. Mox tried to pull her up, but every time he pulled her, she pulled Jasmine. Priscilla was continuously banging the side of her face on the cold hospital floor. Blood shot from Jasmine's nose and mouth.

Uncle Earl tried to intervene but his disabled shoulder and arm prevented him from doing so.

Brandi stood in the middle of the corridor, crying, begging her mother to stop. Priscilla looked up and saw the guards getting closer. They were on their walkie-talkies, calling for back up, and she was pretty sure their back up was the police. She looked the other way and saw the hurt and embarrassment on her daughter's face.

Mox couldn't take it anymore. He grabbed Priscilla in a chokehold, pulled her off Jasmine and yelled for uncle Earl to get Brandi as they made a dash for the emergency exit.

"DAMN SON, that nigga got you good." Six teased as he stared at Tyrell's bandaged leg.

"Fuck you, Six. I'ma kill that muthafucka, and that's on everything I love. He can't walk these streets no more."

"That nigga outside right now. Want me to handle that?"

"Nah, this shit is personal. I wanna look that nigga in his eyes before I squeeze one in his dome."

"Here, hit this shit... take your mind off the pain." Six insisted.

Tiny pieces of sunlight crept through the small slits in the curtains as the two friends talked. Tyrell took the joint, hit it, and exhaled the smoke through his nose. He was sitting on a sofa with his leg propped up on an ottoman, and the only thought running through his mind was revenge. He was disgusted at himself for letting Gahbe catch him off point, but he wasn't taking it lightly. While he was laid up, he plotted.

"I got something nice for him... something real sweet for that bitchassnigga."

"What's that?" Six asked.

"Yo, Tia!" he yelled. "Hold on... watch this shit."

Tia came from the back room. She was tall, brown skinned and slim; like a runway model. Her hair was cut short, and she had thick full lips that longed to be kissed. She was one of the girls that Tyrell and Six used to transport their product from state to state. She was book smart, street smart, pretty, and she had her own car and apartment. She moved to New York a year ago so she could work in a strip club. When Tyrell met her, he took her out the club and made sure she didn't want for anything. He set her up with an apartment and kept her secluded from the street life. She was his favorite Mule.

"Yes, baby."

"Bring me that thang." Tyrell said.

Tia left the room and returned holding a long red box. She placed it on the floor in front of Tyrell and took the top off.

"Goddamn!" Six caught a glimpse of the heavy machinery that the box held. "Nigga, you plan on killing everybody on the block, huh?"

"Hand me that, baby," Tyrell said to Tia. He held the assault rifle in his hands and looked at Six. "They fucked up, Six... anybody out there when I come through is a target. Women, kids, innocent bystanders... I don't give a fuck. He violated, and I'ma deal wit' 'em the right way. I'ma show that faggot how to lay the murder game down, cause it's obvious he don't know what the fuck he doing."

"No more kids, Rell. That shit was fucked up." Six tried his best not to think about what happened to the young boy the day they hit the Telescos, but the image of his small frame sprawled across the concrete in a pool of his own blood was embedded in his mind. Since the day it happened, he hadn't had a good night's sleep, and he was sure he wouldn't get one anytime soon.

Tyrell grilled Six. He hated to be told what to do. "Them ain't your muthafuckin' kids, nigga, fuck is you worried about them for?"

"They kids, Tyrell, that's why. Shit, they could be mines, maybe yours... who knows. All I'm saying is... if there's kids out there, you need to rethink the situation."

Tyrell looked at Tia. "You hear this muthafucka? Who the fuck this nigga think he is, Tia?" Tia didn't answer; she just nodded in agreement. She didn't want to make the situation any worse than it already was. "Nigga, like I said... anybody out there is subject to get it. I don't give a fuck who it is." Tyrell placed the weapon back in the box and sent Tia to the back.

"We still making that move south?" Six asked. He wanted to change the subject.

"Yeah, after I murder this nigga."

49

After Vinny Telesco buried his eldest son, he waged war and severed every tie he had to anybody that wasn't of Italian descent. Bodies started dropping up and down the eastern seaboard, and everyone knew why, but nobody could stop it. He didn't know who pulled the trigger, but sooner than later stories started circulating. The first name to be mentioned was Mox Daniels.

Vinny relaxed in his leather lounge chair with his right leg crossed over his left. He held a burning La Gloria Cubana in one hand and a chrome and black Smith & Wesson in the other. He knew he wasn't supposed to be smoking, but the added stress had him caring less about his health. He looked around the room. There were six guys; all hit men—all trained and ready to kill at the given word. The sweet stench of cigar smoke filled the air as he stared each man in the eyes.

"I'm gonna say this one time," he puffed the cigar, savored the flavor, and let the smoke escape his mouth. "If you guys don't bring me that fucking nigger's head, I swear before God I'll kill each one of you... now, get the fuck outta my face."

None of the men said a word. They just left the room.

A few hours later, three of Vinny's men entered Frank's spot, Club Red and opened fire. Five people were shot and two were killed, one of them was Nate.

PRISCILLA'S LIPS were poked out and she refused to step foot out the car. "I'm not going." she insisted.

"This is the only choice we have, Priscilla, and you know as well as I do this visit is long overdue. Now, c'mon." Mox insisted.

"I'm not leaving my daughter with that lady. You must be outta your mind. I don't even know the last time I saw her. And now you want me to go up there and ask for help... you can't be serious, Mox."

Mox was becoming frustrated and the scorching sun was not helping. "I'm very serious, Priscilla. We can't have her seeing all this crazy shit. She's better off here with your mother."

Priscilla stared out the window at her mother's apartment building. She couldn't believe she was even thinking about what Mox was saying, but he was right. Their daughter had seen enough. The streets weren't the safest place to have your child out at all times of the night, and them being in the bind they were in caused Brandi to see more than her young eyes imagined.

Mox was fed up. He opened the passenger side door and grabbed Priscilla's arm. "Let's go..." he pulled her from the car. "C'mon Brandi, let's go see Nana."

Priscilla rolled her eyes as they walked to the entrance of her mother's apartment building. "She doesn't even know her, Mox. You can't force her to stay there."

"She's a child, Priscilla, she's gonna do what I tell her to do. And I think it's about time she get to know her."

"Get to know her, for what?"

"Because, that's her grandmother, that's why. Don't you think it's a little selfish to not let her meet her grandmother? Just because you two had your differences doesn't mean Brandi has to suffer. She should know who her family is."

"She does know who her family is," Priscilla replied. "We're right here. We're the only family she needs."

As they were walking into the building, Mox stopped short. He stopped and thought about what Priscilla just said. He thought hard about it. He held Brandi's hand, looked down at her precious, innocent face, and then he looked at Priscilla. "Well, what if something happens to us, then what? What would she do then?"

The thought hadn't even crossed her mind. "Ain't nothing happening to us, so we don't even need to discuss that," Priscilla looked down into Brandi's big beautiful eyes and wanted to cry. She couldn't fathom the thought of being separated again, and she would go to great lengths to make sure it didn't happened a second time. She bent down and kissed her daughter's forehead. "You know Mommy loves you, right?" Brandi nodded yes. "And you know I would never let anything happen to you, right?" She nodded yes again. "Mommy needs for you to stay with your grandmother for a little while until things get situated. You okay with that?" Brandi half smiled and nodded yes once again.

They entered the building and took the elevator up. The ride was a silent one. Priscilla tried to encourage herself to be open minded and not dwell on the past, but it was difficult. It was a struggle for her to let go of the heartache caused throughout her childhood. She still felt a bitter taste in her mouth towards her mother. It was something that should have been addressed a long time ago, but wasn't.

Before the elevator opened, Priscilla closed her eyes, took a deep breath and prayed that everything would be fine. She prayed that the slight amount of love she did have for her mother would override the hate and uneasiness she felt towards her. She prayed for her anger and emotions to remain intact, and she hoped she could stay calm and at least try to listen.

When the elevator stopped and the door opened, Priscilla watched Mox walk out while she stood in a daze. Brandi—more anxious than both of them—tugged at her hand as she stepped off the elevator.

"Mommy, c'mon... we're here."

Priscilla snapped out of her trance and stepped off the elevator. The three of them stood in front of the door, but no one knocked. Priscilla looked to Mox and he looked at her. Brandi looked at them both and figured she'd do what they didn't.

"Who is it?" Ms. Davis asked, hearing taps on her door.

Priscilla looked at Mox again.

"Mox," he answered. "I brought you a gift."

Ms. Davis undid the locks and slowly pulled the door open. It was only cracked enough to see the face of the person knocking, because she hasn't heard the name clearly. "Oh, that's you," she said, seeing Mox's face. "I wasn't expecting any company today. I thought you was one of those people selling something." As she spoke, she opened the door all the way and when her eyes met Priscilla's, it was like everything around them came to a pause. They stared at each other for more than sixty seconds, just gazing—amazed, astonished and baffled, all at the same time. "Y'all come on in and have a seat," she said. "Hurry up and close my door, you letting all the good heat out."

"It's nice out, Ms. Davis. What you doing with the heat on?"

"I ain't as young as I used to be," she replied with a slight giggle. "Time catching up to me, baby. I'm not that spring chicken any more."

"Hi, Grandma," Brandi mumbled as she stepped into the doorway.

"Oh my God," Ms. Davis covered her mouth with one hand and tossed the other into the air. "Is that my grand baby?"

Brandi's tight frown turned to a full-blown smile. "Yessss," she sang.

The corners of Priscilla's mouth went up. She couldn't hold back the smile if she wanted to. She watched Brandi embrace her grandmother. It was a first. It was the first time she had the chance to see how much love surrounded her. It was the first time she got to see her daughter interact with her mother—something that was long overdue.

Ms. Davis hugged her granddaughter for the first time, and realized how much she missed her. She hadn't seen her since she was born, and hadn't touched her until today.

"We're not staying long." Priscilla said, taking a seat on the sofa in the living room. She looked around at the pictures on the wall, and the ones on the mantle. Most of them were of her, and even though she had been taking care of her mother, she rarely visited and almost never called to check on her.

Mox snatched a picture off the top of the television, looked at it, and then handed it to Priscilla. "Remember this?"

"Of course," she said, marveling at the photo. "This was the day you got your car. I could never forget this day."

Ms. Davis sat in her favorite chair, with Brandi in her lap, watching Priscilla and Mox. She could see the love radiate from their bodies. She knew it was a true love they shared, but they had a problem, and she also knew they needed her help. "So, what brings you all by here to see me?"

Mox placed the picture on the table. "We got a little problem, Ms. Davis," he turned to Priscilla. "Tell her," he said.

Priscilla hesitated.

"Tell me what?"

Priscilla stared at her mother's face. She was taken aback by how much she resembled her. She never wanted to look like her mother. She hated her mother. "I know you've seen the news, because that's all you watch." she said. "I need you to take care of Brandi for a few days while we figure this thing out." Ms. Davis heard her daughter talking, but acted as if she wasn't paying attention. Her focus was on Brandi. Priscilla got annoyed. "See," she said, standing up from the sofa. "This is why I don't come here. She pays me no mind. Like I'm not even here."

Mox grabbed her arm. "Sit down and chill out."

"You know, I had a feeling you would come by here after I saw you on the news." Ms. Davis said. "Y'all done got all them people searching for y'all... you know that's dangerous, don't you?. And you can't be running around here with this baby..."

"That's why we came to you, Ms. Davis. There's no one else we can trust to watch over Brandi." Mox told her.

Ms. Davis looked at her daughter. "Only if she apologizes."

"What?" Priscilla was livid. "Apologize, to you? You should be the one apologizing, not me."

"Priscilla, calm down."

"No, Mox. Mind your business."

"I'm not doing it unless you apologize."

"I can't believe you." Priscilla got up from the sofa again, this time she reached for Brandi, but her mother pulled her back. "Give me my daughter, please. I'm leaving."

Mox stood up and put his hand on her shoulder. "Hold on, Priscilla, wait..."

"Get off me, Mox."

"Brandi is staying with me, but not under your circumstances, under mine." Ms. Davis picked her telephone up and dialed some numbers. "They're here." she said, and hung up. "See, I knew you two would come here, so I called the police."

"You did what?" Mox ran to the window and looked out. He didn't see any police.

Priscilla went to grab Brandi's hand, and Ms. Davis pulled a small knife from her brassiere. She wrapped one arm around Brandi's neck and held her close. "You make another move, and I'll cut her throat."

Mox was stunned. He couldn't believe what was going on. "What the fuck is wrong with you?"

"Reward money, Mox. You think I'ma let fifty thousand dollars go to someone else, when I can use it." Ms. Davis was serious.

"Fifty thousand?" Priscilla was raging. "I told you we shouldn't have come here." She shook her head, reached into her purse, and pulled her gun out. "If you don't let my daughter go in two seconds, I'ma shoot you right in your fucking head."

"Priscilla, drop the gun. Don't do this. Think about Brandi. Think about our daughter, Priscilla."

"Shut the fuck up, Mox!" She turned and pointed the weapon in his direction.

Ms. Davis snatched Brandi off her feet and pulled her into the bedroom a few feet way. Mox backed away and put his hands in the air. "Priscilla... listen to me."

"No, Mox." A river of tears poured from her eyes as she clutched the weapon in her hands. I listened to you enough. That's the reason we're in this situation now."

A knock at the door made their heads turn. They looked at the door, and then at each other.

50

P
ieces of pure white clouds were scattered throughout the
crystal blue sky as a soft spring breeze rustled the leaves on
the trees. School buses were pulling up to the entrance of
the Hartley Housing Projects, and kids were jumping through the
doors like they had been held captive for years. School was nearing its
end, and the weather was getting warmer each day. Tenants sat on
wood benches in front of their building, gossiping about the
previous night's endeavors—anxious to hear a story other than
their own.

Tyrell leaned against the black gate in front of building 70. He
had on a pair of black jeans, a white t-shirt, and black and white Air
Max 95's. It had been three weeks since he was shot, and he was
healing much faster than expected. He held a cane in his right hand
and a blunt in his left. "Yo, Six, send one of them little niggas to the
store."

Six was a few feet away, sitting on a crate, drinking a Pepsi and
talking to his young boys.

"Yo, one of y'all run to the store real quick." Six pulled some
money from his pocket and gave it to the closest person to him.
"Here..."

"Why I always gotta go to the store?"

"Yo, Grasshopper, shut the fuck up and take yo' ass to the store before I slap the shit outta you." Grasshopper looked at the seriousness on Six's face, sucked his teeth, and took a walk to the store.

Since the incident with Tyrell and Gahbe, the hood was on high alert. Everyone knew retaliation was a must, and they were waiting in the wind for it to happen. A few people other than the young boys wanted to see Gahbe dead too. He owed a few old heads some money and was hesitant to pay. If Tyrell didn't get the job done, someone else would.

A black Cadillac STS slowed to a stop and pulled to the curb. Wise Earl stepped from the driver's seat, hit the alarm, and walked into the projects. He spotted Six and the young boys as soon as he hit the strip, and then saw Tyrell leaning against the gate.

"Tyrell, let me talk to you for a minute," he approached the young hustler.

Tyrell looked around and followed Earl into the little park. "Wassup, old man?"

"You hit the Italians, didn't you?"

"Yeah, and?"

"And? Tyrell, you killed a kid."

"Yo, listen man, it is what it is. That shit is done with... you good?"

Earl pulled a cigarette from his pack and lit it. The thought of a child being murdered for no reason was heavy on his brain. He couldn't stop thinking about it. "Hell no. Look at me." He raised his shirt so Tryell could see the bandages.

"Damn... what the fuck happened?"

"It don't matter what happened. I'm bowing out the game. This shit is too much. My purpose for getting back in was to get rich, not shot."

"C'mon, old man, you know that's part of it. Look at my shit." Tyrell pulled his sweat pants halfway down and showed Earl his wound. "Niggas get shot... but life goes on. It's still money out here to get."

"Yeah, but it comes with a price. And that price is usually your life. I wanna be living for the next twenty years. Not wearing a colostomy bag."

"So, what you saying, old man?"

"I'm saying, I'm out. Done. Waving the white flag. I think I'ma start going back to church."

Tyrell burst out laughing. "Church? Yo, Six... you hear this nigga? He talking 'bout he going back to church. You can't make no muthafuckin money in the church. Fuck is wrong wit' you, old man, you tripping."

Earl didn't appreciate being clowned. "That's the problem wit' you young punks, you think you know every fucking thing, but you don't. I bet you didn't know the church is a billion dollar business."

"Fuck the church." Tyrell replied. "I know one thing, I hope you got that muthafuckin' bread you owe me."

"That's why I'm here." Earl reached into his pocket and pulled out a roll of money. "I'll see you with the rest in a few days."

Tyrell snatched the wad of cash from Earl's hands. Earl sensed the hostility, but kept his cool and let it slide. He didn't come for a problem; he came to let it be known that he was stepping away from the streets.

Tyrell shuffled through the bills counting each one. "Nigga," he threw the money in Wise Earl's face. "You owe me fifteen stacks, what the fuck is that?"

"That's all I got right now. You see me, I'm fucked up."

"Fucked up?" Tyrell took a step forward. "I ain't tryna hear that fucked up shit, everybody fucked up. I'm fucked up... nigga just tried to kill me and you talking 'bout you fucked up." Tyrell was about to reach for his gun, but had second thoughts. "Yo, Earl... get that to me, dog. I'm giving you three days. I want my bread."

Earl got ready to say something slick, but didn't. He swallowed his pride and chose to be the bigger man, but inside he was boiling. He was fuming—ready to explode. Within those split seconds, he envisioned himself whipping his knife from his pocket and jamming it in Tyrell's ribs. But he wouldn't get far. He wouldn't get but a few steps before Tyrell's entourage would pounce him like wild hyenas on helpless prey. So, he played the sucker role. "Three days... I'll have it for you, don't worry."

"I ain't the one that should be worried," Tyrell responded. "Get the fuck outta here."

Earl shook his head, turned and walked off. When he walked

past Six and the young boys, Grasshopper had just come back from the store. He saw Earl had a cigarette in his hand and he wanted one.

"Yo, old timer... can I get cigarette?" Earl kept walking. "Yo! Old timer!" Grasshopper jogged to catch up with him. "Nigga, I know you—"

He touched Earl's shoulder and a second later, his back was on the concrete and he was staring up at the clear blue sky.

"Oh shit! He knocked that nigga the fuck out!" Six and his crew started keeling over from laughter. But Grasshopper's little cousin didn't like that, and he wanted to do something.

Six saw him reaching for his gun and got up from the crate. "Hold up, son, we ain't doin' that. That nigga a old school cat. Let 'em live."

"Let him live?"

"That's what I said. Do I need to repeat myself?"

The young boy dropped his head and walked off in the opposite direction. He wasn't about to challenge Six's authority.

"I CAN'T BELIEVE you left my daughter back there with that fucking physco!" Priscilla banged the top of the dashboard with both hands.

"We'll get her back, don't worry."

"Don't worry? I want her back, now!"

"We can't go back there, Priscilla. You killed a fucking cop!" Mox was doing 70 MPH in a 50 MPH zone, swerving in and out of the congested highway traffic.

"How do we know he was a cop? He didn't show us a badge."

"Cop or not, Priscilla... it's still a body. We gotta leave New York."

"Leave? I'm not going anywhere without my daughter. Pull over, Mox."

"I'm not stopping, Priscilla. You're buggin'." When she saw he had no intentions on slowing down, she leaned over, grabbed the wheel and almost caused a major collision. Luckily, Mox was a skilled driver and was able to avoid a wreck. "What the fuck is wrong with you, Priscilla? You tryna kill us?"

She sat impatient in the passenger seat, tight lipped and furious. "Stop the car, Mox." He ignored her and kept his eyes on the road ahead. "Mox, stop the car and let me out. I'm not leaving New York without Brandi. You can do what you wanna do."

"Priscilla, put your seat-belt on."

"Fuck the seat-belt, Mox. Stop the car."

"The fucking police are behind us, put your seat-belt on."

As soon as Priscilla pulled the seat-belt across her chest, the cop hit the sirens.

"Fuck!" Mox looked at Priscilla and shook his head. "You see this shit..."

Priscilla turned in her seat to see where the cop was. "He's on us, Mox. You gotta go faster."

Mox checked the rear-view and saw how close the patrol car was. "You gotta get 'em off me, Priscilla. They're too close."

"What am I gonna do?"

"You still got bullets in that gun?"

Priscilla released her seat-belt, stuck her body halfway out the window, and aimed her gun at the police car. She squeezed the trigger and let three slugs fly from the barrel into the windshield. The window shattered and the officer jerked the wheel and swerved out the lane like he'd been hit by a bullet. Mox maneuvered through a few more cars, hit the gas, and sped down the highway.

After driving for six and a half hours, Mox hit the blinker and merged with the light traffic that was flowing off 95. He looked to his right and Priscilla was sleeping, like baby—feet up in the seat with her knees to her chest. Mox made another right turn onto West Broad Street, and kept straight until he saw the Hess gas station to his left. He tapped Priscilla's leg. "Wake up."

She squirmed in her seat for a moment and then wiped her eyes free of sleep. "Where are we?" she asked, looking around.

"Virginia," Mox answered. "Richmond."

"Richmond, Virginia? What are we doing here?"

"I got a few people out here I used to deal with. I know we can blend in and move some of this work."

"What about Brandi?"

"We're gonna get Brandi back. Stop worrying. It won't do nothing but stress you out. Lemme get things in order, and I promise we'll get her back." Mox cut the ignition and exited the car to go into the store. "You want something?" Priscilla shook her head no. She was upset they had to leave their daughter behind. She couldn't believe it. She couldn't understand how someone could leave their child and be okay with it. It was disturbing her nerves.

On his way out the store, Mox's phone rang. It was new and he had given only a handful of people his information. The number that showed up on the caller ID wasn't familiar. He let it ring until it stopped, and then got back into the car. As soon as he pulled off, it rang again, same number.

"Why aren't you picking your phone up?" Priscilla questioned.

"Because, I don't know who it is."

"It could be Brandi, pick it up."

Mox thought about what she said. She could be right. He did make sure Brandi knew the number in case of an emergency, and this whole situation was an emergency. He looked down at the phone ringing and finally picked it up. "Hello?"

"Goddamn, nephew, how many times I gotta call yo' ass before you answer... shit."

"I ain't know it was you Unc, wassup?"

"I need you baby, where you at?"

"I'm OT right now, but what's good?"

"Goddamnit!"

"What's wrong, Unc, you got a problem?"

"A small thang, baby boy. But ahh... I need to see as soon as possible. When you coming back?"

"Gimme a few days and I'll meet you somewhere."

"Okay, nephew. I'll see you then. Aye, listen, be careful out there. Keep your eyes open."

"Aight, Unc, peace." Mox hung up and they pulled off.

51

After one month living in Virginia, Mox and Priscilla were back in the game. This time; even deeper. Richmond was a foreign playing field they had to get familiar with, and even being slightly familiar, it was still a task trying to adjust, especially for Mox. But he intended to keep his cool and stick to his plan. It was only so much he could do without drawing attention to himself, so he chose to play incognito and shy away from the limelight.

On the other hand, Priscilla was slipping back into some of her old ways. Somehow, she managed to befriend two females she was introduced to, and lately, she'd been hanging out, a lot. When confronted about it, her excuse was, she missed her daughter and couldn't function without her.

Mox saw the switch in her demeanor, but didn't pay it much attention. The money was coming in and he was ready to make his next move. Just a few more pieces needed to be put in place, and everything would be all good.

Despite its vast population, Richmond, Virginia is a small, close-knit city. If something happened in north Richmond, the south and the west side would find out about it immediately. There was little that went unknown in the city, so, when the word on the street was a new face was in town; everybody knew who it was—everybody but the one person who should've known.

QUIANE and two of his partners relaxed on the posh sofas in The V.I.P area of Club Bliss. It was a Friday night, and as expected, the spot was jam-packed. A barrage of six to eight women bombarded the V.I.P entrance with the hopes of someone spotting them and inviting them in. Quiane glanced down the stairs at the small crowd of barely dressed women and shook his head. "Bitches do anything to get in V.I.P."

"That one right there, with the blue dress on, she's bad." Kyle said. He was sitting to the right of Quiane, sipping his drink.

"That's Toya, I know them." Kurt told them. He was sitting on the opposite side of Quiane, going through his phone.

"Kurt, call 'em over here. I like the one in the blue, she can get it." Kyle said.

Kurt was about to call for Toya, but Quiane stopped him. "Why every time we come to the club y'all niggas gotta invite these broke ass bitches to V.I.P? Fuck that... I'm paying for their drinks tonight. You niggas want 'em up here, y'all pay for their shit."

Kurt smiled at Quiane, stood up, and then pulled a roll of cash from his front pocket. "You ain't saying nothing, nigga... I got money," He let the bills fall from his hand, and onto the table in front of them. "What's the price, my nigga? Two, three thousand?" Hundred dollar bills covered the table. "We getting money. This shit don't mean nothing to me, and it shouldn't mean nothing to you... you rich muthafucka."

"Yeah, and I'm trying to stay that way. I'm not tricking on them bum ass bitches. Y'all crazy." Quiane replied.

"It ain't tricking if you got it." Kurt sang while pouring himself a drink. He tapped Kyle on the shoulder. "That bitch, Toya a freak too, son." he laughed.

"Word? Go get 'em. Fuck what he talking about. I'm tryna score tonight."

Quiane shook his head at his homeboys and watched as Kurt made his move on the ladies.

On a regular night, Quiane would stop by Club Bliss, have a drink, and keep it moving. Tonight was different. Tonight, the club scene was a spectacle for all to see, and the entire city had come out to have fun.

Looking down at the crowded dance floor from where he stood, Quiane watched the crowd party hard. The music was blasting, fog filled the air, along with smoke from the hookahs, and the women were coming in by the bunches. Quiane finished his glass of champagne and thought he saw a face in the crowd he recognized, so he started making his way to the dance floor.

"Where you going?" Kurt asked. He was coming up the stairs, followed by four women in tight dresses and mini-skirts.

"Be right back. I'm going to the bathroom." he lied.

By the time he reached the floor/bar area, the face he'd been looking for was mixed into the crowd of hundreds. It was almost impossible to find someone you thought you saw. He stood in the crowd and continued to survey the area.

PRISCILLA FIXED her titties in her bra and then summoned the bartender. "Can I have a vodka with a splash of cranberry and pineapple, and two straight shots of Patron? What y'all drinking?" she asked her two friends.

"Same as you," they replied.

The downstairs bar area was overcrowded. It was only by a miracle Priscilla and her girls managed to get some seats. Just as they were walking up, two men and a female were leaving, so Erin, the youngest of the three, rushed over and secured the three bar-stools. Not even five minutes passed and they were turning down advances and free drinks from every dude that walked by. Priscilla's other friend, Ariel, was getting frustrated.

"Why is it every time we come to this spot, these weak dudes always pressin' us?" Just as she finished talking, a tall, light-skinned guy with curly hair brushed against her. He acted like it was an accident, and then asked to buy her a drink.

"No, nigga... I don't want you to buy me a drink," she told him. "And you didn't get the memo, huh?"

"What memo?"

"Light-skinned niggas been outta style since eighty-eight!" The three women broke out in laughter while curly hair eased off to the next group of females. It was routine for the girls to turn down more than twenty guys in less than an hour, but after a while, it became irritating.

Priscilla downed her two shots of Tequila, tapped Erin on her arm and the two of them walked towards the bathroom. "We'll be right back, Ariel. Gotta use the little girls room." she said, but Ariel knew why they were going to the bathroom. It wasn't something she participated in.

"Okay, hurry up. I'll be right here."

When they got to the restroom, there was a line that stretched to the back exit. A hoard of scantily dressed women waited for their turn to use the bathroom.

"There's too many people on this line to be standing around waiting. C'mon, Priscilla." Erin snatched her friend's hand and they maneuvered to the front of the line.

"Ungh Ungh, bitch. I know you ain't cuttin' the line!" Someone shouted.

Erin and Priscilla kept moving, and as soon as the restroom door opened, they slithered by the female exiting and scurried in.

"Damn, girl... you gonna get us jumped in here." Priscilla wasn't accustom to Erin's way of doing things. She had an *I don't give a fuck, I'ma get mine'* attitude, and it seemed to work for her, but Priscilla couldn't get familiar with it. It wasn't her style.

Erin was a true country girl from Tallahassee Florida. When she was 14 years old, her mother was diagnosed with pancreatic cancer, and 9 months later, she was dead. From that day on, Erin would learn to fend for herself. With no knowledge of who her biological father was, and her mother in a grave, she did what she felt was best for her. And what was best for her was the streets.

"Please... these bitches just be talking. They ain't gon' do nothing." She pushed the stall door open. "C'mon... get in here."

Priscilla followed her into the stall and fiddled through her Chanel purse, looking for something. "I don't know where it is." She panicked.

"Bitch, you better find it. We ain't got all day."

"Oh, here it is." Priscilla pulled a piece of aluminum foil out, unfolded it, and sprinkled a tiny amount of the white, crystallized powder onto the back of her hand. Quickly, she shoved it up her nose and passed the foil to Erin, who did the same. When they finished, they washed their hands, fixed their hair, and made their exit.

On the way back to the bar, Priscilla felt someone tap her shoulder, but she kept walking. She knew how dudes in the club got after a few drinks, and she wasn't about to blow her high, arguing with some nigga. But once he grabbed her arm, she had to turn around.

"Get the fuck—" When she saw the smile, she could do nothing but laugh. She tried to remember his name as she stood there, gazing into his eyes. "Umm... umm..." She couldn't get it. "What's your name? Honestly, I forgot."

"You forgot, huh?"

"Yeah, I mean, it's normal to forget a person's name if you haven't seen them since the day you met them."

"So, you remember meeting me?"

"Yes. But I don't remember where. Enlighten me, please."

He smiled again and then looked at Erin. He'd seen her around before. "Quiane." he said, extending his hand to Priscilla.

"Yes. Quiane... now I remember. How are you?"

"I'm good, and yourself? I see you're looking sexy as ever."

The compliment made Priscilla blush, which was rare. "Thank you," she replied. "I'm okay, just enjoying the weekend."

"Ughmm... excuse me," Erin butted in. "You're not gonna introduce me to your little, friend?"

"Oh... Erin, this is, Quiane. Quiane, this is my friend, Erin."

"Why don't y'all come upstairs? We got drinks and everything."

Priscilla looked at Erin. "I can't leave my girls,"

"They can come too. Don't worry about it."

"Oh, y'all ballin', huh?" Erin joked.

"Nah, ma, we just like having fun... that's all. Now, y'all coming or what?"

"Yes, we're coming. I just have to get my other friend. We'll meet you up there."

Priscilla and Erin rushed back to the bar area where Ariel was waiting. "C'mon, we out!" Erin grabbed her arm and pulled her off the barstool. "We going to V.I.P."

"*V.I.P,* with who?"

"Priscilla's friend..." She tried to remember his name, but couldn't. "What's his name, Priscilla?"

"Quiane."

"Who?" Ariel didn't hear her.

"Quiane," she repeated. "I met him a while ago in New York. He helped me one day."

The three women looked up to the V.I.P area, and Quiane was staring down at them. He waved, telling them to come upstairs.

"Look, c'mon... " Erin pointed. "They're waiting for us."

Smiling, the three of them walked towards the stairs.

"Yo, Q... come here." Kyle was standing at the railing in the V.I.P overlooking the dance floor. "You see that nigga right there?"

"Who?"

"The nigga with the patch on his eye... right there."

"Yeah, yeah... I see him. Who is he?"

"That's the nigga I was telling you about. He out here getting money."

Quaine smirked as he peered down at the overcrowded club. He tipped the bottle of champagne to his lips and drank. After he wiped his chin, he looked at Kyle, and then over the crowd again. He wasn't too fond of new faces in his town, but tonight he was more focused on Priscilla. He'd deal with his new problem whenever he saw fit. "Get all the info you can, and I'll take care of it on another date. Tonight," he watched the three women walk. "I'ma take care of this right here."

As soon as the girls reached the stairs that led to the V.I.P area, Ariel made a swift turn on her heels and started to go back downstairs. Priscilla chased after her to see what the problem was. "Ariel, what's wrong?"

"Do you know who he is, Priscilla?"

Priscilla looked back. "Who?"

"Quiane."

"Oh, you know him?"

"*Know him?*" Ariel's eyes got big. "He's only *the* biggest drug dealer in Richmond. Duh... everybody knows him."

"And, what... that's a problem?"

"My boyfriend's not going like the fact that I'm hanging out with his arch enemy."

"C'mon, just have one drink with us and then we'll leave."

"I can't, Priscilla... I gotta go." Ariel didn't waste another second. She knew what Quiane was about. In fact, she'd seen him and his cronies in action more than once. Richmond Virginia was her home, and she knew every player in the game. She also knew Quiane had a reputation for making trouble in the streets. It was something he liked to do.

"Where that bitch going?" Erin questioned, watching Ariel walk back down the steps.

"She said she had to go. Her man called."

Erin rolled her eyes and went back to the sofa where Quiane and his boys were sitting. She knew why Ariel left, but she didn't care. Erin was out to enjoy herself.

Priscilla and Erin stayed in the V.I.P with Quiane and his boys for an hour. They had drinks, laughs and more drinks as they partied the night away.

Quiane and Priscilla were engaged in conversation the whole time. She could tell by the way his peers acted around him that he had power, and she knew he had money from the watch he was wearing.

"That's a nice watch."

Quiane smiled. "What you know about watches?"

"I know a lil' something. Not much, but enough."

"Enough, huh?" He smiled again, but this time Priscilla was blushing. "So, how you been, Ms. Mysterious?" Quiane giggled.

"Ms. Mysterious? What's that supposed to mean?"

"It means exactly what it means. Listen, I saw you in need of help, so I helped you. But after I dropped you off, you got locked up and I never heard from you again. I would say that's kinda mysterious, wouldn't you?"

"First of all," Priscilla rolled her eyes. "You hit me with your fucking truck, so don't act like you did some Superman shit and saved the day." She bent down and grabbed at her leg. "I have the scar to prove it, too."

They laughed when Priscilla couldn't keep a straight face.

"I really didn't mean to hit you. But you darted into the street like someone was chasing you. I always wanted to ask; what that was all about?"

"Nothing."

"Nothing? It looked like something to me. You was running for your life." Quiane laughed.

"Oh, that was funny to you, huh?"

"Nah, I'm saying..." he couldn't stop laughing. "You hauled ass up outta there."

"Well, all that's over and done with. I got new problems now."

Quiane sipped his drink. "Don't we all."

For the next forty minutes, Priscilla and Quiane talked about everything that came up. They discussed life, and she badly wanted to let him in on her secret, but she was skeptical. She really didn't know this man, but she felt comfortable in his presence. It was something about the way he spoke. It was his aura—his swagger.

"So, where's your girlfriend?"

The question surprised Quiane and he almost spit his drink out. "*Girlfriend?* Who said I had a girlfriend?"

"Are you telling me you don't?"

"That's exactly what I'm telling you. What's good with you, where's your man?"

"At home."

"Oh, so you do have one?" Quiane nodded his head. "He let you come out all sexy like that by yourself?"

"I'm not by myself... and he doesn't *let* me do anything. I do what I wanna do."

"I hear that. You a big girl, huh?"

They laughed together.

In the middle of their conversation, Erin walked up, sipping her drink. She nudged Priscilla on the arm and gestured for her to look downstairs. "We got trouble at twelve-o-clock," she warned.

At that moment, Priscilla had no idea what Erin was talking about; that was until she saw him with her own eyes.

"Oh shit." she placed her drink on the table. "Sorry," she said, looking at Quiane. "We have to go."

Erin looked at her like she had two heads. "We?"

"Yes, we." Priscilla snatched her arm and tried to pull her towards the stairs, but Erin jerked from her grasp.

"*You* gotta leave," she stated. "I'm staying. I'm enjoying myself, thank you." Erin rolled her eyes and took another sip from her drink.

"But, we came together."

"Yeah, we did... but that's *your* man, so it's *your* problem."

Priscilla sucked her teeth and stormed off. She couldn't believe her so-called friend was acting this way, but there was nothing she could do. Erin had her mind made up, and nobody could tell her otherwise.

"Wassup wit' your girl?" Kyle asked. "She good?"

"Yeah, she'll be fine... her man downstairs."

"Her man, who that?"

Erin pointed to a table that was occupied by two guys. One of them had a shiny, bald-head and a patch over his eye, and the other had short, black hair and a pair of dark shades.

"Which one is her man?"

"The one with the patch."

"Oh, word?" Kyle downed his drink and stepped to where Quiane stood. He got close, leaned in and whispered in his ear. "You heard what that bitch jus' said, right?"

"Yeah... I heard." Quiane answered. "Send them niggas some champagne... it's time for us to get acquainted.

MOX CROSSED his left leg over his right knee, lit his cigar, and savored the sweet taste of the hand rolled leaf. He let the smoke out of his mouth and into a crowd of more than 200 people. The heavy bass thumped in his ears as he surveyed the jam-packed club.

"It's packed in here tonight," Travis said. He was sitting opposite Mox in a black Calvin Klein sport jacket. "I never saw it this crowded."

Mox nodded and continued to blow smoke in the air. With the overflowing crowd, he hadn't noticed the young lady creeping up on his left side, but Travis spotted her from ten feet away and gave him the warning.

"You got company."

Mox turned and saw Priscilla standing there, with a half-smile on her face. "You told me you weren't coming out,"

"I changed my mind."

She rolled her eyes. "Yeah, now, if I did that it would be a problem."

"It wouldn't be a problem. You do what you wanna do anyway."

"Please, Mox."

"Listen, Priscilla... I hope you didn't come over here to start arguing n' shit."

"I don't wanna argue with you, Mox. I came over to say hi." She reached down and gave him a hug and a kiss on his cheek.

"Excuse me, sir..." A female attendant interrupted. "Those gentlemen up there sent this to you." She placed a tin bucket filled with ice and a bottle of Moët Rosè on the table in front of them.

Mox looked up to where she pointed, but he didn't recognize the men standing against the railing. "You know them niggas?"

Travis raised his shades and peeked upstairs. "Yeah, that's the kid I mentioned the other day, Quiane... He moving a lotta weight out here. He from up top. I'm surprised you don't know him."

"Nah... I don't' know him." Mox rubbed his chin. He couldn't understand why complete strangers would send over a $350 bottle of champagne. He puffed his cigar, let the smoke flow from his mouth, and slowly turned to Priscilla. She had a blank stare on her face—confused, like she was hiding something. "You know them niggas?" he asked, looking straight in her face.

"No."

Mox shook his head. He knew she was lying because she couldn't look at him when she answered. "If you're lying to me, you know I'm gonna find out. It's only a matter of time, Priscilla." he called the attendant who brought over the Moët and asked her what their most expensive bottle of champagne was.

"I believe it's the Remy Martin Louis the thirteenth."

"And how much is that, love?"

She pulled a small pad from the pocket on her shirt. "It's five thousand."

Mox pulled three stacks of money from a small black bag and passed one to the attendant. She ripped the band off and counted out five thousand in hundred dollar bills.

"Do me a favor." Mox picked up the bucket with the Moët and gave it back to her. "Send those back up there, and tell those guys... if they're gonna send something, make sure it cost more than a thousand dollars." He looked up at the three men and smirked.

"Priscilla, get your shit. Travis, let's get outta here."

52

E arl stood in front of the full body mirror and looked over himself. He was sharp as a tack. He placed his cufflinks on and straightened his tie. It was almost time to go, and he didn't plan to be late for his debut. He brushed some lint off his pants, checked his shoes, and then kneeled and said a prayer.

"God, I know you're up there watching down on us. Especially me..." he smirked and continued. "I just wanna ask for your guidance and support while I travel this long, tedious journey. Please, Lord, give me the strength, courage and wisdom to preach the word to the people. I know I haven't been the best person... but, I also know I'm not the worst. In Jesus name... Amen."

After a few moments of silence, Earl got back to his feet, snatched his keys and headed out the door.

Summer was withering away, and autumn was tapping on its front door. A fall breeze brushed past his face as he walked down the street to where his car was parked. Earls' stomach was in knots. The last time he felt like this was more than twenty years ago when he met his first wife, Estelle.

He jumped into the driver's seat, put the key in the ignition and slowly pulled off down the road. Twelve minutes later, he was parallel parking in front of Shiloh Baptist Church on Lincoln Avenue.

Earl killed the engine and sat for a moment, watching all the churchgoers enter the House of the Lord. He thought about all the wrong he'd done; all the pain, heartache and misery he caused was coming back to haunt him. It had been days since he had a good night's sleep. Physically, he was drained, and mentally he was scrambled. His thoughts were a scattered mess. The demons he once suppressed were rising from the pits of his hell, and transforming his life into something that was becoming unstable.

A tap on the passenger side window interrupted his daze. He recognized the woman's face and rolled the window down. "How you doin', Mrs. Bailey."

"Just fine, baby. Are you ready?"

"A little nervous, but I'm sure I'll be okay."

"All you have to do is let God guide you in the right direction. I see he got you this far. Leave all your worries to him. Don't even think about 'em." she replied.

Her kind, soothing words brought a tight smile to Earl's face. He was appreciative of Mrs. Bailey's encouragement, and felt it was just what he needed, so he stepped out the car and headed into the church.

As he walked up the steps to the entrance, his stomach tightened and he felt queasy. Sweat built in his armpits and on his forehead. It had been years since his last church visit, and he had no idea what to expect.

He reached the door, and a small crowd of older women was lined up, entering the church one by one. Earl felt a hand on his shoulder and turned to see who it was. "Mrs. Garrett, how are you?" he tried to be calm.

"Fine, and yourself?"

"Not too good," he said, laughing it off. "I think I'll be okay... what you think?"

Mrs. Garrett smiled. She could see the sweat trickling down the side of his face. "Being nervous is natural, baby. You just go on in there and speak from your heart. God don't judge."

Earl agreed, and they walked into the church side by side.

Mrs. Garrett was one of the oldest sisters to attend the church, and she was also the one who convinced Earl to attend. After some much needed conversation, she was able to encourage him to share his story with the congregation.

When Earl stepped into the lobby, he signed the guestbook and an usher escorted him to his seat. Earl sat through the entire two and a half hours of service until they called his name. He closed the Bible he was holding, scooted past the two people sitting next to him and walked down the aisle to the pulpit.

He was dressed sharp in his new Brooks Brothers suit and matching wingtip shoes. The pastor stepped to the side and let Earl have the microphone.

Prior to him speaking, he scanned the crowd in hopes of seeing his nephew in attendance. The moment he realized there was no sign of him, he immediately changed his mind. There was no way he could go through with his plan if Mox wasn't there.

"Umm..." his nerves were again getting the best of him, and the sweat was starting to reappear. "I had a few things I wanted to say to you all, but unfortunately, there's been a change in my plans. Forgive me for the inconvenience... I apologize."

As he stepped away from the pulpit, he noticed Tyrell standing at the back of the church. His stomach dropped and the sweat came down heavier. Earl was in debt to Tyrell, and he knew the only reason he was there was to collect. The problem was; he didn't have it.

Mrs. Garrett got up from her seat and went over to where Earl was. "What's the problem, baby?"

Earl shook his head. "It's not the right time, Mrs. Garrett."

"Okay, baby... I guess the only time it's right is when God say it is. Until then, I'll keep you in my prayers." She moved to the side, and Earl hurried down the aisle. He had lost track of where Tyrell was in those few seconds, and he tried to rush out the door.

"Wassup, old man, where you headed?" Tyrell stepped out of a dark corner in the lobby.

Earl jumped at the sound of his voice and stopped dead in his tracks. He was terrified. "Ahh... ahh..." The words weren't coming out.

"I see you been playing hide and seek, huh? This is what it's come to? This is what gotta happen for me to get mine? You owe me, Earl. I told you, I want mine."

"Listen, Tyrell..."

Tyrell stared into Earl's eyes. The look was pure hate. He eased his right hand underneath his shirt, but before he got the chance to retrieve his gun, Mrs. Garrett interrupted them.

"Tyrell, is that you?" she moved in closer.

"Yes, Mrs. Garrett." He answered, fixing his shirt.

"I can't believe how big you've gotten." She spread her arms and hugged him. She felt the bulge on his waistline. "How's your mother? She doesn't come to the church anymore, is she alright?"

Tyrell knew she felt the gun, and he wanted to get out of there as fast as possible. "Yeah, she's fine, Mrs. Garrett... thanks for asking." He took a step towards the exit, but she grabbed his shoulder and whispered in his ear.

"You know God don't like ugly."

Tyrell looked at Earl, and then at Mrs. Garrett. He wanted to say something, but chose not to and walked out.

53

"Fill it up... and keep the change." Mox told the attendant as he handed him a hundred dollar bill. He turned the radio down and removed the key from the ignition.

"Why you always come to this gas station?" Priscilla asked. She sat in the passenger seat wearing a pair of dark sun glasses, covering her swollen, red eyes, a tight short sleeve shirt, and a pair of fitted jeans.

"Because, they have the best service, and it's the safest."

"The safest?"

"Yeah, you didn't notice there's always a patrol car at those other gas stations?" Priscilla shook her head no. "That's because you don't pay attention to your surroundings. You too busy doing other shit."

"Whatever, Mox." she sucked her teeth.

As the attendant finished pumping the gas, Mox's phone rang. He took a quick glance at it, looked at Priscilla, and then put the key into the ignition.

"Your phone is ringing."

Mox ignored her and continued to exit the gas station. When she went to reach for it, he pushed her hand away. "Don't touch my shit, Priscilla. We went through this before."

"So, pick it up," she said. "It's probably your lil' fucking girl-friend... what's that bitch's name?"

Mox was silent for a few seconds. He kept his hands on the steering wheel and his eye on the road. "Priscilla, cut it out, alright. Every day you wanna start an argument over nothing."

"Over *nothing?*" the phone was still ringing. "So, why don't you pick the phone up? Because you know I'm right." As soon as she saw the opportunity, Priscilla reached over and hit the *'Answer Call'* button on Mox's phone and a female answered.

"Hello?"

Mox slammed on the brakes and almost caused a collision. He snatched the phone from the middle console and quickly hit the *'End Call'* button.

"What the fuck is wrong with you, Priscilla?" He tried to grab a handful of her hair, but she fought him off and swung an open palm that connected to the side of his face.

"I knew it was that bitch, you lying muthafucka!"

In the midst of their squabble, Mox was able to put the car in park. He jumped from the driver's seat, rushed to the passenger side, and attempted to snatch Priscilla out of the car, but she was putting up a resistance that he wasn't expecting.

"I told you about putting your fucking hands on me." He struggled to pry her body from the vehicle, and the only thing stopping him was the seatbelt.

Priscilla tussled to stay on the inside the car, but once Mox got the seatbelt loose, there wasn't much she could do.

"Mox, stop!" She cried as he pulled her hundred plus pound body from the automobile. Once he got her out, he dragged her through the middle of the street and onto a patch of grass.

"Why are you doing this?" she sobbed. "I love you... please... stop."

Mox was oblivious to her pleads and cries. "I'm not dealing with this shit no more, Priscilla."

Priscilla wiped the tears from her face and tried to catch her breath. "Why do treat me like this, Mox? You know how much I love you."

Mox turned and started walking back to his car. He knew what he was doing was absolutely wrong, but at the time, he felt there was a justifiable reason behind it. He loved Priscilla, unconditionally—but the drama he could do without.

As he got closer to the car, her screams got louder. "Mox, please, please don't leave me!" She jumped up from the grass, but by the time she reached the car, he was pulling away. Priscilla stood there, in the middle of the street—withered, humiliated, and sobbing like a spoiled baby.

Ten minutes went by and she gathered herself and pulled her phone from her purse. She dialed a number and it rang several times. No one picked up, but less than a minute later, her phone rang.

"Hello?" she answered.

"Who is this?"

"It's, Priscilla."

"Oh... hey, wassup, baby?"

"Hey, I umm..." She was hesitant, but he was her only option. "I'm in a little dilemma and I need a favor."

"What is it, babe?"

"Can you come and get me?"

"Where are you, everything okay?"

Priscilla looked around for a street sign so she could tell him where she was. "I'm okay. I'm on the corner of Judah and Leigh Street. You know where that is?"

"Yeah, I'll be there in fifteen minutes. Stay there."

FIFTEEN MINUTES LATER

Priscilla found a shaded spot underneath a tree where she sat and cried until her eyes hurt. When she picked her head up, she saw a burgundy Jaguar pull up twenty feet from where she was. The passenger side window came down, and when she saw who the driver was, she began walking towards the car.

"Are you sure you alright?" Quiane asked after she entered the vehicle. He could see she'd been crying. Priscilla was mute. She wiped her face and shook her head no. Quiane wanted to ask what happened, but he knew it wasn't the right time, or the right place, so he turned the volume on the radio down and drove off.

Two hundred feet away, across the street from a kids playing park, Mox sat in his car. His eyes were glued to the burgundy Jaguar and he had a strong feeling of who it was. He started the car when he saw them pulling off, and followed at a respectable distance. While driving, he dialed Travis' number.

"Mox, what's good?" Travis answered.

"Ol' boy that was in the club... what he driving?"

"Umm..." Travis thought on it for a few seconds. "I saw him in a few different joints. Most recently a white drop, and a burgundy Jag... I think."

Travis just confirmed Mox's suspicion. "Okay, cool."

"Why, wassup?"

"I got the drop on this dude. I'ma follow him for a minute and see what it is."

"Oh yeah," Travis laughed. "Be careful though, you heard? I'll see you later."

54

Cleo was out of breath as he stood over the wounded man, sweating, clutching a hot pistol in his right hand. "You got one more chance to tell me where that money is, or it's over for you," he told him.

The victim, a 25-year-old young black male by the name of Jamal, was lying face down on his living room carpet. His hands were rope tied behind his back, and black electrical tape covered his eyes while faint sobs and pleas for help escaped his lips. The bullet hole in the back of his right thigh was leaking blood all over the rug. Jamal was silently praying for God to spare his life.

Since migrating south, Cleo figured he'd try his hand in the drug game. That only lasted a few months before some stick-up kids kicked his front door in and robbed him of everything but his life. He was able to escape a tragic situation by the skin of his teeth, but that particular incident is what made him take a different turn in his career choice. It wasn't long after, he started robbing the drug dealers himself. In his mind, it was easy money. Much easier than selling the drugs, because all he had to do was find a potential target, plot on him for a few days, and then attack.

The change in occupation was lucrative. Cleo had more money than he'd ever had, and was feeling like he was on top of the world.

"Turn over, nigga!" He kicked Jamal in his left rib and he rolled onto his back. "All you gotta do is tell me where it is, Jamal... you making this real difficult."

Whoadie, Cleo's partner, was tossing the house, looking for anything he could find—money in particular. So far, he'd come up with nothing. After ransacking the closet in the master bedroom, he lifted the mattress on the king sized bed in hopes of finding something underneath—but he came up empty handed again. He stood in the middle of the bedroom, looking around. He knew something was there, but he just couldn't pin point it. His eyes searched the room for the tenth time, and then fell upon the painting that was hanging over the headboard of the bed. It was slightly crooked and looked out of place.

Whoadie jumped onto the bed. As soon as he touched the painting, the right side fell down, revealing a hidden safe that was built into the wall. "Jackpot." he mumbled, and then called for his partner. "Yo, Cle!"

Cleo was still towering over Jamal, continuously kicking him in his stomach and ribs—so much that he threw up the previous night's dinner. He looked up when he heard his name. "You found something?"

"Yup!" Whoadie was examining the safe, trying to figure out how to get it open. It didn't have a keypad or any visible locks. He jumped off the bed and ran downstairs to where Cleo was. "I found the safe." he said.

Cleo's eyes got big and he smiled. "I knew there was something in here. You been playing games wit' me all fucking night." He raised his leg and stomped on Jamal's testicles. "What's the combination, muthafucka?"

Jamal grunted in pain but never once screamed. He hadn't said a word since they entered the house. He knew if they were lucky enough to find the safe, they wouldn't be able to open it unless he was there—alive.

Cleo bent down and shoved his pistol in Jamal's mouth. "Stop making this so hard, and give up the combination."

"Yo, Cle..."

Cleo ignored Whoadie. He was too focused on obtaining the combination to the safe.

"Yo, Cleo!" he yelled.

"What, nigga?"

"Ain't no keypad or lock on that joint... Go check it out."

Cleo looked down at Jamal. His lip was busted and blood was trickling down the side of his mouth. "You gonna make me kill ya' stupid ass, Jamal." He turned around and ran up the stairs to the second floor where the master bedroom was.

When he entered the room, his eyes went straight to the safe. He jumped onto the bed to get a good look at it, and it didn't take long before he figured out what he needed to open it. He rushed back downstairs.

"Pick this nigga up," he told his partner.

Whoadie struggled for a moment, but eventually got Jamal to his feet. "What you want me to do wit' him?"

"Bring his ass upstairs... he's gonna open that safe for us."

They dragged Jamal up the stairs and Cleo had him stand on the bed in front of the safe. He ripped the electrical tape from around his eyes, grabbed his neck and shoved his face right into the safe. After holding his head there for ten seconds, a green light appeared at the top of the safe. Jamal wasn't even putting up a fight. He knew it was over. There was nothing he could do.

Cleo wrapped the tape back around his eyes and then pulled a knife from his pocket and cut the rope that was tied around his wrist. He snatched Jamal by the arm and placed his right hand onto the handprint that was on the safe. Ten seconds later, another green light came on and the safe opened. Before seeing the contents, Cleo shoved Jamal off the bed and emptied his clip into his back. The shots echoed throughout the moderately furnished home, but no one for at least a quarter mile would hear them.

"Empty this shit and let's get outta here." On their way downstairs, Cleo heard a key enter the front door lock. "Oh shit... go back, go back." He whispered as they darted back up the stairs and into the master bedroom.

The front door opened and then closed, and a female shouted, "Jamal!"

Cleo and Whoadie panicked. "Why the fuck you didn't tell me somebody else would be here with him?"

Whoadie looked confused. "I didn't know," he whispered back. "Every time I came here he was by his self."

The female shouted again, but this time, her voice was getting louder because she was walking up the steps.

"Yo..." Cleo whispered. "She's coming up here. Stand on that side."

They stood on opposite sides of the door, so in case she decided to enter the room, she wouldn't be able to see them.

Cleo gripped his pistol. He released the empty clip and pushed a full one into the bottom of the weapon. The only thing they could do was wait.

The footsteps were getting closer and closer.

"Jamal, I just had the most stressful day at work... ughh... I'm starting to hate my job," she said. "Jamal?" she checked the bathroom. "You in there, babe... I had to arrest this young black kid today.

Cleo's eyes bulged at the word 'arrest'. He looked at Whoadie. "This bitch is a cop?"

Whoadie looked even more confused. He just shrugged.

The doorknob of the bedroom turned and the female cop entered the room. The first thing she saw was the painting on the wall. It was leaning to the left, and the safe was wide open—emptied of its contents.

She rushed over to the bed and almost tripped over Jamal's bullet riddled corpse. She immediately went to reach for her service weapon.

"You touch that gun, you gon' be laying next to him." Cleo had his weapon aimed at the female cop's head.

Once she turned, she saw the two men standing there, pointing guns at her. "Put those guns down guys... c'mon, let's not do this the hard way."

"Shut the fuck up, I'm giving out orders 'round this muthafucka." Cleo replied. He took two steps towards her, holding the gun with both hands.

"She's a cop, Cle... we need to get outta here." Whoadie suggested.

"Listen to your boy, Cle..." she said, repeating his name. "Put the guns down and walk out of here. I'll act like I never saw anything."

"You must think I'm stupid, huh?" Cleo took another step towards the officer, raised his pistol, and slapped her on the side of her face with it. "Lay the fuck down!" he demanded.

She stumbled into the dresser, holding her cheek. Blood oozed from her nose, through her fingers, and down her hand as she pleaded for her life. "Please, don't do this. I'ma cop..."

Cleo glanced at his partner and then down at the female officer. He hated cops. He hated their uniforms and everything they stood for. Never did they protect and serve—only harass and arrest. He held the gun in his sweaty palms—itching, anxious to take the shot. He took a deep breath, looked directly into the eyes of the female officer, and shook his head. "Wrong place, wrong time." he mumbled.

The shot burst forth and the first slug ripped into her shoulder, pinning her to the carpet. She collapsed and landed right beside Jamal.

Whaodie followed suit and squeezed the trigger on his weapon, releasing hot lead into her chest cavity. Her body jerked and shivered each time a bullet entered her. After the third or fourth slug, she was dead and blood was seeping from every hole in her body.

"Whoadie, let's make a move!" Cleo shouted. The two shooters dashed from the house and into their car that was parked out front.

They hit the highway and drove 30 miles without saying a word. When they felt they were in the clear, smiles danced across their faces.

"This shit is too easy," Cleo expressed. "It can't get no easier than this." he looked over to his partner. Whoadie was smiling, but he wasn't as excited as Cleo. "What's the problem?"

"Man... we just killed a cop, Cle... that's serious shit. You know we can't go back there... ever."

Whoadie was right and Cleo knew it. "Be easy, man... we good. Fuck it, we just go somewhere else. It's niggas getting money all over the globe. Fuck you tripping for?"

"I ain't tripping, nigga... I'm just saying... where the fuck we gonna go?"

Cleo turned and glanced at the duffle bag in the backseat. "I'm pretty sure we got enough money to go where ever the fuck we wanna go."

Whoadie sat quiet in the passenger seat. He was thinking hard. "Oh," he said, sitting up in his seat. "My cousin."

"Your cousin who?"

"Remember I was telling you about my family from up top... the nigga, Quiane."

"Oh, yeah... the fly, pretty muthafucka."

"Yeah, him. He's in Virginia gettin' it, I spoke to him a few days ago."

"Oh word," Cleo kept his hands on the steering wheel, but his mind was in Virginia. "So, call that nigga and let him know we on our way."

"Aight." Whoadie replied.

"But yo... what part of Virginia is he in?"

Whoadie rubbed his chin, trying to remember the city his cousin was staying in. "Umm... hold on... oh, I think he said Richmond... yeah, Richmond Virginia, that's it."

"Richmond, huh?" Cleo pressed the gas harder and the speedometer reached 90 MPH. "I bet there's a whole lotta niggas getting money in Richmond."

55

SOMEWHERE IN NEW JERSEY

A stint of light from the flickering flame atop the candle on the television stand was all that could be seen. The rest of the room was black. The scent of sweaty sex was prevalent in the air and the sounds of repetitive moans filled the atmosphere.

"Yeah, baby, ride that... show daddy you know how to work the stick." Priest was lying on his back, in his plush king sized bed, holding onto the slim waist of his young companion, while she bounced on his hard dick.

"Ooh... I feel this dick in my stomach, daddy... ooh!" April arched her back and slid up and down Priest's rock hard shaft until she felt her climax building up. She licked her lips, pressed her chest against his and shoved her tongue into his mouth. They exchanged hot saliva for a few seconds, and then she kissed his neck and went down to his chest. When she flickered his nipple with her tongue, he jumped from the pleasure. "You like that?" she asked.

Priest moved his hands from her waist and palmed her ass cheeks. "Yeah, stay on that dick... just like that." he moaned.

April slid up and down a few more times, and slowly slid off.

"Whoa... whoa, what you doing?" He tried to grab her ass.

"Shhh... I got this," she whispered and slid between his legs. She pecked his hard-on with her soft lips. "You like that?" Priest nodded yes. April cupped his balls with her left hand, stroked his shaft with her right, and slurped on the head of his dick like it was her favorite Blow-pop.

"Oh shit, I'm 'bout to cum, baby." Priest's body tightened up and he exploded in her mouth.

April didn't budge. She swallowed every drop that came out, looked up at Priest, licked her lips and smiled.

Suddenly, the bedroom light came on. "Bravo! Bravo! Encore! Encore!" Two white men in suit jackets, jeans, and boots stood at the bedroom entrance, clapping as if a show had just ended.

"What the fuck!" Priest shoved April off the bed, rolled over to the opposite side and went to reach for his gun, underneath his pillow, but he was too slow. One of the agents rushed over with his weapon drawn and put the barrel to the tip of Priest's nose.

"Reach for it, I dare you," he said, gripping the weapon with both hands. "Get the fuck on the floor."

Priest eased his hand away from the pillow and took a deep breath. These guys sounded like cops, and if the sounded like cops, more than likely they were.

"Aight... don't shoot, just calm down." Priest begged, sliding off the bed. He lay flat on his chest with the side of his face pressed against the hardwood floor.

The second guy in the suit jacket came to where Priest lay. "Get up," he said, kicking his leg. "It's time you and I have a conversation." He turned to April, who was crouched in the corner, covering her naked body. "Here, put some fucking clothes on." He tossed a t-shirt at her.

Priest got up slow. He was butt naked, standing face to face with the guy in the suit jacket. "Conversation? I don't even fucking know you."

A quick, sharp right hand connected to his lower abdomen and he went down to one knee.

"Good, because I didn't tell you my fucking name, smart ass. Now, listen here, Mister Priest. We can do this the easy way or the extremely hard way. Your choice."

Priest raised his head and glanced at the other guy in the suit jacket. He still had his gun in hand. He weighed about 220 pounds and stood over six feet, which made him slightly bigger. Priest contemplated a rumble with the two men, but he honestly knew he didn't stand a chance. He understood the end result would not be a good one.

"What the fuck you want?" he held onto the spot where he got hit.

The white dude in the suit jacket reached inside his pocket and pulled out a badge. He tossed it at Priest and it hit his chest and fell to the floor. "I'm Agent O'Malley, and that's my partner, Agent Havoc.

Priest turned and glanced at Havoc. He was still clutching his weapon. "I ain't did nothing for the Feds to be fucking with me." he said.

Agent O'Malley grabbed a pair of pants that were on a chair in the corner of the room. "Here," he tossed them at Priest. "Put the pants on and we can talk."

Priest slid into the jeans and then fished for his tank top that was hidden underneath the covers. Once he found it, he put it on. "So, wassup?"

Agent O'Malley pulled the chair to the bed and faced Priest. "We got you on an attempted murder of a federal informant, but I think we can work something out."

Priest smiled, showing his pearly whites. He didn't believe a word that came from O'Malley's mouth. In fact, he was starting to think they weren't even cops. "Fuck outta here," he said. "Y'all fucking crazy. I didn't attempt to murder anyone, you got the wrong person." He went to stand up, but O'Malley pulled his piece from his waistline.

"Sit your black ass down before I put a bullet between your fucking eyes."

"Aight, chill." Priest put his hands up and sat back on the bed. "I'm telling you... you got the wrong person. Whatever you're talking about, I didn't do it."

"So, who the fuck is this?" O'Malley whipped out a picture of Earl, lying in a hospital bed.

Priest swallowed the lump in his throat. "I don't know that nigga."

As soon as the last word rolled off his tongue, O'Malley's right palm was connecting to the side of his face. "Don't fucking lie to me!"

Agent Havoc stepped up and pushed his gun in Priest's face. "Let me shoot this piece of shit, O'Malley."

"Stand down, Agent."

"Wait..." Priest was regaining his equilibrium. "Wait... aight... hold up." He touched his jaw because it felt like he got punched instead of slapped. He looked at O'Malley's hands. They were huge. "Aight, I know that muthafucka, but he ain't no federal informant."

"You sure about that?"

"Man, that's Earl. I known that nigga all my life, and I ain't never heard of him being a rat."

"Yeah, well, certain circumstances will make a person do things they normally wouldn't do."

Priest looked around the room. April was still crouched in the corner. "I ain't no snitch."

O'Malley glanced at Havoc and laughed. "Don't they all say that in the beginning?" He got up from the chair and stood over Priest. "Listen, asshole. I know more than you think I know, believe me... but our problem ain't with you."

"So, why you fucking with me?"

"Shut up and listen," O'Malley demanded. "This little attempted murder situation, this is nothing. You'll do what, ten... fifteen years. Not to mention this is fed time, not that state shit you did before." He sat back in the chair. "You're too old to be going back to jail, Priest. Help us help you."

Priest sat in silence for a moment. Of all the crimes he'd committed, and all the times he's been interrogated, never once had he been asked to cooperate. It was as if they knew he wouldn't do it, so they never asked. Priest was a stand up dude, and as far as he knew, so was Earl. That's why it was hard to believe what O'Malley was saying. "I don't know about this..." he rubbed his head. "It just don't sound right. Why the fuck would Earl be working for the Feds?"

O'Malley pulled his phone from his pocket. "Earl done got

himself into something he can't get out of." He passed the phone to Priest. "You know him?" It was a picture of Tyrell.

"Nah." Priest lied again.

"That's Tyrell Michaels. We got him on a murder charge and a few drug cases. Young muthafucka thinks he's Nino Brown or something." O'Malley shook his head. "Anyway, Earl owes the kid some money and hasn't paid yet. Word is, Tyrell put some money on his head."

"And being that you guys have this information, you went to Earl with it, and he's willing to help y'all if y'all help him, correct?"

"Exactly." O'Malley answered.

"So, what I got to do with this?"

"I'm getting to it, I'm getting to it." O'Malley took the phone from Priest, moved to the next picture, and handed it back to him. "There's our problem, and I'm pretty fucking sure you know who that is." It was a picture of Mox.

"Nope."

O'Malley used his other hand and slapped the opposite side of Priest's face. "You keep lying to me and I'll keep fucking you up."

Priest felt his cheek and smiled. It didn't matter how many pictures they showed him, the answer would always be no.

"Now, here's what it is..." O'Malley stood up again. "Our only concern is him, right there," he pointed at the phone and then to Priest. "Your son. Your one and only biological son, Mox Daniels."

Priest took a deep breath and dropped his head.

"C'mon, Priest, we know everything. Earl's sister's murder on down to Mox's little brother's murder... even Brandi's kidnapping... all of it." O'Malley scooted the chair closer to the bed, leaned in to Priest's ear, and whispered. "We even know it wasn't you who killed Mox's mom. Believe me, Priest, we know every-fucking-thing."

Priest closed his eyes and fell back onto the bed. He couldn't believe how much information they had.

"Help us help you, Priest... do the right thing." Agent Havoc instructed.

"We want Mox and Priscilla, Priest. Bring them to us and all this will go away."

Priest sat up, wiped his face and laughed. "I guess y'all don't know everything, huh?"

"What's that?" O'Malley asked.

"How do you expect me to get close to Mox, when he thinks I murdered his mother. He wants to kill me."

"Don't worry about that."

"Don't worry about it?"

O'Malley was getting upset. "Yeah, what are you hard of fucking hearing now? I said don't fucking worry about it." he reached down, picked up his badge and holstered his gun. "Let us worry about everything else, you just bring them back here."

Priest was confused. "Bring them back, from where?"

"Richmond, Virginia."

Priest scratched his head. "Y'all want me to go to Richmond, Virginia, find my son and his girlfriend, and bring 'em back to New York, so you can lock 'em up?"

O'Malley tapped Priest shoulder. "There you go... see, you're picking up quick."

"Suck my dick, you cracka muthafucka. I ain't doing—"

Those were the last words Priest got out, before Agent Havoc smashed him in the back of his head with the butt of his service weapon.

"What the fuck did you do that for?"

Agent Havoc shrugged. "Fucking guy kept talking smack, O'Malley. How much of that shit am I forced to listen to?"

"Goddamnit!" O'Malley kicked the chair. "We didn't get him to say yes."

Agent Havoc stared at Priest knocked out on the bed. "I bet his ass says yes when he wakes up."

They laughed. "Aye, you..." O'Malley called to April. "Get dressed and get the fuck out of here. Don't ever let me see you around this fucking piece of shit again."

April snatched her belongings and dashed out the house half-dressed.

"Aye, Havoc... you got a real fucking grudge against black guys, huh?"

"Leave it alone, O'Malley." Havoc knew exactly where his partner was trying to go with that remark.

"I'm just saying... your wife still banging that drug dealer guy?" O'Malley burst into laughter.

"Fuck you, O'Malley."

"Yeah, try going home to fuck your wife, asshole."

56

"**D**amn Unc, I hear you... stop yelling in my ear." Mox held his phone in one hand and the steering wheel in the other.

"Well, I'm jus' making sure, nephew. How long before you get here?" Earl asked on the other end.

"I'll be through in like, twenty minutes. I'm starving too... been driving all fucking night." Mox turned his lip up and side eyed Travis, snoring in the passenger seat. "I should'a stopped in Harlem and got something to eat, but I said fuck it, I'll just get something when I get there."

"I got food here, don't worry."

"Aight, Unc, I'll see you in a few." Mox hung up and continued north on the highway.

The sun had just come up and the highway was empty of traffic. Mox pushed the rented Porsche truck to 80 MPH, clutching the steering wheel, and at the same time, keeping an eye out for lurking law enforcement. They were known to be hidden in certain spots off the road—camouflaged—waiting to catch someone moving above the speed limit.

"The Glamorous Life," by Sheila E came on the radio, and Mox raised the volume. Travis squirmed in his seat, trying to get all the rest he could, but Mox had different plans. The loud music wasn't enough, so he tugged at Travis' arm and rolled the windows down. The fresh November winds smacked his face and he jumped to attention, wiping his eyes, looking around.

"Wake up, nigga. We in New York."

Travis looked at his watch. It read ten minutes past six am. "Damn nigga," he said, stretching. "You was flying, huh?"

"Hell yeah. I did ninety the whole way."

It was a few minutes past midnight when he and Travis got on the highway in Virginia. Due to the light traffic, he'd been able to make the trip in one of his fastest times.

Travis slipped his sneakers back on and sipped his water. "I know one thing, I'm hungrier than a muthafucka. I hope we going to get something to eat."

Mox agreed. "Me too. You already know. My uncle said he got some grub at the crib, so we good."

They cruised the remaining distance until exit 16 came up and Mox veered to the right and got off.

As far as Mox and Priscilla's relationship, the past month and a half had been rough. The strain was beginning to put distance between them. Priscilla would come in at the wee hours of the morning, several times during the week. Mox knew what it was, but he didn't want to let go, and neither did she.

Mox's trips to New York became more frequent, and were no longer just business. More than often, he would mix his business with pleasure, and he knew better than to do that.

Despite the altercations and the drama, Mox was still seeing Jasmine. Only now, it had become more normal and serious. He purchased a three-bedroom condominium in Hartsdale, New York, and she was living in it. Jasmine was satisfied, and for the time being, they lived a drama free life, but those moments don't last long.

"When was the last time you was in New York?" Mox asked Travis.

"Shit... I ain't been back here since I was six years old."

"Damn, that's a minute. Your family ain't out here?"

Travis gazed out the window at his birthplace. "Nah, my mother didn't have any brothers or sisters, it was just us. Once we moved south, she never looked back. I don't know who my father is..."

Travis paused. "Fuck that nigga... and my grandmother died five years ago."

"Yeah, I be feeling the same way. You know what's real though?"

"What's that?"

Mox tightened his grip on the steering wheel and glanced at Travis. "I just hope my daughter don't say that shit about me."

The rest of the ride to uncle Earl's house was silent. They pulled up to the address he'd given them and Mox parked the truck.

"This your uncle's crib?" Travis asked.

Mox shrugged. "I guess so. This is where the GPS brought us. I never been to this spot. He do so much moving around, you never know what this dude is into."

The property they were in front of was a one family townhouse style home with a short driveway and a small front yard. Mox and Travis got out the car and walked to the front door, but before he got a chance to knock, the door opened, and uncle Earl was there to greet them.

"Nephew, wassup?" he said with open arms.

"Whaddup, Unc." Mox hugged him, patted his back, and got a good look at him. "You looking good, Unc... I see you," he smiled.

Earl looked at Travis. He'd never seen him before. "Who's your homeboy?"

"That's my road dog, Unc, Travis,"

Earl extended his arm and shook Travis' hand. He pulled the door open and let the two men inside.

"So, what's the emergency, Unc?" Mox looked around the nicely furnished house. His uncle always had a good sense of style.

Earl took a seat on his leather couch and picked the Bible up from the coffee table.

"Did you ever read this book, Mox?"

"Bits and pieces. Why?"

Earl opened the Bible to a page he had bookmarked and recited a passage to himself. After he finished, he looked up at Mox. "This is the most powerful book you could ever read. You know why?"

"Nah, why?"

"Because, it can change your life, Mox." Earl looked down at himself. "I'm living proof, nephew. I found my calling... and this book right here is the reason."

Mox had a stunned look on his face. "I don't understand where you going with this, Unc. What, you read the Bible... okay."

Earl shook his head. "You don't get it, nephew," he tried to explain. "I found God, Mox. I accepted Jesus Christ into my life, and ever since that day, I pray and worship him every minute of every hour. I thought you were gonna be here a few weeks ago, and I had something set up. I need you to come to the church with me."

"To the church?"

"Yeah, next month, on Christmas Day. I'm getting baptized and I want you to be there. I also got a few words to say."

Mox stared at his uncle to see if he was joking or not, but Earl kept a straight face. "You serious, huh?"

Earl nodded yes. "Excuse me for being rude. Y'all want something to drink?"

"Yeah, get us some water, Unc... and bring some food."

Earl went into the kitchen to fix some drinks and a few snacks for his houseguests while they sat and relaxed on the couch. Almost ten minutes went by before he returned, carrying a tray with two glasses of water and two plates of food.

"Unc your phone was ringing, somebody named O'Malley called." Mox pushed the phone to the other side of the table.

Earl's eyes popped wide open at the mention of O'Malley, but neither Travis nor Mox caught it. "Yeah, umm... that's the guy from the church. I'll give him a call back in a few."

The deception was making Earl extremely uncomfortable. This was his nephew—his bloodline. And although he had't snitched on him, he was still a rat because he was going to snitch on someone else. He knew how Mox felt about rats; in fact, it was one of the most important rules of the game he learned from Earl. But circumstances were different now. Tables were turned, and the cards that were dealt were now being played. Earl was still coming to terms with the decision he made. He felt it was best for his well-being. He was afraid for his life.

"So, Unc," Mox broke off a piece of the grilled cheese sandwich and tossed it in his mouth. "You really getting baptized?"

"Yeah. I need to make a change in my life style. I need some stability—some direction."

Mox listened to his uncle, and he sounded sincere. It was the first time he'd heard him speak about religion with such passion. "I respect it, Unc, shit... I got no choice but to respect it, but you already know how I'm living. I really don't do the church thing."

"You telling me you not coming?"

"Nah, I'm not saying that. I'll be there, don't worry."

Mox and Travis sat with Earl for an hour before they left. Hartsdale, New York was one of the few stops he had to make before going to see Juan Carlos, to handle his business.

HARTSDALE, NEW YORK

Mox hit the lights and pulled into the gated community. He punched his code in the panel at the front gate and continued up the winding road until he was at his front door.

A black Mercedes Benz and a blue Corvette occupied the two guest parking spaces next to Jasmine's Range Rover, so he knew she had company. He parked a few spaces down and he and Travis got out the car and walked to the house. Before he stuck the key into the door, he could hear the music playing from the inside. "They probably in there drinking n shit." he said to Travis as he opened the door.

Mary J Blige and Lil' Kim's video, "I Can Love You," was playing on the flat screen television and blasting through the surround sound. Jasmine's two friends were in the middle of the living room, dancing and singing along.

"Y'all having a party, huh?" Mox said. Jasmine looked up, smiling. She knew her man's voice anywhere. She lowered the music and got up from the sofa to greet Mox. "Wassup, babe?" He wrapped his strong arms around her soft, warm body. "You miss me?"

Jasmine kissed her teeth. "Nope," she joked, kissing his lips. She reached down and cuffed his sack. "I miss him, though."

"Yeah? I bet you do." Mox looked at her two friends. "Wassup, Melonie?" He had no idea who her other friend was, so he just waved. "Jasmine, this my homie, Travis. Travis this my boo, and her crazy ass friend, Melonie."

"How you doin?" Travis shook Jasmine's hand and waved at her two friends.

"Are you staying for dinner, Mox?"

He wanted to say yes, but time wasn't permitting. He had a couple more stops before his meeting. "Nah, babe... I told you, I gotta take care of something. Next time I come up, I'll be able to stay."

No, was exactly what Jasmine did not want to hear. She told Mox she was comfortable with their situation, but honestly, she was jealous of Priscilla. She was annoyed that he constantly expressed his love for her, but woke up every morning to someone else. Jasmine no longer wanted to be viewed as second in line; she wanted the top spot. But to even be considered for that spot, she needed a relevant explanation—a sure reason for him to leave the person he was with.

"Mox, I need to tell you something." Jasmine grabbed his arm and led him into the kitchen, fifty feet away.

"I'll be right back," he told Travis. When they entered the kitchen, Jasmine grabbed the lump in Mox's pants and massaged it. She got close to him and slipped her tongue into his mouth. Mox cupped her ass cheeks as he felt his dick hardening. "Chill... you gonna get him hard," he whispered in her ear.

"That's exactly what I wanna do." She whispered back, pulling his zipper down. Jasmine started to go down on her knees, but Mox stopped her.

"Not right now, babe... I told you, I gotta go."

"Shh..." She put her finger to her lips. "It won't take long. I got you." she assured.

Mox couldn't resist seeing her soft, wet lips around his hard dick. Jasmine gave the best head. It was one of the many reasons he kept going back. And he agreed with her. The way she worked those lips, it wouldn't take long at all. Seconds later, he succumbed to her sweet seduction. He leaned his back against the seven-foot refrigerator and let Jasmine take control.

She released his medium hard-on from his boxer briefs and let it fall over her hand. Jasmine loved chocolate, but she loved Mox's chocolate pipe even more. She licked her lips at the sight of his muscle hardening in her grasp, kissed the tip, and then took as much into her mouth as she could.

The music came back on. Mox jumped and turned to see if anyone was coming. Jasmine kept sucking. She held his stiffened manhood in both of her hands while she slobbed on his sack.

"Relax, baby," she said, jerking and sucking his shaft. "They're not coming in here, we're alright." Her motion sped up and Mox let his head rest against the refrigerator. His eyelid shut, and he felt his climax building up. Minutes later, he opened his eye and watched Jasmine with her pretty face, slob all over his dick. She stopped and looked at him. "Am I doing it good, baby?" Mox nodded yes. "I want you to cum in my mouth, and all over my face." Mox nodded yes again. He couldn't seem to get any words out of his mouth.

Jasmine continued stroking Mox's long, log third leg. He snatched a handful of her hair once he felt his nut coming and she kept her lips wrapped around his head.

"Ooooohh... I'm cummin', baby."

Jasmine opened her mouth, and got ready for his load to shoot down her throat, and Mox exploded. She jerked faster, catching everything that came out. It was in her eyes, dripping off her chin, and even in her hair. "Damn, baby, that was a lot." She wiped the cum from her face. "I still haven't told you what I need to tell you."

Mox smiled. "I thought this is what you needed to tell me?" He looked down at his dick.

"Part of it," she answered. "But not the most important part."

"Important part, what's that?"

Jasmine snatched a paper towel, wet it, and then wiped her face clean. She was hesitant on revealing the news to Mox. She didn't know how he would react, and the last thing she wanted was to push him away. She gazed into his eye and tried to read his thoughts.

"You know I love you, right, Mox?"

Mox smiled. "I love you too."

"You know I understand our situation, but to be honest, I want more of your time."

"Babe, I can't—"

"Wait," she cut him off. "Let me finish saying this. Mox, I haven't been with a man that made me feel this good in a long time. I can honestly say I trust you, I love you, dearly, and I want us to start a family together." She paused and waited for his reaction.

Mox was silent. He didn't know what to say. He loved Jasmine, and had strong feelings for her. But for them to start a family, they would have to make a child, and that was something Mox hadn't planned.

When she saw he wasn't going to say anything, she blurted out. "Mox, I'm seven weeks pregnant."

"You're what?"

"I'm seven weeks pregnant," Jasmine grinned. "We're gonna have a baby."

"A baby?"

"Yes, Mox... a child, you know... an infant. How does that make you feel?" Mox was stunned. He didn't know whether to be happy because of the blessing or upset because of his situation. "Well, say something."

"I guess, I feel good," he paused. "Yeah, I feel good... I mean, there's a life growing inside of you, how can I not be happy?"

"So, you're not mad?"

"No," he said, wrapping her in his arms. "Not at all. It's a surprise, but, it's also a blessing. I'm very happy that you're carrying our child."

"You being happy makes me happy, Mox." She leaned in and kissed his cheek. "I love you and there's nothing that can make me change the way I feel."

"I love you too, babe. Listen, I got some important business to take care of, so I gotta get outta here. I'll call to check up on you and make sure you all right. Cool?"

"Yes," she answered. "But I would be much better if you stayed."

"You know I can't stay, baby. Next time I come up, I'll stay for a few more days than I usually do, how's that?"

"I don't have a choice, do I?"

Mox shrugged and kissed her cheek. "I'll see you in a few weeks." Before walking out, he looked in her eyes and placed his hand on her stomach. "Take good care of our baby," he said, before he and Travis made their exit.

57

A fter visiting Jasmine, Mox floored the $90,000 vehicle up the highway to New Rochelle. It had been months since he walked through the projects. The memories served as horror stories that he felt he could live without. His reluctance was built mostly on fear; he was afraid to face his reality and deal with the issues at hand, he kept dodging them—eluding the truth, running from his own shadow.

He tapped the blinker, got off at the exit and navigated his way through the back blocks and onto Webster Avenue. Once he reached Horton Avenue, he parked, and he and Travis got out the car. "This is my hood, this is where it all started."

It was two days before Thanksgiving and the hood was empty. A cool breeze whizzed by and blew some leaves into the street as the two men entered Hartley Projects.

"I know that's not that nigga, Mox!" Someone shouted.

Mox and Travis turned their heads at the same time, trying to see who was speaking, but no one was on the street; just parked vehicles. Mox saw someone wave their arm out the window of a red Mercedes Benz, three cars from where they stood.

"Who is that?"

"Come and see!" The person yelled back.

Mox looked at Travis and walked towards the parked car. When he got within ten feet, he heard the door pop open and the driver stepped out.

"Whaddup, nigga?" Tyrell threw his arms up.

"Oh shit, Rell... whaddup?" A smile came across Mox's face. He hadn't seen Tyrell in almost a year. The last time they spoke, it was about Dana's murder. "Okay, I see you lil' nigga." he nodded. To see Tyrell doing good for himself brought joy to his heart. He could tell by his demeanor and the car he was driving what type of business he was into, but Mox never judged. "You got your weight up, huh?"

Tyrell smiled. He had a certain respect for Mox. He knew everything he told him was to benefit him in the end. In the short time they did spend around each other, Tyrell soaked up plenty of jewels. He learned a lot and saw a lot. "Yeah, something like that." he answered modestly. "I'm just out here tryna eat like everybody else."

"Trying? Mox smirked. "Stop fronting, nigga, I see you... new Benz n' shit," He pointed to the car Tyrell got out of. "You fresh, probably fucking all the bitches... I know, nigga."

Tyrell laughed. "Yo, chill... you wild." He pulled a roll of money from his pocket and held it up so Mox and Travis could see it. "Fuck them bitches though, this is what it's all about."

Mox was impressed. The young boy was coming into his manhood. "Take a walk with me real quick." he said. "Oh," he turned to Travis who was standing off to the side. "Yo, Rell, this my homey, Travis. Travis, this my lil' man, Rell."

"Peace." Tyrell gave Travis a pound. "C'mon, Mox, we can walk up the block." He turned and yelled down the block. "Yo Six! Yo Six!"

"Yo!" Six screamed from a few feet away.

"Keep ya' eyes open!" Tyrell tapped Mox and they walked off. "So, what's good?"

"Wassup with the white boys?"

"Them niggas is history. I handled that."

"You handled that, handled that?" Mox repeated.

"I handled that, my nigga. Trust me, newspaper clippings and all." Tyrell reached into his back pocket, pulled his wallet out, and showed Mox the newspaper clipping. He took a few seconds to read it through. The only light on the street was from the street lamps, and he had to squint to see the words on the paper.

"You killed a kid, nigga."

Tyrell dropped his head in shame. Out of the many things he'd done in the street, that was something he wished he could take back. "I didn't mean to do it. I thought he was gonna stay inside. That's my word, Mox... that shit be fucking wit' me too."

"What about, Vinny? I don't see anything about him."

"I don't think he was there, and if he was, he was inside."

Mox didn't like that a kid had been killed, but he was satisfied. Mikey and his brother were dead, and if need be, he would deal with Vinny when the time came.

"Have you seen or heard from Frank or Nate?"

Tyrell dropped his head again. "You don't know, huh?"

"Know what?"

"The Italians hit Nate in Frank's club, a couple months back."

"Get the fuck outta here..."

"Word."

Mox couldn't believe it. "Not Nate, Nate was tough as nails."

"They caught him slipping... fucking wit' them bitches in the club and not paying attention to his surroundings."

"Damn," Mox shook his head. "So, where the fuck is Frank?"

"Shit... I don't know. Police shut the club down and nobody seen that nigga. Like he disappeared off the face of the earth."

"Dissapeared, huh?" Mox laughed. "Yeah... so, wassup? You wanna make some real money?"

"What's real money?" Tyrell asked.

"A hunit... hunit and fifty a day."

"Every day?"

"Every day."

"You telling me I can make a hunit thousand dollars every day of the week... even Sunday?"

"Nigga," Mox paused and looked Tyrell in his face. "Even on Sunday."

The headlights from a dark colored car at the stop sign up the block caught Tyrell's attention. "Watch this car coming down," he warned. "Niggas ain't gon' catch me slipping." He pulled his gun off his waist and cocked it.

Mox took a few steps back, between two parked cars, and watched as the vehicle cruised down the street. It seemed to slow up once it reached Tyrell, but then it kept cruising by.

"Them niggas come back around this block, they gon' get it."

Mox looked down at the gun in Tyrell's hand. "You can't get money and be out here on some gun ho shit... it's not gonna work."

"It's been working."

"How long you think it's gonna last? Not long at all. A few more months and you'll either be dead, or locked away for the rest of your life."

"Mox, I ain't tryna hear this shit right now. I'm out here. Any nigga disrespect me or mines, and they gettin' it. Straight like that. I ain't got time to be playing wit' these niggas."

"And that's exactly what I'm tryna tell your hard headed ass. You wasting your time out here, you could be living like a king if you wanted to."

"I'm already living like a king," Tyrell flashed the Oyster Perpetual Rolex on his wrist. "This ain't no regular nigga shit. Grown men can't even afford the kind of shit I be rocking."

Mox chuckled. He had no choice but to respect the youngster. He was holding his own. "I see you, and I also see you ain't gonna change your mind, but that's cool."

"It ain't broke, Mox. You know as well as I do, If it ain't broke, don't fix it."

Mox agreed. "You're right." He gave Tyrell a pound and he and Travis walked to the truck.

"What that lil' nigga talking about?" Travis asked.

Mox started the car and pulled off. "He doing his own thing; I respect it though, I can't be mad at the lil' nigga, he getting a lil' money so he feeling good... fuck him."

THE NEXT MORNING, Mox and Travis met up with Juan Carlos in the Bronx to handle business. As instructed, the Porsche truck with

$160,000 in it was left parked in front of an auto repair shop on Jerome Avenue. After that, he and Travis took a cab across town to pick up the mini-van with the drugs. Soon after, they were back on the highway, headed south to Richmond Virginia.

58

W hile Mox ventured to New York, to attend to his personal and business issues, Priscilla stayed in Richmond. She had a gut feeling Mox was doing more than what he told her, but she didn't have evidence to make an accusation. The only thing she knew was he took these trips every so often to meet up with Juan Carlos. Anything after that, she was oblivious to.

But Priscilla was far from an angel herself. She had secrets too. Once again, she relapsed and was back to sniffing cocaine. It was gradually taking its toll on her—eating away at her brain and causing her to make bad decisions. Her vision became shaded and no longer did she worry about how she would get Brandi back. Her only concerns were money and drugs.

For the past few weeks, Priscilla and Quiane had been seeing each other more than often. She started to catch feelings for him—something she vowed to not do. She also understood the consequences of her actions could be deadly.

When she was with Quiane, she was happy. She felt wanted and appreciated, loved and connected; desired.

Quiane was smart, handsome, and to top it off, he had a lot of money—lots of money. His nickname on the streets was, The Million Dollar Man, and some say that was just being modest.

Born and raised in New York, Quiane was the youngest of his

brothers. His mother was a retired school teacher who devoted herself to church, and his father had just come home from a twenty year bid in the Feds for drug trafficking.

Quiane was introduced to drugs as a child, and ever since, it's been the only living he's made. Everything he got and anything he has, came from drug money.

He owned a $300,000 five bedroom mini mansion he had built from ground up on three acres of land, in Highland Springs. It contained all the amenities of the most lavish homes in the area. An indoor/outdoor swimming pool, a professional sized tennis court, a gymnasium that housed a basketball court, and a 17 hole mid-sized golf course. It was a drug lord's lair—the king's castle.

Priscilla relaxed in the Jacuzzi with her hair tied in a bun, wearing a one piece Christian Dior bathing suit. She popped a strawberry into her mouth and took a sip of her mimosa as she smiled, watching Rhianna's music video on the television mounted to the wall.

She felt the presence of someone in the room and she turned to see who was there.

"Gotcha!" Quiane shouted, popping out from behind the door. He was holding a bouquet of pink and white roses in one hand and a bottle of champagne in the other.

Priscilla almost jumped out of her skin. "Boyyy... don't be scaring me like that. What's wrong with you?"

Quiane laughed. "I'm sorry. You looked a lil' bored in here, I was tryna liven you up."

"Liven me up with some of that," she replied, pointing at his dick.

Quiane bent down, kissed her lips, and handed her the roses. "If I didn't have this business to take care of, I would have no problem doing that. But wait until later... I'ma come back and wear that ass out."

"I'm not gonna be here later."

"Why not, where you going?"

"Quiane, it's Saturday. I'm pretty sure my man is back at home. I don't want any problems and I do not wanna hear his mouth."

"Oh, that nigga. Fuck that nigga." Quiane didn't like Mox. He barely knew anything about him, but Mox having something he desired was enough. "Tell him you was with me and see what he say."

"Yeah, right." Priscilla stepped out of the Jacuzzi, snatched a towel off the rack, and started drying off. "You tryna start trouble."

"That's something I'm good at," he said. "Oh, I forgot... you don't want your little boyfriend to get hurt."

"Fuck you, Quiane."

He laughed. "I must've struck a nerve, I'm sorry."

"Kiss my ass."

"Bend over."

"Grow up, okay. You're fucking forty years old and yet you still act like a child. "

"I'm acting like a child, but you're the one keeping secrets from your man. You might as well tell him. Sooner or later he's gonna find out. I just hope he can accept it."

"Accept what?" Priscilla questioned.

"Accept the fact that I have his bitch now."

"*Bitch?*" She rolled her eyes. "Ain't nobody's bitch here, you better go find one of them hoodrats. You got me confused, boo boo."

"So, why haven't you told him?"

"Because, he doesn't need to know."

"How about I tell him? I would love to see his reaction." Quiane reached for Priscilla's arm, but she pulled away and started walking out the bathroom.

"You know... sometimes you say the lamest shit," she mumbled.

"What you say?" Quiane caught up to her.

"You heard me."

Slap! His right palm met the side of her face. She grabbed her cheek in shock; surprised that Quiane put his hands on her. "Watch your fucking mouth when you talk to me."

Priscilla stood there in a stupor—speechless and unsure of how to react. A tear slid down from the corner of her eye, but she wiped it away before it reached her cheek. Her thoughts were scrambled and she was confused. She believed Quiane was different, but she'd been proven wrong; he was just like the rest of them.

"PRISCILLA! PRISCILLA, YOU HERE?" Mox yelled as he stepped through the front door. The house was quiet and didn't smell of food, so he knew she wasn't cooking. "Priscilla!"

"Yes! I'm upstairs!" she answered. She took her time coming down because she had a pounding headache from the slap Quiane had given her earlier. She even missed the bruise on her face when she checked herself in the mirror, but Mox caught it.

"You miss me?" he asked, holding two Gucci shopping bags in his hand.

Priscilla smiled when she saw the bags. Gucci was one of her favorite stores to shop in, and Mox knew it. "Just a lil' bit," she said, showing him the amount with her fingers.

"Well, that ain't enough," he hid the bags behind his back.

"Pleeeease..." She begged, getting closer. Priscilla wrapped her arms around Mox's neck and pecked his lips.

"What the fuck happened to your face?" he saw the light bruise on her cheek.

Priscilla's eyes widened and her instinct caused her to touch the exact spot where the bruise was. "Huh, what?" She acted as if she didn't know what he was talking about.

"What you mean, what? You put your hand right on it." Mox's mood switched. "Don't fucking play with me, Priscilla."

"Mox, I don't know what you're talking about." She lied, and rushed to the mirror that was next to the front door. "Where? I don't see anything."

Mox shook his head and dropped the bags on the floor. He knew she was lying and he was fed up with her dishonesty. He was tired of the falsehood they were living—the backbiting, deceit and deception. It was time to come clean; time to lay all the cards on the table and man up. Time to tell her the whole truth.

"You're fucking him, ain't you?"

An eerie silence swept the entire house. Not even the sounds of nature could be heard. Priscilla turned to Mox with a confused look on her face. "What are you talking about, Mox?"

"You know what the fuck I'm talking about, Priscilla."

She tried to laugh it off like it was nothing. "You're buggin, Mox."

"Oh, I'm buggin... I'm buggin', right?" Mox pulled his phone from his pocket, went through his pictures, and held it up to Priscilla's face. "Tell me I'm buggin' again and watch what the fuck I do to you."

Priscilla's lip dropped when she saw the picture of herself and Quiane, getting out of his car and getting ready to walk into his house. "Mox... I..."

"Shut the fuck up. You tell another lie and I'ma—"

"I didn't fuck him, Mox."

"Stop lying to me, Priscilla. You was in there for three hours. What the fuck you doing in that niggas house for three hours?"

"He only gave me a ride home, Mox. I swear." Tears started to build in her eyes. "I swear. He only gave me a ride because you left me. I didn't have any other way to get home."

"Three hours, Priscilla?" Mox smiled, but inside he was crying. "You stayed at that nigga's house for three hours and you expect me to believe y'all didn't do anything? You lied to me that night in the club and said you didn't know who he was. " Mox stood in the middle of his living room, looking around. He just purchased the house with cash, over a hundred thousand. "All this shit," he said, waving his hand. "I did it for you... for us, and what you do? You go behind my back and fuck with some lame ass nigga who probably sold you a dream."

"*For me?*" Priscilla was livid. "Fuck what you did for me, Mox. Where's Brandi, huh? Where's our daughter, Mox? Oh, did you forget you had a daughter? Don't fucking stand here and criticize me like I'm the only one who did some fucked up shit in this relationship." The tears poured from her eyes. "You did me wrong, Mox, and you know it. I loved you and you did me wrong. You told me you loved me. What's this tattoo we got, " she pointed at her neck. "I guess this shit don't mean nothing, huh? I thought it was let no one stand before we... before us, Mox, you and I. You don't love me, you just say that shit to appease me."

"I do love you, Priscilla."

"No you don't!" she screamed. "You don't continue to hurt the person you love. You don't do that, Mox."

Mox knew she was right, and there was nothing he could say. The only thing left to do was to tell her everything. Tears were falling from Priscilla's eyes like a waterfall. She could barely catch her breath. "Priscilla..." Mox called her name and she tried to ignore him. "Priscilla, look at me."

"What, Mox?"

"Jasmine is pregnant."

59

"You sure this the right address?" Cleo asked.

"It has to be. This is the address he gave me."

Cleo pulled up to the trailer home and parked in the grass. It looked abandoned. The small, shack like trailer was rundown and dilapidated, but there were two cars parked in front. He snatched the key from the ignition. "Well, go see if he's in there." he said to Whoadie.

Whoadie stepped out the car, walked to the door, rang the bell and waited. He could hear people shuffling around inside.

"Who is it?" A female asked from inside the trailer.

"It's Whoadie, is Q here?"

The locks came off and the door opened. Standing in the doorway was a short, brown skinned female who was naked from the waist up. Her breasts were perky, her hair was in a ponytail, and she had a white dust mask over her nose and mouth. "He back deer," she said, in a heavy southern accent.

Whoadie turned and waved to Cleo who was standing by the car. "C'mon," he told him.

The trailer home had very few pieces of furniture; a table, a couch and some chairs. Four half-dressed women sat around the mid-sized wooden table, sifting cocaine, cutting it, and placing it in plastic lunch baggies.

"Ladies…" Cleo greeted, smiling from ear to ear.

He and Whoadie were escorted to the back where Quiane sat on a twin-sized bed, tossing stacks of money into a black duffle bag on the floor. "Cousin, what's good wit' you?"

"Same shit, looking for a come up. Wassup wit' you?"

Quiane smiled. "Who's your boy?" he ignored Whoadie's question.

"This my nigga, Cleo."

"What's good?" Cleo extended his arm to shake Quiane's hand.

"What y'all niggas doing in Richmond? Ain't shit out here."

"Came to see you."

Quiane looked at his cousin and smiled again. "Nigga, what the fuck you done did?" He knew his cousin's only reason for being there was because something happened.

"I didn't do nothing I wouldn't usually do. You know how I get down, boy."

"Yeah," Quiane nodded. "I know exactly how you get down. I need a favor."

"Anything for you, cuz. What you need?"

Quiane pulled a piece of paper from his pocket and passed it to Whoadie. "Drop this bag off at the address and bring the other bag back. Can you handle that?"

"I got you, cuz."

Quiane tossed two more stacks of money into the bag and pushed it towards his cousin. When they got back to the car, Cleo jumped in the driver's seat and Whoadie put the bag into the trunk and then got in on the passenger side.

"How much you think is in the bag?" Cleo started the car.

"I don't know… couple hunit thousand prolly."

Cleo thought about the amount of money in the bag. They already had over a hundred thousand in cash, two guns, and some jewelry from their last robbery, but he wanted more. He was greedy and never satisfied. Before they reached the address Quiane gave them, he pulled over to the side of the road.

Whoadie looked around; he was confused. "Why you stop? This ain't the address." They were on a dirt road, surrounded by thick woods on both sides.

THE UNION | 415

"I gotta check that tire on your side. I think it has a leak." He lied, grabbing the gun that was underneath his seat. Cleo got out the car and walked to the passenger side. He bent down to act like he was checking the tire, and when he came up, the gun was in his hand and it was pointed at Whoadie.

Whoadie tried to duck, but the bullet crashed through the window and hit him in his ear. He was slumped over the middle console with blood coming from the hole in the side of his head. Cleo put two more slugs in his chest to make sure he was dead, and then opened the door, dragged his limp corpse from the vehicle, and left him in the woods. He then continued to the address that was on the paper.

Cleo rang the bell, and as soon as the door opened, his gun went off. Flame shot from the barrel and several shots followed. The other two occupants of the house tried to scurry to safety, but Cleo was swift. He moved through the small trailer, clutching the pistol, pumping lead into any moving figure in his sight. When the shots stopped, there were three dead bodies in the trailer.

He looked around. The setup was identical to Quiane's with a table, chairs and a couch. When he walked into the kitchen, there was a duffle bag that looked exactly like the one Quiane had given Whoadie. He unzipped it and smiled. It was full of cocaine. With both bags in his possession, Cleo got back into his car and drove off.

THE NEXT DAY

"This ain't like my cousin, he don't do shit like this." Quiane explained. He got up from the chair he was sitting in and paced the floor. Kurt and Kyle sat on the sofa across from him, and Priscilla was walking in from the kitchen. "Kyle, did you get in touch with Tammy?"

"Nah, not yet," he answered. "I called a few times but no one answered."

Quiane rubbed his hands together, trying not to think about the worst case scenario. "I know something happened... Y'all niggas take a ride over to Tammy's spot and see what's up. Call me as soon as you get there."

"How much was in the bag, babe?" Priscilla inquired.

"About, two hunit."

"And you trusted him with all that money?"

"It was times I gave him more than that. I know my cousin. Whoadie don't get down like that. I been around him all my life..." Quiane paused and collected his thoughts. "That nigga he was with though... I don't know about him."

"Who was he?"

Quiane tried to recall the name. "Umm... I don't know. I forgot what Whoadie said his name was... fuck!"

"Calm down, babe. We'll get to the bottom of it... trust me." Priscilla massaged his shoulders and then sat in his lap. "The last thing you need to be stressing over is money, we'll get it back."

"It ain't the money I'm worried about, it's the product. The only place I can get high quality product like that is in New York, and right now, I can't go back up there. I gotta take care of this shit down here."

"Can you get someone else to go up there?"

Quiane thought about it. "Nah, Kurt and Kyle got warrants in damn near every state, so I can't ask them to do it. Besides them, I don't trust no one else."

"I'll do it for you." Priscilla said.

Quiane stared her; she wasn't smiling, she was dead serious. "Do what?"

"I'll go to New York and handle whatever you need me to do. I'm capable."

Quiane grinned, but Priscilla kept a straight face. "You're serious, ain't you?"

"Why wouldn't I be? I mean, it can't be that hard of a task, right?"

"You don't even know what you're getting yourself into. This shit ain't no game, Priscilla. You can get fifty years doing this." Quiane explained.

"Can I ask you something?"

"Yeah."

"Do you love me?" Priscilla looked into Quiane's eyes.

"Yeah, I love you."

"Do you trust me?"

Quiane hesitated. "Until you give me a reason not to."

Priscilla brushed the side of his face. "Quiane," she whispered. "If I give you my heart, would you protect it with your life?"

"Of course I would, Priscilla." Quiane leaned in close, kissed her lips and she kissed him back.

"So, let me do this for you."

Before he could answer, his phone rang. "Hello?"

"This shit is ugly, Q... blood everywhere, no bags, and no sign of your cousin, Whoadie."

"Fuck!" He slammed the phone on the carpet, took a deep breath, closed his eyes and tried to figure out a solution.

Seconds later, when his eyes opened, Priscilla was standing directly in his face. "All you gotta do is tell me who I need to see."

60

M ox hadn't heard from Priscilla in almost a week. He was starting to believe it was over for them; their relationship was finished. He felt in his heart he had done the right thing by exposing the truth and telling her what it was, but never did he think she would leave. He loved Priscilla and would do anything for her. But to wait in the wind for her to come back from who knows where, was something he wasn't going to do.

"What if she comes back and you're gone?" Travis asked, watching Mox put the last bag into the car.

"That's her problem. I'm going back to New York. Christmas is two days away, Jasmine is pregnant, and my uncle Earl is getting baptized."

"What about the work that's on the streets?"

"You take care of that. Handle it how you see fit." He snatched the last of his belongings and piled them into the rental car. "I'ma see you when I come back, Travis... and keep my muthafuckin' house clean too." he laughed and jumped into the driver's seat. Right before he put the key in the ignition, his phone rang. "Hello?"

"You have a collect call from an inmate at a Westchester County Correctional Facility. To accept this call, please press three. If you no longer wish to receive..."

Mox pressed three and cut the recording short. He had no idea who it was, but he wanted to find out. "Hello?" he repeated.

"Yooo, Mox what's good... it's Bing."

"Bing, what's good, boy... damn, nigga, they got you again?"

"Yeah, man... serious shit this time. Them alphabet boys snatched me up two weeks ago. I just moved out here to White Plains n' shit... I was chillin', but I guess they had other plans. These muthafucka got me in the federal hold, here in Valhalla."

"Damn, son. What you need? You know I got you."

"I'm good. Only thing I need you to do is get a message to my sister. She stay over there by the old Yankee stadium."

"I got you."

"Good looking, Mox, I appreciate it. You know how we do."

"Aight, Bing... hold your head, peace." Mox hung up the phone, started the car and pulled off.

NEW ROCHELLE, NEW YORK

"I told you I was going to get yo' punk ass." Tyrell cursed. "Six, bring that nigga over here."

Gahbe was naked as a newborn baby, shivering and shaking in the winter frost. It was so cold the tears and snot coming from his eyes and nose was freezing on his face. Six held him by the back of his neck and walked him to the edge of the roof where Tyrell was standing.

"Kinda cold out here, huh?" Tyrell joked. "Check this out though... I'ma give you an ultimatum. Either you can jump off this muthafuckin' roof , or you can take the bullet that's gon' come out this pistol."

Gahbe's hands were shaking as he wiped the snot from his face. "Fu... fu... fuck you, nig... nigga. Ki... kil... kill me, mutha... muthafucka!" he spat.

Tyrell grinned and glanced at Six. "This nigga talking big shit, huh? Move Six." He pulled a black 9-millimeter from his coat, cocked it, walked up on Gahbe and pressed the barrel against his forehead. "I'm starting to like this shit, Gahbe... you know... this murder shit. You should'a killed me when you had the opportunity, you bitchassnigga." He stared into his eyes and squeezed the trigger. The echo from the blast was heard throughout the entire projects, and Gahbe's body fell to the pavement.

CHRISTMAS DAY
2012

Mox woke up at 5am Christmas morning. He brushed his teeth, showered and got dressed to go out and get an early breakfast. Light snow flurries fell from the clouded skies, blanketing the cold pavement as he cruised the empty streets of New Rochelle.

After a light breakfast, Mox went to pick Jasmine up so they could get ready to attend church services. It was a special day. A special day for Mox because it would be his first time in church in years, and a special day for his uncle, Earl, because today he would turn over a new leaf and begin a new life.

While they sat in the car at a red light, Jasmine stared out the window at nothing in particular. She was in a deep trance. She rubbed her stomach and thought about the life that was growing inside of her. She thought about starting a family with Mox, and a smile appeared on her face. It was all she wanted; all she longed for.

Right before the light turned green, Mox's phone rang. He looked at it and saw it was Priscilla, so he picked it up. "Hello?"

"I'm in New York. I wanna see you."

"For what, Priscilla?" As soon as Mox mentioned her name, Jasmine's head turned.

"Because, I love you, Mox, and I want us to be together."

"You shoulda thought about that before you started fucking around on me."

"We both did wrong, Mox. Let's put the past behind us and move forward."

"I am moving forward."

"What about our daughter? You're just gonna leave us in the wind like we ain't shit?"

"You were fine without me, you'll be alright. I gotta go." He said, trying to get her off the phone.

"Mox, wait..." Priscilla sniffled. "Are you going to church for uncle Earl's baptism?"

"Yes, Priscilla."

"Will you talk to me, please? I just need to say a few words to you, that's all. I think you owe me that."

"Owe you?" Mox looked at Jasmine in the passenger seat. She had a disgusted look on her face. "Listen... Priscilla, I gotta go. Bye."

AGENT O'MALLEY and Agent Havoc pulled into Priest's driveway. His car was parked in the garage, so they had a strong feeling he was home. They hadn't heard from him since their visit, and they were highly upset because he hadn't followed their orders to find Mox and bring him to them.

They exited the vehicle and walked to the front door. After banging for two minutes, Agent Havoc decided to walk around the house to see if the back door was open. He checked the knob and to his surprise, the locks were off, so he called to his partner. "O'Malley, I got an open back door over here!"

O'Malley walked to the back of the house and they pushed the door open. The stench was atrocious. Both agents covered their mouths and rushed out the door.

"What the fuck is that smell?" Havoc yelled.

"Smells like somebody got to Priest before we did. Shit... C'mon, let's go back in and find him."

"Fuck no! I'm not going back in there, that shit is horrendous." Havoc complained. "If he's dead, what the fuck we going in there for? Call the coroner."

"Stop being a pussy and get your ass in here."

The agents searched the house for Priest's body. They found him in his bathroom, slumped in his tub, with a bullet in his head.

"Oh my God, I think I'm gonna throw up." Havoc turned around and hurled on the floor.

"Jesus Christ, Havoc... get it together." O'Malley said. He stepped inside the bathroom covering his nose and mouth and looked down at Priest's decomposed corpse. "Probably been in here a few days... fucking guy stinks."

"What's that?" Havoc asked, seeing a note sticking to the mirror.

O'Malley ripped it off the mirror and read it.

THEY COULD NEVER SAY I WASN'T A STAND UP NIGGA. TELL MOX I DIDN'T KILL HIS MOTHER, AND I LOVE HIM.

EARL KILLED the ignition and stepped from the vehicle. He had ten minutes before church started and he was nervous as hell. He wiped the beads of sweat from his forehead and walked up the stairs and into the church.

"Good morning, Earl." Mrs Garrett greeted. "You ready?"

Earl nodded and continued into the church. It was packed. Since he'd been coming to the church, he'd never saw it this crowded. The whole neighborhood attended. He scanned the crowd, looking for the people he invited. He saw Mox sitting in the front row, next to Jasmine and he smiled. He knew his nephew wouldn't let him down.

Earl also spotted Tyrell and Priscilla in the crowd, and thought he saw someone who had a striking resemblance to Cleo. He took a deep breath and walked down the aisle to the pulpit. Dressed in his best suit and shoes, Earl was ready to let the truth be told. The congregation quieted and when he stepped in front of the microphone, he cleared his throat and began.

"Good morning, ladies and gentlemen, and merry Christmas to all. Today is a very important day for me. Not just because it's a holiday, but because this is the day I rejoice and confess my sins." He paused, looked over the crowd, and continued. "I've done a lot of good, but there's one thing I can't seem to erase from my brain, and that's the murder of my sister." Earl looked down at Mox sitting in the first row. "I think I owe my nephew an apology."

Mox didn't understand what his uncle was trying to say. He just listened.

"I've been living a lie for thirty years, and I can no longer live like this." Earl placed his hand on the Bible and closed his eyes. "If we confess our sins, he is faithful and just, and will forgive us our sins and purify us from all unrighteousness."

Mox's heart dropped when he heard his uncle Earl reciting the prayer. It was the same prayer the killer said the night his mother was murdered. He stood up and stared at Earl on the pulpit.

"I'm sorry, Mox." A tear fell from his eye and splashed the Bible. "I'm sorry for taking my sister's life, I'm sorry for lying to you... I'm sorry for everything. I hope you can forgive me." Earl stepped back from the pulpit, reached for his waistline and pulled out a black revolver. Before anyone could react, he put the barrel of the gun to his temple and hugged the trigger...

EPILOGUE

F ederal agents had the church surrounded, waiting for Mox to come out. After the shot went off, they stormed the church, and in the mix of it all, Priscilla, Cleo and Tyrell were taken into custody. Authorities were never able to locate Mox.

VALHALLAH CORRECTIONAL FACILITY

"Yo, Rell, tell the C.O. to crack my gate!" An inmate yelled.

"He ain't gon' do it unless you signed up for sick call." Tyrell replied.

"You the trustee, make it happen!"

"I don't even fuck wit' you like that, homey." Tyrell continued mopping the tier floor.

The C.O. shouted from inside the bubble. "Cell twenty-one! Daniels! Sick call!"

Tyrell dropped the mop he was holding, waited until he heard the cell door open, and then started walking down the tier. He dug his hand inside his sweatpants and fetched his prison gun. When he reached the front of cell twenty-one, the inmate had just stepped out. Tyrell gripped the handmade shank in his palm, bit down on his lip and approached the inmate. "I got a gift from Mox," he shoved the sharpened tip of the shank into the target's abdomen. He pulled it out and stuck it in his chest, directly over his heart and blood squirted from the hole and splashed his t-shirt.

Cleo pulled the shank out of his chest and the blood poured out even faster. On his way to the floor, he looked up and saw was Tyrell's back as he walked off.

SUMMER 2013

Illuminant rays burst out the sun, giving the sky a bright yellowish tint. Not a cloud was in sight as the children played amongst themselves on swings, monkey bars, and in the sandbox. Parents and siblings sat on benches and stood against fences, watching their little ones have the time of their life.

Ms. Davis sat on the bench she always sat on when she brought her granddaughter to the park. It was the shadiest area of the playground, and she could see the entire park from her sitting position. With her newspaper in hand, she skimmed through the day's topics, searching for something interesting to read.

"Crime, crime and more crime." She mumbled to herself, flipping through the pages. A droplet of water landed on her arm and she looked around to see if one of the kids was playing with a water gun, but she hadn't spotted any. Suddenly, another droplet hit her and then three more. When she looked up, she saw dark clouds forming in the sky, and before she knew it, thunder was roaring and lighting struck down from the heavens.

Parents scurried to find their children, grabbing them, rushing to their vehicles before the torrential rains fell.

Ms. Davis stood up and walked to the swings, where she last saw Brandi. "Brandi!" she called. "Brandi, where are you?"

JASMINE KEPT her foot on the brake with the car in drive. "Hurry up, c'mon!"

"Where we going, Daddy?" Brandi held onto Mox's hand as tight as she could as they ran to the waiting car.

"We're going home, baby... we're going home..."

CPSIA information can be obtained
at www.ICGtesting.com
Printed in the USA
LVHW100508090222
710589LV00011BA/873